Critical praise for

RUTH AXTELL
MORREN

DAWN IN MY HEART

"Morren turns in a superior romantic historical."
—*Booklist*

LILAC SPRING

"*Lilac Spring* blooms with heartfelt yearning
and genuine conflict as Cherish and Silas
seek God's will for their lives. Fascinating
details about nineteenth-century shipbuilding are
planted here and there, bringing a historical
feel to this faith-filled romance."
—Liz Curtis Higgs, bestselling author
of *Whence Came a Prince*

WILD ROSE

"The charm of the story lies in Morren's ability
to portray real passion between her characters.
Wild Rose is not so much a romance as
an old-fashioned love story."
—*Booklist*

WINTER IS PAST

"[This book] inspires readers toward a deeper trust in the transforming power of God.... [Readers] will find in *Winter Is Past* a novel not to be put down and a new favorite author."
—*Christian Retailing*

"[The] faith journeys are so realistic all readers can benefit from the story. Highly recommended."
—CBA *Marketplace*

RUTH AXTELL MORREN

WILD ROSE

Steeple
Hill®

Published by Steeple Hill Books™

STEEPLE HILL BOOKS

Steeple
Hill®

ISBN-13: 978-0-373-78609-1
ISBN-10:   0-373-78609-3

WILD ROSE

Copyright © 2004 by Ruth Axtell

www.SteepleHill.com

Printed in U.S.A.

Here's to you, Dad.
A "down-easterner" in spirit if not by birth.
And to Mom, who probably rejoiced as much as I
did when I got "the Call."

Prologue

Haven's End, Maine, August 1872

Geneva felt the push from behind, a blow between the shoulder blades. The next instant she lay flat on her face against the rough, gray wharf, her toes caught in the spaces between the worn wood slats, her brimming baskets wrenched sideways. Helpless, she watched their contents scatter. The fruits and vegetables she'd taken such pains to arrange that morning in neat, concentric circles tumbled across the sun-bleached planks.

Heads of cabbage rolled like croquet balls off the edge of the wharf to land with a *plop* into the awaiting tide. The smaller items—the precious raspberries she'd handled so gently to prevent bruising and the bright green string beans—disappeared down the cracks to join the bobbing cabbages below. The shriek of gulls mingled with the cackle of laughter around her, as the birds were alerted to the treasures floating on the sea.

"Salt Fish Ginny! Salt Fish Ginny! How come you're so skinny?" The teasing chant resonated above the laughter. "Salt Fish Ginny! Dirty as a hog, mean as her dog!"

Geneva glared at the trio of village boys stampeding by her, shouting the hated words that described her occupation, fishing for cod.

She forgot the boys as the thump of footfalls farther down the wharf reached her ears. Her glance passed the pranksters to the group turning down the wharf from the street. Rusticators! Her face flamed in humiliation as she watched the smartly dressed ladies and gentlemen on holiday, the very ones who bought her produce, stroll down the pier from the quaint, white clapboard village.

Before she could do more than pull herself to her knees, they had reached her, and stood hesitating as if looking for a way to pass through the mess. Wrinkling their noses, the ladies lifted their skirts to avoid soiling them.

Only one gentleman moved. His boots resonated against the wood, but as soon as Geneva saw who it was, her heartbeat muted the sound. She stared openmouthed as Captain Caleb Phelps came and knelt beside her. She had never been in such close proximity to him before.

Geneva found herself looking straight into the bluest pair of eyes she'd ever seen. They were the blue of the open ocean off Ferguson Point after the morning fog burned off and when the noon sun hung high overhead. Not a cloud diminished the hue of the vast, flat expanse of sea then, but its inky blue depths sparkled with a thousand lights and depths from the reflecting sun.

Captain Caleb's eyes danced with a mixture of concern and amusement. It wasn't the sly amusement of the onlookers, she realized, but a companionable sort, as if he and she were sharing some private joke. His eyes' wry twinkle was telling her that he had been in a similar predicament in another time and place, long ago enough to look back with humor.

Geneva blinked to break the spell. *Don't be a fool.* Captain Caleb didn't care what she was thinking. His world was so far removed from hers, it might as well be across the sea. She needed to get back on her feet and quick. There'd been enough damage done already, and she had to see what she could salvage.

But her commands didn't reach her legs. Geneva caught sight of the untidy patchwork on one threadbare knee of her overalls and suddenly became conscious of her appearance. She cringed in shame at the contrast between the man's easy elegance and her own homespun looks. The seams of her pa's old flannel shirt were visibly frayed, the color faded from numerous washings.

Geneva glanced down at the hand the captain placed on her forearm. Despite the tanned skin, it was the hand of a gentleman. His fingernails were clean and neatly trimmed. She curled her own hands into fists to hide the broken nails, traces of garden dirt still clinging to them.

"Are you all right, miss?" After a cursory glance over her as he asked the question, his gaze returned to her face.

Miss. It sounded so respectful. He might be talking to a fragile, young lady.

Geneva nodded and mumbled something, hardly believing what she was experiencing. For the first time, a man wasn't undressing her with a look. No matter how oversized her pa's old shirts or thick the bib of her overalls, they never did enough to flatten her bosom. Everywhere else she was bone thin, an unfortunate circumstance that only served to make the fullness of her chest more apparent.

Geneva flushed, meeting the intense indigo gaze focused on her. Captain Caleb scarcely gave her body a glance. He seemed to look beyond her features to the person within.

Although the captain's face was one she recognized, she'd only seen it two or three times in her life, from afar. "Cap'n Caleb," as he was known in these parts, hailed from Boston and rarely came to port in Haven's End.

Geneva couldn't help staring at it now, from the deep chestnut-colored hair brushed back from the bronzed forehead, to the strong jaw and rugged cleft chin, every feature in perfect proportion as if the artist's hand hadn't faltered once in executing his work.

Not like her uneven features: too-sharp nose, eyebrows arching like bird's wings across her brow, stick-straight dark hair and eyes black as pitch, attesting to her half-breed status.

She broke away from his grasp and pushed herself to her feet. Taking a step away from him, she forced herself back to the situation at hand. Her heart sank as she contemplated the wreckage around her. Well, it would do no good to cry about it.

She stooped to gather her baskets, but was stopped by Captain Caleb's firm grasp. He spoke with a tone of authority so different from the one he'd used with her, she had to look twice to make sure it was the same man speaking.

"Come here, lads, and rectify the damage you've inflicted on the lady."

The boys hooted at this. "But, Cap'n Caleb, that ain't no lady," one of the boys protested. The others doubled over in amusement at the very thought. "That's Ginny. Salt Fish Ginny!" Their laughter was joined by the discreet titters of the ladies and gentlemen still standing there.

Geneva wished the planks beneath her feet would widen enough to let her through so she could join her vegetables on the incoming tide. Of all the people to witness her disgraceful fall and hear that odious nickname, why did it have to be Cap'n Caleb?

"Young men—" the voice grew softer "—if I have to repeat my request, you'll find yourselves floating alongside those lettuces down there."

"Yessir," the trio mumbled, shuffling forward.

"Wait," he added. "Apologize to the lady first."

Their eyes looked just about ready to pop out of their heads. Under other circumstances, Geneva would have laughed out loud at their amazement.

The boys bobbed their heads, each in turn. "Sorry, Ginny." "Beg pardon, Ginny." "No offense, Ginny." Then, their natural exuberance restored, they bent to collect what remained on the dock. Geneva, stunned by what had just occurred, stood motionless. When she recovered from her surprise and moved to help, the captain's grip tightened on her arm.

The boys finished quickly. Proudly, they handed her the two baskets, only half full now, the bruised and battered fruits and vegetables a jumble. Geneva took them without a word, anxious to be out of sight as quickly as possible. She'd forget her deliveries in the village today, and continue on up the coast, where no one would know of the incident.

But she wasn't allowed such a quick retreat.

When everything was set to rights to his satisfaction, Captain Caleb turned to her and took off his cap. "Caleb Phelps, at your service, as you can see."

He smiled, and the warmth of his smile gave her the sensation she was the only human being worth knowing on the face of the earth. Now she understood why everyone in the village thought so highly of him and had nothing but good to say about "Cap'n Caleb" whenever he came to port.

"Whom do I have the pleasure of assisting?"

He was asking her name! "Geneva Patterson," she croaked, her throat so dry that she didn't know how she managed the syllables.

By this time, a pretty young lady came to stand beside the captain, taking his arm as if it was her rightful place to do so.

He turned to her, his voice tender. "Arabella, may I present Miss Geneva Patterson? My fiancée, Miss Arabella Harding."

The blond woman was dressed in a light blue suit that matched her eyes. "Pleased, I'm sure." Her glance slid off Geneva before she turned her attention back to the captain. "Caleb, we must be on our way while the day is so pleasant."

Geneva dodged aside before the captain could say anything more to her. But he reached out one last time, detaining her by holding the handle of one basket.

"I'd like to purchase these from you."

Geneva stared down at the crushed raspberries staining the wilted radish tops and lettuce leaves.

"How much are the two baskets worth?" He was already reaching inside his jacket to pull out his wallet.

Geneva shook her head, horrified at the completion of her shame. She backed away, bumping against a piling just in time, before she toppled over the edge of the wharf like her produce.

"I don't mean to offend you, Miss Patterson. I realize you won't be able to deliver them wherever you had originally intended—"

"They're not for sale. Thanks just the same, Cap'n." She stumbled toward the ladder and, reaching it, scurried over the side, afraid the captain would insist further.

Geneva dropped the baskets into her boat, not caring what tumbled out now. When she climbed back up the catwalk to free her line, she saw the captain and his betrothed standing where she had left them, their backs to her.

Miss Harding's cultivated tones reached her ears. "Caleb, sometimes your sense of chivalry goes too far. What possessed you to aid that creature? I could hardly distinguish whether it was a man or woman. She looked perfectly capable of picking up that dirty rubbish herself." Miss Harding's back shuddered.

Geneva watched the impeccably dressed young lady clutch the captain's arm more closely as she propelled him back toward their friends. Miss Harding's soft laughter floated to her. "That poor thing. She'll probably dream of your attentions for weeks."

Geneva didn't wait to hear the captain's reply, but slipped back down the catwalk, unable to bear it if she heard an answering chuckle. She jumped into the boat. Unmindful of its rocking, she set the oars in the pins, pushing one against a barnacle-encrusted piling to shove herself out into the harbor as quickly as possible.

The memory of Miss Harding's words burned on Geneva's heart like lye as she recognized the prophetic truth of them.

Chapter One

Haven's End, June 1873

The door to Mr. Watson's general store banged shut behind Geneva. She paused a few seconds at the door to give herself time to adjust to the dim light. The sweeter smells of spices, tobacco and new leather mingled with the more pungent odors of pickling barrels, hard cheeses and salted fish.

Three women leaned over one end of the long counter that ran the width of the store, examining lengths of ribbon and lace. At the sight of Geneva, they drew in their ranks, as if afraid of contagion in such close quarters. Used to such a reaction to her presence, Geneva ignored them and strode to the opposite end of the counter. She would state her business and leave as quickly as she had come.

Leaning her hands against the counter, she drummed her fingers lightly against the scarred, wooden surface.

"What can I do for you, Geneva?" Mr. Watson approached her with a smile.

Geneva didn't smile back, lest she give the storekeeper any encouragement. Suspicious of the teasing look in his eyes, she deemed it best to keep him at a distance.

"I'll take two dozen long nails."

Mr. Watson slapped the counter with his palms. "Two dozen nails it'll be."

When he turned his back to her to rummage in the keg, Geneva could hear Mrs. Bidwell's voice at the other end of the store.

"I hear tell he begged and pleaded with his intended to forgive him."

Geneva glanced toward the speaker, whose bonnet nodded up and down, giving the impression she had been in the very room at the time, an eyewitness to the scene she was describing. Her listeners seemed to think so, too, the way they drank in her words.

"Poor Miss Arabella Harding must have been brokenhearted." Young Annie Chase, who was engaged to one of Mrs. Bidwell's boys, expressed this opinion. "Such a pretty woman. So ladylike."

At the name, Geneva's fingers stopped their drumbeat against the countertop. She'd never forget that name. Nor the way Captain Caleb had looked at its owner when he'd introduced her, as if she were an angel.

Annie was soft-spoken, and everything she said came out sounding tenderhearted. "I don't know what I'd do if my Amos ever did anything dishonest like Captain Caleb." She hugged herself. "But Amos would never dishonor his family name in such a despicable manner."

"Of course not! Amos would never do any such thing," his mother answered, aghast at the mere notion. "He hasn't been brought up that way."

Geneva could feel every fiber in her body poised to attack. What gave these biddies the right to pass judgment on Captain Caleb? She bit her lip, holding in her anger, when Mr. Watson set the nails down in front of her.

"These long enough?"

She glared at him, as if he, too, were guilty of blaspheming her sacred memory of the captain.

"Anything else?"

She shook her head, her reasons for being in his store pushed aside by the more pressing matter of Captain Caleb's reputation.

"How could anybody be so foolish?" Mrs. Bidwell's voice carried the clearest. Geneva knew she prided herself on her opinions, and she gave full voice to them now. "Embezzling company money! Didn't he think he was going to get caught? He was Phelps' heir. Had everything he could wish for. If anyone was ever born with a silver spoon in his mouth, it was Caleb Phelps III. To go and steal from his own father! Why, it's wicked!"

The thudding between Geneva's temples drowned out their voices. She was sick and tired of hearing the captain gossiped about. It seemed she couldn't come into the village anymore without hearing the accusations hashed and rehashed. Didn't people have anything else to talk about?

"He had to pay for that big, fancy cottage on the Point," Mrs. Webb reminded the others. "The old farmhouse wasn't good enough for him. Oh, no. He had to tear that down. He probably ran short of money to pay for it all."

Mr. Watson looked toward the women and gave a chuckle. "I hear Phelps Senior's a mite close to the bark. I figure he kept young Phelps on a tight leash with his salary. The young captain probably got impatient, wantin' to give that pretty Miss Harding all that money can buy. After all, he had to fight off her other suitors. She was the belle of Boston, I hear."

Geneva told herself to turn around and march out of the store, but her feet seemed stuck to the floor with spruce gum.

Mrs. Webb tapped the counter with a large knuckled forefinger. "That doesn't excuse what he did. If he was short on money, he should have gone straight to his father. What did he do with all the money he earned as a captain? Look at our own captains—they live well on their shares the rest of their lives."

Mrs. Bidwell sniffed. "They don't squander their wealth on extravagant living. I saw the wagon-loads on their way to the Point to build that grand summer cottage of his. Cap'n Caleb only bought the best for his place. No hand-split shakes for his roof. Only slate all the way from Wales. And the glass! Enough panes you'd think he was going to live in a greenhouse. Mahogany shipped in from Santo Domingo. And that's not sayin' a thing about his residence in Boston. He overreached himself, all right!"

"I hear he up and left everything in Boston." Mrs. Webb snapped her fingers. "Just like that. If anything's proof of guilt, it's running. Now he's buried himself up in that mausoleum. Thinkin' he can hide himself here." She sniffed. "We're honest, God-fearing folk. He'll find that out in short order."

Mr. Watson nodded. "What I always say is, money's the root of all evil." He wrapped up the nails in brown paper. "That'll be twelve cents," he told Geneva, then turned back to the ladies. "You know how rich folks think they can be above the law, but things have a way of catchin' up with 'em." He gave a final nod of emphasis.

Geneva slapped her coins onto the counter. Mrs. Bidwell opened her mouth to speak. Before she could draw breath,

Geneva turned to the three women, hands on her hips, her back straight, her eyes narrowed.

"Poor folks seem to think they're above mindin' their own business. Guess they've never heard gossipin's a sin just like stealin'. Nor 'bout hittin' a man when he's down, even though he's never done nothing to them. I seem to recall just a while back, nothing but praise for Cap'n Caleb. Now he's tarred and feathered with your tongues when no one knows what really went on down there in Boston. Why, he's never treated any one of us but kindly and fairly, even some that don't deserve it!"

She glared at each one in turn. They stared at her, their jaws slack. These women probably hadn't ever heard her say so much all of a piece. Deciding the sooner she was away from these old harpies the better, she turned back to Mr. Watson.

Stifling the urge to tell him to wipe the smirk off his face, she picked up the parcel of nails. "Good day to you!"

She shoved away from the counter. It was then she noticed the silence. Not one of the women had said a word, not even the outspoken Mrs. Bidwell. In fact, they weren't even looking at her. Everyone was staring at the door.

Slowly Geneva turned. There, his dark form silhouetted against the sunshine of the open doorway, stood Caleb Phelps. She couldn't make out his features, but she could feel his gaze on her, as intense as it had been that day last summer.

Hugging the parcel to her chest as if it might conceal the workings of her heart, Geneva took a step forward, then another. The pounding of her heart was so loud, he must surely see the bib of her overalls flapping up and down clear across the store. She kept on marching until she reached the captain's looming figure. She'd forgotten how tall he was, a good head above her, and she was as tall as several men of her acquaintance.

He moved aside just as she approached and tipped his hat to her as she passed. Touching her own hat briefly at the brim, she lunged through the doorway into the sunshine. She took the steps down two at a time, her boots clattering on the rickety wooden planks.

Why was it that every time she ran into the captain, she felt compelled to flee afterward, as if she were guilty of something?

Caleb Phelps turned toward the banging screen door, the only sound in the small village store. He watched the long strides of the overalled figure taking her rapidly away from the store and toward the wharf.

Only her voice gave her away as a woman.

In the couple of weeks he'd been back to Haven's End, he'd felt a distinct chill every time he was in the presence of the villagers.

Funny how quickly bad news traveled. He had thought he'd become inured to suspicious looks—or worse, those self-righteous, smug expressions that said more clearly than words, *Well, he got his just deserts!* He'd certainly endured enough of them in Boston.

Somehow he'd thought this little village where he was scarcely known, but where he'd always had pleasant if superficial dealings with the residents, would welcome him differently.

The woman's harsh words to the villagers rang in his ears. She'd expressed more clearly than he ever could exactly what he'd felt.

Strange, how belief in one's integrity could come from the strangest quarters. What did she know of him or of events in Boston?

From her yard farther up the road from Ferguson Point, through the thin screen of hackmatack trees, Geneva watched her new neighbor with a frown. Ever since Captain Caleb had begun to turn the soil in a portion of his yard, she'd started to worry. When it became clear he was making a garden, her concern deepened. As she hoed her own young plants, she fretted that her neighbor wouldn't have the same success, not knowing the land in these parts.

"If I was plantin' a garden on the Point," she told her black Labrador, Jake, "I'd make it on the other side. For one thing, it'd get sun there the whole day. I remember Pa telling me there used to be a chicken yard nearby, so the soil'll be rich over yonder."

She banged her buckets together. "Ain't none o' my business what he does. Even if nothin' comes up, he won't go hungry. Isn't as if he depends on his garden to live, like most of us."

But no matter how much she debated with Jake over the next few days, Geneva couldn't help observing Captain Caleb each time she went outside. And the longer she watched him bent over his fork, the more she itched to offer her advice. He had helped her out of a mess once. She told herself she owed it to him.

Finally, making up her mind, she threw down the pump handle. "No, you stay here," she told Jake. "Don't need you scarin' him before I can get a word out." She wiped her hands down the sides of her trousers and headed for the dirt road. When she saw Jake at her heels, she stopped once again and shook a finger at him. "Now, do I have to chain you up, or are you going to obey?"

The dog whined, but after another stern look from Geneva, he stayed put. Her tone softened. "That's a good fellow. I knew I could count on you."

She walked down the sloping dirt road to the end of Ferguson Point, where a gate stood. The newly erected barrier, the lumber still raw and unpainted, matched the house beyond it. Together, house and gated fence stood out like intruders against the familiar landmarks of the Point. Geneva's gaze swept the vista before her, never tiring of it. She'd always thought this the best location in all Haven's End.

A large expanse of cleared land descended toward the sea. Below was a sheltered cove with dark, rocky cliffs curved around, protecting it from the open sea. Tall, ancient firs and spruce, their long, thin peaks looking black against the sky, grew down to the very edge of the cliffs, like multi-tiered sentinels standing guard against the sea.

Above the cove, where there had once been an old, abandoned house, now stood an imposing, new structure. Despite its freshness, there was something sad about it, Geneva thought as she observed the overgrown grass in the yard. It wouldn't take long for the bright reddish-brown luster of the cedar shingles to take on the faded gray of her own shack. The curtainless windows stared back at her like empty eye sockets.

Shaking aside the morbid thought, Geneva opened the forbidding gate. Spying her target at the far side of the yard beyond the barn, she walked resolutely toward the new owner of Ferguson Point.

The captain squatted by the half-turned garden plot, a clod of dirt and grass held in one hand. He was studying this as if it held the answer to a mystery.

Already she regretted coming. What in the world was she going to say to him now? So she stood, not saying a word, until he raised his head. His initial glance was startled, but it quickly changed to one of suspicion.

He sat back on his heels, pushing his hat away from his eyes to observe her. The sun shone full on his face, and Geneva struggled to hide her shock. Was this the same gentleman who'd helped her last summer? It wasn't just the absence of a smile, but the complete lack of welcome. His dark hair hung long and shaggy over his collar, his jaw shadowed with several days' growth of beard. Sweat and dirt stained his shirt. Only the color of his eyes remained unchanged—the same hue of the ocean.

But now they were no longer crinkled at the corners with mirth, but narrowed in bitter distrust. They gave her no encouragement to proceed.

Well, she was in for it now. Best have her say and be done.

"Be lucky to get much of anything to grow here." She kicked a clump of dirt with the toe of her boot.

After several seconds of silence in which Geneva wasn't sure whether he was going to order her off his land or just plumb ignore her, he answered in a quiet voice, each word carefully modulated as if he was holding on to his patience with an effort. "Why is that?"

Geneva made an abrupt gesture with her hand. "Poor soil." She jerked her head sideways. "Get half day's shade from those trees."

She watched him swallow as he digested her words. By the set of his unshaven jaw, she could tell he was having a hard time just being civil to her.

"Where do you propose I plant?"

She moved her chin forward. "Over yonder."

The captain turned his head in the direction she indicated, his mouth a stern line.

"Why?"

"My pa used to tell o' folks had a turnip patch there. Fine soil, full sun the whole day. Used to be a chicken yard right next to it. Lots o' manure." When he didn't reply, she made another motion with her chin. "You're late plantin'. Short growing season 'round here."

He turned back to her, giving her a look that told her he welcomed her advice about as much as he would a skunk under a house.

"I'm certainly obliged to you for telling me at this late date that I should abandon one field for another that looks identical to it." He threw aside the clump of turf he'd been holding and took a deep breath, as if continuing the conversation was an effort.

"I realize I'm nothing but a sailor who doesn't know a spade from a hoe, but I didn't have much choice about planting time."

She'd been right—he didn't know a thing about gardening. She kicked at the dirt again. "Awful shame. But 'twouldn't take you long with two people. I've already planted my garden. Could come over here tomorrow morning and help you till up yonder."

He let out a breath—whether in annoyance or amusement, she couldn't tell. "Are you proposing to help me dig up a field of the toughest, most rock-ridden sod I've ever encountered in my life?"

She went on as if he hadn't spoken. "If we prepare the soil good, I can give you some o' my seedlings. Have more'n I can use, anyway. That'll make up for lost time."

He paused as if considering. "That would be very generous of you."

She hurried on, afraid he'd change his mind. "You can still plant carrots, taters, squash, beans, greens." She nodded. "It'll do you for the winter."

"In that case, you'll probably have to show me how to put them up as well," he replied, the first hint of a twinkle beginning to thaw the chill in his eyes. Geneva felt something inside her begin to melt, too, and felt a profound relief that the man she remembered had not disappeared entirely.

A second later his eyes resumed their coldness. "I'll let you know when I'm ready to plant." He stood and, once again, she was conscious of his height.

He picked up a fork. "By the looks of it, I have a few days of hard labor ahead, so if you'll excuse me..." Without waiting for her reply, he began to walk toward the field she'd indicated.

"I'll come by tomorrow to help you with the tilling," she muttered to his back.

He heard her and turned around. "I will *not* have a woman wielding a fork alongside of me." He enunciated like a teacher to a stubborn pupil.

"Suit yourself. If you want to be a fool, ain't no concern o' mine."

"No?" His voice reached her. "Seems to have concerned you the other day."

So, he *had* heard. She could feel the blood heating her face up to the roots of her hair. She kicked at the tough grass. "Folks should mind their own business."

"What they ought to do and what they do are frequently two different things." He tipped his hat to her. "I want to thank you for your kind if unnecessary defense of me."

Wrestling with something inside herself, Geneva gave an abrupt nod and turned to begin her trek back to the gate.

She'd spent too many years protecting her own hide to know how to reach out to anyone. The captain would have to learn to sink or swim on his own. She'd help him with his garden. That was all. She owed him that much.

Caleb sat on the veranda, staring out at the silvery sea, the hot coffee cup enveloped by his hands. He couldn't see the horizon this morning. It was obscured by the milky white fog that lay offshore and high overhead.

The sun was already visible, its strong yellow orb promising to burn through the white film shrouding but not obliterating it. He listened to the movement of sea against rock, its sucking, rushing sound ceaseless.

He'd been listening to it off and on all night.

Finally the nausea he had felt since rising began to ebb. He took a cautious sip of coffee, feeling as if he were just finding his sea legs.

In truth, he knew his physical condition was the result of more than rising too early and sleeping too little over several days.

He ventured another sip of the scalding coffee, needing something—anything—to wash out the vile taste in his mouth.

Lost in thought again, the knock didn't penetrate his consciousness the first time. It was only at the second knock that it intruded like something at the periphery of his vision gradually taking shape.

He got up slowly at the third knock, his head shifting like sand, his body weak and wobbly like one who hasn't eaten in a few days.

Caleb walked back inside, following the echo of the now silent knock. His footsteps reverberated against the polished wood floor as he walked through the wide living room, into the dining room, and finally reached the kitchen. He approached the door leading out into the shed and opened it a crack.

The tall woman wearing men's attire—denim overalls and a straw hat—was just turning to leave.

He opened the door wider. "Good morning," he said, immediately clearing his throat as he heard the raspy sound of the syllables emanating from it.

She nodded by way of greeting. "Brought you some loam."

He frowned. "Loom?" He repeated the word the way she'd pronounced it.

"Topsoil. And dry manure," she added.

"Oh." Was this supposed to mean something to him?

The way she waited, just staring at him, made him conscious of his appearance. His fingers touched the collar of his shirt, and he realized the top buttons were undone.

She shifted in her boots. "I'll bring the seedlings 'round as soon as we work in the loam. Thought you'd want to get started early with the planting."

He finally nodded in understanding, remembering her offer of seedlings. Somehow it had slipped his mind amidst the backbreaking labor of the last two days.

"And so I do." He yawned. "Excuse me. I didn't get to sleep until late." When she said nothing, he asked, "What time is it anyway?"

He saw her blink at his question. She was younger than he'd imagined. In her men's getup and her clipped sentences, she had seemed ageless to him.

Not waiting for her to answer, he pulled out his watch. "Eight o'clock. It feels more like daybreak." He looked at her questioningly. "Don't you have your own work to do? I don't want to keep you from it."

She shook her head. "Already weeded and watered this mornin'."

He nodded. "Of course." If her speech was anything to go by, she wasn't a person to waste time. "I suppose if I am to accept your generous gift, I should at least know your name. You seem to know mine."

All he understood of the mumbled words was "Neeva Patterson."

"Pleased to meet you, Miss Patterson." He took a last swallow of coffee. "Well, let's be at it, then."

He followed her out into the yard. The morning was still cool and he shivered slightly in his thin shirt. She marched ahead of him, straight toward the garden patch. Once there, she looked it over like a general reviewing his troops.

She turned to him. "What made you decide to turn your hand to gardening?"

"Sheer boredom."

As if finding no response to that, she pointed to the wheelbarrow. "We've got to spread this over the garden and then use the fork to dig it in deep. I'll empty it out and go bring some more. You'll need to cover the garden good."

As she reached for the handles of the barrow, Caleb came alive, realizing she'd meant what she'd said the other day about helping him. He got to the handles first and flipped the contraption over.

Then he turned toward the barn. "I'll go get the shovel and fork," he said over his shoulder.

It was after noon before Geneva judged the soil ready for planting. She stood back from where she had been working the manure into the soil with her fork. "Reckon we can rake it smooth now."

The captain stopped his work at once, and she wondered whether he was as glad of the respite as she.

She hadn't liked his pallor this morning. She'd kept telling herself it came only from lack of sleep, but being out in the sunshine hadn't improved it. Now his paleness was overlaid with a sheen of perspiration.

The noonday sun burned down on their backs. They'd spent the morning carting manure and compost from her yard and forking it into his newly tilled garden. The captain hadn't even stopped to drink a dipper of water. The back of his shirt was wet, and every so often he'd stop to swat at the blackflies that hovered around him in a cloud and remove his hat to wipe his brow with a handkerchief, or just straighten up, as if his back pained him.

He worked steadily, almost as if he was trying to prove something, but she couldn't fathom what a gentleman like himself wanted to prove by bending over a garden patch.

Whatever the reason, she admired him for it. He had grit. Not like her pa, who'd bullied her ma all the time she was alive, but when she was gone, he'd just given up. Not all at once, but gradually, taking to the bottle until he was no longer fit to carry out the logging work that was his livelihood. One day they'd carried his body home after he'd slipped from a log into the rushing river on a spring log drive....

Geneva shook away the memories and sneaked another peek at the captain. She bit her lip to keep from voicing her concern. She'd had long years of practice keeping silent. The captain had made it clear this morning that he was not interested in chitchat.

Her own throat felt parched and her belly empty. She leaned against her rake. "I think we oughtta quit for dinner."

Before he could refuse, she added, "We can plant the seeds this afternoon, but it's not a good idea to plant the seedlings in full sun. Best thing is to set them tomorrow morning, early."

He considered a moment, looking over the neatly tilled plot. Finally he gave a short nod, and Geneva breathed her relief.

She gave a doubtful look at the seedlings. "I don't like setting everything out all at once, but guess it can't be helped, it being so late for your first planting."

"What do you mean?"

"All your stem vegetables should be planted when there's a moon, and all the root crops, 'cluding your taters, when it's dark."

He gave the little plants, which were already beginning to droop, an uninterested look. "I don't think it'll make much difference to these plants one way or another. They should be grateful just to be planted." He gave one of the pots a kick.

Instead of showing outrage, Geneva smiled. The contrast between the sweat-stained man before her and the polished gentleman who'd helped her on the wharf was too great.

He caught her smiling at him and frowned. "What's so funny?"

"Nothing." She pinched her lips together. "I'm just glad those seedlings are hardy things."

He looked at her for a second without reacting, then slowly he smiled. Her own lips relaxed in answer. Suddenly she felt like his partner in the garden.

"You've helped me more than I had any right to expect," he said. "The least I can do is offer you some dinner."

She stared at him, too startled by his invitation to answer.

"What's the matter? Have I offended you?"

She shook her head. How could she explain it to him? To eat at someone's table was truly to be accepted as his equal. He didn't know what he was offering. Captain Caleb Phelps III, son of a Boston shipping magnate, dining with Salt Fish Ginny, pariah of Haven's End? No, she'd spare him the humiliation. He was suffering enough at the hands of the villagers with his own troubles. She wouldn't add to them.

With a heavy heart she said, "Much obliged, Cap'n, but I better be getting back. Got to feed Jake."

"Jake?"

"My dog," she added.

"Certainly. Well, perhaps another time." He began picking up the tools, as if the invitation was already forgotten.

She hurried to help him, dumping the smaller items into the wheelbarrow. "I'll just keep my things in your barn, if you don't mind. That'll save hauling everything back tomorrow."

"You won't need them yourself?"

She shook her head. "Not for a couple of days, anyhow."

He pushed the wheelbarrow while she carried the long-handled implements toward the open barn door. He showed her a space inside where she could set the things, then went back to the garden for the remaining tools. Geneva took a turn about the barn while she waited for his return. She wanted to thank him again for the invitation.

She shook her head. No one in Haven's End had ever invited her to eat. Even when her ma died, and then her pa, her nearest neighbor had brought a few covered dishes, but no one had invited her over.

They'd tried to force her to the Poor Farm when she'd been left with no living relatives, but she'd had none of that. She'd fended off the town do-gooders with the help of her pa's rifle and hounds. Since then, she'd been pretty much left to herself.

Geneva kicked at the wisps of hay on the wooden floor, trying to understand how Captain Caleb could treat her the same as he would one of his own world.

She reached the doorway leading to the shed that connected the barn to the house. There in the dim corridor sat a wooden crate. Its yellow slats of new wood made it stand out.

Geneva stepped back when she saw what it contained.

The crate was filled with empty bottles, stacked every which way, right side up, upside down, sideways. The sickly sweet smell of liquor reached her nostrils. She knew that odor well. It had lingered for months in her own one-room house after her pa died. Geneva held her stomach, feeling as sick as if she'd drunk the contents herself.

Chapter Two

Caleb swung the scythe back and forth across the lawn at the side of the house. It had taken him the whole morning to learn to wield it properly, but now he began to see some progress on the grass that reached his knees and gave the house a derelict appearance. *Just like its owner,* his mind echoed. He glanced down at his work clothes—denim trousers and rough cotton shirt, its sleeves rolled up on his forearms, revealing the undervest beneath—what would his father say of him now?

Nothing that he hadn't heard his whole life.

Caleb abandoned that line of thought and concentrated on his strokes. He hadn't had such a workout since he'd climbed the ratlines of a ship. He turned to look with pleasure at the swath behind him, ignoring for the moment the much larger portion that remained to be cut.

Just then, he saw his neighbor coming down the road toward his property. Caleb wiped his brow with his bandanna, wondering what the strange Miss Patterson was coming to see him about now. He hadn't spoken to her in over a week. Occasionally he'd glimpsed her at her tasks, up beyond the field and trees that separated their two properties or out on her boat, but she'd made no more silent ventures into his territory since the day she'd helped him prepare the soil for planting.

The two of them had worked hard that day. Caleb chuckled, remembering how he'd felt when she first appeared at his door. He'd about forgotten her promise of seedlings.

Working in a field in the full sun was not a remedy he'd recommend to anyone after the amount of alcohol he'd consumed the evening before. But he didn't let on about his physical condition, though he suspected her sharp black eyes didn't miss much.

He watched his neighbor open his gate now and wondered what sage advice Miss Patterson was going to offer him on this occasion. At least he knew her name properly. He'd found out the last time he'd been to the village.

She was making her way toward him with her purposeful stride. Did she ever wander aimlessly?

She'd probably take one look at his garden and make a dour prophecy of doom. At least the seedlings had survived his inexperienced planting; several rows of seeds and the quartered potatoes with their eyes had sprouted as well. Except for that one row of beans, everything had looked promising to him this morning. Now he wasn't so sure. His plants began to take on a thin and sparse appearance as he tried to picture them through Miss Patterson's experienced eyes.

"Morning." She wasted no excess words in greeting.

Caleb leaned against the scythe and touched his hand to his hat brim. "Good morning to you, Miss Patterson." She gave him a sharp glance, as if his words held some double meaning. He returned her look blandly. "What can I do for you?"

"Came to see how the seedlings were doing."

"Just getting around to worrying about their fate?"

She flushed at that and looked away from him. "I been busy. Couldn't make it back the other day."

"You were under no obligation. I am grateful enough for all your help."

"Still, it wasn't right. I should'a finished what I begun."

"Shall we have a look?" He invited her to go before him with a gesture of his hand.

Giving an abrupt nod, she turned and led the way to his garden, saying along the way, "You can set out seeds every week for another couple o' weeks. That'll give you crops right through the summer and into the first frost."

When she got to the plot, she walked the length of it, silently inspecting the inch-high rows of peas, the tiny pairs of leaves on the sprouted radish and beet seeds, the feathery carrot tops, the pale gray-green of the cabbage and turnip sprouts. She nodded at the taller seedlings she'd given him to transplant from her own supply, which showed a few new leaves. Caleb hadn't felt so nervous since holding out his slate for his tutor's scrutiny.

"You water 'em when they're dry?"

"Yes, miss."

She gave him another glance, then bent down to pull out a thin weed Caleb could have sworn hadn't been there that morning. "Hoe around the bigger plants after it rains?"

"I will now."

Then she came to the pole beans. She squatted down beside them and took one little stem between her thumb and forefinger. It was thick and green, but where its two first leaves should have been was a shriveled, brown stump. Before Caleb could offer any explanation, any denial that he'd treated these seeds with any less care than the others, she pronounced her verdict.

"Cutworms."

The word conjured up an image of a pair of shears going through all his rows, hacking the tender plants to shreds.

"We'll have to replant 'em. This time we'll sprinkle some wood ashes all along the rows. If that don't do it, I'll mix up a mess of cornmeal and molasses. That should keep 'em off. Lucky they haven't gotten to your other plants." She stood once more, thrusting her hands into her back pockets. "Everything else is coming up fine. You did a good job planting," she acknowledged.

She didn't give him much chance to enjoy the sense of victory that filled him.

"If you notice anything else eating the leaves, let me know."

"Yes, ma'am," he answered automatically.

Again she narrowed her eyes at him, as if suspicious of his tone. When she didn't say anything more, Caleb tried to think of something to add. For some reason, he didn't want her to leave just yet. Up to now, he'd avoided all company.

But he was intrigued. Perhaps it was because she seemed as content to leave him alone as he was to be left alone. Or perhaps it was the fact that she'd defended him that day in the store.

He still wanted to know why.

When she started walking away from the garden patch, he spoke up. "I'm thinking of buying a boat. Know anything of Winslow's Shipyard?"

She nodded. "Don't think much of old man Winslow, but young Silas'll build you a good craft. He's got a gift."

"A gift?"

"It's in his hands." She looked briefly down at her own dirt-stained ones. "Anything he builds is light, easy to handle, seaworthy. He won't charge you much for a small vessel. What are you looking at?"

"Nothing too big. Something I can handle myself. I noticed your little craft. She serves you well. Where do you take her?"

He couldn't tell whether she was pleased or not by the compliment. "Up and down the coast. She's just a double-ender, but that's all I need." She nodded. "Silas built her for me. In his spare time." She made a sound of disgust. "Winslow wouldn't let him waste his time on a little peapod for the likes o' me. Farmers usually build their own. Folks use 'em for fishing and some lobstering."

"I'll have to see him. I don't believe I've ever met him, although Phelps Shipping has commissioned the Winslow Yard for schooners."

"Silas has been with Winslow for a long time. Ever since he was a boy. Apprenticed with him. He isn't from these parts. Comes from one of the islands—Swans or Frenchboro."

Another pause. Silence filled the space between them like a physical presence. Caleb still didn't want her to leave. Maybe it was just boredom. He felt as if he had all the time in the world on his hands.

"You wouldn't have any extra seeds?" he asked on impulse.

"Seeds? Oh, sure, I'll see what I have."

"Mind if I come along?" *Now, why had he said that?*

But she just shrugged. "Suit yourself. I have a little bit o' everything."

Caleb walked beside her across the lawn, but as they neared the gate, he heard the sound of a wagon coming down the road toward them. He shaded his eyes against the sun, trying to see who would be coming out to the Point.

It was old Jim, the man who'd driven him out the first day, with another man beside him. Caleb felt his gut tighten as soon as he recognized Nate, his former first mate, now a captain on a Phelps bark.

What did Nate want? Was he bringing a message from Boston? Caleb steeled his features to betray nothing, but he couldn't silence his heart as it began to hammer in anticipation.

He stood, bracing himself to face the man who was like a brother to him. The only one who'd believed in him throughout. If anyone knew him, it was Nate. If it hadn't been for his friendship on Caleb's first voyage, he didn't think he would have survived the trip in the forecastle of one of his father's square-riggers.

How would Caleb stand up to the coming encounter? Could he really convince his friend all was well with him at Haven's End?

As the horse and wagon ambled slowly forward, Caleb glanced over at Miss Patterson. She stood, silently watching the two men, nodding a greeting to Jim when he drew up.

Nate thanked the driver and descended, retrieving his bag from the back.

Before Caleb had a chance to introduce her, Miss Patterson muttered, "Be seeing ya," and walked off.

Caleb's glance flickered briefly to her, but he made no move to stop her, his attention centered on Nate.

The two men stood watching the horse and driver depart. When they were alone, Caleb turned to Nate. "What are you doing here?"

Nate removed his blue cap and scratched his head. "I'm glad I wasn't expecting a warm greeting, otherwise my feelings might be hurt."

Caleb looked hard at his friend. "I thought I made it clear I didn't want you or anyone else feeling obliged to come and check up on me."

Nate ignored the remark. "How was your journey?" he asked himself, then answered, "The seas weren't too rough."

Caleb crossed his arms and remained silent.

"We had a good passage. Would you like to come in? Yes, thank you kindly, I've had a long journey. Can I get you some refreshment? Why, yes, if it wouldn't presume on your hospitality."

Caleb turned on his heel, ignoring Nate's soliloquy, and walked toward the house, knowing his friend would follow.

Once inside, Caleb left Nate in the living room and went to the kitchen to fetch him something to drink. When he returned, Nate stood with his back toward him, admiring the view from the rear windows.

"I can see why you came here." He turned around with a smile. "Ahh! Just the thing for a parched throat." He smacked his lips after the first long sip of the cold tea. "Wonderful." He looked around. "Would you like to have a seat? Why, thank you." Seeing only the one armchair in the room, he raised an eyebrow. Caleb fetched a straight-backed, wooden kitchen chair and gestured for Nate to take the armchair.

"Now, are you ready to tell me why you've come? Or do you need some food first?"

Nate smiled. "Perhaps a little later, if it's not too much to ask." He set his glass on the wooden crate beside the armchair. Then he looked straight at Caleb, his expression serious for the first time since he'd stepped down from the wagon. "Your father needs you."

"Did he send you?" The words were out before Caleb could stop them.

"You know him better than that. He wouldn't send for you even if he were gasping his last breath. That doesn't change the truth. He needs you. The firm needs you. Not to mention countless others. Your mother, for one."

When Caleb made no reply, Nate stood and raised his voice. "What is it going to take to get you back? This place is beautiful, I'll grant you that," he said, motioning toward the ocean view, "but what are you *doing* here? You don't belong here. You belong in Boston, taking over the reins of a shipping empire, not in some tiny harbor hardly visible on a map."

Caleb rubbed his hand against his jaw, holding his emotions in check. He'd made his decision and was not going to defend it to anyone. Not anymore. "If *you* don't understand why I won't go back, you who know me, then I can't explain it to you."

His friend continued in a more reasonable tone. "I know how these little villages work. The people living here don't accept outsiders. Their families have been living here for centuries. It's all right for summering, but to *live* here… You have everything waiting for you in Boston. You can't just walk off and leave it all!"

The ship's clock above the mantel ticked in the silence. "Are you finished?" Caleb asked, his calm tone belying his inward turmoil.

Nate scowled at him in outrage for a second. Then he grinned. "Yes, sir. Are you ready to talk?"

Caleb sighed. He'd been foolish to think he'd be able to draw a line between everything in his previous life and his reclusive existence now in Haven's End. "None of what happened in Boston matters anymore."

"In a pig's eye."

"Maybe," Caleb conceded, "but I'm settled here now. Whatever goes on back in Boston is no concern of mine."

"Your father is sorry for not trusting your word. He realizes he shouldn't have condemned you out of hand on the basis of circumstantial evidence. But you know him. He'll never be able to tell you that. But let him show you. He'll never doubt your word, nor your loyalty, again."

Why was it too little, too late? Caleb stood, unable to contain himself within the confines of a chair.

"It won't work, running away." Nate's tone was soft, persuasive.

"It's called renouncing," Caleb said quietly.

"Is nothing I say going to make any difference?"

"No." The one syllable conveyed finality. He had thought long and hard about his decision.

Nate took up his glass and tilted it, watching the circle of liquid around its edge. He met Caleb's gaze over its rim. "I'm not giving up, you know." Without allowing the other a chance to reply, he changed the subject as if he hadn't just thrown down a serious challenge.

"So, what do you find to do in this place?" He looked around the sparsely furnished room and added, "What do you do when the fog rolls in?"

"I sleep."

Nate threw back his head and laughed. He took another sip of his drink before placing it on the crate and rising to stroll the perimeters of the room. "Glad to see you didn't renounce every last remnant of your past life," he said, stopping by the sea chest and picking up the spyglass sitting atop it. He focused it out the window.

"At least you shall never be bored with this view before you. I envy you that."

"How reassuring there's something you find redeeming about my new home."

Nate lifted his brow at the word *home*. He replaced the spyglass and continued his perusal of Caleb's belongings, fingering sextant, chronometer, compass—those tools by which a captain located his position at sea.

At the bookcase he examined Caleb's pitiful collection of books, which filled only half a shelf. Leafing through Becher's *Navigation,* he said, "Arabella has set a date for her marriage."

The news hit Caleb like an unexpected blow to the gut. His muscles hadn't had a chance to tense and form a wall rigid enough to withstand the assault.

Well, it was done. He should have known it was coming. Now he could get on with his life, knowing this chapter was irrevocably closed. *What life?* a part of his mind countered, taunting him with the emptiness of his days.

As if in reply to a question, Nate continued. "August twenty-fifth. Three o'clock. At the Congregational Church. Reception to follow at the home of the bride's parents."

Once again, the only sound in the room was that of the clock. "There's still time to do something about it. She continues in ignorance of Ellery's role."

Caleb turned to look beyond his back lawn, beyond the cove, to the sea. Cloud cover gave the ocean a silvery green appearance. A small whitecap here and there signaled the stiff breeze blowing in from the Atlantic. A few islands lay directly in front of his cove, outcroppings of rock more than real landmasses. The larger one was flat, like an old man lying half submerged by water.

He watched a wave curl against one side of its forbidding gray rock, then slip back down into the ocean in defeat. His soul felt like that rock. Assaulted. Barren. Alone.

Knowing Nate waited for him to say something, he asked, "Why shouldn't Arabella continue in ignorance about Ellery? What went on in the firm has nothing to do with her."

Nate slammed the heavy tome shut and turned to Caleb. "*Nothing* to do with her that the man she's planning to marry is the man who did everything in his power to make you look guilty? *Nothing* to do with her that the man who could have cleared you with one word was silent throughout the whole ordeal? And that you've done nothing to make her see the truth? Caleb, why do you insist on continuing the martyrdom? Wasn't it bad enough when you had no choice? Now you've got your father behind you."

Caleb tightened his hands into fists against the windowsill. Hadn't he had the same discussions in his head over and over?

"Arabella made her decision."

"She made a *mistake*." Nate's voice softened. "We all make mistakes. Is that a reason for condemning her to a lifetime shackled to a weak, envious, backstabbing—"

Caleb turned toward the room once more.

"You forget, Ellery is my cousin." When Nate made a sound of disagreement, Caleb held up a hand. "*I* made the decision to leave." He looked steadily at Nate, reminding him of his promise not to interfere. "My decision was final. What Ellery chooses to tell Arabella, or anyone else, is no longer my concern. It's not the reason I left Boston. You and I both know why I did that."

Nate replaced the book on the shelf. The care he took in putting it back exactly where he'd taken it told Caleb that his friend was using the time to compose himself. When he faced Caleb once again, his tone was calm.

"You're still letting your father rule you. Even way up here, where you can't see him or hear him, he continues to be a tyrant over you. I just wonder how long it's going to take you to figure that out."

* * *

Caleb awoke and looked up at the whitewashed ceiling, orienting himself. His mind was permeated with a feeling of anticipation, and he had to think a minute, wondering at its origin.

Nate had stayed until the day before, when he'd left on a schooner to Eastport, where he'd catch the overnight steamer to Boston. Caleb spent the two days of his visit showing him around. They had hiked and explored the coastline the same way they'd done as young sailors exploring the various ports of call.

Caleb stretched, reaching his arms up behind him, wondering at the sense of purpose he'd awakened with. He lay back on his pillow, the sunlight streaming in through the bare panes, until it came to him. The seeds!

Like an interrupted conversation that needed to be picked up where it had broken off, Caleb felt the need to follow through on his last encounter with Miss Patterson. She'd offered him seeds, and he was going to see about getting them.

Caleb threw back his sheet and blanket and jumped up from his bed, glad he no longer had to pretend that everything was all right, or weigh each word to make sure his faithful friend wouldn't pounce on it, ready to use it as ammunition for Caleb's return to Boston.

Glancing outside, he saw the sun shimmering off the blue Atlantic. Suddenly he felt a desire to plunge into it. He needed the cold, clear water to wash his mind of all the debate Nate's visit had threatened to resurrect.

Grabbing a towel, he headed outside in his drawers and undervest across the remaining knee-high grass of his back lawn, down the rickety wooden stairs to the beach below. He flung the towel onto the round stones, stripped off the undervest, and began walking toward the surf. Immediately, he had to slacken his pace, his feet finding it hard going over the stones. They were as round and smooth as ostrich eggs, originally a slate hue but now bleached almost white by the sun.

When he first entered the water, the cold almost made him turn back, and as he went deeper, his ankles and feet grew numb. The rubbery rockweed covering the stones beneath the surf made walking precarious. When the water reached his thighs, Caleb braced himself for the impact and plunged in.

He swam straight out against the tide, then, turning, he veered to the side, swimming parallel to the shore, up and back, until his body recovered from the shock of the icy water and the exertion made him impervious to the cold.

He emerged from the water, feeling a release from the past. Thoughts of Arabella's impending wedding could no longer threaten the equilibrium he'd achieved for himself.

Equilibrium? Since when? Certainly not since coming to Haven's End, when he'd tried to drown his sorrows in drink. As he rubbed himself vigorously with the towel, he tried to pinpoint the moment he'd begun feeling a semblance of peace.

Since beginning the garden.

A gust of breeze raised the gooseflesh on his skin, so he turned his feet away from the cove and back toward the stairs.

After shaving and dressing, he headed up the road to his neighbor's. She'd disappeared the day Nate had arrived, and Caleb hadn't seen her since.

He proceeded in a leisurely way up the slope toward her place. A row of hackmatack trees, their sparse needle-clad branches interlocking, created a windbreak between his land and hers. A thicket of low-growing wild rosebushes clustered along the edge of the road, but they had not yet blossomed.

The sound of the wind was constant, offering today a soft, steady sifting through the fir trees.

Miss Patterson's front yard was edged by a crumbling stone wall, which was almost buried in wild rose and blackberry vines. Beyond this barrier, the yard was neat, the grass short and green, with a profusion of flowers blossoming around the well and at a window box. The house itself was a small, weathered shingle-box, surely not containing more than one room.

The first thing that greeted Caleb was the loud bark of a dog. As soon as he'd stepped onto the path of crushed, bleached white clamshells that led to the front door, his neighbor's large, black dog bounded toward him. He was a black Labrador with enough other traits to deny any purity in his lineage. An old wound crumpled one ear, and an ugly pink scar disfigured the fur of one of its haunches.

Stopping a mere foot or so from Caleb, the dog kept up his barking. Caleb stood still, speaking to the dog in soft tones. Each time Caleb attempted to take a step forward, the dog dodged in front of him, his black eyes trained on Caleb.

Geneva walked around the side of the house, an empty pail swinging from each hand, heading toward the well. She stopped short at seeing Captain Caleb. What was he doing here? And Jake!

Recovering, she rushed toward the dog. "Down, Jake. That's enough! I said hush!" When the dog continued barking and running back and forth, Geneva turned to Caleb. "Don't pay him no mind. He won't hurt you."

The captain looked dubious. "Are you sure *he* knows that?"

"He just acts fierce. You won't hurt the captain, will you, boy?" She bent over and rubbed Jake's neck, seeking to ease the tension she felt in his muscles.

Caleb took a few cautious steps toward Jake and held out his hand for the dog's inspection. "Your mistress is right. I won't hurt you." Jake would have none of it, but continued his incessant barking.

"He don't take easily to strangers," she explained, wanting so much for Jake to take to the captain. Her fingers continued running down the dog's black hair in long, soothing strokes. "He had some bad times 'fore I got him, and he's still not over them—are you, Jake?" She bent her head over her pet.

She could feel the captain watching the rhythm of her fingers down the dog's haunches and she struggled to maintain their steadiness.

"Did his owner neglect him?" he asked gently.

Relieved that his focus was on the dog, she answered with a short laugh. "He probably wishes he had. No, his owner liked to take a stick to him and beat him 'til he could hardly stand." She gave him a sharp look. "The man liked to drink."

He didn't react to her pointed reference, but said, "You ran off the other day."

With a final pat, she straightened and picked up her buckets. "I didn't 'run off.'" She threw the words over her shoulder as she walked toward the well. "You had company. Figured the best thing I could do was stay out of your way."

She set the pails down on the wet slats and began pumping the handle. When she'd filled each, she took them up and headed back around the house.

"Here, let me." The captain reached her, ignoring Jake's immediate menacing bark, to grab one of the pails.

Surprised at the gesture, she didn't let go of the handle, but gave it a tug toward herself, sloshing water over the side of the rim. Jake immediately stood beside them, giving the captain a low-throated growl.

"Hush, Jake." Geneva took the bucket from the captain's loosened fingers. "Don't worry, Cap'n, I got it. I'm just taking it to the garden. It hasn't rained in a few days. Soil's getting dry." She heard the sentences coming out one atop the other in an effort to overcome her confusion at his gentlemanly gesture. Why did he treat her like a lady? Didn't he see she was more like a man than a woman?

When she realized he hadn't followed her, she had to swallow a sense of disappointment. She began watering her plants and was startled again at the sound of a whistle behind her.

The captain stood staring at her garden, a bucket in his hand. "Everything looks twice as high as in my garden."

She shrugged, hiding her pleasure. "Yours will catch up."

"Where do you want the water?" He held up the bucket.

She blinked. "You don't have to help me with this."

"You've helped me. And I'm sure to need your help again."

For a moment she looked at him, then finally turned away. "Suit yourself."

He took the bucket down another row of plants, watching and listening as she explained which way she watered what, taking care not to wet the leaves of some plants, not worrying about sloshing others, and crouching low to inspect the underside of a leaf here and there, looking for hungry caterpillars.

"By the way," he said when they'd each emptied their last bucketful, "you said something about seeds the other day. Do you still have any to spare?"

"You still want 'em?" she asked doubtfully.

The captain nodded. "You told me to plant something every week, didn't you?"

"Yep. I just figured since then—" She shook her head, falling silent.

"You figured what?"

She could feel a flush covering her cheeks. "Nothin'—you having company and all."

"Nate? He just stayed three nights."

She turned away, saying with a shrug, "Thought you'd be heading back to Boston by now."

Leaving him, she headed toward the lean-to attached to her house. She unlatched the door and entered its shadowy interior. Firewood lined most of the walls, floor to ceiling. The air was redolent with the spicy scent of drying spruce and balsam. She turned to the shelf holding gardening implements and took down a jar. From it she extracted a folded paper. Inside it were minute specks. She refolded the paper and handed it to the captain, who had followed her into the shed.

"You can bring me back what you don't use."

He nodded absently and took the paper. "What did you mean—you thought I would be returning to Boston the first chance I got?"

She continued uncorking jars and extracting folded packets of paper. "It's where you're from. Didn't think you'd stick it out here if you didn't have to."

The captain thrust out his hand to stop the motion of her hand on a jar. "I *chose* to come here. I didn't *have to.* Do you understand the difference?"

She raised startled eyes to him. For a second their gazes met and held. The sunlight sliced through the open doorway, cutting a path across her face, leaving her feeling exposed, yet helpless to look away. His eyes traveled across her face, almost as if he were seeing her for the first time.

"I jus' thought—I mean—I didn't think anyone'd come here to live. Not from Boston, anyway. Ain't none of my business, anyhow."

His hand still held her wrist. She jerked it away, and he immediately let it go.

He looked at the seed papers in his other hand. "How do I tell what is what?"

Again he'd caught her off guard. "Uh, I jus' know by looking at 'em." She unfolded one and said, "This here's lettuce. It'll grow quick. You should get enough through the summer if you plant some now, and then again in a week or so."

"I should write the names of each on the papers."

She bit her lip. "Uh, sure. I don't have a pencil with me."

He took one from his breast pocket. "Here."

She looked at the pencil distrustfully. "You write. I— I'll tell you what they are."

"Good enough." He unfolded the first paper and showed her. Then he refolded it and wrote the name she gave him on the paper. They continued until they'd labeled all the packets, though she gave him only the seeds she thought he should plant.

When they finished, he thanked her and left. She watched him walk back down the path to the road. Shame engulfed her.

What a fool she felt, not even being able to do so simple a task as write down the names of the seeds.

Chapter Three

Caleb walked down the dirt road that descended into the village. He'd hiked the three miles into town from the Point, enjoying the droplets of mist on his face the entire way, and now his clothes and hair felt damp.

Gradually the number of white clapboard houses increased until he was in the center of town, which consisted of a post office, a small store, a newly opened hotel, and a few warehouses along the three piers jutting out into the harbor.

Caleb entered Mr. Watson's store and carefully shut the door behind him. He was glad to be out of the fog. The woodstove radiated heat throughout the store's interior. A group of men sat around it, their eyes turned to him.

He nodded to them before turning to the storekeeper. "Afternoon."

"Afternoon, Captain," Mr. Watson answered.

Caleb ventured in a few feet. One woman looked at him over some bolts of fabric spread out before her. He removed his hat, acknowledging her. With a quick little duck of her head, she turned her attention back to the calico prints.

The men leaning back in their chairs by the potbellied

stove continued eyeing him with undisguised interest, their boots propped against the fender of the stove. Although none of the men said a word, their mouths weren't still. Two moved in rhythm working over plugs of tobacco and the third sucked on the stem of a pipe.

Caleb gave his list to Mr. Watson.

"Good summah we've been havin' up until today," one man in bib overalls commented.

"Yup," another answered, his plump fingers interlaced atop his stomach. "I seen summahs the sun didn't come out atall."

"Was gettin' a bit dry for the plantin', though," Mr. Watson put in from across the room.

"I seen you got a garden started down at the Point." One of the three by the stove turned his light blue eyes on Caleb. He stood out from the other two by his neater appearance. His red beard was trimmed and his hair slicked back. He wore a suit and string tie in contrast to the others' overalls and open collars. "It's been quite a few yeahs since anybody's tried to grow anything up theah."

Caleb nodded, wondering when anybody had been by his place to notice his garden.

"Didn't evah get your house finished, did ya?" the red-bearded man asked when Caleb didn't volunteer any more information.

"No." Caleb moved to examine the fishhooks at one end of the store. "But it's fine for myself."

"Ain't too lonely for ya, after Boston?" one of the men in overalls asked from around his pipe.

Caleb shook his head without offering any comment.

"You could always knock on your neighbah's door if you're hankerin' aftah some company," the man with plump fingers laced atop his belly suggested. He seemed the boldest of the three, if the angle of his tilted chair was any indication.

The other two chuckled. "Hankerin' after a bullet in his chest, you mean," Bib Overalls put in.

"'Less, o'course, she was particularly ornery that mornin' and aimed lowah," Red Beard added, punctuating his remark with a well-aimed stream of tobacco juice at the spittoon.

All three men, as well as Mr. Watson, laughed at the implication.

"First he'd have to get past Jake," Bib Overalls warned.

"Ain't as if no one around here hasn't tried to get past ol' Jake." Plump Fingers angled a sly look at Red Beard. "Remembah the time Elijah tried to sneak into her shack after dark? Wasn't long aftah her pa passed on." The others nodded, chuckling at the story to come. "Came back out in short ordah, a hole shot clean through his straw hat. We ribbed him some about that hat." Plump Fingers slapped his knee, and the others laughed at the memory.

"I think ol' Elijah learned his lesson," Red Beard said with a nod of his head, shifting the tobacco from one side of his mouth to the other.

"I'll wager not everyone's learned his lesson." Plump Fingers lifted his sandy-haired fingers and stared at them, then looked across at Red Beard.

"I ain't heard o' no man who's snuck past ol' Jake at night, though it ain't been for lack of wantin'," Red Beard answered placidly, but with a gleam in his eyes that testified of his own desires in that direction.

"Gotta be careful o' Ginny. Her ol' man had a mean streak a mile wide and I think she inherited a good portion of it," Mr. Watson explained to Caleb.

"She probably needs it, by the sounds of things," Caleb said quietly, looking at the three men around the stove as he spoke.

All three chairs stopped rocking and hung tilted in mid-air as the men stared at Caleb. He could hear the murmur of the lady and Mr. Watson behind him die down.

Bib Overalls' chair was the first to resume its rocking. "I think Genevar's just waitin' for someone who's man enough to tame her," he said, pointing his pipe first at Red Beard and then at Caleb. "What do you think, Cap'n?"

Red Beard's smile had something nasty in it. "The cap'n has already lost one good woman. Just think, if he was to get turned down by Salt Fish Ginny, how'd he be able to lift his head up in public?" He slapped his knee and chortled. The other two men laughed more guardedly, awaiting Caleb's reaction.

"It's been my experience that the more a man boasts about his conquests, the less they exist in truth," Caleb commented, leaning his back against the counter.

All the men except the red-bearded one laughed heartily.

When their laughter subsided, Mr. Watson smiled. "We've got some fresh eggs. Would you like me to add a dozen to your order?" he asked Caleb.

Caleb turned back toward the shopkeeper. "Half a dozen will do."

"It'll cost you more that way. Two bits a dozen, but fifteen cents for half."

"I'll take the half," Caleb repeated.

When he faced the room at large again, he discovered the topic of Miss Patterson was by no means exhausted.

"You mustn't blame Geneva for the way she's turned out," the woman from the other end of the counter piped up. "She used to be black and blue from the beatings her pa give her. It's no wonder she's unfriendly."

Deciding he'd had enough village gossip, Caleb moved away, hoping that would end the subject. Looking at several stacks of denim overalls, he began to finger through them until his order was filled.

"Those are fine quality denim. Just the thing for gardenin'. Is there a particular size you'd like to look at?" Mr. Watson came to stand behind the stacks of trousers.

"Is my order ready?"

He watched the friendly expectancy on the shopkeeper's face turn to surprise and end in frosty politeness. "Yes, of course. Is there anything else you be needin' today?"

Caleb shook his head and walked back to the center counter.

"The way ol' Jeb Patterson kept her out of school, it was disgraceful," the woman said. "We tried to reason with him, but anytime anybody would come by, he'd wave that shotgun at us from the doorway, and all his hunting dogs would bark something ferocious. There was nothing to do but leave him to his own devices."

Caleb watched Mr. Watson add the column of numbers on a piece of paper. He didn't want to hear anything more about Geneva Patterson. The men's conversation sickened him. He'd been curious about her. He'd realized the other day that she wasn't as self-assured as she'd first appeared to him. She was also kinder-hearted than her gruff manner suggested. It was evident in her manner toward her dog.

He'd been intrigued about why she dressed like a man and hid any feminine charms she might possess. Now he understood why.

"And her mother, poor woman, Canuck—"

"Half-breed," Bib Overalls put in. "Woman could barely speak English."

Caleb ignored their talk. He paid his bill, aware of the silence that had returned to the store, knowing everyone was just waiting for him to leave so they could begin commenting on his past.

He put his hat back on at the door, tipping it to the general company. "Good day." He heard the door bang behind him as he walked down the worn steps.

After he had arrived home and put everything away, he felt at loose ends. The fog had lifted but the day remained cool and overcast. Without a conscious decision, he found himself directing his feet back up the hill toward Miss Patterson's. He'd seen her working in her front yard when he'd passed. He had no valid reason for visiting, but something drew him.

Jake started barking the moment Caleb came in sight. As he came up the path, the dog ran up and down alongside him.

"Hello, boy. Whatcha got there?" He examined the old buoy Jake had brought him.

Miss Patterson, her back toward him, was sawing a board on a sawhorse. Caleb went up to her and pushed her gently aside. "Here, let me do that for you."

She jumped when she felt his touch. "Hey, what're you doin'?" she demanded when his hand touched the handle of the saw.

"I can finish it for you."

She scowled. "I can do it fine myself."

"Give me that," he insisted, trying to pry the handle away from her. Her fingers only tightened on the handle as she attempted to continue the sawing motion. They began a brief tug-of-war for the saw, but when Caleb realized how ludicrous it was, he let go and stepped back.

"Did anyone ever tell you you're about as stubborn as a mule?"

"When they bother to talk to me, yes," she answered shortly above the rasp of the saw.

At the words, Caleb felt a curious link with her. He knew how it felt to be singled out. He shook his head, never having imagined in Boston that one day he'd find something in common with a person such as Geneva Patterson. Taciturn, ornery, proud…

Caleb thought about what he'd heard at the store. He found it hard to fathom the men's salacious gossip. If there was a spark of femininity in Miss Geneva Patterson, he couldn't see it. He stepped back and watched her finish sawing the board. Without a word she carried it past him, to the front stoop, where she'd already pried off an old plank.

Carefully she placed the new board over the hole and lined it up with the rest of the steps. She took some nails from a piece of paper and picked up a hammer from the grass. As usual she was wearing that beat-up old hat, so Caleb couldn't see much of her profile. Her eyes were fine, really, not black as he'd supposed, but deep brown, as he'd seen the other day in the light, like polished mahogany, and fringed with inky black lashes. They were about the only feminine feature she possessed, besides the braid that fell down her back like a black rope.

She had on her habitual flannel shirt, buttoned to the very top. His gaze wandered farther down. The bib of her overalls curved over her bosom. The baggy pants didn't reveal much of her legs; he imagined they must be long and slim, like her arms and fingers. He remembered her gentle strokes over Jake's fur.

The only woman he could really compare her to was Arabella, and the two were so different it hardly seemed a fair comparison. Caleb watched Miss Patterson's long fingers position a nail and grip the hammer. *Whack!*

When she'd pounded in the first nail, she suddenly took off her hat and wiped her forehead with a sleeve. She didn't put the hat back on, but proceeded to line up another nail on the board.

Her hair was pulled straight back into that one long, thick dark braid, giving credence to the gossip that her mother was a half-breed. She had high cheekbones, as well. But her looks were just as much Gallic—pale skin and dark hair and eyes—reminding him of the women he'd seen at the ports of Bordeaux and Marseilles.

The only thing relieving the sharpness of her features was the widow's peak above her forehead. It occurred to Caleb that she used her entire mode of dress to hide behind. With those men hanging around like a pack of hungry wolves, she probably had no choice.

Caleb's eyes narrowed as a memory teased the edges of his mind. Suddenly it came to him—a young woman tripping at the wharves, spilling all her vegetables, the last time he'd come to Haven's End. On that occasion he'd played the gentleman, coming to her aid.

Before he could recollect further, Miss Patterson spoke without looking at him. "What're you starin' at?"

"Nothing. I'm just admiring your work."

"If you're so all fired to do some carpentry, why don't you finish that mausoleum of yours?"

Her words brought him up short. "An apt description," he said, glancing at the house he had planned with such enthusiasm. "Is that what they're calling it around here?"

She didn't look at him from where she was kneeling at the steps, but he could tell he had her attention. She took a nail out of her mouth, her eyes focused on some point on the steps, and replied in a mumble, as if she were ashamed to admit it. "I just heard the word used once. Folks were sayin' as how you've buried yourself in the place."

He said nothing, but watched her position the nail on the board. Above the intermittent whack of the hammer, he heard her words. "They say your lady—" *bang!* "—broke off the engagement." *Bang!* "What's the matter?" *Bang!* "She decide—" *bang!* "—she preferred someone else—" *bang!* "—after you run into your troubles in Boston?"

Silence.

To his own surprise he found himself answering as he watched her pick up another nail from the paper. "As a matter of fact, she did."

He wasn't sure if she could hear his quiet words, but her immediate reaction told him she had. She looked up at him, hammer and nail forgotten, her expression stunned as if that was the last thing she'd expected to hear.

"You're serious." Her words were as quietly spoken as his own. At his nod, she remained silent a moment, as if truly stumped for the first time.

Finally she just shook her head. "Don't fret, Cap'n," she said softly. "The woman's clearly got no sense." With those words she turned back to her work.

Caleb was amazed to feel no resentment at her tone of sympathy. In fact, he actually felt comforted. He didn't have the foggiest idea how some rustic, uneducated woman's simple words could reach him. Perhaps because for the first time in his life he felt someone's complete acceptance of him. Even with his friend, Nate, Caleb had struggled to prove himself since the day they'd met. Caleb had been a lad of eight, and Nate, at thirteen, had appeared to him a hero. Caleb had been playing catch-up ever since.

But with the woman kneeling at the steps in front of him, there was no censure, no judgment, and no expectations he had to fill. It didn't seem to matter to Miss Patterson what his background was, whether he was innocent or guilty of wrongdoing. She accepted him just as he presented himself. No past, no gossip, no stories that had reached her ears seemed to affect her opinion.

Caleb had never experienced this kind of acceptance, and he didn't know quite what to make of it.

The next day Caleb was thinning his thriving seedlings when he heard Jake's bark. He turned, amazed to see the dog bounding across his yard making straight for him. The bark sounded exuberant, and Caleb sat back, curious to see what his neighbor and her dog were coming for. Geneva walked more slowly behind her pet, slower than Caleb had ever seen her walk. She always seemed so purposeful, and today, he'd venture to say, she approached hesitantly.

Caleb had begun calling her Geneva to himself. He liked the sound of it. It suited her.

Jake ran around Caleb, and Caleb turned, afraid the dog would step on his new plants, but Jake didn't even touch the edge of the soil. Caleb glanced up at his mistress, realizing, despite appearances, how well trained the dog must be.

Geneva was carrying a basket in one hand. When she stopped, still a little distance from him, Caleb pushed his hat back. "Good morning. Come to inspect your little ones?"

She looked surprised at his remark. "What's that supposed to mean?"

He made a motion with his head toward the row of plants. "You've got a stake in these crops. I expect you want to see how they're doing."

She flushed. "'Course not. They're yours."

After a short silence, he said, "I wish there was something I could do for you in return. You've helped me immeasurably. If you hadn't come over that first day, I'd have nothing but a big weed field by now and a sore back."

She shook her head. "I didn't do nothin' special."

"I wouldn't be too sure of that," he answered. Their gazes met, and he realized she was the only villager who hadn't once looked at him as if he were guilty. "Thank you."

She gripped the handle of her basket with her two hands, clearly uncomfortable with his gratitude. He knew he'd offend her if he offered her money in payment for her help. "What have you got there?" he asked to distract her.

"This?" She looked down at the basket before holding it out to him. "Brought you some strawberries. They're wild, my crop's not ripe yet. But these are better anyway. Sweeter."

To ease her obvious embarrassment, Caleb stood and took the basket from her. Inside, nestled in some hay, sat a dish full of the reddest, tiniest strawberries he'd ever seen. He popped one into his mouth, smiling at the burst of sweetness and juice. "These are good. Where did you pick them?"

She motioned off to a field up the road. "Up there by the edge of the woods. I'll show you, if you like."

"They probably make good jam," he added, still hoping to put her at ease.

She nodded and looked toward the ocean. "I just picked 'em this morning. Thought I'd bring you some."

Caleb's eyes narrowed in sudden suspicion. "You wouldn't be taking pity on me now, would you, after what I told you yesterday?"

Her reddened cheeks made her look so guilty, Caleb felt

sorry immediately. Clearly she wasn't used to offering a person comfort.

Her denial came swiftly, cutting off any chance Caleb had of making amends. "Ain't none of my business why you're here or what your lady done to you." She stuck her hands in her back pockets and looked down at the toes of her boots.

"Forget about all that. It doesn't matter anymore anyway." Caleb set the basket down on the ground, then straightened, rubbing his two hands together, deciding it was better for both of them if he changed the subject. "I'd like to repay you for all the help you've given me with the planting. You seem bound and determined not to let me help you with any physical labor. Isn't there anything I can do for you, in return for all you've done for me?" He laughed ruefully and gestured toward the basket. "Including these beautiful berries you picked for my breakfast?"

"You don't have to do nothing for me."

"I know that. But neither do I want to be in your debt. I'll never feel I can ask you another favor, not even to show me exactly where you picked these berries—"

"You could teach me to read," she blurted out before he could finish persuading her.

"What?" She'd said it so fast, he wasn't sure he'd heard correctly.

She continued looking stubbornly at her feet. "You heard me."

Caleb hid his surprise and said in a neutral voice, "I thought I heard you say I could teach you to read."

"That's right." She began tapping one foot, as if at any moment she'd be off.

"I'm not sure whether I could teach anyone to read or write," he said carefully.

She finally looked at him, jutting out her chin. "What's the matter? It's not too difficult, is it?"

Her tone was belligerent, but that didn't fool Caleb. He realized what treacherous ground he was treading on. "No, it's not too difficult. It's just that you have to be specially trained to teach someone to read."

Her focus returned to her feet. The toe of the boot that had been tapping now began to dig into the dirt. "You think I'm too stupid to learn."

Caleb held back a sigh. Whatever he said would probably be wrong. "I think you're very intelligent."

At that she looked at him.

"I'm the one who's probably too stupid to teach you. It's like planting. Did you think it would be so easy to teach an ignorant seaman to plant a garden?"

She considered, then shook her head. "But I did, didn't I?"

Poor example, he said to himself. To her he said, "Yes, you did, and you did a fine job. Except for neglecting to warn me about those cutworms." He let out a breath at seeing her reluctant smile, a smile that transformed her from dour farmer to fresh-faced lass.

Against his will, knowing it would probably end badly, he said with a sigh, "If you're willing to risk it with me, I shall try to teach you. Only, I don't guarantee anything. You must promise me that if I can't teach you, it doesn't mean you can't learn, just that I'm not a very good teacher. Is that agreed?"

She nodded.

"I only have a few books and they wouldn't be suitable—technical things on sailing."

"That's all right," she interrupted. "I have a book."

He raised an eyebrow.

"It was my ma's."

He wondered what kind of woman her mother had been. He'd heard about her father from the villagers, but he hadn't heard much about the maternal influence in her life. Whatever it had been had made an impact, judging by the reverent tone of voice she used when she mentioned her mother's book.

"Good enough," he agreed. "It's settled." He held out his hand.

After a second's hesitation, she brought forth her own hand. He felt the long, slim fingers wrap around the edge of his palm, and he remembered once again their soft touch upon her pet.

"Bring the book this afternoon and we'll start with our first lesson."

Geneva took the cloth off the rough-hewn chest and lifted the lid. The pungent smell of cedar brought back a sharp reminder of her mother. Geneva had knelt at her feet whenever her ma had opened the chest. Geneva's pa had made the chest for his bride, and in it she'd kept the few items of her former life. Over the years, her mother had added the quilts she'd made. Geneva lifted those out first, remembering her mother's hands as she'd sat in her rocker and sewed the squares together. Bits of pale yellow and lavender and moss green formed a pattern of flowers against a white muslin background.

Next came a couple of woolen sweaters her ma had knitted for herself and her husband. Geneva often wore them in winter now. There at the bottom of the chest lay her mother's few personal possessions—some old dresses, the cloth worn thin from so many washings. Geneva had never been able to bring herself to cut them up for rags.

Geneva's hand smoothed the brown wool skirt of her mother's best dress, the dress she'd been married in. She and Pa had married in November. The sisters at the convent had made the dress for her. That was the last thing they'd given her before sending her back out into the world. They'd received her as a little girl, from her Indian father who'd just lost his white wife.

Geneva set the dress aside. Below it was a thick roll of fabric, which her mother had purchased for a new dress. She remembered her excitement as a little girl that last spring before her mother had become bedridden, as her mother told her she'd bought enough fabric to make a dress for the two of them for summer. She'd told Geneva they'd be like twins instead of mother and daughter. The fabric had remained in one piece and would probably stay that way until it began to crumble at the folds with decay.

Geneva pushed aside the fabric and uncovered the object she'd come to get. A soft, brown, suede-bound volume with gilt letters. Geneva opened the book upon her crossed legs. Neatly printed letters in black upon white. She could recognize most of the letters, but could make nothing of the groupings. She'd tried and tried over the years.

What had made her think that this time it would be any different? What had possessed her to ask the captain to teach her to read? She could feel the heat suffusing her face as she thought once again of her request. The captain had acted so cordial. He'd seemed practically like his old self, the man she remembered on the wharf, so genuinely interested in doing something for her. But to spill out her most shameful secret? What had possessed her?

Having already spent the day agonizing over her behavior that morning, Geneva gave herself a shake and replaced everything in the chest, except the book. She stood and straightened her shoulders. She'd already washed her hands and face and combed her hair and changed her shirt. There was nothing left but to face the situation head-on. She gripped the book and marched to the door.

The afternoon sun was still high in the sky, causing the ocean at the end of the Point to shimmer in a thousand brilliant lights. Geneva could list a dozen things she should be doing instead of whiling away the afternoon poring over a book.

Jake started to follow her. "No, boy. You'd best stay home," she told him, giving her yard a look of longing. How much she'd give to take her foolish words back and spend the afternoon on her soil, with the things she knew. "Your mistress has got to have all her wits about her this afternoon."

Jake was no longer listening to her words. He turned his head away from her and began to bark. Geneva followed his gaze.

She stifled a sigh of annoyance at seeing her neighbor, Mrs. Stillman, bearing down her way, carrying a bundle wrapped in a dishcloth.

"Geneva!" Mrs. Stillman's shrill voice reached her from the road.

Geneva sighed again and walked to meet the woman.

"Good afternoon." Mrs. Stillman's voice was breathless from her hike down the road.

"Afternoon." Geneva remembered too late that she was still holding her mother's book. She didn't know whether to rest it on the stone wall in back of her, or just hang on to it, hoping it would go unnoticed. She decided the less movement she made with it, the better.

"You haven't been by to collect any milk." The farmer's wife readjusted one of the pins in her abundant gray roll of hair. "I brought you some fresh butter. Sarah just churned it this morning."

Sarah was Mrs. Stillman's oldest daughter and Geneva's age. Geneva had detested her since the two had walked to school together and Sarah had whispered things to her sisters, pointing and giggling at Geneva the whole way.

"Thank you," Geneva mumbled, reaching out to take the proffered butter, laying the book on the stone wall in the process.

Mrs. Stillman smoothed her starched apron. "Is everything all right with you? You haven't been by the farm."

"Right as rain. Been busy with the garden is all."

Mrs. Stillman nodded.

Geneva shifted the covered crock of butter from one hand to the other.

"Your new neighbor hasn't been botherin' you, has he?"

Geneva glanced at her. "Who?"

Mrs. Stillman's glance strayed down the road to the Point. "The captain. I've seen you over there."

Geneva started. "What's wrong with giving him a hand?"

"Now, Geneva, I know you don't like anyone interfering with what you do, and land sakes, you don't live the kind of life I'd like to see any of my daughters live, but listen when I tell you, that man's not someone you should get friendly with."

Geneva straightened her shoulders. "There's nothing wrong with Cap'n Caleb. He's a decent, honorable gentleman."

Mrs. Stillman's lips tightened. "A woman's got only one reputation and she'd better do her best to keep it spotless."

"I ain't doin' nothin' to be ashamed of. That's more'n I can say for the rest of Haven's End."

"Don't get your dander up. I'm not saying you are. But the less time you spend over there, the better."

Geneva glared at her but decided she'd said enough.

When Mrs. Stillman saw that Geneva wasn't going to say anything more, she sighed and smoothed down the front of her apron once more.

"Well, I've spoken my piece. I'll leave the butter with you. You make sure you come by and get a pail of milk. Need to put some meat on your bones." Her neighbor looked her critically up and down. She'd long ago stopped admonishing her to wear a dress, but never managed to hide her looks of disapproval.

"What's that you got there?" Mrs. Stillman's chin jutted toward the book perched on the flat stone.

"Just a book."

She chuckled. "Where are you going with a book?" Her eyes narrowed in suspicion. "You aren't going…to lend it to a neighbor?" Her gaze traveled down the road toward the captain's house.

Geneva looked down at the broken clamshells at her feet, noticing how green and damp the grass was along the edges of her path.

"A young woman oughtn't be visitin' a man alone. It's not proper."

Geneva wished she could just walk off and leave her nosy neighbor, but she didn't want to do anything to cause harm to the captain. People were condemning him enough as it was. She thought of the way he'd told her that Miss Harding had broken the engagement and gone with another man. He had stated it so simply, but Geneva had sensed the pain behind the admission.

The captain didn't need her adding to his woes. He needed her protection from the villagers' gossip.

She cleared her throat, looking Mrs. Stillman in the eye. "Cap'n Caleb hasn't done nothin' that wasn't proper and decent. I just offered some help to start his garden. There hasn't been any more to it than that."

"Well, you take care, my dear. I know you have no one in the world to speak for you. I feel it's my bounden duty to look after you as if you was my daughter."

"Yes'm." Geneva looked at the butter. "Well, I'd best get this out of the sun." She gave her neighbor a final nod. "I'll be seein' ya. Thank you kindly for the butter." She turned back toward her door, hoping that by the time she came out, Mrs. Stillman would be gone.

She could feel her neighbor's gaze on her until she closed the door behind her. She waited, peering through her curtain until the older woman climbed back up the hill, before venturing out again.

Captain Caleb was nowhere to be seen outside his yard, so Geneva headed toward the kitchen door, forgetting about Mrs. Stillman as her thoughts turned to her impending reading lesson. Her heart began pounding with each step she took closer to the house.

She heard the captain's voice immediately after her knock, bidding her come in. She turned the doorknob and entered his kitchen. It was a large room, larger than her entire house including the lean-to. Not as large as the big hotel kitchen down at the harbor, but larger than any other kitchen she'd seen.

"Come on in. I'm back here."

Geneva followed the captain's voice through a dining room and into a long, airy room at the back of the house. Her first impression was space. So much empty space. Space and light. The room had a clean, swept feeling. It contained very little furniture. The walls that faced the windows were lined with empty bookcases. She ventured farther along the shiny wooden floors. Two framed pictures hung one atop the other on one wall. Square-rigged ships. She wondered whether they were from his father's line.

The focal point was the windows, a whole row of them overlooking the sea. It was exactly what she'd imagined it would look like, the view from a house right at the end of the Point.

"That's the reason I bought this piece of land."

Geneva jumped at the sound of the captain's voice behind her.

He came and stood beside her. "I took one look at the view from the old house that used to stand here, and knew this was where I wanted to build my home."

Geneva just nodded, too awed by the fact that the captain's thoughts and hers had coincided so perfectly. "It's the most beautiful spot in Haven's End."

He glanced at her. "You're just up the hill."

"I look out onto the bay. I like it well enough. But this is the wide-open sea."

He nodded in understanding. "I imagine the gales blow fierce in winter."

"You keep a good fire goin', you'll be all right."

He motioned to her book. "Shall we get started? Come, I've set up a table out here on the porch. As long as the weather is so nice, I thought we might as well be outside." He led her through a glass-paned door to a veranda.

Geneva sat and looked from the captain, seating himself so close to her, to her mother's book in her hands, and finally to the shimmering sea beyond the two of them. Mrs. Stillman, the rest of Haven's End and Miss Harding were all somewhere far behind them. Only she and the captain existed in this world. Suddenly, she felt as if she were tasting a little bit of heaven.

The captain held out a hand. "May I?"

She nodded and handed him the book.

He laid it on the table and opened it. She saw him frown and began to worry that something was wrong.

He looked at her. "This is in French."

She stared at him, her thoughts tumbling around, but all pointing in one direction: once again she'd failed.

When she didn't speak, he asked her, "Do you understand what that means? It's written in another language. It wouldn't do you much good to learn to read in French."

"It was my ma's. She spoke the language."

"Your mother was French?"

"Only half. But she was raised in a convent, in *Québec*. I reckon that's all they spoke to her up there."

The captain smiled at her. "You say it like a native. Did your mother teach you her native tongue?"

Geneva shook her head. "No. I heard her say a word now and then, but I didn't understand it. Pa made her speak English whenever he was around." She looked beyond him toward the sea. "I remember she'd call me *chérie*. And she gave me a long, funny-sounding name."

"Your name is not Geneva?"

She shook her head. *"Geneviève."* She pronounced it just the way she used to hear her mother say it, with the airy *g* sound and the last syllables all running together like a softly expelled breath. "Trouble was, Pa couldn't say it right, and ended up deciding it should be plain old 'Geneva,' but Ma always said it the French way. *Geneviève*," she repeated. She turned to see the captain looking at her in wonder. She felt the heat steal into her face. "What's wrong with that?"

"You say your name exactly as a Frenchwoman would. Your accent is impeccable."

Her chagrin turned into pleasure. But she just shrugged. "That's about *all* I can say."

The captain closed the book, resting his hand atop it. She remembered his hands, large and capable-looking, from the first time he'd touched her, back on the wharf. They were not so much the gentleman's hands as they had appeared then, but still appealing, probably more so now that they were toughened by the soil.

"It's a Bible, you know."

She pulled her gaze away from his hands. "What? Oh." She focused on her mother's book again. "I should have figured. She was always reading it. Especially once she was bedridden."

"Was she ill very long?"

"Just a year."

"I'm sorry. How old were you when you lost her?"

Geneva shrugged. "Eight, nine, near as I can reckon."

"You don't remember exactly how old you were then?"

"Not exactly. Pa didn't believe in celebrating things like birthdays." She gave a bitter laugh. "If I could read, I'd know exactly how old I was. Ma wrote it all down here." Geneva reached for the Bible, and Captain Caleb pushed it toward her. She opened it to one of the front pages where she knew her mother's handwriting appeared. She flattened the pages and turned the book back toward the captain, beginning to feel the excitement of uncovering a long-held secret. He leaned over it, seeming as eager as she felt.

"Geneviève Samantha Patterson. Née 5 Mai, 1850." He looked at her triumphantly.

"You speak French," she said.

"Just what I learned in school." He smiled at her. "You, Miss Patterson, were born on May fifth. You just turned twenty-three last month."

She nodded slowly. "I knew it said five, but I wasn't sure of the rest."

"Now that we've solved that mystery, we still have the problem of how we're going to find you something to read. Did you never have any schooling at all?"

"Just a couple of years. Then Ma got sick, and Pa took me out of school to tend to her."

"You must have been rather young for such a burden."

"She was no burden. I was glad to do it." Geneva looked down at the painted wooden table. "Wish I coulda' done more."

The captain's hand covered hers. For an instant she felt an overwhelming desire to turn her hand over and receive his comfort, but she held back. Life had taught her not to rely on anyone or anything.

So she pulled her hand away and clasped it rigidly on the tabletop with her other hand. "When's this lesson going to begin?"

Captain Caleb withdrew his hand with a chuckle and sat back. He lifted a stone paperweight from the center of the table and removed a sheet of white paper from a small stack. "Let's see what you remember from your school days."

Chapter Four

Caleb looked at Geneva's departing back as she climbed up the slope to her house. He didn't know which of them felt the more exhausted, pupil or teacher. He tried to look on the bright side. At least she had mastered the alphabet back in school and could form the letters fairly well. She recognized several one-syllable words, though anything more complicated was beyond her. He felt sorry for her, seeing her struggle.

He felt almost as helpless, not sure how to approach teaching her. He tried to remember how he'd been taught in school. School! Like Geneva, he'd only had a couple of years of formal schooling before being yanked out and shipped off to sea. But at least his father had provided a tutor on those journeys. A man who was quick to rap an eight-year-old boy on the knuckles at the slightest sign of fidgeting. And who was fonder of sitting in the captain's quarters over a glass of brandy than of overseeing a boy's lessons.

He smiled, understanding the frustration Geneva tried to control but which was so evident each time she missed a word or copied his example incorrectly. It was going to be an uphill struggle—but worth it.

He could feel something stirring in him at the effort to help someone. She was obviously bright, but had suffered nothing but disadvantages since her youth. From the little she'd told him, he could form a vivid picture of the rest. A little girl struggling to nurse a dying woman, left at the mercy of a hard, unfeeling woodsman. No wonder she'd rejected Caleb's offer of sympathy so emphatically. She probably didn't know how to accept anyone's helping hand.

After the lesson and once Geneva had disappeared over the ridge, Caleb watched a buggy come down the road. It held a lone woman, Maud Bradford. He felt mixed emotions at seeing another acquaintance from Boston.

He'd forgotten she summered at Haven's End. She was an old friend of his mother's. Part of him yearned for news from Boston, yearned to see a friendly face. But just as strongly, he wished to put everything from Boston behind him. He didn't want to be reminded of all he'd left behind, to question his decision to leave. Still, he'd survived Nate's visit. Surely, this would be easy in comparison.

The horse clip-clopped to his gate, and Caleb took his time walking toward it.

Mrs. Bradford waited patiently for him, her face wreathed in a smile as he approached. Despite her gray hair, her face was unlined and held a serene quality that Caleb found hard to resist.

"Hello, Caleb."

He nodded to her and proceeded to open the gate. When the buggy pulled up at the house, Caleb helped Mrs. Bradford down from her seat.

She looked him up and down. "You're looking well, Caleb. I must confess I wasn't quite sure what to expect."

It was impossible to feel any resentment toward this elegant lady who was his mother's age, and whom he'd known since he was in short skirts. She'd always spoken her mind, but in such a simple, gentle way that it was impossible to take offense.

"And I must confess," he told her, "I'd forgotten you summered here in Haven's End."

She chuckled. "Am I welcome? I heard from Nate that you weren't entertaining."

Caleb smiled at the understatement. "You're always welcome, as long as you don't expect too much."

She gave him a look of sympathetic understanding. "I won't expect you to do or say anything you don't feel inclined to."

"Good. Now, can I invite you in for a cup of tea?"

"That sounds most welcome."

They walked together into the house, and Caleb guided her toward the back. After he'd brewed a pot of tea, the two sat in two chairs overlooking the sea.

Mrs. Bradford sat back with a sigh of contentment. "I didn't mean to put you to any trouble, my boy, but this tea is just the thing after my ride out here." She stirred the spoon around in her cup.

"No trouble at all." Caleb wanted to ask her about his mother, but held back, reluctant to bring up anything pertaining to Boston.

"Your place is lovely. Lovely, indeed." She looked around with a smile, not appearing to notice the scant furnishings. She gestured toward the view outside. "The location is simply breathtaking."

She took another sip of tea. When Caleb made no effort at small talk, she replaced her cup in its saucer. "I promised your mother I'd look in on you."

He appreciated her directness. "How is she?"

"Don't you know?" Her clear gray gaze made him feel uncomfortable.

"I haven't received any news."

"Nor have you sent her any."

He rubbed his cheek. "I've tried to write on a few occasions. Truly. But the words don't seem to come."

She smiled sadly. "I understand. I think she does, too. That's why she's giving you time. And that's why she sent me. I shall give her a full report. It will ease her burden. I'll say I found you fit and in good spirits, living in a very salutary location."

"Thank you. It will help knowing she's not worrying."

She lifted her eyebrows in a look that said more clearly than words that keeping his mother from worrying was another matter.

They continued drinking their tea. After a few moments, Mrs. Bradford spoke again. "Your father's firm has issued a formal statement to the press that any allegations against you were completely unfounded. Investigations are continuing to uncover the real perpetrator."

She looked down at her cup and saucer. "Details were very sketchy, however, to explain how there could ever have been a breath of suspicion surrounding your name. Errors in judgment…hasty accusations…"

Caleb sat still, not sure how the news affected him. So, his father had respected his wishes and not exposed his cousin's part in the calumny against him. At least Caleb could be grateful for that.

The only thing he felt was the same hollowness he'd experienced from the moment his father had revealed how little he believed in Caleb's integrity. "Errors in judgment… hasty accusations. How awkward for the firm."

"It is unfortunate that your father's formal statement only succeeds in raising more questions than it answers."

Caleb leaned his head back against his chair. "People will say old man Phelps is covering up for his only son."

"Oh, no. Surely not. And whatever you may think to the contrary, most people, after having had a chance to consider it well, don't really think you had anything to do with any irregularities at the firm."

Caleb raised an eyebrow. "No? I beg to differ. You weren't the recipient of their looks."

"Oh, I know it must have been dreadful for you." She raised a finger to her mouth, touching her lip gingerly. "But don't you think it made things worse by leaving Boston? Coming here might have helped you in many ways, but it gave the impression to people who don't know you very well that you were…well, running away from something."

"At the time, I no longer cared how my actions would be construed."

"I know you suffered a terrible disappointment."

Caleb didn't know whether she was referring to the one with his father or the one with Arabella. Most likely the latter. For all her friendship with his mother, Mrs. Bradford didn't know him very well. He hadn't been around Boston for much of his youth, thanks to his father.

"You could return to Boston now, you know," she continued calmly. "It might be a little difficult at first, but eventually you could pick up where you left off."

"Pick up where I left off?" Caleb turned to the window, no longer wishing to discuss his life. "It's beautiful here, isn't it?"

Mrs. Bradford followed the change in subject without missing a stride. "Yes. That's why I've been rusticating here every summer for the last twenty years. Phineas discovered it with me, although he wasn't able to enjoy it long thereafter."

"I'm sorry." He'd hardly known her late husband.

"Don't be. He's in a better place. And I shall join him again someday soon." She smiled as if in absolute tranquility at the inevitable eventualities of life.

Caleb had achieved no such equanimity as yet. He got up from his chair, suddenly restless.

As if sensing his change in mood, Mrs. Bradford set down her cup and saucer. "Who was that person walking up the road when I drove up? He seemed to be coming from here."

Caleb turned back to his visitor in surprise. "That was my neighbor. Miss Patterson."

"A woman?" Mrs. Bradford looked puzzled. "How strange. The way she was dressed…from a distance…that hat shading her features…" She shook her head with a chuckle. "You see a lot of odd characters in these parts. I should be used to that by now." She tapped her finger against her lip. "Patterson…Patterson. That's a common family name around here. Wait a minute. She isn't Big Jeb Patterson's little girl, is she? He was a woodsman who lived down this road."

"Sounds like the one, from your description," Caleb answered.

She shook her head. "My, my. I remember her as this quiet, shy little thing, always looking underfed, wearing faded calico dresses and going around with dirty, bare feet. What was she doing here?"

For some inexplicable reason, Caleb didn't like the way the conversation was going. "She's my neighbor. From time to time she's offered me advice on my garden." At the question in her eyes, he smiled. "I have to do something with my time, so I thought I'd try my hand at gardening. I enjoy it, actually."

"I'm glad to hear it. Gardening can be soothing to the soul. How nice that your neighbor has proved helpful."

It was on the tip of Caleb's tongue to ask Mrs. Bradford's advice about some primers for Geneva's lessons, but he stopped himself before voicing the question.

Perhaps as a reaction against having undergone Mrs. Bradford's gentle, yet discerning, probing of his own affairs, he felt suddenly protective of Geneva. Her secrets were her own, and he respected that.

He was also getting tired of hearing only negative things about Geneva every time her name came up. Mrs. Bradford's recollection brought to mind a hungry, unwashed young waif.

He'd order the reading books through the company's agent in New York, bypassing any questions that would come up through the shipping company's Boston office. Yes, that was what he'd do.

Jake's barking alerted Geneva before she heard the crunch of wheels or the clip-clop of hooves, telling her that Captain Caleb's visitor was departing.

"Hush, Jake," she said automatically, though she knew he wouldn't be still until the buggy had passed. Geneva went on with her task, picking off the dead pansy and marigold heads from the flowers she had planted in her front yard. The sweet smell of pinks mingled with the pungent odor of the broken flowers in her hand.

When the sound of buggy wheels stopped and Jake stood stiff-legged by the road, barking for all he was worth, Geneva finally looked up.

She rose at the sight of the buggy at her entrance and dusted off her knees. The woman handling the reins was clearly a lady. Geneva went to Jake and took him by the collar. "Hush, boy. Sit." Although he obeyed her, she could feel the tension in his body. He was itching to be up again. She soothed him with her hand, running it down his neck, while observing the elegant-looking lady in the buggy. Her dun-colored jacket and skirt were simple, almost mannish, yet they looked well tailored and did not detract from the lady's femininity.

Geneva watched her loop the reins around the whipstock. When she stood to descend, Geneva stepped forward, holding out a hand to help her down. At the sight of her leaf-stained fingers, and the thought of what they would do to the woman's hand, Geneva pulled them back.

But the woman held out her hand with a smile, and slowly Geneva reached out once again. The woman was as tall as she was. Geneva always felt awkward, dwarfing most of the women she talked to, yet this woman exuded elegance rather than ungainliness.

"You have a fine watchdog," the lady said, eyeing Jake approvingly.

It was the first time anyone had ever given Jake a compliment. "Always raising a racket," Geneva answered, "but he don't mean no harm."

"What pretty flowers you have growing," the lady continued, smoothing down the lapels of her jacket.

"Just ordinary flowers."

"They make a pretty effect, nonetheless. You have an eye for color."

"Thank you, ma'am," she mumbled.

The woman looked at her with frank curiosity. "You wouldn't be Jeb Patterson's daughter, would you?"

"Yes'm," she answered in surprise, unable to imagine this lady acquainted with her father.

"He used to bring me some fine trout. I remember you as a young child."

Geneva shook her head, still amazed. "Sorry, ma'am, I don't recollect."

"No, I don't expect you do. My name is Maud Bradford. I've been coming up here for a good many years during the summer months. I have a house in the village, the yellow one up on a hill, up past the hotel."

Geneva nodded. "I know it. If you ever be needin' some fresh fruits or vegetables, I supply some of the summer folks with produce once a week."

"That would be lovely. Come around anytime." She looked back down the hill toward the Point. "I was just paying a call on your neighbor, Caleb Phelps. I'm an old friend of the family."

Geneva looked at Mrs. Bradford, hoping she'd continue talking, yet afraid to make any comment lest the lady think her curiosity unseemly.

"He seems to be doing well here. He mentioned you had helped him with his garden."

He had talked about her? To hide her surprise, Geneva shrugged. "I didn't do nothin' much. Guess he'd never done any gardenin' before, and it's not easy up here."

"No, I imagine not. He appreciates your help." Mrs. Bradford smiled. "I'm glad he's found a good neighbor."

Geneva returned the smile, feeling accepted by the lady as she never had by any of the village women. At the enormity of the thought, she stepped back. She must be imagining it! She shoved her soil-stained hands in her pockets and looked away.

Mrs. Bradford didn't seem to notice the motion but continued speaking. "Growing up here, you're no doubt well acquainted with the woods and trails, as well as the seashore?"

"A fair amount, I'd say."

"I enjoy bird-watching. But as I'm growing older, my family back in Boston tend to worry, thinking of me out alone anywhere." She smiled, her gray eyes crinkling at the corners. "It doesn't matter how many times I tell them I'm not alone, that the good Lord is ever present." She sighed. "At any rate, to ease their minds, I've decided to hire a companion, a guide of sorts. I suspect you'd be too occupied in summer to consider such a position?"

Geneva's mind had ceased taking in much of the conversation. When she realized Mrs. Bradford was looking at her, expecting an answer, she could only say, "Beg pardon?"

"I said you were no doubt too busy to consider any sort of additional occupation during the summer months."

"I fish during the summer months mainly, but I'm always lookin' for ways to make a few dollars. The winters are mighty long, without much chance to earn anything."

"Would you consider acting as a guide a few times a week, the weather permitting, for my expeditions?"

Geneva nodded, not quite certain to what she was committing herself.

"Good, then. Shall we say, a week from Thursday, in the morning, if the weather is clear?"

"I'll be there next Thursday morning. I'll come around to the harbor in my boat."

"A boat? How lovely. Perhaps we could go for a sail around the coast. Maybe we'll spot a few eagles?"

"Sure. I'll take you to Seal Island and you can see the puffins nesting."

The woman gave her such a gracious smile, Geneva couldn't help smiling again in return.

"You have a lovely smile, my dear. I shall see you on Thursday." Mrs. Bradford turned to climb back into the buggy. With a final wave, she was on her way. Geneva watched her until the buggy was out of sight, wondering at how much had occurred in the space of a few short minutes.

She patted Jake. "What do you make of all that, boy? Your mistress has gone and gotten herself a job without even trying."

Geneva knocked on the captain's door but received no response. He'd told her, after their first lesson, to come over after lunch the following afternoon, so she knew he expected her. Today, she'd brought Jake with her.

To keep him from pawing at the door, Geneva turned the knob and pushed it open. She'd just glance around in the kitchen, give a holler if necessary.

At the sight of the silent kitchen, she paused. Entering it without the captain present was like catching a glimpse of him without his being aware of it. Although her mind told her to retreat the way she'd come, a part of her heart urged her forward until she stood in the center of the room. His abode.

Everything looked bare and clean. A lone teacup and saucer stood on the counter by the soapstone sink. The curtainless window above it was a quarter of the way open and the sound of waves came up from beyond the backyard.

She wondered how the captain managed his meals on his own. She knew he had deliveries made from Mr. Watson's store every few days. But how did a gentleman's son survive all by himself? Although he called himself a sailor, she was certain he knew nothing about sea life below the rank of captain or first mate.

Geneva grabbed Jake's collar in an effort to suppress the temptation of nosing around in the captain's cupboards. She tore her gaze from the kitchen and headed toward the veranda.

"Cap'n Caleb?" she called out. "It's me, Geneva." When nothing but silence greeted her, she said, "Anybody home?" By then she was in the large living room. "Cap'n Caleb?"

Seeing the door onto the veranda ajar, she walked toward it. Jake broke away from her and reached it first, shoving the door open and bounding joyfully toward one end of the porch. Geneva was quickly after him. She saw the hammock and Captain Caleb lying in it, but wasn't in time to reach Jake as he jumped up to it, barking, and set it to rocking violently.

"Hey! What—" The captain's hands came up around Jake's head. "Hey, boy, down." Captain Caleb looked up at her as she reached the hammock.

"Jake! Down! What's the matter with you? Get your paws off the cap'n." She spoke to Jake more harshly than she had intended, trying to hide what she felt at seeing Captain Caleb lying there. It was clear he'd been sleeping.

This impression intensified when he smiled up at her. "It's all right. He meant no harm. At least he's warming to me." He patted Jake's head as he talked. Long, sun-browned fingers ran over Jake's ears and down the sides of his neck, large palms cupped the sides of his head. "What are you doing here, boy?"

Geneva could feel the heat rise in her face as she observed the captain. Thick, wavy hair swept back untidily from his high forehead. His face, just wakened from sleep, had a freshness and an openness that she hadn't seen since he'd come back to Haven's End.

"Uh, I jus' came in by the back. Shouldn'a brought him, I guess—I thought you'd behave yourself, Jake." She fixed her eyes on her dog.

"No more scolding. There, that's a good boy." The captain continued talking to the dog, rubbing his head and neck all the while. "I'm glad your mistress thought fit to bring you. It gives us a chance to get acquainted."

"Thought it was time, you know, for the lesson," Geneva explained, shoving her hands into her back pockets.

The captain pulled out his watch. "So it is." He smiled at her again, transfixing her. "I just lay down a minute after my lunch to watch the sea, and must have fallen asleep. Went to bed too late last night, I guess. Come on, get your dog off me, and help me up."

Geneva swallowed and took hold of Jake's collar, ordering him to sit. Not sure whether the captain had meant it seriously, she stuck out her hand. He grabbed it firmly and held out his other hand. Geneva offered hers more tentatively, but he clasped it readily. When both her hands were ensconced in his, she felt joined to him in a way more profound than the simple touch warranted.

She pulled him forward.

"Thanks." Once he was standing, the captain held her hands an instant longer before letting go. Geneva stepped back to dispel the feeling of abandonment.

He ran his hands through his hair and then smoothed his shirt down. Geneva just stared. He was wearing a white cotton shirt with a barely visible, blue line threaded through it. Geneva thought she'd never seen any material so fine. His collar was open, revealing the brown skin of his neck.

Her own collar felt constricting. Giving herself a mental shake, she walked toward the worktable. Her hand trembled as it reached for a pencil. The captain seemed so at ease; clearly he had no idea what he did to her.

During the lesson Geneva felt more ignorant than she'd ever felt during her short time up the road at the schoolhouse. She couldn't seem to make sense of anything this afternoon. She mixed *b*'s and *d*'s, *m*'s and *n*'s. She stumbled over words of more than three letters.

It was worse than when she'd had to trudge to school each morning, wearing the same dress, until Mrs. Stillman's daughter, Sarah, started spreading the rumor that she had fleas. After that, no one wanted to sit with her.

She vowed never to set foot inside the schoolhouse again, but then Pa demanded to know why she was hanging around at home. When she told him she wasn't going back, he hauled her up the road to the schoolhouse, vowing no offspring of his was going to grow up into a lazy, worthless, good-for-nothing.

By the time they entered the schoolroom, she was late, everyone else seated and quiet. All the children turned around, staring at her, then shifting their gazes to follow her father. His black hair and beard always spooked the little ones. The older ones said he'd probably been sired by one of the black bears he always hunted in the fall.

She'd hated her father for the shame he caused her, especially when he'd gone and pulled her out of school himself the following year.

Captain Caleb's sigh jolted her back to the present. "Let's try this word again. *Ap*—" he began sounding out for her.

"*Ap*," she repeated, then struggled with the other letters his fingers had formed on the paper. Another *p*. "*Puh*," she expelled the sound. That other letter, what was it? Two sticks. *L*. "*Lll*." Then *e*. What did that sound like again? "*Eee*." Now, to put it together. By this time she'd forgotten how the beginning sounded.

"That *e* is silent," the captain corrected.

"Why'd they put it there, then?" she asked in annoyance. She looked at Jake sleeping so peacefully on the gray porch floor, his tail thumping every once in a while, while she was strung so tight she was afraid she'd spin around like a top if the captain so much as touched her. Why'd she ever get herself into this?

"I don't know why it's there. Usually if there's an *e* at the end of a word, it's silent. So, let's begin at the beginning. *A-P-L.*" He said it more quickly, "*Apl.* What is it?"

"*Apple!*"

The captain sighed with relief. "Good. Maybe this will help to remind you of the sound." He took the pencil and began drawing a little circle beside the word. When he added the stem on top, Geneva recognized it as an apple.

"An apple," she guessed, looking in awe at the neat little picture.

He nodded, continuing to draw. "This should help you remember the *a* sound in apple. *A* makes a whole lot of other sounds, but we'll worry about those later. There." He put the pencil down and moved the paper toward her. She saw he'd added a little worm coming out of the apple. She looked up to find him grinning at her.

"I don't know why you bother with me," she said with a shake of her head. "If I haven't learned this stuff by now, I don't think I ever will."

"Nonsense. People learn new languages every day, and it's the same thing. It takes a lot of practice and patience. Now—" he took the paper back and began forming a new word "—*B* comes next. Ball, that's easy to draw."

Geneva watched his fingers curve around the pencil, and knew exactly why nothing would come to her that afternoon. She could think of nothing but him sitting there so close to her. Her gaze traveled up to his head bent over the paper. The dark hair glinted reddish gold in places.

She was going to have to stay up real late every night poring over those letters he was writing to make up for her wandering thoughts during lesson time.

As if reading her mind, he said, "I shall have to get you a slate so you can practice making these at home. Now this one's easy." He finished printing the letters and moved the paper toward her.

She stared at the letters, willing her mind to concentrate. *"Kuh…Kuh,"* she repeated. *"Uh…rr…ll."* Then she tried putting the sounds together as the captain was teaching her. *"K-uh-r-l.* Cuhrl. Curl!" She looked at him in triumph, meeting the look of satisfaction in his eyes.

"Good." He wrote another word. "This should be familiar."

She looked at the three-letter word. *"D-d…"* She took a stab at the vowel, *"aw…guh.* Dawg. Dog!"

"All right. Let's try something harder." Again he took the paper back and bent over it.

That night she took out the list of words and copied them out on a separate sheet of paper by the glow of her kerosene lamp. She wrote each one and read it over and over until she knew it perfectly. As she sat on the edge of her bed in her nightgown, she took one last look at the paper, smiling at the captain's pencil drawings. A curl of hair, a little dragon, its spiked tail curved upward, a flame coming out of its mouth. She traced the drawings with her fingertip. An oblong circle for an egg, a squatting frog. Silently she mouthed the words, vowing she'd master each lesson, if it meant receiving the smile of approval the captain had given her this afternoon.

Chapter Five

"Hello there, Geneva. You must be pleased about somepin'."

Geneva jumped at the sound of Lucius Tucker's low drawl. Her knife nearly sliced off her finger as it slid through a stalk of rhubarb. She scowled up at the red-bearded man, annoyed that he'd caught her kneeling.

Despite his new suit and starched shirt, something about Lucius Tucker reminded her of her father. Ever since he'd been appointed overseer of the poor at the last town meeting, he thought he was somebody.

She placed the stalk of rhubarb in the basket at her side but kept the open jackknife in her hand as she stood. Meeting him at eye level, she no longer felt at a disadvantage.

She'd been so wrapped up in thinking about the captain, she hadn't heard Lucius approach. Where had Jake gone off to? She made out her dog's bark off in the meadow, but didn't take her gaze off Lucius.

She glared at him. "What do you want? I got work needs doing."

Lucius just smiled and pushed back his hat. "Sure sounded pretty what you were hummin'."

Her scowl deepened as she felt the heat rise up to the roots of her hair. She'd been humming to herself, anticipating the captain's pleasure when he saw how well she'd learned her lessons over the past week. "Ain't none o' your business what I was doing."

"You gotta learn to curb that tongue o' yours." He pushed his hat farther back on his head. "If I told you once, I've told you a thousand times, I jus' want to help you out."

"You don't have a charitable bone in your body, Lucius."

"Now, there you go again, lettin' that tongue o' yours loose."

Lucius eyed her up and down, his pale blue gaze coming to rest on her chest. "Look at you. Grubbin' around in the dirt. Coverin' yourself up so a body can't hardly tell whether you're a man or a woman. But ol' Lucius can tell. You're all woman, Geneva. It's time you began showin' off your assets 'stead o' hiding behind those clothes o' your pa's."

"You better watch your mouth," she answered shortly, keeping her knife poised.

Lucius ignored it. "Look at you slavin' away here. I been offering to take care of you since your poor pa passed away. He'd be grateful to me, I know, if he knew my intentions."

"Your intentions! There's nothing decent about your intentions."

"Now, Ginny, just because I don't offer you a wedding band don't mean I wouldn't if I could. You know how it is—"

"Quit your whinin' around me. You got a wife and three kids. She's doing her duty to you. I'm sick of your pestering me with your filthy offers. Callin' yourself an upstanding member of the community."

"I don't call it filthy, offerin' you a snug little cabin up on Whittier's Lake. I'd come up to see you when I was huntin'. No one'd know a thing."

"I've told you before, no. You deaf as well as stupid? *No means no.*"

Lucius just rocked back on his heels, his smile never wavering. He removed his hat and scratched his head with a thumbnail. His pale red hair was combed back in wet strands, revealing a pink scalp beneath.

"The selectmen voted at last night's meetin' to set aside the money raised at the Fourth o' July celebrations for the widows and orphans of this town." He chuckled, continuing to scratch his head. "Widows and orphans." He paused and let the significance of the words sink in. "I have sole discretion over those funds." He winked at her. "Seems to me you're an orphan."

Geneva looked at him in disgust. "You better get off my property."

"Now, Geneva, simmer down. You know I only want to help you out. You don't have no man to lean on. It breaks my heart thinkin' of you holed up here all winter. Up to the cabin, I'd see you every day when I'd come up to cut timber. You could cook me dinner then." He sidled up closer.

"We'd cozy up in the afternoon. I could ease your toil if you'd jus' let me. The ride's much pleasanter if two enjoy it."

She brought the knife up to chest level. "You step back. I don't need no man to lean on, least of all the likes o' you."

His blue eyes hardened. "I told you, you better watch that tongue o' yours. I'm a patient man, but…" His finger snaked out to grab hold of the buckle of her overalls.

Geneva pushed the knife against his hand, but before she could free herself, he'd twisted her wrist and sent her knife spinning away from her.

"Careful you don't push me to my limits." His breath was hot against her face. "You might jus' find yourself on the losin' end." He considered her. "You're about tall as I am. I wouldn't mind puttin' your strength to the test. I think I might just enjoy a contest with you."

His eyes challenged her. "I hear tell some women like a man who can beat them." He smirked. "Maybe your ma was one of 'em—"

"Why, you low-down skunk!" Geneva lunged at him. Lucius took advantage of the moment to grab her around the waist and pull her to him. For a while, she held her own, but then he did a fancy move with his foot and had her on the ground. He lay on top of her and grabbed one of her breasts. She yelped at the pain.

The next thing she knew, Lucius was being hauled up by the collar and pitched on the ground like a forkful of hay. Geneva pushed herself up on her elbows and stared at Captain Caleb, towering over her.

"What are...you...doin' here?" she gasped out. At the same instant, she heard Jake's barking as her dog bounded over the fields.

The captain didn't look at her. "Mister, if you ever show your face around here again, you'll wish you hadn't. I can promise you that."

The fallen man pulled himself up, dusting himself off in the process. "Me an' Geneva wuz havin' a private conversation. I'll thank you, Captain—" he spit the title out "—to keep outta what don't concern you."

Jake stood growling at Lucius.

Lucius turned back to Geneva. "You think about my offer. It's more'n generous. It's downright magnanimous." He said the word as if he'd just learned to say it and enjoyed the exercise it gave his mouth. His eyes narrowed at the threatening dog.

"Call off your cur." Lucius took a step closer to her. At the captain's menacing look, he said, "I'm goin'. I'm goin'. Just remember, Geneva, one word, *one word,* to the selectmen is all it takes and you might find your taxes raised. They might be raised so high you can't pay 'em anymore. And you know what that means. Goodbye to your pa's land."

"You raise Miss Patterson's taxes, and I'll see you never sell another cord of lumber on Phelps' Wharf." Captain Caleb's words were spoken low.

"Don't get all bent outta shape, Cap'n Phelps." Under the pretense of picking up his hat and dusting it off, Lucius bent close enough to Geneva to say, for her ears only, "You keep your captain away from me. Or next time you're out fishin', you might come home to find your precious cur has eaten some poison meat. I don't take kindly to a common thief—" he glanced at the captain "—come tellin' me who I can and can't speak to."

Lucius straightened, and with one final thump of his hat against his leg, he set it back on his head with all the dignity of a parson leaving a congregant's house.

Jake barked after his retreating back but didn't leave Geneva's side.

Geneva took a deep breath, feeling a trembling begin within her. She felt like bursting into tears. To quell the impulse, she knelt beside Jake, taking hold of his fur. His body felt warm, his panting steady. "Where did you go off to?" She remembered Lucius' threat and squeezed Jake harder. No one was going to harm him, even if it meant taking him with her everywhere she went.

"Are you all right?"

The captain's impatient voice broke into her worries and she turned to him, still afraid to speak, for fear her voice would tremble. She nodded.

"What were you thinking of to entertain that man alone?"

She could only stare at the captain as if he'd gone mad. "Entertain him! I didn't invite him here."

"Where in thunder was Jake?"

"How should I know? Off chasin' some rabbit."

"How long has that man been pestering you?"

Geneva gave a bitter laugh. "If it wasn't him, it'd be another one. This town is so full of worthless men that think jus' 'cause I live alone it means I want company."

"If that's the case, you shouldn't live alone. Can't you live with some woman or family in the village?"

Geneva looked up at him, dumbfounded. There she sat on the ground, and he hadn't even given her a hand up yet, which wasn't like him at all. He sounded angry at *her,* as if it were all her fault! What had gotten into him?

"Why should I live with some family?" She raised her voice to match his. "This is my house, my land. No one has any right to come around telling me how I should live."

"You'd rather be here at the mercy of any man who wants to molest you? You have no protection—"

"I got Jake. And my shotgun."

It was his turn to laugh. "A lot of good they did you just now."

Geneva was beginning to get angry herself. "I been taking care of myself just fine plenty long enough."

He gave her an exasperated look. "If I hadn't come when I did, what would have happened? I'll tell you exactly what would have happened. That man would have had his way with you, and there's nothing you could have done about it."

She refused to let him see that his words had any effect on her. She looked around the grass for her jackknife and snatched it up. "I had a knife."

Captain Caleb gave another strangled laugh and turned away, his hand rubbing the back of his neck. "I don't know why I bother with you. You won't listen to reason."

Geneva shot to her feet, alerting Jake, who gave a bark. "Why you *bother* with me? Why you *bother* with me?" she repeated, her voice rising. "I should ask why I bother with you! I was just fine 'til you came along. I been living here by myself since Pa died. 'Fore then, I was as good as on my own most o' the time. Then you come along, pretendin' to be a farmer."

Even as she said the words, she was ashamed of them, knowing they were untrue. But she wanted to hurt him before he hurt her. "Farmer!" She gave a scornful laugh. "You didn't know how to do nothing. Running away from your troubles. Look at you, sittin' all alone in that great big house, not even bothering to furnish it! You don't mean to stay here. You're all set to pull up stakes whenever things get rough! You, the son of a big important ship owner. You don't belong here! Why don't you go back to your riches and easy life and save us all some trouble?"

Geneva was horrified with herself. She stood staring at him, telling herself, good riddance, she'd never see him again, and that was what she wanted.

The captain just looked at her for a moment, then he bent down and picked up a few books and a slate off the ground. She hadn't noticed them until that moment. He must have dropped them when he grabbed Lucius. Geneva swallowed, wondering what they were and why he'd brought them to her place.

"I beg your pardon for intruding into your well-ordered life. I should have known better than to try to help someone who clearly needs no help." His lips stretched in a bitter parody of a smile. "I've made the mistake countless times before. I don't know why I'm so pigheaded."

He looked down at the books, as if uncertain what to do with them. Then he gave a shrug. "You can do what you like with these. I have no use for them. Give them away, for all I care." He placed them back down on the grass.

"Goodbye, Geneva."

Geneva watched him leave. Her whole being ached to call him back, but her vocal cords refused to move. She heard Jake give a couple of uncertain barks, clearly confused as to what had just transpired. He took a few steps forward, then turned back to his mistress, but she ignored him. She couldn't help herself, much less him, at that moment.

"Look!" Mrs. Bradford pointed upward with her finger. She was gazing through her binoculars, but Geneva didn't need the glasses to see the eagle soaring through the sky. Not even the bird's majestic flight could break through Geneva's melancholy since Captain Caleb had left her yard a couple of days ago.

The two women watched the bird's flight until it disappeared out of sight, across the straits and over the tall firs outlining the coast. Mrs. Bradford lowered the binoculars and smiled at Geneva.

"My morning is complete. Thank you for bringing me here, my dear."

They stood on the edge of a rocky cliff of an island across from the mainland. Geneva and Mrs. Bradford had spent the morning on the small, uninhabited island, hiking the trails Geneva was familiar with and sitting to watch the birds.

"Shall we have some lunch?" asked Mrs. Bradford.

"Sure. I'll go fetch the basket." Geneva turned and made her way back down to the beach where her peapod lay. From under a tarpaulin she retrieved her satchel and the larger wicker hamper Mrs. Bradford had provided. She climbed more slowly back up the pebbly beach to the larger rocks edging the shoreline, then up the needle-covered earth, using the tree roots as her stepping-stones.

The summer smells of sun-warmed vegetation reached her nostrils—ferns, bunchberries, and carpets of damp moss—all growing silently in the patches of sunlight that reached the forest floor. The delicate pink-white blossoms of the ground-hugging cranberry plants contrasted with its dark green, waxy leaves. Geneva's footsteps stirred up the scent of balsam needles drying on the ground. Usually these scents—scents she had known since childhood—soothed her. Today they could not ease her troubled spirit.

"Oh, there you are," Mrs. Bradford exclaimed when Geneva emerged from the forest. "I've found a good spot to spread our lunch. Maybe we'll spot another eagle."

"They've got their nests somewhere around here." She reached the edge of the land again, where the granite and slate ledges formed a natural barrier against the assaults of the tides below.

Mrs. Bradford sat on a nice flat ledge. She patted the place beside her. Geneva let the hamper fall with a *thud.* She could hear the jangle of cutlery inside.

"The stone is nice and warm here," said Mrs. Bradford. "And we have a magnificent view of the shore opposite." She reached toward the hamper and unclasped its lid. Geneva couldn't help glancing inside before retrieving her own lunch. Mrs. Bradford removed a neatly folded red-checked tablecloth, which she shook out. She spread it between them, smiling gratefully as Geneva caught two corners and pulled them toward herself. Then came the cutlery and glassware, which Geneva had heard rattling. Heavy-handled silver knives and forks and snowy linen napkins, rolled up like sausages. When Mrs. Bradford handed one to Geneva, she accepted it without thinking. The napkin was large enough to cover her lap from waist to knee, although it seemed ludicrous to cover her dirty overalls with such a spotless cloth. It seemed more appropriate that her pants should protect the napkin.

There was enough food for twice their party. Another linen napkin was rolled up around a jar of ice-cold lemonade. Last came the plates of white china.

Geneva turned back to her own satchel. With a sigh, she undid the string clasp and retrieved her lunch: two slices of old bread spread with lard, a piece of dried salt-cod sandwiched in between, and a handful of her first radishes, which she'd dug out that morning and washed at the pump. For the rest, she'd planned on picking up some goose grass on the beach, and any wild strawberries she spotted.

"I hope you don't expect me to eat all this by myself," came Mrs. Bradford's soft voice. "I should have told you not to worry yourself about packing your lunch. I'll be responsible on all our excursions. After all, I have more time on my hands than you, as well as Beacon Hill's finest cook, according to her own words."

Geneva hesitated.

The older woman smiled. "Now, come, if you'll share your radishes with me, I'll pass you some of this cold chicken salad."

"Thank you, ma'am. The gulls will appreciate this," Geneva said as she tore a piece of her bread off and flung it toward the ocean. It didn't take long for the sharp-eyed scavengers to circle and dive. Geneva finished breaking up the bread and throwing it out to them before she gave her attention back to Mrs. Bradford. The older woman had already prepared a plate for her and set it beside her.

Geneva took it gingerly, conscious of her stained fingers against the gleaming china plate. She laid it on her lap, and then took the glass Mrs. Bradford held out to her. It was already damp from the cold drink in it. Geneva set the glass down beside her, afraid it would tip over and crack at any moment. She fingered the knife and fork in each hand, watching Mrs. Bradford's every move.

Before she began eating, the older lady bowed her head. *"We thank You, Lord, for the meal we are about to enjoy. Bless it, Lord, for our bodies' use, and multiply it for those who haven't any. Amen."*

Not until Mrs. Bradford had stuck the tines of the fork into her food did Geneva dare begin eating. She took a forkful of chicken into her mouth.

When Mrs. Bradford continued eating and regarding the scene before her, Geneva finally relaxed and began enjoying the exquisite flavor of the food. She couldn't remember the last time she'd had chicken. This one was tasty, coated in some kind of tangy sauce and mixed with celery.

Besides that, there were rolls so soft Geneva supposed you could chew them even if you had no teeth. And different kinds of pickles, and deviled eggs, and the lemonade—just the right combination of sweet and acid, and icy cold.

Halfway through the meal, Geneva had the sudden urge to laugh out loud. Who would've thought a month ago, she'd be sitting atop of Seal Island, eating a meal fit for a queen, off real china with real silverware? What would Pa say if he could see her now? Or Ma?

She sobered. Ma had probably seen real china at the convent, perhaps even silver. Geneva knew her ma would smile and be happy for her today.

All in all it had been a pleasant morning. After the awful

things she'd said to Captain Caleb, she never thought to find peace again. She felt a terrible sadness inside her, a terrible ache when she thought about him, but for some reason Mrs. Bradford's presence soothed her. This expedition had been an escape for Geneva. Soon she'd have to return and pick up where she'd left off, carrying out her daily chores as if she'd never known the existence of Captain Caleb Phelps. She looked down at the remains of chicken on her plate. She didn't think she could swallow anything more past the lump in her throat.

After the captain had left, Geneva finally pulled herself together enough to pick up the books he'd brought. Leafing through the first one, she immediately saw they were reading books. They resembled the books she'd had only a short time to use at the schoolhouse, except these looked so much finer. Brand-new, for one thing—and the pictures inside! Beautiful drawings, some in rich colors.

Geneva put her plate down. Mrs. Bradford had already finished and was brushing the crumbs from her skirt. "How nice to eat with genuine hunger and have one's appetite satisfied."

"I didn't know there was any other way to eat."

Mrs. Bradford chuckled. "Oh, yes. Where there is plenty, people eat for different reasons. As part of one's entertainment or to ease sorrow or simply to overcome boredom."

Geneva looked down at the food she'd left on her plate. Mrs. Bradford had heaped it with more than she was used to consuming. But not knowing when she'd ever have such a tasty combination again, she took up her plate once again and didn't pause until every last morsel had been tucked into her mouth.

By then Mrs. Bradford was putting some of the things back in the hamper. "May I offer you anything else? I've left out the fruit for dessert."

"Oh, no, ma'am, I couldn't eat a speck more. It was delicious, though. Thank you."

"You're very welcome. Although, I mustn't take the credit. My cook, Bessie, did the work, and you carried it up here, so there's very little to thank me for."

"Well, thank your cook for me. And thank you just the same for providing it. It was worth the hauling up here." Geneva collected the two plates. "I know a little brook close by. Would you like me to rinse off the dishes?"

"That would be excellent. Bessie would appreciate that." She handed Geneva the cutlery.

When Geneva returned with the rinsed things, Mrs. Bradford took them from her and wrapped them in one of the linen napkins. "There, now have a peach and let's enjoy this beautiful spot before it's time to return."

Geneva took the peach. Not bothering to peel it and cut off a section as she saw Mrs. Bradford do, she simply bit into its juiciness.

As she ate, she thought it was now or never. If she didn't speak up now, she'd have no further opportunity. She sucked on the peach pit, then tossed it out over the ocean. She wiped her hands and mouth on her napkin and then refolded it and tucked it inside the hamper. Rubbing her hands up and down her trouser legs, Geneva rehearsed her question.

Mrs. Bradford was sitting, calmly gazing out to sea. Geneva had never known such a peaceful presence. Not that she'd been close to enough people to form a valid basis for comparison. But instinctively she felt Mrs. Bradford would steer her right.

"Ma'am?"

Mrs. Bradford turned to her with a smile. "Yes, dear?"

Geneva cleared her throat. "If—" She began again. "If you've wronged somebody, what do you do?" There, she'd said it out in the open.

Mrs. Bradford looked at her. "Why, you make it right as soon as you can."

"How can you make something terrible right again? I mean, if you've said things—if the person won't ever speak to you again... And you deserve it," she added immediately.

The older woman smiled. "First, you go to your Father."

"Ain't got no father. He died a few years back."

"Not your earthly father. I was referring to your heavenly Father."

"Don't know if Pa ever made it as far as heaven," Geneva mumbled.

"Your heavenly Father is God, the Father, our Creator. You must first tell Him of your wrong and ask His forgiveness. Then ask His help in making it right with the one you wronged."

"That'll work?" Geneva asked doubtfully. It sounded too easy. "Don't think God pays too much attention to the likes o' me."

"You'd be surprised. You know what Jesus tells us about the Father?"

Geneva shook her head.

"He says He's numbered the very hairs on our head. And that not even a sparrow shall fall on the ground without His knowing it. Best of all, He tells us not to be afraid, because we are of more value to Him than many sparrows."

It sounded too good to be true. "He said that?"

Mrs. Bradford smiled. "Truly."

"Jesus. Ma used to mention him a lot. 'Cept she called Him *Jesu*."

"She was French?"

"Canadian French."

"Ah, *Québécoise.*"

Geneva came back to the subject of Jesus. "Ma used to talk about Jesus. But I didn't understand too much about it all. I know He died on some cross. Ma had a wooden cross at the head of her bed. She used to take it down and hold on to it when—when she got worse."

Mrs. Bradford patted her hand. "I'm sure Jesus was there with your mother at the end, showing her the way."

"I don't know, ma'am. Didn't seem like there was nobody there. We sure did need someone. I hope Ma was able to see her Jesus and that He showed her the way."

"Jesus promised us, 'I am the way, the truth, and the life: no man cometh unto the Father, but by me.'" Mrs. Bradford's eyes took on a light as she recited the words. "'Yet a little while, and the world seeth me no more; but ye see me: because I live, ye shall live also.'"

She smiled at Geneva, a smile that reached down into Geneva, comforting her more than anything had since Ma had been taken away.

"You don't have to worry about your mother. Jesus took her to be with our heavenly Father. He promised not only to show us the way, but that He *is* the way."

"Your words are the best ones I've heard." Geneva tried to explain what they meant to her, but couldn't articulate exactly what they made her feel. "I still don't rightly understand it all, but it sure sounds nice."

Mrs. Bradford gave her hand a final pat. "That's all right. I'll tell you more about Jesus the next time we're together. In the meantime, when you go home you pray to God to soften that person's heart that you hurt. And pray in Jesus'

name. Say something like, *'Father, I've injured somebody,*
but I'm sorry, and I ask Your forgiveness. But I need that
person's forgiveness, too. Help me make it right with that
person. I pray this in Your dear son, Jesus', name.'
Remember, Jesus is up there in heaven, pleading your case
with the Father."

Geneva had been following the words closely, trying to
engrave them on her memory, afraid she'd forget them by the
evening. Instinctively she felt that the most crucial part came
at the end, so she mouthed those words to herself as soon as
Mrs. Bradford had stopped speaking. *In Your dear son, Jesus',*
name.

"You'll see. It will prepare you to go to the person and ask
her forgiveness."

"It was a man I wronged."

"Oh. Well, then, when you go to him."

"I don't know how God can change this person's heart, as
you say. I said some pretty mean things. Things I wish I
could take back."

Mrs. Bradford laid her hand back on Geneva's. "No matter how that person receives you, it's still up to you to ask
forgiveness. Because it's really between you and God. If
you've acted wrongly and don't try to fix it, it creates a sep-
aration between you and God. And He can't help you, then.
That's the problem with so many people. They've let so many
things come between themselves and God, they're not even
capable of hearing His voice.

"Come on." Mrs. Bradford rose to her feet. "Let's enjoy
this day that the Lord has made before it's time to go
back."

"Thanks to you, I can enjoy it. You've eased my mind
greatly, ma'am."

"Then I'm doubly thankful to the Lord." She chuckled. "I'm curious to see how your dog has made out with Bessie while we've been away."

"I'm grateful I could leave Jake tied up in your yard. He gets lonely when I'm away for so long," she said, knowing it was only a half truth.

"That's quite understandable. My cat stays inside, and she'll ignore me for a little while when I first return, to let me know she's cross."

As they were making their way down the path, back to the beach, Geneva ventured one last request. "Ma'am? There's one other thing I'd like to ask you."

"Ask away."

"Can you stop me every time I say somethin' I ain't supposed to?"

"What do you mean?" Mrs. Bradford stopped and faced Geneva along the sun-dappled path.

"When I don't talk the way you do. Grammar and suchlike."

"Oh, I see, you'd like to learn to speak correctly. How about if I begin by correcting the big things, and later on, when you've mastered those, we'll work on the small things?" She smiled. "That's the way the Lord works in our lives. He needs to remove the biggest stumbling blocks first before tackling the lesser faults."

Caleb walked up the road, the sea to his left, pastures to his right. Beyond them loomed the ever-present dark fir forest. He passed Geneva's house, wondering at the absence of Jake's bark. She didn't usually take him with her when she went out fishing. Then he heard it, barking coming from the bay. Shading his eyes against the hazy sun, Caleb made out

Geneva's peapod, leg-o'-mutton sail hoisted, a dog seated forward. Caleb marveled; it was almost as if the dog spotted him all the way up there from the boat.

He shook his head, continuing on his way. Geneva had made it clear more than a week ago that she didn't want him interfering in her life anymore. He walked past a white clapboard farmhouse up the hill past Geneva's fields. A woman stood on the porch, sweeping. She stopped her broom to watch him. He gave her a nod, and after a second, she nodded back. Caleb wondered once again how much of his reputation had preceded him from Boston. A fair amount, he suspected.

The road dipped and then climbed upward once again. At the juncture of the peninsula to the mainland, the road curved eastward, past a schoolhouse. Caleb's thoughts flitted to his erstwhile pupil, trying to picture her as a little girl in pigtails, walking to and from school until her father pulled her out.

He determined to put Geneva out of his mind. He had to get over this habit of sticking his nose in where it didn't belong. He'd done it with Ellery, and look where that had got him. The image of Ellery, his young cousin, as the little boy who'd been brought to live in his home after being orphaned, rose to his mind. He'd seemed so weak and pitiful, Caleb hadn't been able to help feeling sorry for him. He felt so hale and hearty, fresh from his sea voyages, beside his pale cousin.

So, whenever Caleb was home from the sea, he had taken little Ellery under his wing. Caleb had always found it easy to make friends. He smiled sardonically now. Whatever else the price of being Phelps Senior's son, it also meant that every social door had opened on well-oiled hinges.

But he'd learned firsthand how quickly those doors closed, how quickly those friends vanished.

Caleb's thoughts came back to Geneva. His anger had long since evaporated, her hurtful words ceasing to rankle. He couldn't really blame her for them. He realized now that he'd treated her pretty roughly. And she was the type of person who came back fighting.

It was just that when he'd seen that animal, Lucius Tucker, on top of Geneva, he'd felt a sudden, blinding fury. He couldn't stand seeing a woman ill-treated. But his anger had turned as quickly to Geneva for forcing him to come to her rescue. He was through playing white knight. He'd come to Haven's End to get away from people. Noble and gentlemanly behavior was a waste of time. Ellery and Arabella had made that abundantly clear.

He'd known them practically his entire life. And in a matter of a few weeks they'd shown him he'd never known them at all.

Caleb was sorry he'd lashed out at Geneva. She'd had enough knocks in her young life to warrant her touchy pride. But he was also sorry he would no longer be able to help her to read. Perhaps she would find someone in the village who would do a better job. Even as the thought crossed his mind, he knew her stubborn pride would never permit her to go to anyone there. The fact he was an outsider was the only reason, he guessed, that she'd ventured to ask him for help.

The road wound through a stretch of balsam and spruce forest on either side, brightened by the white trunk of an occasional paper birch. The scent of evergreen was carried along the breeze. Along the edges of the dirt road daisies, clover and buttercups bobbed up and down. Blackberry bushes, covered in a cascade of white blossoms, grew thickly in any patch of sunlight they could find.

About a mile farther on, the trees cleared and dwellings began to reappear along the edges of the next bay. The tide was out, leaving its upper reaches mudflats and drained salt marshes. Caleb walked past the white, steepled church and a few houses at the head of the bay, until he reached the boatyard.

Even from the head of the bay, a ship's hull was visible. Standing in the stocks, looking like a skeleton with vertical ribs, the new schooner dwarfed the men busy along the lumber-strewn beach.

Caleb made his way to the shingled building marked Winslow's Shipyard, which sat above the beach on pilings. Before entering it, his eye was drawn to the activity along the beach. He loved the atmosphere of a boatyard. Full-length logs, the height of the trees they'd been cut from, lay everywhere. Along the embankment they were piled up, but along the sand, they lay spread out in disarray. The rest of the beach was covered with pieces of lumber, cut in all sizes and shapes. Men worked on the stocks of the ship, shouting to each other and to the men below them, as they walked up and down the ramps leading to the top of the hull. The sound of the caulkers' mallets pounding against the wood echoed the length of the beach.

Caleb observed the scene. What in the world was he doing shut away on Ferguson Point, tending a garden? The feeling of impotent rage at the events in his life welled up inside him. It pressed against his rib cage, finding no outlet. He clenched his fists in frustration.

The feeling lasted only a few seconds. With a quick shake of his head, as if to drive away the thoughts trapped inside, he turned away from the sights and sounds of activity.

He gave his attention to the building before him. The door stood open. Holding on to the doorjamb, he leaned into the cluttered but airy workshop. "Excuse me. Is there someone named Silas around here?"

A man turned from the long table strewn with drawings. "Silas? Who's looking for Silas?" As he spoke, the man came forward, placing the pencil he'd been holding behind an ear and peering sharply over half-moon spectacles. He was in his shirtsleeves and wore a leather apron.

Caleb recognized him as Mr. Winslow, the proprietor, a man in his early fifties, though his full head of dark hair showed only a few strands of white. Caleb's father had had dealings with him. He remembered Geneva's words of dismissal about him.

"I am. Caleb Phelps." Wondering whether he should stick his hand out, he decided against it. If the farm woman's curt nod were any indication, this man probably wouldn't even take it.

"Phelps? Young Caleb Phelps?" As Winslow looked closely at him in the light coming in from the doorway, his whole manner altered from sharp inquisition to hearty welcome. "Come in, come in, my boy. I knew you were here, but I haven't had a chance to drive down to the Point to pay my respects. I just received a note from your father with several news clippings." As he spoke he dusted the sawdust off a chair and motioned Caleb to it. Caleb shook his head to signal that he preferred to stand.

"I must say I'm relieved to hear everything's sorted itself out in Boston." He shook his head. "Awful business. I was sorry to hear about it all, but now it's behind you. I hope it doesn't mean we'll be losing you to Boston?"

Caleb ignored the question. "May I see the clippings? I haven't received the papers from Boston."

"Sure, sure. Let me see where I put them." He went over to a desk and rummaged around the top. After a few minutes, he came back carrying a large envelope, and slipped out the clippings.

Caleb recognized his father's strong handwriting on the company's stationery clipped to the top of them. "Thank you," he murmured, taking the papers toward the window. "Shipping Heir Cleared of all Charges," "Caleb Phelps III Found Innocent," "Phelps Senior, Vehement in Defense of His Only Son." Despite the bold headlines, the articles were scant in their reporting of how Caleb Phelps could have been under suspicion in the first place. As far as Caleb was concerned, as many unanswered questions remained for the public to unravel as before.

The only difference was that now the entire firm of Phelps Shipping & Co. stood solidly behind him, declaring his innocence without giving a clear explanation of what had actually occurred, except that "officials" were hard at work to bring the real criminal to justice.

If his father believed this to be the way to exonerate his son's name, Caleb thought he'd only succeeded in resurrecting the whole sordid business over again.

Mr. Winslow's next words confirmed Caleb's fears. "You may be sure I'll spread the word in the village of your innocence. It will come as a relief to everyone to know the truth."

Understanding Winslow's friendliness more clearly now, Caleb lifted an eyebrow. "The truth? What truth?"

The older man looked confused for a second. "Why, your innocence! We've always had the highest regard around here for both your father and yourself. Your father and I go back quite a ways—"

"I was told you had a young man working for you named Silas."

Once again he'd succeeded in catching the shipwright off guard. "Silas? Why, he's just a hand. What would you want with him?"

"I'd like to have him build me a boat."

Mr. Winslow smiled in relief. "A boat. Why, certainly. We'll build you the best you could wish for. We've got the best reputation around here."

"May I speak to this Silas about my requirements?"

Mr. Winslow cleared his throat. "Oh, no, you'll need to speak with me. Silas has no knowledge of naval architecture. He's just involved in the carpentry end of things."

"Very well. Here's a rough plan of what I'd like." Caleb took a rolled-up paper from his trousers pocket.

"What exactly are you looking at?" Winslow asked as he accepted the paper from Caleb and motioned him to one of the drafting tables.

"A small-size sloop, about eighteen feet at the waterline."

"I'll draw up the necessary lines plan. Silas, of course, can assist in the building of it, but he knows nothing of design."

They discussed the details of Caleb's plan a little further, then Caleb told Winslow he was heading down to the yard to have a look around.

"Good enough. Young Silas'll be down there—a fair-haired young fella, but as I said, he knows nothing of the design end of things. I'll go over this drawing in detail and draw up the plan and contract and have them sent around to the Point. How's that?"

"Fine." Replacing his hat on his head, Caleb ducked back out the doorway. The wind had picked up and felt cool on his arms. Farther down, the mouth of the bay was cloaked in fog. Wisps of it were already wafting toward the head of the harbor.

He eyed the boats in the stocks below him, feeling again the yearning to be on the sea, or at least involved with things of the sea.

Spotting a young man with dark blond hair, Caleb walked down the grassy embankment to the beach, fixing his thoughts firmly on the goal before him. He'd made his choices. He'd better learn to live with them.

An older man was speaking with the young man, who was perhaps in his early twenties. It was clear, after listening to just a few words of their conversation, who was consulting whom. The design was clearly the young man's, and the older man was seeking clarification. When he left satisfied, the young man looked questioningly at Caleb.

"May I help you, sir?"

"Yes. Are you Silas?"

He nodded.

"I'm told you're good at your craft."

"Who told you that?"

"Geneva Patterson."

The young man smiled. "I just helped her with her little boat. Nothing any farmer or fisherman around here couldn't do."

"I've given my plans to Winslow inside. I'd like you to take a look at them when you get a chance and tell me what you think."

"Sure."

"You have a nice boatyard here."

The young man shrugged. "It's not mine. I merely work here."

"So Winslow told me. You ever thought of designing a craft?"

The young man pointed to his temple. "I already have. Up here."

Caleb smiled. "Maybe we could go over your designs one day."

"I'd be glad to."

"You've been with Winslow long?"

"Since I was a lad. I apprenticed under him. Winslow's is the biggest shipyard around here."

"There are opportunities elsewhere. Know anything about building yachts?" Caleb wasn't sure why he was pursuing the topic, but something about the young man appealed to him, especially after Geneva's recommendations and Winslow's behavior.

Silas looked interested. "No, sir, but I've seen some at anchor here. I wouldn't mind working on one."

"Maybe you will. Do you have time to show me around?"

"Sure." The young man, who had been so serious up until now, smiled and gestured for Caleb to accompany him. Caleb thought of the people he could recommend the youth to, people who wouldn't hold him back the way Winslow was clearly doing.

Stop it, he told himself.

Wasn't one failed project—Miss Geneva Samantha Patterson—enough for his first month at Haven's End?

Chapter Six

Geneva hauled up the cod line, the thick, wool nippers encircling her palms protecting them from the coarse rope. She loosened the hooks from the cod and haddock gullets with the gobstick and let the fish flop into the bottom of her boat and turned her attention to rebaiting the line.

She spared a glance for Jake, who sat at the prow. "You've been good, boy. I know you must be gettin' restless. Like to stretch your legs, huh? So would I." She didn't know what she was going to do with him. She wished she hadn't— No, she wouldn't start with regrets about Captain Caleb. It was too late to think about how he would have been the natural person to leave Jake with.

She filled each snood with pickled clams from the bucket at her feet. After securing the net bags to the line and adjusting the hooks, she heaved the line back down over the side. Then she brought up the second line and repeated the procedure, all the time reminding herself that she still hadn't followed Mrs. Bradford's advice.

"Don't look at me like that," she told Jake, who was staring at her dolefully. "I did the first part, didn't I? You saw me get down on my knees just like Ma used to do before she got too ill to leave her bed. I asked God's forgiveness. I pretty near begged Him to help me make things right with the cap'n."

But that's as far as it had gone. "I just didn't have the courage to say 'I'm sorry' to his face."

She'd seen him at work in his yard countless times. And how many times had he walked by her house? But she'd always made sure her back was to him as he passed.

She dearly hoped Mrs. Bradford had forgotten all about their conversation. She wouldn't want to disappoint the old lady by telling her the praying hadn't worked. She was beneath God's notice, just as she'd always suspected.

Geneva turned her attention back to her catch. With her knife, she sliced off the fish heads and threw them overboard. Another slit down the belly and out went the guts, everything but the liver, which she dropped into a bucket. Jake looked longingly at the scraps, but Geneva just shook her head. "You've had enough, boy. Get yourself sick."

The gulls screeched and circled overhead, diving for the scraps with the precision of an arrow heading straight for its target. Geneva pulled her boots up over her thighs. She ignored the apron of oiled canvas splattered with blood and fish guts. Only when she'd filled half her boat did she stop for a break. She retrieved the flask of tea from under the thwart and removed the sailcloth she'd wrapped it in to keep it warm. She drank straight from the flask and munched on some hard crackers, all the while keeping an eye seaward, where the fog obscured the horizon. Jake got up and took a few turns around the small space allotted to him, then sat back down.

After her meal, she pulled up the lines a last time, before shipping anchor and hoisting her sail to head to the next bay. She navigated through the Juniper Island Narrows between a few small, uninhabited islands scattered between the jutting point of the mainland and the larger Juniper Island opposite. Past them lay Hendricks Bay, a large expanse of water dotted with several small islands.

Saluting to a distant fisherman, with Jake standing up straight to bark his own greeting, Geneva made her way to her favorite fishing grounds, and proceeded to bait her lines and cast them overboard.

When the fog began to roll in, in billowing clouds, she put on her oilskins and sou'wester and kept hauling her lines. The fog crept in over the ocean, first blanketing one island, then another, swallowing each one up, then obscuring mooring posts and buoys. Not until it began edging the beach and forests and fields above it did Geneva pull up her last lines and head homeward.

She made her way by sound, recognizing the bells along the inlet and the sounds of cows lowing at the Roberts' farm, until passing close enough to spot a buoy in her own bay. She eased up on the sail, peering through the shrouded world until she made out the boulders looming darkly through the fog and heard the barking of the Stillmans' hounds, which Jake returned.

At last she reached her strip of beach. Jake was ahead of her, jumping out while they were still in a few feet of water. He immediately disappeared up the trail to the house. She followed him more slowly, sloshing through the water until the boat scraped the stones on the bottom. She pulled it up above the tidemark, where the rockweed was stiff and black and tangled with bits of rope and pieces of driftwood. Before she'd finished securing the line to a gnarled tree branch that bent low over the stones, she heard Jake's joyful bark coming nearer once again. Behind his quick, pattering footsteps, she heard another set crunching down the path.

For a second Geneva froze, remembering Lucius. But, no, Jake wouldn't bark like that for him.

The dog came bounding out of the fog, and right behind him, his dark head and pea jacket visible through the mist, came Captain Caleb.

Geneva sagged in relief. Never had she been so glad to see him. Maybe God did answer prayer. She vowed silently to ask the captain's pardon, no matter what the outcome.

But the next moment he stood beside her, and she lost her nerve. Instead, she bent over the line, her numb fingers fumbling with the knot.

"Hello there."

His voice sounded friendly. She stole a look at his face. It looked calm. His dark hair was edged with drops of moisture. Her glance darted to his deep blue eyes. He didn't look angry. He had every right to be, yet his whole demeanor spoke nothing but acceptance.

Without asking for permission, he gently pushed her hands away from the half-formed hitch and finished the job for her. She didn't argue.

"Your hands are cold" was his only comment.

When she didn't say anything, he cleared his throat, "I know I shouldn't be intruding, but I saw the fog and knew you'd gone out." He smiled sheepishly. "I just wanted to make sure you'd gotten back all right."

That smile was the loveliest thing she'd ever seen. Suddenly Geneva couldn't talk for the lump in her throat. No one had ever cared about her whereabouts before. Why, if she went down in a storm or got lost in the fog, folks probably wouldn't notice it for days. She looked down at the rope, trying to form some words.

"It'd take a little more'n fog to keep me from coming

home," she said gruffly, still not looking at him. Why couldn't she say what was in her heart and be done with it?

She heard his chuckle, deep and reassuring. "I'm sure it would, Miss Patterson. I'm sure it would."

"Wish you wouldn't call me that."

"Call you what? Miss Patterson? It's your name, isn't it?"

"Always sounds like you're making fun o' me when you call me that. Nobody else calls me that."

"Perhaps it's time somebody did." His voice lost its mirth. "I'm not making fun of you when I say it." His finger came up and hooked her chin.

She couldn't breathe, looking into his blue eyes.

"What would you like me to call you?"

"Geneva," she whispered.

"That's fine with me. It's the way I think of you anyhow."

Before she could fathom the meaning of that, he let her go and looked toward the boat.

"Can I help bring anything up? Or would that be interfering where I shouldn't?"

She shook her head mutely. This was the opportunity she'd been hoping for. But the words of apology still wouldn't come.

"No, no," she said quickly when she realized he was still awaiting a reply. "Just got my catch in there, but it's awful smelly. You look so neat and clean."

She looked down at herself, suddenly aware of what a sight she must appear. She began tugging at the knot of her sou'wester.

"I've handled worse things than a mess of cod. Come on. It'll be quicker with two." Without waiting for her answer, he went to her boat and looked inside.

Geneva collected the tubs from the shore and brought them to the boat. "I fill these and carry them up."

He didn't even let her load, but took off his jacket and started filling a tub with fish. Geneva followed suit. When both tubs were full, she led the way up the path.

"I'll start splittin' these," she told him as he turned to get another load. Her hands shook while handling the first fish, but as soon as Captain Caleb was gone, she calmed down a bit and began gathering her usual speed. She'd just store them in saltwater tonight and lay them on the racks to dry tomorrow.

When he'd brought the last of the fish up and filled a hogshead for her with saltwater for storing the fish, he watched her work for a few seconds and then said, "I'll clean out the boat." Before she could reply, he was gone.

When he returned, he washed out the emptied tubs and stacked them by the shed. "All shipshape and accounted for," he told her when he'd finished, his eyes twinkling with humor, the same way they had when he'd rescued her on the wharf.

"I'm just about finished with these," she said, not knowing how to thank him, wishing he would stay, wishing for so many things....

"Can you spare any of those, or are they all for the market?"

"Uh, no, I save some for myself. Why?"

"How would you like to give me a piece of haddock and I'll give you the best-tasting fish chowder you've had all month?"

She had to smile at that. "Who's going make it?"

"You're looking at him."

She laughed out loud.

"You're going to regret that laughter. You think I'm from Boston and don't know how to prepare a fish chowder, do you?"

"Stop ribbin' me, Cap'n. You're…a gentleman—a ship's captain—"

"Who has held just about every other position aboard ship—" he cocked his head "—except perhaps cook. But as cabin boy, I hung around the galley long enough to learn to fend for myself."

"You expect me to believe you've swabbed the deck and climbed the rigging?"

"My father believes in learning from the bottom up." His smile disappeared. "I told you I've gotten a lot more than cod on my hands."

She shook her head, not able to adjust her picture of the captain so quickly. His next words jolted her still further.

"If I'm to address you as Geneva, you must call me Caleb."

She reddened. "I couldn't do that."

"Why not?" His blue eyes pierced through the fog.

"Don't sound right. I've always thought of you as Cap'n."

"Well, I haven't always been a captain. I was only captain for a relatively short period. If you don't want me going back to 'Miss Patterson,' you'll have to overcome your aversion to 'Caleb.'"

"Very well, Cap—" She could feel her cheeks grow hot again, and hoped the fog muted their color. She cleared her throat. "Caleb."

"That's better." He took a few steps closer to her, and Geneva tensed.

"Let's have a look at that catch. This one looks good." His hand scooped up one of the smaller fish.

"What do you have in that garden of yours now? Nothing in mine is ready."

Geneva could hardly keep up with the changes in the conversation. She struggled to think. "I have some radishes, peas, a few heads of lettuce, might have a few spears of asparagus still left."

"Perfect. Would you trust me in your garden to get what I need?"

"Sure. You'll find a bushel basket in the lean-to." At the moment, she was willing to give him whatever he wanted. He could go in her garden and trample all her crops down for all she cared. She rummaged in her pocket. "Here's a knife."

"No need." He patted his own pocket. "I have my own." He grinned. "A sailor always goes prepared."

"I still think you're ribbin' me about all that."

"I'll prove you wrong with my chowder."

"We'll see about that."

As he turned to go, she remembered something. "You can skip the asparagus."

He looked back over his shoulder at her. "Why's that?"

"Never eat it. I just grow it to sell."

"You don't care for it, or it doesn't agree with you?"

"Don't care for it. Can't see all the fuss summer folks make about it."

"You wait until you've tried it the way I'll fix it for you, and then decide."

She nodded, resigned.

"Come down to the house in a couple of hours, how's that? Does that give you enough time to finish up?"

She nodded again, unable to believe she would be dining at the captain's table. "I'll be there."

Geneva had finished splitting the fish. She'd gone into the garden and found everything in order. No boot prints where they shouldn't be, no crushed leaves or blossoms. She decided to cut some rhubarb and make a cobbler for the captain—Caleb, she reminded herself, feeling the color steal through her cheeks at the name.

While the cobbler was baking, she went out to the pump and hauled in buckets of water to heat. She filled the tin washtub and began scrubbing herself until she was sure the smell of fish was off her. Her stinking clothes were now in the washtub, to soak overnight. She put on her only remaining clean shirt, looking in distaste at the frayed collar and faded plaid.

It was nothing like the outfit Miss Harding had worn that afternoon on the wharf. Now, why did she have to go and think about that? All her pleasure at the thought of dining with the captain dissolved at the memory of the captain's former betrothed.

Miss Harding had worn a light blue suit. Once, up at the hotel to deliver some vegetables, Geneva had seen a little girl carrying a porcelain doll, a doll much finer than any owned by the girls in the village. Miss Harding's outfit had reminded Geneva of that doll. Its little skirt and jacket had been trimmed in a darker shade of velvet. Miniature buttons, covered in the same fabric as the suit, formed a row down the little doll's front. The skirt was meticulously pleated. Pale lace peeked out from its collar and cuffs, which matched the miniature suede gloves and buttoned boots. A saucy little hat perched atop its blond ringlets.

Geneva tugged at her cuffs and looked at her image in the tiny square of mirror on the wall, in which she could see only a portion of her face at a time. Just as well—she'd never liked what she saw, ever since she was a girl and climbed up on the chair and peered in the glass and had her first glimpse of herself.

A thin face had stared back at her, its black eyes frowning, her hair so straight she couldn't do anything but braid it.

No, neither features nor hair had been anything like the plump, curly-haired, peaches-and-cream faces of the girls who walked to school each morning.

Geneva turned from the mirror, beginning to dread the coming hour. There was nothing left to do. She'd washed and changed her clothes. She'd even washed her hair, putting some vinegar in the final rinse. She'd heard somewhere that lemon juice was good, but since she didn't have any of that, she'd decided to try the vinegar. Anything that might wash away the smell of fish.

Why was she so scared? she chided herself. She'd been to the capta—Caleb's—home before.

The name made her feel self-conscious. It sounded different by itself. She was used to rattling it off, as an appendage to "captain." By itself, the two syllables *Ca-leb* made themselves felt, calling attention to the man who bore them.

In a few moments, she would be sitting across the table from this man, attempting idle conversation. Something about eating a meal with him frightened her. She was used to taking her meals in the solitary confines of her one room.

The captain would watch how she held her knife and fork. She remembered her picnic with Mrs. Bradford. That had been merely a picnic, with Mrs. Bradford, a woman of extreme kindness and tact. Geneva couldn't bear it if Caleb, with only a look, expressed displeasure—or worse—distaste over her manners.

Geneva folded her arms across her waist, beginning to feel sick to her stomach. How was she ever going to swallow down even a mouthful of chowder?

The thing that scared her most was knowing she couldn't sit down to a meal with him without apologizing to him first.

The captain had done nothing but give and give and give, and what had she done in return?

Smelling the cobbler, Geneva got up from her rocker and walked toward the oven, her footsteps slow and heavy. The cobbler was bubbling, the pastry golden brown and beginning to scorch a little around the edges.

It was now or never.

Geneva marched up the steps toward the etched glass doors. Jake had arrived ahead of her and was already scratching at the entrance.

"Hold on." Grasping the cold brass knocker as if it might lend her strength, she tapped it against the door, hearing its knock echo within the house. An instant later, Captain Caleb stood before her.

She swallowed, already feeling in the wrong place. He looked so neat and polished in a pair of charcoal-gray trousers instead of his usual denim dungarees. The flannel shirt had been replaced with a crisp white shirt and dark vest. Before Geneva could back away, he was inviting her in.

She gestured toward Jake, not knowing how to explain his presence. "Hope you don't mind my bringing him along. I can leave him in the barn."

"Nonsense. Hi there, boy." Caleb was already squatting before Jake and rubbing his fur. He gave her a sheepish look. "I never had a dog of my own."

She looked at him in astonishment. "Well, you're welcome to Jake's company whenever you want. I wouldn't want him becoming a nuisance, though."

"I don't think he'll become a nuisance—do you, Jake?" He gave the dog a final rub before standing. "I noticed you took him out with you today. Is that usual?" He motioned her inside as he spoke.

Geneva didn't know how to answer. If she told him about Lucius' threat, there was no telling what Caleb would do. She didn't want to make trouble for him.

"No," she answered finally, standing awkwardly in the entrance hall, the dish of cobbler balanced atop the reading primers and slate that Caleb had left with her.

"Here, let me take that." Before she could stop him, he had relieved her of the cobbler, exposing the books underneath. He couldn't help but see them, but he made no comment. Geneva clutched them to her side.

"I—I—" She tried to regain her train of thought. "I don't like leaving Jake alone so much. But a small boat's no place for a dog."

"Would you like to leave him with me when you go out?"

She stared at him. The invitation seemed to slip from him so easily. "Do you mean it?"

"Of course I do. What did I just tell him?"

He bent over Jake. "You'll never be a nuisance." Caleb gave her a sidelong wink. "He'll keep me company."

Before Geneva could express her gratitude, he held up the dish of cobbler, taking a deep sniff.

"I thought I was doing the cooking tonight."

"It's just a cobbler. I didn't want to come empty-handed."

He gave her an understanding look. "It smells good enough to eat right now and skip the chowder."

Geneva began to relax slightly. "You just don't want to admit you can't make a chowder."

"That's what you think. I'll put this cobbler on the shelf and bring out my five-course dinner."

Geneva followed him down the hall to the main room as they talked. When she entered the room, she stopped short. Wooden crates and boxes lay everywhere. Stacks of books sat upon the bookshelves. A few oriental vases and a pair of carved ebony elephants with ivory tusks joined the ship's clock on one shelf.

Large Persian carpets, navy blue and burgundy, unlike anything Geneva had ever seen, covered the wooden floor. She felt as if she'd stumbled upon a treasure trove of exotic booty. Her gaze traveled slowly around the room, her eyes widening when she noticed the walls. Where there had been whitewashed plaster, now there stood a section of muted striped wallpaper. The reading table was loaded with rolls of wallpaper and a bucket of glue and brushes. Jake was already busy sniffing around the new items.

"What's all this?" she blurted out when Caleb returned from the kitchen.

Caleb came toward her with a smile. "Like it? It's called settling in. I've ordered some furniture as well. It'll be coming in on the packet from Boston. The books just arrived yesterday."

Geneva stared around her, not knowing what to say, not knowing what to think. "Where did you get so many... treasures?"

Caleb smiled at the word. "I've collected many things over the years during my sea voyages. I never had a place to put them. They've been sitting in a warehouse in Boston until now."

After a moment he said, "You were right the other day about my not having a stick of furniture in here." He held up a hand before she could speak. "Actually, I'd already sent for these things before you spoke. I told my friend, Nate, to ship them when he got back to Boston."

He smiled. "I was probably trying to prove to him that I was here to stay. He didn't believe me, either. And he tried his best to persuade me to come back to Boston."

Geneva swallowed, feeling worse than she had when she'd made the remark. Then her thoughts shifted to his friend's visit. She forced herself to ask. "He didn't succeed?"

Caleb shook his head. "I know it will take more than a few pieces of furniture to prove my staying power here, but I also have a few plans for this place."

Geneva shifted her books from one hand to the other. "I had no right to—"

Caleb stopped her attempt at an apology. "Forget it. I already have." He chuckled. "Up until now I had no heart for doing much of anything. You could thank your gardening for saving me. It inspired me to begin rebuilding my life."

Geneva's words weighed more heavily than ever now. "I spoke outta turn the other day, Cap'n. I didn't know what I was talking about."

"You spoke the truth as you saw it. You stick to your directness. It's one of the things I like about you. And what happened to calling me Caleb?"

She could feel herself flush. "Sorry. It takes some getting used to." She cleared her throat. "I guess I'm not used to seeing newcomers around here. Most everyone's family's been around since the place was settled."

He smiled again, that rich smile that crinkled the edges of his eyes and reached down to her very insides. "So, a few pieces of furniture won't do it? My name shall have to span a few generations before you're willing to consider me part of the community?"

"You're making fun of me again." She moved away from him, farther into the room, still clutching the pair of books at her side.

"I told you you could keep the books," he said quietly.

She stopped and looked down at them. "They're beautiful. Better than any readers we ever had in school." She met his gaze. "But they wouldn't be any use. After I left school, I tried learning on my own. But it didn't do no—any—good. I tried and tried but I just couldn't make sense of the letters all strung together."

The way he was looking at her, she became embarrassed by her confession. She glanced back down at the books, her fingers outlining the gilt lettering on the top cover.

"Geneva, do you want to learn to read?"

She nodded without looking up.

"Are you willing to give it another try with me as your teacher?"

She looked at him then. "Yes." The sound was a choked whisper, but that's all he required.

His tone became brisk. "Good. Now that that's settled, I'll expect you here tomorrow afternoon." He rubbed his hands together. "If you'll excuse me, I have to get dinner on the table. I don't know about you, but I'm famished. Do you want me to give Jake something?"

At the sound of his name, the dog came over to Caleb, eagerly stretching his neck upward.

Geneva felt such a relief that things were back to normal between her and the captain, she was afraid her legs would collapse under her. She took a deep breath and slowly loosened her grip on the books. To keep the captain's attention on Jake, she spoke sharply to her pet, "Get your muddy paws off the captain."

"Listen to your mistress, dressing you down like that. Your paws are clean. Look at that silky coat of yours. I bet you've just had a bath." Caleb's voice was warm and affectionate, his hands echoing his tone as they scratched Jake's head. "So, have you had anything to eat?"

Geneva forced her mind to what he was saying. "He's eaten. I—I fed him before we came over."

"Do you want to come out to the kitchen with me anyway?" Caleb continued to address the dog. "Sit by the warm stove?"

Jake followed Caleb as if he'd found a new master.

Glad of the time alone to put everything back into perspective, Geneva took a slow turn around the room. Hesitantly, she walked first toward the shelves. She fingered one of Caleb's books with awe, wondering if she would ever come to read well enough to make head or tail of the words in them. A few looked like stories, with an interesting picture here and there throughout the text.

She could hear Caleb going from the dining room to the pantry and kitchen, and asked him if he needed any help. When he declined, she walked over to one of the carpets. She didn't dare walk on it. It looked exotic, thick and soft, appropriate only for soft slippers such as she imagined Miss Harding wore indoors.

To dispel the image of the woman who had been meant to be mistress of this house, Geneva kept moving. She went up to the wall that the captain had started papering.

"Like it?"

She jumped at the captain's voice behind her, then looked more closely at the paper. Little sprigs of blue flowers and ribbons formed vertical stripes against a creamy background. The blue was the same periwinkle shade as Miss Harding's suit.

"Pretty enough" was all she said, but in reality she'd never seen anything so lovely.

"Come on. Your dinner is served."

"Where's Jake?"

"Curled up in front of the stove."

Caleb had set up the small kitchen table in the dining room and covered it with a cloth. Fine china and crystal goblets and silverware adorned it. A small vase of daisies sat in the middle. It looked elegant and inviting at the same time, and it took her breath away. She gave a rapid glance toward the captain. He'd done this for her.

Caleb held out a chair at one end for her, and she sat down carefully. At least she wouldn't be balancing fine china on her lap above the cliffs on an island. Making it through this meal without disgracing herself shouldn't be so difficult after her picnic with Mrs. Bradford. The memory of it made her smile.

"What are you thinking about?" Caleb asked as he took the seat opposite her.

"If someone would'a told me that I'd be dining off fine china and linen, using real silver, twice in two weeks, I would'a laughed in his face."

He looked interested. "This is your second time?"

Geneva told him about her employment with Mrs. Bradford.

"Maud is a wonderful lady. She'll teach you a lot of things if you spend some time with her." Caleb lifted the bottle. "Would you care for a glass of wine?"

She looked away. "I never drank much spirits. Pa...well, he...liked to drink, and it used to make him mean." Those were the times Geneva would wake up the next morning to find her ma with black-and-blue marks on her arms. Once he'd given Ma a black eye.

"I'm sorry."

She shook her head. "It's all in the past now."

"Too often, people think they can run from their situation through liquor. I can tell you from firsthand experience, it doesn't work."

She looked at his twisted smile, wondering at his admission. Did that mean he no longer drank? "Pa never could give it up. Not that I ever saw him try," she added dryly.

He met her gaze. "I'm sorry. He was probably one of those unfortunate men who become slaves of the bottle. And you and your mother suffered for it."

He glanced at the bottle in his hand. "Unfortunately—or fortunately, I should say—drinking myself to oblivion did nothing to ease my pain. It only made waking the next day more agonizing than I care to remember."

He set the bottle back on the table. "Would you like a glass of water or tea?"

"Anything would be fine."

After he'd served her, she looked down at her place. Four spears of asparagus lay against each other on a small plate, which sat on a larger plate. A thick yellow sauce had been poured on the asparagus.

Carefully she took the linen napkin from under her fork and unfolded it. She draped it on her lap as she'd seen Mrs. Bradford do, and waited. Caleb took up his fork and knife and began cutting. When he was ready to take the fork up to his mouth, she blurted out, stalling for time. "Mrs. Bradford prayed. Before the meal, that is," she added at his look of inquiry.

He set his fork back down. "By all means." When she didn't say anything, he prompted, "Go ahead."

She didn't know what to say and tried to remember Mrs. Bradford's words. *"Thank You, Lord, for this food. Uh, please bless it, uh, in Jesus' name,"* she ended in a rush, remembering those three words.

"Thank you." Caleb proceeded to take up where he'd left off. After his first mouthful he looked at her. Wiping his mouth with the napkin, he said, "Try it. Just one bite."

She cut through the bright green stem.

"Try it with the sauce."

Obediently, she dipped the piece into the creamy sauce and then brought the fork to her mouth.

She looked at him in surprise. "It's good."

"Of course it's good. I told you I could cook."

When they'd finished the asparagus, Caleb removed the top plate. He brought in a steaming soup tureen and bowls. The fish chowder was rich and delicious, and she told him so.

"You really do know how to cook," she said, looking at him in awe, trying to reconcile what he'd said about his background with her own assumptions.

She marveled at how he put her at ease, talking about things she knew about. He asked her about her fishing, about how she spent the winter, without asking her anything personal that might be difficult for her to talk about, such as her father or mother, or the way the villagers viewed her.

He, in turn, told her about his visit with Silas, the boat builder, and recounted some of his adventures at sea with his friend Nate, all without saying anything about the troubles in Boston that had brought him to Haven's End.

The room around them grew darker until only their own small area lit by the kerosene lamp on the table was visible. Jake had wandered in at some point during the dinner and now sat asleep at their feet.

Caleb drained his glass. "Now that I've proven I can make a passable fish chowder, I'm looking forward to judging your efforts at cobbler."

"It's nothing special. Just some rhubarb and the last strawberries."

"How about having it in the other room with our coffee?"

"That sounds fine with me." She stood and helped him clear the table. Jake stirred, but did not stand, only watched his mistress's movements as if it were the most natural thing in the world to see her in Caleb's house doing household chores.

Geneva tried to begin washing up, but Caleb stopped her. "Just put them to soak."

She noticed the pump he had right at his sink.

"Yes, nothing but the best for this place," he said with a trace of irony in his tone, as he filled up the coffeepot with water.

"Why don't you serve the cobbler, while I get the coffee cups?" he suggested, reaching above her head to open one of the cupboards.

Working alongside Caleb in his kitchen felt as right as tilling his garden or bringing in a smelly load of fish with him. Geneva stared at the crust of the cobbler, willing those kinds of thoughts away. But it was getting harder and harder not to imagine such things as natural.

She scooped out a generous portion of the cobbler for Caleb, knowing by looking that it had turned out well. She carried the two plates into the sitting room, Jake at her heels, and set them on the crate by the armchair, while Caleb waited for the coffee to boil.

She lit the sitting-room lamp and adjusted the flame. The crate held a spyglass, a book and newspapers. As she removed these to make room on the surface for the coffee that was to come, she saw the locket.

It lay open, and she could see a woman's photograph within. She stared at the locket as if it were a vial of venomous poison, one drop capable of destroying all the well-being she'd gained during the meal. It was probably a portrait of a family member, she told herself, her hand already reaching for it. She must know.

She had known all along what she'd find. Arabella Harding's sepia image stared back at her, those same blond curls framing a heart-shaped face under a pert little hat.

Those few weeks last summer flooded Geneva's memory. Just as Miss Harding had predicted, Geneva had fallen much harder than against the planks of the wharf. She'd done nothing but dream of the captain day and night during his short stay at Haven's End. She'd been obsessed with catching a glimpse of him around the harbor, without being seen by him. She hadn't wanted to risk another humiliating encounter.

She shook her head, trying desperately to chase away the shameful memories. But they refused to flee. The most embarrassing was of the night she stole out to the village, when she'd heard of the dance the captain was giving at the hotel in honor of his bride-to-be. Geneva had stood outside in the dark, peering through the long windows. She'd watched the captain dance with his fiancée.

The two had circled around and around, clearly the most elegant couple in the entire room. She saw how he bent his head to hear what Miss Harding had to say, watched his tender smile—and imagined what it would be like to be the recipient of that smile.

"What are you doing?" Caleb's sharp question brought Geneva up short. The locket clattered against the floor.

"Nothin'. I… I…was just clearing…" Geneva stuffed her hands in her pockets and took a step away from the crate, feeling as guilty as if she'd been caught stealing something.

Jake, who'd found a comfortable spot near the armchair, immediately stood and growled low in his throat.

Caleb stepped forward and set down the coffee cups. Very deliberately, he picked up the locket, snapped it shut and put it in his pocket.

Geneva took a few more steps back. "I better be off," she muttered, not even sure he heard her. "Thanks for the meal." She spun around and headed for the doorway.

"Wait, Geneva."

Geneva turned. Caleb looked at her across the length of the lamp-lit room, his eyes pleading. She hesitated, knowing to stay meant disaster for her. Unable to leave, she berated herself for the worst kind of fool as she hovered on the threshold.

The captain walked toward a window. He stood there so long, staring at the black panes, that she thought once again he'd forgotten her existence.

"Forgive me, Geneva. I didn't mean to bite your head off."

She stayed where she was, neither advancing nor retreating. "I shouldn'a been nosing into things that don't concern me."

"The locket was lying there. It was natural to take a look."

Geneva's foot was raised behind her, poised for flight.

"Do you realize how difficult it is to get used to the fact that the goddess you worshiped has feet of clay?"

Caleb's words stopped her.

He gave a harsh laugh, raking a hand through his hair. "That's not the best part. The best part is, you still want her. You'd do anything to have her back."

Chapter Seven

Geneva watched the angles of Caleb's shoulders jut forward as he leaned his palms against the windowsill. His back was broad, making her think of a large beast trying to escape from its very body, but finding it impossible.

He gave another bitter laugh. "Well, you'd do *almost* anything to have her back. Unfortunately, a few remaining scruples prevent you from abasing yourself completely."

Geneva's stomach began to twist, but she stood rooted, no longer able to move. Jake, believing that all was well, returned to his place by the chair.

"That locket shows the woman I intended to marry." His voice was flat.

"Miss Harding." Geneva spoke the name softly, amazed at how calm her voice sounded, when the name was the one thing capable of awaking her from her dream.

Caleb looked over his shoulder at her. "You met her?"

Geneva cleared her throat. "Yes. Once. You…introduced us."

He nodded slowly, comprehension dawning in his eyes. "At the wharf. You were tripped."

So, he remembered. Her deepest fear now scarcely mattered. His memory of that day was obviously fixed on Miss Harding.

He faced the black window once more. "She wanted to go sailing that day. An excursion with the friends she'd insisted we bring along." He talked about the event as if he were watching it through the panes of glass, instead of seeing only the point of light reflected from the lamp.

"I was so eager to please her in everything. As long as she would be happy summering here at Haven's End after we were married, I didn't care if she dragged half of Boston along with her."

Geneva could hear the smile in his voice, even as his words sliced through her heart the way her knife gutted a cod.

Why hadn't she left while she could? Now it was too late to save herself.

"It was worth it that day to see her happy." Another silence followed. "I thought my enthusiasm for this place would be enough for both of us," he continued, his lean forefinger tracing the edge of the windowsill. "How easy it is to ignore all the little signals of discontent when it's to our advantage to remain in ignorance."

"Haven's End isn't for everyone" was all Geneva could think to say. How ironic that all the time she'd agonized over her embarrassing fall on the wharf, Caleb had been worrying about making Miss Harding happy. When he'd looked into Geneva's eyes, making her feel so special, he hadn't seen her at all. He'd had eyes only for his fiancée.

"No, I suppose not." He leaned against the window sash, his head resting on his forearm, his gaze directed toward the floor. To Geneva he looked like a man weary of puzzling things out, yet still the conundrum wouldn't let him be.

"How can a man be such a fool as to think he knows a person, when all the time he's seen nothing but his own fantasy?" His head moved back and forth slowly.

"I remember when Arabella was born. I was eight years old. Our families were friends, our fathers business associates. Arabella was like a little sister or cousin.

"It wasn't until I came back from a voyage, after I'd been made first mate, that I found Arabella had blossomed into a young lady. I'd left her a year previously a little girl in pigtails and came back to find a young lady of fifteen, her hair up, dressed in the latest fashion, the young men flocking around her like bees to honey.

"It was that day I made my decision to have her for my wife. I knew I'd have to wait years. I knew I'd have to win her against all the competition. I knew I had to remain true to her, no matter how tough that would prove."

Geneva knew enough about men to understand what Caleb was telling her. She closed her eyes. How could a woman inspire such devotion from a man and not prize it? Didn't she understand how precious such a love was?

"All the young men who'd been teasing her and treating her like a little sister suddenly were fighting for her attention. I walked into the room and thought she was the loveliest thing I'd ever seen." Caleb gave a laugh. "I was only one of a string of admirers."

Geneva thought bitterly of the pure sort of admiration Miss Harding must have attracted, not the lecherous advances she herself received.

"When I told my father that Arabella was the woman I wanted to marry, imagine my surprise when he actually approved. He not only approved, he encouraged me wholeheartedly."

Geneva's attention was caught by his words. "Why wouldn't your father approve?"

He gave a grim laugh. "You don't know my father. He is not an easy man to please."

Geneva looked at the outline of his bowed back. He was telling her things about himself that she had never dreamed she'd be privy to. She'd always imagined him as a man who'd had it easy his whole life. But tonight she was being allowed glimpses of another picture. His father sounded a bit like her own pa. Instinctively, she knew Caleb was revealing things he'd told no one else. But what good did these facts do her? Another woman completely possessed his heart.

Geneva cleared her throat again. "But your father did approve of your marriage. That was the important thing."

Caleb turned to face her. "Oh, yes. It would have been good for business. He and Arabella's father had been talking about a merger for years. Our union would have been the culmination of two shrewd businessmen's ambitions." He smiled. "Father must be relieved the merger will still be possible."

She didn't understand what he meant.

"She's getting married next month."

Geneva started, her hand going to her throat. Was it possible? Was he going to—?

"To my cousin, Ellery. So, you see, it all still stays in the family.

"August twenty-fifth." His fingers gripped the sill behind him as he looked at her, his eyes glittering in their intensity. "Do you know what it's like to know you have the power to stop something—and yet know you will do nothing?"

Her own throat was so dry she could scarcely speak the words. "You can stop the wedding?"

"One word. One word, and I can stop it. But I won't."

She stared at him. He could have his heart's desire, and he wouldn't do what he needed in order to have it? Her heart thudded, knowing the fulfillment of his desires meant the end of hers. The more she was in the captain's company, experiencing a companionability she'd never known with anyone, the more her soul yearned for the kind of complete union he sought with Miss Harding.

"Why won't you stop the wedding?" she whispered finally.

She could see his fingers white-knuckled against the edge of the sill. His head jerked back against the pane, the skin drawn tightly across his cheeks. He clenched his eyes shut, and his words came out an agonized whisper. *"Because I don't want her that way!"*

She recoiled at the violence in those barely audible words. In the stillness that followed, he opened his eyes and looked at her, although she doubted he really saw her.

"I waited so long for her." His voice regained a calmer tone. "All those years, I thought I had her love. That's what made it all worthwhile—her love and belief in me. Do you know what that means, Geneva, to love and honor someone and think you have the same from them?"

His eyes asked her for understanding, and all she could do was shake her head dumbly.

"I'm thirty-three years old, and what do I have to show for it?" His arm encompassed the room. "All those years wasted on nothing but a dream." His voice continued, dispassionate now as he proceeded with his story. "When Arabella's love was put to a test, it just wasn't strong enough. Maybe it never existed in the first place. The moment she thought I was guilty of all that—" he gestured in disgust

"—rubbish, she walked away from me and turned to someone else."

Geneva wanted to run to him. She wanted to draw him into her arms and give him the kind of love he sought. She wanted to shout to him, *I believe in you! Put my love to the test! I'll stick with you through thick and thin, till death do us part!*

Before she could be tempted to do anything so foolish, Caleb sighed and moved away from the window. As if finally realizing to whom he was talking, he gave a laugh. "Listen to me. Going on about things that don't concern you in the least."

He took a turn about the room, as if to compose himself. Finally, he came back to the crate and saw the plates of cobbler and cups of coffee. "We forgot our dessert. Come sit down, let's have some of that cobbler."

Her toes curled within her boots, her hands formed fists in her pockets. How she wished she could roll herself up into a little ball and disappear under that plush blue carpet. He couldn't have any idea how cruelly he'd hurt her with that last offhand remark. *Going on about things that don't concern you in the least.* No, he could have no idea how much his pain concerned her.

And he must never know.

Geneva shoved her hands deeper into her pockets. "I'd better be off. It's getting late and I gotta be up 'fore dawn. Goin' clamming." With each word, she backed farther down the hallway. "Come on, Jake."

At her command, the dog lifted his head. She was sorry to make him move when he looked so comfortable and…at home.

The thought mocked her.

"Jake!" she called sharply, knowing if she didn't get away soon, she'd disgrace herself in front of Caleb.

No matter what happened, she must never let the captain suspect her true feelings.

"'There be three things which are too wonderful for me, yea, four which I know not: The way of an eagle in the air; the way of a serpent upon a rock; the way of a ship in the midst of the sea; and the way of a man with a maid.'"

Mrs. Bradford's soft voice soothed Geneva as the two of them perched quietly upon the granite cliff, watching the soar of an eagle. Geneva had been lying back against the stone, her eyes closed against the sun, but she'd propped up on an elbow when Mrs. Bradford sighted the eagle. They'd waited all morning and were now amply rewarded as they watched his broad-winged flight across the sky. The sky was so blue it hurt Geneva's eyes.

Geneva asked Mrs. Bradford to repeat the words she'd recited, liking the sound of them.

"I know about the way of an eagle in the air," Geneva said afterward, shading her eyes to watch the great bird soar above them. "I haven't been aboard one of those ships that come into port, but I've been on a boat enough to understand what it means to be in the midst of the sea. And I guess a serpent upon a rock feels a bit the way I'm feeling right now."

The tranquility she'd been feeling in Mrs. Bradford's presence evaporated at the last image. "As for that last one, I can't say I know much about that."

The older woman smiled, her eyes still on the eagle. "'The way of a man with a maid.' That, perhaps, is the most beautiful of all. The most beautiful and mysterious of all."

The two women had been quiet most of the day. Geneva had never known a woman who could sit so still, except perhaps her ma, and Geneva didn't know how much that was because she'd been ill. But Mrs. Bradford wasn't like the women Geneva knew in the village, who did nothing but chatter whenever they got together.

They had arrived at this spot where they could watch the puffins nest along the tufts of grass atop the cliffs and keep an eye out for eagles. They had disturbed the seals when they'd first beached their boat, but after a while the seals had come back to shore, and now lay sprawled along the rocks below them.

Mrs. Bradford sat patiently, her hands clasped lightly in her lap, her hat shading her eyes from the sun. From time to time she'd take up her binoculars to observe the spruce trees behind her, to search for a nest, or to watch the flight of a tern over the water.

"I don't know about the beauty and mystery between a man and woman," Geneva commented. "I didn't see nothin' but rough language from my pa toward my ma...when it wasn't something worse."

"*Anything,*" Mrs. Bradford corrected. "I'm sorry it was like that between your father and mother. It's a pity so few unions achieve the ideal God would give us."

Geneva thought back on Caleb's words. He'd desired the kind of union to which Mrs. Bradford undoubtedly referred.

The older woman looked down at her hands. "I count myself very blessed to have known true love and companionship with the man I shared a good part of my life with." She glanced at Geneva. "I would wish you to have the same happiness. When you experience the love of a good man, you'll understand what a wonderful gift the Lord has given us in 'the way of a man with a maid.'"

"Seems to me it's nothing but feeling sick at heart," she said without thinking, remembering Caleb's anguish, and her own.

Mrs. Bradford looked at her in compassion. "Troubles of the heart, my dear?"

"Oh, no, ma'am, not me. Just what I seen in others."

"*I've* seen in others. It's from 'I have seen.'"

"Yes, ma'am. *I've* seen in others." Geneva's mouth bore down on the *v* sound, stressing it the way she'd heard Mrs. Bradford do.

"The road to true love can be fraught with many obstacles," Mrs. Bradford continued. "That's why it's so comforting to know we have the love of Jesus to see us through the times when we doubt the love of others."

"How's that?" Geneva gazed upward at the blue sky, hoping that its vast expanse would make what she was feeling for Caleb seem small and puny.

"If we are sure of God's abiding love for us, then no matter what trials we experience in the world, they will pale in comparison."

Mrs. Bradford's words paralleled Geneva's thoughts so closely that Geneva rolled on her side to look at her. "Can God's love really make our troubles seem small?"

"Oh, yes, dear. When you know the love of God for us frail human beings, you'll feel special no matter how anyone treats you. You know how the great King David prayed? He asked the Lord, 'Make me to know mine end, and the measure of my days, what it is; that I may know how frail I am.'"

Geneva gave a bitter laugh. "I think most of us are trying to forget how frail we are. All I have to do is go out in my boat and see nothing but blue sea and sky around and above me, the land too far away to do me any good, and I know how frail I am. What good does that do me?"

"Because, my dear, knowing our frailty shows us how utterly we depend on God's grace to see us through. Any other thing we choose to lean on is false, like the man who built his house upon the sand, and when the storms came, it was quickly swept away."

Mrs. Bradford's eyes and tone had taken on a certainty as she spoke, a certainty that drew Geneva. "'The man whose house was built upon the rock stood fast.'" The older woman patted the slate-gray rock beneath her hand. "That rock is Jesus. He is God's grace toward us, proving God's love for us, lifting us out of our condition."

Geneva could scarcely believe such a thing was possible, but she was desperate for some kind of cure. "How do you know all this?"

"Because His Word testifies of it."

"You mean the Bible?" she asked, her heart sinking.

"That's right."

Well, that did it for her. By the time she learned to read well enough, she'd be so consumed with her feelings for Caleb, it would take a mighty powerful word to save her.

"It's more than just a book, Geneva. It's Jesus Himself. The Bible says, 'In the beginning was the Word, and the Word was with God, and the Word was God.'"

Well, she'd just have to keep learning to read. Even if it meant continuing to see Caleb and be so near him she could touch him—except that she'd never have that privilege.

"I sure hope God really does love me."

"'For God so loved the world, that He gave His only begotten Son, that whosoever believeth in Him should not perish, but have everlasting life,'" Mrs. Bradford quoted quietly.

The words sounded so beautiful, "…so loved the world…
his only begotten Son…not perish…everlasting life." Geneva
didn't understand this kind of love, but she did know one
thing—whenever Mrs. Bradford talked with her, she soothed
Geneva's troubled soul.

When they returned to Mrs. Bradford's summer cottage,
which perched high on a bluff overlooking the harbor,
Geneva accompanied Mrs. Bradford to fetch Jake.

Jake came bounding out to greet Geneva, and she stooped
to rub his neck. "Had a good day? I hope you've been
behaving yourself."

"Let's get him a snack in the kitchen," Mrs. Bradford suggested. "We'll see if Bessie has a nice soup bone to spare."

Geneva followed the older woman around to the back
porch. She hadn't ever entered the house. Inside, the kitchen
looked inviting. Yellow gingham curtains framed the
windows; a sink with a skirt of the same material over-
looked one of those windows; a large, black, iron cookstove
stood at another wall and a pine hutch beside it was filled
with china. A long, work-roughened table stood in the
middle of the room. The table was covered with bowls and
utensils. A woman in an apron, her hair pulled back into a
gray bun, sat behind it, eyeing Geneva as she passed through
the doorway.

"Hello, Bessie. We're back," Mrs. Bradford said as they
entered the kitchen, clearly the other woman's domain.

"So I see. Who've you brought with you there?"

"This is my guide, Geneva Patterson." Mrs. Bradford
turned to her. "Geneva, this is the woman responsible for the
delicious picnics we've enjoyed. Geneva has told me how delicious the food is, and I keep telling her that I'm not responsible for any of it. It's all your doing."

The cook didn't return Mrs. Bradford's smile, but continued eyeing Geneva. Geneva removed her hat and stared straight back at the woman called Bessie.

"Come, sit down." Mrs. Bradford motioned to one of the cream-colored kitchen chairs at the table.

"I think I better be going along," she replied, feeling the lack of welcome in the seated woman.

"But we promised Jake a snack. What do you say, Bessie? Any leftover bones in your larder?"

Bessie sighed and pushed herself up from her chair, leaning one arm against the back to propel herself. "I'm up to my elbows in potato peels."

Mrs. Bradford's clear laugh filled the kitchen. "You just sit still where you are. I'll go rummage around myself. And get my guest something cold to drink while I'm at it."

Bessie waved Mrs. Bradford away. "You go into the parlor, ma'am, and lie down. It's time for your nap. What you need to be traipsing around cliffs and forests for at your age, I'll never know." She walked to the pantry, mumbling under her breath, "Bringing home every sort of creature…"

"I do feel a little tired. If you'll excuse me, my dear." She looked apologetically at Geneva. "Please stay and get acquainted with Bessie. Her bark's worse than her bite, I promise," she said in an encouraging undertone, while the cook was in the pantry. "I'll see you next week, then?"

With a final nod and smile, she left the kitchen.

Geneva drummed her fingers against the painted table, wishing she could be gone but not wanting to hurt Mrs. Bradford's feelings.

"You're still here?" Bessie glared at her from the pantry doorway.

Geneva glared back at her. "Yes, I'm still *here*."

Bessie sniffed. When she saw Geneva wasn't moving, she came in with a platter in one hand, a pitcher in the other.

"Take that to your cur." She held out an enamel dish.

Geneva walked over to her, glad of an excuse to leave the kitchen. The dish contained a good-size bone that still had some meat on it. Jake would enjoy it.

"Thank you, ma'am."

"I was saving that for a nice pot of soup."

Geneva shoved the dish back toward her. "You can have it. I can feed my own dog. Don't need no one's help."

Bessie pursed her lips, her hands folded across her ample bosom. Suddenly she smiled. "You go give it to that dog of yours. Don't let your pride keep him from enjoying it. After all, he's earned his keep here, chasing every rabbit from the garden the whole morning."

Geneva backed away from Bessie, wondering at the sudden change in the woman's manner.

When she came back, Bessie had resumed her place at the table. She gestured to Geneva's seat with her paring knife.

"Sit down and have your refreshment."

Geneva walked over and took her seat once more. Set before her were a glass of lemonade and a plate of marble cake. She ate silently, eyeing the cook every once in a while.

"Mrs. Bradford's taken a liking to you," Bessie commented, heaping a pile of potato peelings off to one side. "She's a kindhearted woman. People like to take advantage of her sort. I try to look after her."

Geneva nodded, watching the woman slice the peeled potatoes into a buttered dish.

"I don't know what she sees in you, but I'm bound it's something most others don't see. She's got an instinct about people."

Geneva took a sip of the lemonade, which tasted astringently sour after the sweet cake. "Most folks don't bother lookin' farther'n their own nose, so there's not much they see."

Bessie chuckled. "That's pretty wise for a girl who dresses up in men's trousers."

Geneva shrugged. "Can't go fishin' in skirts. I'd probably fall overboard and drown."

Bessie laughed then. "You keep an eye on Mrs. Bradford when you're out on your expeditions, you hear? She's not as spry as she used to be. Watch she doesn't overdo."

Geneva promised, feeling afraid suddenly, hoping she hadn't already overtaxed the older woman, taking her over steep rocks. "Is she ill?"

Bessie shook her head. "No, she's healthy enough, but she's no longer a young girl. And she isn't afraid of anything. I worry about her."

Geneva nodded, thinking how much she'd like to be like that, not afraid of anything.

Chapter Eight

Caleb swung the scythe, admiring the broad swath before him. Behind him the hay lay spread like a field of tin soldiers fallen in battle. The scent of sweet grass and clover rose into the warm air, combining into an almost tangible thing, earth and air together creating the essence of summer.

He inhaled deeply, reveling in the pungent scent, feeling the warm sun on his back and the pull of his muscles against the scythe.

Physical labor was the only thing bringing him any peace these days. Ever since the night he'd prepared supper for Geneva, he'd been feeling out of sorts. Everything had gone well, until...well, until Geneva had discovered the picture of Arabella. Why he'd left it there—his forgetfulness continued to irritate him even now, a few days later.

He'd been sharp toward Geneva—too sharp. And in making amends, he'd had to go and spill his guts. He still winced when he thought of it. He wasn't used to letting people see his feelings, not since he was a lad of four or five and his father decided he was too old to be crying.

Caleb had grown used to masking his true feelings aboard

ship. As the youngest member of the crew, far from home, with no one to run to, he wouldn't have made it too far if he'd shown his fears. As captain of a ship, he'd had to lead. Any sign of wavering would have been fatal. At the firm, he'd taken Ellery under his wing, wishing to spare his younger cousin the brunt of his father's harsh exactitude. He'd felt sorry for Ellery, who'd had to exhibit gratitude for enjoying the family privileges as a penniless relation. Caleb snorted. He'd even asked Arabella to be especially nice to Ellery.

What Caleb wasn't used to was what had occurred the other night with Geneva. He'd never divulged his deepest needs to someone else, much less a woman. Even his closest friend, Nate, knew him more because of Nate's inherent discernment than because Caleb had confided in him.

It made Caleb feel weak to have confessed his feelings for Arabella to Geneva. If she'd stayed much longer, he'd have probably begun blurting out all the hurts of his boyhood.

He hadn't seen Geneva since that night, and he was relieved she hadn't come to him for her reading lesson. He wasn't sure what he was going to say to her when she did.

Caleb heard the rumbling of wagon wheels up the road, and he turned to see who was coming down the hill. A man and woman sat in the buggy, a small child between them. He frowned. The last thing he desired was company. He rubbed his face, feeling the stubble of beard. He was hardly prepared for receiving visitors. Well, they were clearly coming to his place. There was nothing left for it but to face them. He set the scythe down, watching the man descend from his wagon and go to open the gate.

Caleb stooped to pick up his shirt. The breeze off the ocean had picked up. He glanced seaward toward the horizon, feeling the weather would soon change. He put his shirt back on, slowly buttoning it, as the wagon proceeded up the drive. He wiped the sweat and grime from his forehead with his bandanna.

When he could put it off no longer, he walked toward the front porch in time to meet the man as he turned from helping the woman down from the buggy. The woman turned to lift the child—a little girl of three or four—down.

The man held out his hand to Caleb. Caleb stuck out his hand more slowly. The man was quite young—in his early twenties, Caleb would guess, or perhaps it was his cherubic face that belied his true age. He was fair and rosy-cheeked, with the heavy fringed blue eyes of a baby, and thick dark-blond hair swept back from a generous forehead. Only the rough darker hair of his sideburns gave him the look of maturity and masculinity of a man in his twenties.

"Pastor Arlo McDuffie."

The man's handshake was firm, a bit on the hearty side. Caleb returned the pressure, saying, "Caleb Phelps."

Pastor McDuffie smiled. "I know, Captain." He turned to the woman at his side. "May I present my better half, Carrie McDuffie?"

"Pleased, ma'am." Caleb shook her hand. She looked more mature than her husband, although he judged her also to be in her twenties. In addition, there was a serenity in her gaze that gave her an ageless quality. She had attractive features, a wide face, a straight nose and a nicely shaped mouth.

"What can I help you with?" Caleb asked, turning back to the parson.

"That should be my question," McDuffie said with a smile. "I've been remiss in my duties. I've been meaning to come and call all summer and have made it out here only now with Carrie to pay our respects."

At Caleb's silence, he added, "We like to welcome any newcomers to the area and invite them to fellowship with us in church."

"I see. Well, I appreciate that, but have no inclination at present to attend church."

The pastor nodded, apparently unperturbed by the frank admission. "In that case, may we come in and pay a simple social call?"

Not wishing to appear completely rude, he nodded, at a loss as to what to say to a country preacher. He was used to the more learned ministers of Boston who had studied in the best theological seminaries. "Very well, come into the house," he said, gesturing them toward the front porch. "I'm sorry I'm not set up to receive visitors."

Mrs. McDuffie spoke up for the first time. "Set your mind at ease, Captain. We require nothing but your company."

When they were seated inside, Caleb stood with his arms crossed in front of him. Catching a glimpse of the woman bending over the child, whispering some caution to her, Caleb's feelings softened.

"I do have tea. May I offer you some?"

He could see the woman was on the point of declining, but the husband smiled and accepted.

Caleb excused himself and headed for the kitchen. As he looked out the window over the sink toward the ocean, waiting for the water to boil, he wondered why they were calling on him. He wasn't accustomed to small-town rituals, but suspected this was one he'd have to submit to. The good pastor would probably leave him alone once he'd fulfilled his obligation.

Caleb turned to the cupboard to dig out enough cups and saucers for three. Then he thought of the little girl, and remembered his own boredom when taken by his mother to pay calls on grown people. Caleb rummaged around for something to offer her. His glance swept over the half-empty bottle of rum in a cupboard. This pastor obviously wouldn't approve of spirits in any shape or form.

The dish that had contained Geneva's cobbler sat in the sink half filled with water, its edges streaked with the dark red remains of the filling. He hadn't gotten around to returning the dish to her, and wondered what she'd say if she knew that cobbler—and not the rum this time—had sustained him for the past few days? He'd eaten it straight from the dish, and had just polished off the last portion at noon.

Caleb opened a tin containing thin square tea biscuits. He set several on a round plate then got a tray and some spoons. When everything was ready, he lifted the tray. At the last moment, some devilry in him decided to add the bottle of rum.

The pastor was standing admiring the view. The little girl sat on the floor at her mother's feet, playing with the fringe of her mother's bag. Upon seeing Caleb, Mrs. McDuffie immediately rose and came to help him.

"Where would you like to put it?" she asked.

"I'll just set it here," he answered, walking to the crate where Geneva had set out their dessert plates a few nights ago.

"Would you like me to pour?" the woman offered.

Caleb nodded, stepping back and allowing the pastor's wife access to the wing chair. "I wasn't sure what the child would like, so I thought perhaps some cookies," he offered.

"That would be fine," the woman answered. "Janey, come here and get a cookie." When the little girl had complied, staring up at Caleb all the while, her mother said, "Say 'thank you' to Captain Phelps."

"Thank you." She nibbled the cookie and, as soon as her mother gave her a nod, skipped to her father's side.

Her father put an arm around the child and smiled down at her.

Ignoring the bottle of rum, Mrs. McDuffie poured Caleb and her husband their tea and handed the cups to Caleb. Last, she poured herself a cup.

"Looks like we're going to get rain," the pastor remarked as he returned from the window.

"The crops could sure use it," Caleb answered.

"How is your garden doing?"

Caleb shrugged. "Between a late start and the cutworms, I don't expect to live on it this winter."

McDuffie chuckled, taking a seat. He crossed his legs and leaned back as if settling in for a good, long chat. "You'll do better again next year, I'm sure. How *do* you like living at Haven's End?" he asked, genuine interest evident in his light blue eyes.

Caleb drank his tea standing. "It suits me."

"It must be quite a change from Boston. I'm from down around Portland myself. I have to admit, it took me some getting used to such a small village, but now we're very happy here. Aren't we, Carrie?"

Mrs. McDuffie smiled and nodded, taking another sip of tea.

Caleb walked over to the tea tray. "Would you like me to fortify your tea?" he asked the pastor very deliberately, raising the bottle of liquor.

The pastor chuckled, holding up a palm. "I choose not to 'get drunk with wine, but be ever filled with the Spirit.'"

That was a new one to Caleb. Without a word, he returned the bottle to its position.

Before he could think of a suitable rejoinder, Mrs. McDuffie spoke up quietly. "Do you have anyone do for you here?"

"You mean housekeeping?"

"That's right."

"No, I've been managing on my own since I arrived." He smiled. "Does it show?"

She returned his smile. "Oh, no, everything looks very nice to me. Neater than my own sitting room, I must admit." She took a look around at the half-finished wallpapering job. "I can see you're even managing to make some improvements as well."

"I guess I just got tired of staring at white plaster."

She nodded. "The reason I ask is I imagine it must be difficult for a gentleman alone, especially with all your outside work in summer. Perhaps you'd like to have a village girl come in one or two days a week to clean and do the week's baking?"

Caleb considered, gazing down into his teacup, remembering how good Geneva's homemade cobbler had tasted. He met Mrs. McDuffie's calm gaze. "Can you recommend anyone?"

She looked thoughtful, then nodded slowly. "I know of several suitable candidates from our own parish. Elder daughters from large families who could use a little extra income." She turned to her husband. "What do you think of Hannah Stearns or Marilla Beaman?"

Her husband quickly supported her choices. "Both excellent candidates. Hardworking, good women. You wouldn't even know they were here. And they have brothers if you need any help around the place."

"Well, have them come up and I'll interview them." He addressed Mrs. McDuffie. "Thank you, ma'am, for your suggestion. I confess cooking for myself has lost its appeal."

She laughed, and changed from a quiet, submissive wife in an instant to a jolly young woman. "And as one whose strong suit is *not* cooking, I confess cooking for a family quickly loses its appeal as well!"

Caleb smiled, taking a liking to the woman in spite of his earlier prejudice.

"Carrie's talents lie in music," Pastor McDuffie told Caleb. "If it weren't for her piano playing, I'd probably have a congregation half its size. My sermons can't compete with her hymns."

"Don't you believe him." His wife turned to Caleb. "My husband has a gift for preaching. If you don't believe me, come hear for yourself."

Caleb looked at both husband and wife. Something about their obvious love and partnership gave him a twinge of envy. He'd never considered marriage in this light—two souls working together at something. For him, Arabella had always been an ideal, a princess to be earned and held high above the mundane and dirty world of men's business. "Perhaps I will come and hear," he replied to Mrs. McDuffie, only half meaning the words.

"We'd be honored if you came to a meeting," she said.

The pastor sat forward, enthusiasm plain in his face. "While we're on the subject, let me invite you officially to our annual church picnic, a week from Sunday. Let me assure you, I don't exaggerate when I say it's a high point in the summer season! I'm sure that's due to the size of this community and not to any special attraction to eating out of doors."

Caleb just smiled and nodded, not committing himself to anything.

They had been silent for a few moments, when over the rim of his cup, Caleb noticed the look that passed between the pastor and his wife, and the slight nod the pastor gave his wife.

She turned to him. "Captain Phelps, would you mind if I take Janey for a turn about your back porch?"

Caleb looked out at the sky, which had filled with gray clouds. "You're welcome to go out, but the weather doesn't look too favorable."

"The porch is covered in case it should start to rain. In any event, we can always come right back in." Rising and holding out a hand to her daughter, she said, "Come, Janey."

The little girl obeyed immediately, clearly relieved for a chance to move about.

When the two men were alone, Caleb waited for the pastor to speak. He was curious to know what the silent communication between pastor and wife had meant.

Pastor McDuffie flicked a finger against his nose as if removing a piece of dust. "Captain Phelps, I don't mean to be impertinent, but it has come to my attention that your young neighbor has been spending a considerable amount of time alone in your company."

Caleb's mind was a complete blank for a few seconds. "My young neighbor?" Suddenly it dawned on him. "You don't mean Ge—Miss Patterson?" He corrected himself in time.

McDuffie nodded. "A concerned parishioner has brought it to my attention. Oh, I know how people gossip, but still, if there's a grain of truth in it, I thought I should caution you."

Even before the pastor finished speaking, Caleb gave a laugh, more amused than outraged. "You can't be serious! Why, look at her!"

The pastor didn't share his amusement. "She's a young woman living alone and you're a single gentleman. In the eyes of most people, that presents a dangerous combination."

"What nonsense! She's given me some advice on gardening and helped me with the planting. Now I'm trying to return the favor, helping her out with a few things. She wants to improve herself, and can you blame her? She's never had the benefit of schooling, and it's not as if your circle has welcomed her with open arms. The village has ignored her her whole life—"

"Now, you don't have to get angry with me. I believe what you're saying. It is unfortunate, her upbringing and all."

Caleb's jaw tightened. "I'm ten years older than she is! How could anyone imagine anything between us?"

The pastor answered him seriously. "Age never stood in the way of two people forming an attachment to one another. Besides, I wouldn't exactly call you a man in his dotage. I'd say you're in your prime. But that's beside the point. As I said, people gossip, and I came here, not to censure you, but rather to caution you."

The young pastor leaned forward. "I'm thinking of the young woman more than you. You can understand that. She's alone with no one to stand up for her. What should happen if you should do anything—however innocently—" he hastened to add "—to compromise her? Think of what her life would be like in such a small town."

Caleb expressed his disgust. "As if her life here is so wonderful at present."

"She might be considered a bit odd by the community, but she is generally left alone to do as she pleases. Think what it would be like if people openly condemned her, walked on the other side of the street if she passed by, refused even to address one word to her? Let me tell you, all it takes is one busybody taking an unhealthy interest in Geneva's affairs and her life here at Haven's End could truly become a living nightmare."

The pastor's words sobered Caleb, and he realized it was useless to be offended. He was merely the messenger, pointing out some very real facts. Caleb sighed. "Very well, Pastor, I'll give your cautions very serious consideration."

The pastor nodded. "That's all I ask."

At that moment, the door to the back porch opened and Mrs. McDuffie reentered with her daughter. "Some drops are just beginning to fall. Perhaps we should be on our way?"

Her husband rose immediately. He was probably relieved that his whole mission had been completed, Caleb thought sourly, and was now anxious to be off. How convenient of the rain.

"My dear wife is right as usual. We should be going. It was a pleasure, Captain." McDuffie held out his hand. "Thanks for the hospitality."

Caleb shook his hand mechanically, his mind on everything that had been said.

Mrs. McDuffie smiled and offered her hand. "I'll send Hannah and Marilla along, and you can let me know which one you prefer to engage."

He nodded, speaking over her head to her husband. "I'll be sure to let you know which one I hire. That'll give you a good reliable source to inform you of what shenanigans are going on here."

"I'm sure nothing of the sort is going on. You're a man of honor—" The pastor flushed, his naturally rosy face becoming completely suffused with color as he realized his choice of words.

He coughed in his hand and looked away, and Caleb knew they were both thinking of why he'd left Boston. The pastor recovered quickly and met Caleb's gaze once more. "As I told you, it's not your conduct I'm thinking of in terms of Miss Patterson. I appeal to you to think of *her.* She could be hurt, shamed or worse."

"You've made your case most plain and I'm aware of all the ramifications. I give you my word I wouldn't do anything to hurt her." Caleb smiled thinly. "Contrary to popular opinion, sailors don't go around as a rule ruining respectable young women. They confine themselves to brothels when in port. Excuse the plain language, Mrs. McDuffie."

Ignoring the comment, she bent down to her daughter. "Say goodbye to the captain, Janey."

The little girl stuck out her hand. Caleb took the little hand in his, and it occurred to him that once Geneva must have looked so, dressed in a little homemade frock, a miniature bonnet covering her hair and ears.

After they'd left, Caleb wandered about the room restlessly, going over and over what the pastor had said. If he'd thought to escape the censure of Boston's Brahmins by coming to a remote Maine village, he'd been gravely mistaken. Within the month and a half he'd been in Haven's End, outsiders—complete strangers—seemed to know more about his life than he did himself. They knew when he planted, what he planted, and now they seemed to know what was going on in his bedroom as well.

He glanced outside, his hand gripping the back of his neck. He wished he could rid himself of the excess energy his anger was causing him. What he needed was a good, long walk. But as the pastor's wife had feared, the rain had begun to come down harder, and it looked as if it were set to rain for the remainder of the afternoon.

His gaze roved across the room. He had two choices: he could pace the floor like a caged tiger, feeling the frustration mount; or he could put his time to good use and finish the wallpapering. He sighed, opting for the more useful occupation.

Once he got started he became quickly engrossed. It had been difficult at first to hang the strips of paper by himself, but now he'd gotten the knack of it and had developed a rhythm of measuring, cutting, gluing and hanging.

He was just flattening out a strip of paper he'd hung, when a knock sounded on the kitchen door. For an instant he thought it was the pastor and his wife, having forgotten something.

Stifling his annoyance, he shouted, "Come in!"

He could hear the person enter and shut the door. As he listened to the distracting noise of footsteps crossing the kitchen floor, his annoyance grew. He was in no frame of mind for any more company this afternoon.

And then, there she stood in the doorway. He didn't know why he hadn't expected his caller to be Geneva. Since he hadn't seen her in a few days, part of him had probably hoped she'd disappeared for good, and that all his problems in that area would be solved.

"What are you doing here?" he asked gruffly, in no mood to coddle her feelings.

She stood resolute, her arms straight at her sides, one hand clutching a book. "Since it begun—began—raining, I thought I'd come by for my reading lesson."

"Well, now that you're here, you might as well come in," he replied ungraciously, turning back to the wall and running his palms once more across its surface.

"If you're busy, I can come back another day."

He pressed his palms against the walls and sighed. "No, I'm not busy. I'm just doing this to avoid perishing from boredom."

"I never knew what it was to be bored. There's always something needs doing."

"No, I'm sure idleness is not a problem for you," he said, walking over to his worktable to begin measuring another length of paper. "You seem to find something to keep you occupied every minute of the day, sunup to sundown."

He cut the paper and glanced up at her, surprised at her control. He was trying his best to drive her away, and there she stood. Why wasn't she storming off in offense?

He cut the paper, then proceeded to brush glue over it.

"Need any help?" she asked from across the room.

It irritated him that she had ignored his invitation to come in and still stood in the doorway.

"No." He carried the paper over to the wall and stepped onto the footstool. He aligned the long strip carefully against the ceiling molding and the length of paper already laid on the portion of wall beside it. Then he began pressing it against the plaster. To her credit, Geneva didn't say anything to throw off his concentration, but when he looked away from the paper, she stood at his elbow, holding out the stiff brush, which he used to smooth down the paper.

"Thanks," he grunted.

He took his time smoothing out the paper, using long strokes of the brush against the paper, making sure the edges had adhered well, then inspecting each corner. When he'd gone over every inch of that strip of paper, he finally stepped back, his decision taken. If she wanted to learn to read badly enough that she was willing to put up with his foul mood, then he was going to teach her to read—gossip or no gossip.

"What do you think?" he asked gently, looking at the blue and cream paper.

"Looks right fine."

Caleb looked over at her profile, feeling ashamed of his earlier rudeness. No matter the pastor's good intentions, Caleb owed Geneva her reading lessons.

"Come on, let's get started on your lesson."

* * *

Geneva gritted her teeth and sat down with her reader. Whatever it took, she'd promised herself she was going to read. It had taken all her resolve to come to Caleb. But she knew if she were ever to read the Bible and see for herself those things Mrs. Bradford had told her, there was only one way to go about it.

Mrs. Bradford had inspired Geneva to reach for things she'd long ago believed were beyond her. How she wished she had the older woman's courage, especially at a time like this, when all her instincts told her to bolt, to protect herself while there was still time.

She stole a look at Caleb, sitting beside her at the kitchen table. He'd acted so ill-humored when she'd first stopped by, she wondered what was eating him. But now he seemed relaxed, waiting for her to begin. She looked down at the large letters on the page.

She cleared her throat. She'd been practicing and practicing, hoping she could gain Caleb's admiration in this one area. "'Tom—sits—on—the—chair.'" Each word was said separately, creating a stilted cadence. She glanced at Caleb again, but he sat expressionless, so she took another breath and began the next sentence. "'Tom—has—a—big—'" She paused, hoping she remembered the sound of *ch* correctly. "'Chair.'"

"Go on." It was the first words he'd spoken since they'd sat down.

"'Sister has a mi-dd-le-sized chair.'" She let out her breath in relief at having reached the end of another sentence.

"'Baby has a li-ttle chair.'" Geneva shifted in her own hard chair, wondering why the captain looked so stony-faced. Suddenly a horrible thought occurred to her and she stumbled in the middle of her sentence. Did he suspect how she felt for him? Had her feelings shown on her face the other night? Geneva struggled to remember what she'd said, how she'd acted.

"Go on."

Caleb's voice prompted her again, cutting into her frantic searching. She looked at him, for a second thinking he'd read her thoughts, but then realized he was only waiting for her to continue.

Geneva turned the page of her reader. "'Tom sits at—'" *th* she confused with *sh* and *ch* "'—the table.'" Since he made no comment, she figured she had it right.

Her thoughts calmed down some, and she tried to concentrate on the letters before her. "'Moth-er brings soup to the table.'" He couldn't suspect anything. No, it wasn't possible. "'Tom has a big bowl. Sister has a middle-sized bowl.'"

She'd done nothing to show her anguish that night. It had only been after she'd run up the hill to the refuge of her own house that the tears had let loose. "'Baby has a little bowl.'" Another deep breath at completing a page.

Geneva flattened down the pages with her fingers and turned her gaze to the facing page. "'The—soup—is—hot. Baby t-a-stes the soup. Baby cries. Tom stands up. The bowl falls down.'"

Geneva wanted to smile at the picture before her. The expression of shock on the little boy's face, the crying baby's crumpled-up features, the obvious concern of the little sister. But one glance at Caleb's unsmiling lips, and her impulse to smile withered up within her. If anything, he looked bored. And shouldn't he be? He was used to so much more.

The rain sounded on the back porch roof, a steady patter. From the window in front of the table, the Atlantic looked gray, sky and sea blending in one grim color. The small islands at the entrance of the cove emerged from the sea like black walruses, their backs slick with the rain. Only the largest was partially covered in grass, a sparse green layer. That island lay the farthest out and had always been called the Old Man, because of the way it jutted out of the sea in two parts, one forming his belly, the other a craggy profile. Now, the Old Man lay sodden and forlorn, like a drunkard on his beam-ends.

Geneva wondered if Caleb was perhaps suffering another hangover, but she hadn't smelled any liquor on his breath.

He reached his hand over to turn the page. Geneva jumped back, removing her own hands from the bottom of the book. She watched his sun-bronzed fingers and heard the crisp sound of the creamy sheet of paper turning. She remembered those strong fingers and palms gripping the windowsill the other night, reflecting his agony of mind.

Her gaze ran upward, along his arm to the rolled-up shirt-sleeve. Farther up, the fabric was stretched taut around his biceps. Her eyes darted from shoulder to shoulder, taking in their breadth, wondering how it would feel to be engulfed by them.

Quickly, she turned her head down to the new page in front of her.

"'Mo-th-er runs in. Mother picks up baby.'" She pressed her finger firmly under each word as she pronounced the syllables, wishing her thoughts would submit as easily as the paper under her finger. "'Baby stops crying. Tom picks up the t-a-ble. Sis-ter picks up the bowl. Mother brings—'" she hesitated at the word, trying to sound it out in her head "'—more soup.'" She let out a sigh and turned the page. The next two pages contained a review of the words used.

"You did very well," Caleb said when she was done.

Geneva swallowed. "I did?"

He nodded, his broad shoulders leaning back against his chair. His inky blue eyes continued regarding her, giving her no clue to what he was thinking. He no longer seemed angry with her. Neither did he seem to be suffering the ill effects of liquor. Despite the day's growth of beard along his jaw, his general appearance was too neat, his demeanor too fresh to denote the rigors of a night of drinking.

What if he wasn't even thinking about her? What if he was thinking about something—someone—in Boston? Maybe he'd had news from there. She remembered the latest rumors she'd heard at the harbor, that he'd been cleared of all charges. He could go back whenever he wanted, with his head held high, and resume his position in the family firm. Miss Harding would probably even take him back.

"Why don't we take a little break before we begin going over the next lesson? Would you like a cup of tea?" Caleb's voice broke into her thoughts, causing her to flush guiltily, afraid he could see right through to them.

She nodded dumbly, relieved when he rose and turned his scrutiny from her to the kettle on the stove. While he got the tea, Geneva jumped up to help him. Remembering where the cups were kept, she reached up to a cupboard.

"You don't have to do that."

"I don't mind. I like to make myself useful," she said with a shrug, taking the cups and a pair of spoons to the table.

"So I've noticed."

His back was turned to her as he filled the china pot with the boiling water, so she couldn't interpret the remark by the tone alone.

While they waited for their tea to cool, Geneva wondered how to fill the silence. It had seemed so easy the other night at dinner. But now, there was an awkwardness, which she knew must be due to what he'd told her. Did he regret confiding in her?

Racking her brain, she finally said in desperation, "The news is all over the village," then was immediately afraid she'd said the wrong thing.

"What news?" He didn't sound particularly interested.

She cleared her throat. "About your…your troubles in Boston." She was making a hash of it. She could feel his blue-eyed stare on her as she looked determinedly at her tea, her fingers curved around the rim of the warm cup.

"What are they saying, Geneva?"

She looked up. "That everything is all right," she whispered. "That you never done—did—anything wrong."

"What do you think? Are they right?"

Their gazes locked. Geneva tried to figure out how to say what she wanted to, without giving away her feelings. Finally she just spoke the truth simply. "I never thought you could do the things they accused you of."

She still couldn't read his expression. Finally he turned his gaze from her and directed it out the window. "You're right. I could never steal."

She felt such a profound relief at hearing those words from his lips. It hadn't been right, his not defending himself against his accusers. But her relief was short-lived. Now he could return to Boston. She felt sick at the thought.

"Geneva, have you ever thought of asking anyone else to teach you to read?"

The question was so unrelated to all they'd just talked about that it took Geneva a moment to answer. "No."

"I've been thinking, you're doing very well. Much better than I would have anticipated." He gave her a half smile, the first sign of welcome he'd shown her since she'd stepped into his house. "You must have learned more than you realized back then when you attended the schoolhouse."

She shook her head mutely, as much to disagree with what he was saying as to negate what she knew he meant: he was going away and was telling her he would no longer be able to continue the lessons.

"What about the schoolteacher? She would be the appropriate person to tutor you. Soon you'll need to learn grammar and spelling rules." He rubbed the back of his head. "Things I haven't thought of in an age."

"You're leaving, aren't you. Going back to Boston." Her voice was flat.

He looked at her with a frown. "What are you talking about?"

She cleared her throat, willing her voice to come out sounding normal. "Now that everything's been made right in Boston, there's no reason for you to stick around here."

"Everything's been made right," he repeated. "Is that what you think?"

She could only nod solemnly.

"Just because my father decided to examine the evidence before him and judge for himself I wasn't guilty, that makes everything all right? My word alone wasn't good enough."

The words were spoken lightly, but she wasn't fooled. His bitterness, his anguish the other evening, were too fresh in her mind.

She remembered what he'd said about his father, that he wasn't an easy man to please. "I never expected anything of my pa, so I was never disappointed." When Caleb said nothing, and looked back out the window, she continued cautiously. "I couldn't say the same for him. He was disappointed from day one. Don't know what he expected—most likely for Ma to produce a half-dozen tall, strong boys to take after him."

She looked down at herself contemptuously. "All she could do was give him a scrawny girl-child, and then go and get sick so she couldn't give him any more. I don't know who he was more angry at, Ma or me."

Geneva could feel Caleb's gaze on her now. "Is that why you go around dressed like a man? Trying to be what he wanted?"

Geneva stared at him. He'd said the words harshly, as if accusing her of something. She should have known better than to compare his situation in any way to hers. She stood.

"Why I dress the way I do ain't nobody's business but my own."

His mouth curled. "Ready to run away again?"

He'd read her intentions perfectly. She gripped the back of the chair, forcing herself to stay put.

He leaned back, his relaxed posture in direct contrast to her own rigid stance. "Don't you think it's about time you got that chip off your shoulder? Did it ever occur to you that if you bothered to dress like a woman now and then, instead of hiding behind your father's clothing, you might actually look like one?"

She recoiled at the words. Unable to hear anything above the pounding between her temples, she turned on her heel and headed for the door.

"That's right, stomp off when you don't like what you hear." Caleb's words mocked her.

In reply she slammed the kitchen door behind her.

Chapter Nine

After being shut in the previous afternoon, Caleb needed to get out. Finishing a hasty breakfast, he set out for the village. Heading toward the harbor, skirting the bigger puddles and muddy ruts, Caleb decided to check on the progress of his boat at the shipyard. He'd signed and delivered the contract to Winslow, who'd promised to begin work on it immediately.

By the time he left the harbor a couple of hours later, Caleb's outlook had undergone a hundred-eighty degree change from frustration to promise. He was through with self-pity and second-guessing.

The day had cleared as he'd expected, leaving a breathtakingly blue sky in place of the scattered clouds. The sun felt warm on his back. Everything looked different from when he'd first arrived at the beginning of the summer. Even the villagers he'd encountered at the harbor had looked at him differently. He thought of Geneva's assumption that he'd return to Boston now that his name was cleared.

He'd considered the question last night until he was sick of it. At the moment, in the glorious midsummer sunshine, he preferred thinking he might make a new beginning for himself right here at Haven's End.

Caleb walked by the farm up the road from Geneva's. Once again, the farmer's wife stood on the front porch as she had when he'd headed to the village earlier in the day. Caleb lifted a hand in a brief salute. He realized how her front porch afforded her a clear sweep of Geneva's weather-beaten house and farther down the Point to his own house.

He had to accept that little was hidden in a small community such as this. No matter how far-fetched Pastor McDuffie's concerns about Geneva's reputation, Caleb admitted the truth didn't matter so much. After his own experience in Boston, he understood that better than anyone.

The best thing for everyone concerned was to have nothing to do with Geneva. But things in reality weren't quite so simple. All it had taken yesterday was a slight suggestion for her to find herself another teacher, and she'd jumped at him.

He'd compounded the injury with that comment about her clothing. He knew as soon as he'd uttered those careless words that he'd breached some unspoken rule. Real hurt shone through her anger.

After putting away his few purchases, Caleb turned toward the garden. The sun had dried the plants by now, though the earth remained damp. Caleb strode toward the rows of green. He shook his head. He'd never have the knack Geneva had for producing vegetables. He was beginning to lose hope that his garden would ever produce more than a handful of radishes. He'd had a brief spurt of enthusiasm when he'd spotted some blossoms on the peas a few days ago, but the sight of the thriving gardens, their rows thick and leafy, in the farmyards along the road had left him less optimistic. Geneva was already selling new potatoes and peas and beans from her garden.

Caleb walked between the rows, crouching here and there to examine a plant more closely or pull a weed. It was when he was bending to look at the pea blossoms that he saw it— a tiny little pod, bright green and infinitely fragile in its newness. Caleb looked farther up the vine and spotted another pod. The next plant over held a couple more. His wonder grew. It was like magic—no, no, more like a miracle of life: yesterday a flower, and today a fully formed fruit. He rose and went over to the pole beans. He had to move the thick growth of leaves out of the way before he saw them. Sure enough, tiny beans were hanging from the plants.

A smile broke out on his face. He'd done it! His seeds had sprouted and grown and now were producing honest-to-goodness vegetables! He stooped over the minuscule bean once more. He could even see the tiny bumps along its edge, promising to grow into fully formed beans inside the pod.

He had to share his joy with someone.

Geneva. Her name sprang immediately into his mind—the person who'd made it all possible. She'd selected the spot; overseen the preparation of the soil, adding her own sweat and toil to it; she'd shared her seeds and plants with him and seen him through the cutworm disaster; and then she'd taught him how to keep a check on the caterpillars. No one would understand his joy right now more than Geneva.

Caleb felt doubly sorry for his rough words to her yesterday. He'd make it up to her. He turned and began walking toward her shack.

"Hi there, big fellow," he said in answer to Jake's bark, giving the dog a pat along his neck. "Where's your mistress? Out in her garden?" He checked there but saw no sign of her. He scanned the fields in back. The fish tubs were washed and overturned, so he doubted she'd be down at her beach. He turned toward her dwelling, sticking his head in at the shed door as he passed it. Everything stood neat and empty.

Finally he came to her door. He rapped just as Jake barked at him. He thought he heard Geneva's "come in" over the dog's bark, so he pushed the door inward.

As he stepped into the dim interior, the scent of roses around the door frame assailed his nostrils. He saw no one at first. Then he heard a soft gasp. His glance went to the far corner of the room.

Geneva sat in a tin tub, her knees drawn up in front of her, shielding her. Her hair, always so severely braided away from her face, was drawn up in a loose knot, and now billowed outward like a dark cloud, framing her face. A few escaped tendrils of dark, damp hair trailed down her long, slim neck, plastered to it, and contrasted sharply with the alabaster skin. Caleb's gaze followed the trail down to glistening shoulders. A pale, gleaming arm gripped still paler knees. Her other hand clutched a sponge. The only sound in the room was the *drip-drip* of the water falling from it back into the tub.

Caleb stood, incapable of moving. He was no longer a seasoned man of the world, but a schoolboy. He found himself unable to act logically. His mind told him to do the gentlemanly thing: apologize and turn around and walk out. Instead, he remained rooted, staring as if he had never seen a woman. He watched her drop the sponge. It fell with a *plop* into the water. With her free hand, she groped for her towel, her gaze all the while locked with his. Her towel lay just beyond her reach on a wooden chair.

Instead of giving her the privacy she required, Caleb found himself advancing, each footstep sounding loud in the still, small room. He reached the chair. She crouched there at his feet, hidden from his view by her drawn-up knees. He swallowed, knowing he was beyond all reason, all thought.

He remembered the way the red-bearded man had pawed at her, and he felt sickened.

Slowly, as if watching a drama unfold, he picked up the towel. He clutched it for a moment, thinking insanely that such a coarse material shouldn't touch her silken skin.

Somehow, he found his wits, knowing he could never dishonor her. With a quick shove, he thrust the towel into her outstretched hand. The moment he did so, it was as if his reason returned.

"I'm s-sorry—please e-excu—" He was stammering like an idiot, his voice sounding as rusty as a stovepipe. He finally managed to transmit a message to his feet and they began backing out awkwardly.

He shut the door softly behind him and stood for a moment to catch his breath. What had he been thinking? All this time it had been staring him in the face and he'd refused to see it. He realized he'd been treating Geneva like a man—no, more like a younger brother, the way he'd taken Ellery under his wing. But this was no Ellery.

Geneva was a woman.

No manly type, either. She was a beautiful, statuesque woman. With the right clothing and coiffure, she would stand out as a queen in any ballroom.

He began walking, his long strides taking him away from the area as quickly as possible, as if distance could erase the image of her womanliness.

Geneva stared out the rain-streaked window, Jake at her feet. The night was pitch black. She could hear the howl of the wind through the trees but could barely see their outline.

The rain fell steadily, thumping against the roof, the muddy earth, the windowpane.

But it didn't matter how dark the night was. Geneva could still see Caleb staring down at her this afternoon. She'd replayed the scene in her mind so many times, but it didn't lessen the intensity of his gaze. Nor her reaction on seeing him looking at her. She kept seeing the look in Caleb's eyes, comparing it to the look she'd fought against in other men. For the first time in her life, she didn't feel repulsed. In fact, she wondered if her own eyes hadn't reflected what she'd seen written in his eyes.

Unable to stop the direction of her gaze, she looked down the road toward the Point. A single golden light shone at a window, visible to her like a wavy torch. It beckoned her cruelly through the darkness, like a beacon she could never hope to reach in a stormy ocean.

Chapter Ten

Caleb picked the bright green caterpillar off the underside of a tender cabbage leaf and squeezed it between his fingernails. On to the next leaf. The tiny worms were hard to distinguish against the leaf, their color blending in so well.

He was tired of checking on the leaves every day and hunting for the caterpillars that were ravaging his otherwise healthy plants. The more he picked off the little beasts, the more they multiplied. By the lacy look of his leaves, the caterpillars were winning the war. He'd have to get some outside advice on a new strategy; he glanced up the hill toward Geneva's house. He hadn't seen her in five days.

Five whole days since that fateful afternoon when he'd seen her crouched in her tub. Five days, which hadn't diminished the image of that strand of hair plastered against her sleek neck.

In those five days, he'd finished wallpapering the main room, in addition to the front room. He'd papered every afternoon, after putting in a full morning outside: weeding and watering the garden, scything the lawn, repairing the fence, cleaning out the shed and barn. He'd interviewed and hired one of the young women Pastor McDuffie's wife had recommended, as well as her brother to cut some timber for the winter months.

All this activity in an effort to erase the image of a young woman crouched in her washtub.

Caleb's gaze strayed again to the unpainted shingled dwelling barely visible across the upward sloping meadow and thin fringe of trees.

In the past week, he'd developed an obsession with his neighbor; that fact couldn't be denied. He knew his reaction was nature's way of telling him he'd simply been without a woman too long. Unfortunately, that rationalization didn't help his body go back to its former state of dormancy.

The evenings were the worst. Long and drawn-out. But he no longer indulged in the bottle. That was the coward's way out, which he'd taken temporary refuge in. Geneva's primer sat on the table, taunting him. All he had to do was pick it up and return it to her if he needed an excuse to visit.

Caleb watched the silent house for a few moments longer, knowing that if Geneva didn't come soon, he'd have to march over there and find out— What?

Find out why she'd stayed away? Was she frightened of him? Did she think he was like the other men in the village, only waiting for an opportunity to take advantage of her lonely situation?

Did he want to find out if his memory had exaggerated what he'd seen? Or was it his own loneliness grasping at any human intimacy available to him?

By the next day, Caleb couldn't stay away any longer. He had to see Geneva alone, and read for himself in her eyes how their relationship had changed. He'd done everything in his power to put her out of his mind, to convince himself they could continue as before.

Before.

His gaze fell on the primer on the table. At least he had a bona fide excuse for seeing her. He picked up the book and headed toward the door.

Jake was all over him when he entered Geneva's yard minutes later. After bounding around him a few times and barking, the dog edged close to sniff at his trousers, his shirt, his hands and shoes.

Caleb bent over the dog and ruffled his fur. "What've you been up to, boy? Found any foxholes? Been out fishing with your mistress?" The dog's fur felt smooth, his body warm.

With a final pat, he proceeded toward Geneva's house, Jake trotting along beside him. Caleb was determined to knock loud and clear several times. Before he reached the door, however, Geneva emerged from the shed, swinging a pail in her hand, a satchel strapped about her front.

She looked the way she normally did—faded blue overalls and a flannel shirt. But Caleb saw her differently now. He noticed the curve beneath the bib and the slim forearms emerging from the rolled-up sleeves.

Upon seeing him, she stopped dead. For a second he thought she'd turn and bolt.

Before she had a chance, he spoke. "Good afternoon, Geneva."

"What are doing here?"

At her abrupt tone of voice, his own became gruff. "I wanted to see if you've given up on learning to read."

She looked down then, as if ashamed. "No. I been—I've been practicing. On my own." She looked at him defiantly.

"Well, let's see how you're doing."

She scowled. "I can't right now. I'm on my way out."

"Where are you headed?"

"Up yonder to a patch of raspberries that should be ripe."

He nodded. "Mind if I come along?"

He thought she was going to refuse, and breathed a quick sigh of relief when she finally gave a quick nod.

"Suit yourself. There's another pail in the shed. Might as well make yourself useful."

He suppressed a smile, suddenly feeling lighthearted, and headed toward the shed.

The two crossed the road and made for the meadow beyond, with Jake running ahead of them, barking joyfully at being allowed to go along. The field was fragrant with clover and daisies, and a host of other wildflowers unfamiliar to Caleb. But the scents were warm and earthy. He yanked a stalk of timothy and stuck it in his mouth, then bent to pick a feathery purple flower and waved it in front of Geneva.

"What's this called?"

She barely gave it a glance. "Vetch."

"And this?" He plucked an orange flower.

"Hawkweed."

"What about this yellow one?"

"They call that 'bread and butter.'"

"And this large white one?" He tugged at the long stem with a wide head made up of tiny white flowers with yellow centers.

"That's yarrow."

"You have a whole flower garden out here, without even planting a seed."

"It'll be mowed soon, so you better enjoy it."

Caleb used the timothy stalk to wind around the flowers to form a posy. With a flourish he handed it to Geneva.

That made her stop. "What's that for?" She looked at the bouquet as if it might bite her.

"A garden of wildflowers for a woman of the wild." He twirled the posy between his fingers. "There's only one kind missing."

"Which one?" Her eyes followed the twirling flowers.

"Wild rose." He held the flowers up to his nose, then toward hers. "None of these have its fragrance. Sweet, but potent. It fills the senses. Like champagne—seemingly harmless—yet heady. You drink a few glasses and suddenly find yourself intoxicated."

Her brown eyes stared at him, as if she were mesmerized by the images he drew. He offered her the posy. "For you."

She jerked away from it. "What am I going to do with those?"

He shrugged and took the bouquet back. Sticking it in his top buttonhole, he smiled at her. She didn't smile back, but turned and continued walking.

They reached the forest in silence. Then Geneva called to Jake, and the dog came bounding toward them.

"I didn't know raspberries grew in the forest," Caleb remarked.

"They don't."

He gave her a sidelong look, and she finally explained.

"There's a glade a little way in. It was struck by lightning a few years back, and now it's full of berries. There'll be blackberries by the end of next month. But the raspberries should be ready now."

The rich, spicy scent of drying sap from fallen spruce trees hit his nostrils as soon as they entered under the canopy of tall, ancient trees, their lower limbs festooned with old-man's beard. The ground was a thick layer of short brown

needles and tiny pinecones. Wherever the light fell, patches
of green, ground-hugging plants grew, some with berries,
some with flowers. A boulder here and there was covered in
a carpet of green moss. Overhead, he could hear the caw of
crows. The white bark of a birch tree stood out among the
hoary, lichen-covered trunks of the evergreens.

Caleb followed Geneva over a fallen tree. "You know
your way around pretty well," he said softly.

"I ought to. Been living here all my life." She turned to
look back at Jake, who was pawing at the base of a tree
trunk. "Come on, boy, we're almost there."

Suddenly they were in the sunlight once again. A large
round glade, completely surrounded by forest, lay before
them. It was filled with waist-high bushes.

Geneva waded in. She parted some branches and examined the fruit. "Yep, they're just right." She stepped aside to
show him how the red berries were found growing under the
leaves. "Hold your bucket under the fruit. Some of them just
drop off, they're so ripe."

"Aye, aye, Captain."

She looked at him sharply before turning away. He
watched her picking for a few seconds, then, with a sigh, bent
down to fill his pail.

"Hey, these have thorns on them."

"Is that so?"

Seeing he would get no sympathy in that quarter, he
began picking.

For a while all he could hear was the buzz of a fly and
Jake's bark from the other side of the clearing. He tasted a
dark red berry and found it sweet and juicy.

"What are you going to do with all the berries you pick?"
he asked Geneva's bent head. He no longer noticed her hat

or severe braid; instead he saw a small earlobe peeking out beneath the dark hair.

"I make jam with most of them."

"How much do I need to pick in order to qualify for a jar?"

She looked at him. "Getting tired already?"

He smiled and watched her, wondering what was going on behind those solemn dark eyes. "No, there's nothing I like better than squatting in the hot sun, trying to locate berries among the thorns, let alone pick them without crushing them."

"Life on a farm means bending over in the hot sun most of the summer."

"So I've gathered."

"I'd think you'd be used to it by now. I seen—I've seen— you do your fair share of working in the sun."

So, she'd noticed him. "Do you notice any improvement, or has my labor been in vain?"

She shrugged and continued picking, her head bent down. "Your property looks tidy and well-kept."

"No longer like a mausoleum?" He couldn't see her face.

"It looks lived-in."

Caleb swatted at a persistent insect. "Hey, this is a hornet."

"Yellow jacket," she corrected. "They're always around anything sweet. Just ignore them and they'll ignore you."

"I hope so. This one seems pretty friendly."

"Just leave it alone."

Caleb continued picking, wishing he'd brought his hat. He hadn't planned on spending his afternoon this way. He'd imagined sitting in a cool interior, teaching someone her letters, not crouched in the hot sun, straining his back. He popped another berry into his mouth. At least he could reward himself every now and then.

"I've engaged a village girl to come cook and clean for me every few days."

She made no comment.

"What have you been up to all this week that I haven't seen much of you?" *Haven't seen you at all,* he amended silently.

She didn't answer right away. Caleb continued picking, wondering whether to repeat the question.

"I been—I've—been out fishing most days. Took Mrs. Bradford out, too. Then delivering vegetables. Summer's a busy time for people around here."

His fingers were stained red. The bottom of his pail was no longer visible. Maybe if he stayed a few more hours, he'd have it brimming full of the plump red fruit. "What do folks find to do here in winter?"

"Mendin' things—tools, nets, boats. Felling trees."

She was silent for a moment, then added, "Folks go visiting, too. Most families put on a party or sociable at least once in winter."

Caleb looked at the top of Geneva's hat, wondering whether she ever attended one of these socials. He knew the answer without asking.

"Readin' would make the evenings go by faster in winter," she said. "That's why it'd be nice to learn."

And so you shall, he vowed.

His pail was now half full, and he and Geneva had covered only a third of the clearing. His scalp burned under the sun. His fingers were full of countless little thorns. His back felt hot and sore. He was thirsty. The juice from the countless berries he'd eaten no longer satisfied. And those confounded wasps just seemed to be getting worse. He swatted angrily, not caring if he angered them or not.

He'd finally given up on trying to draw Geneva out. She seemed intent on picking berries. If she wanted to ignore his existence, that was fine with him. He'd pick until he filled his pail and then go sit in the shade until Geneva was ready to quit.

He got up to ease his legs, hoping at the same time to get away from the persistent wasps. Suddenly his foot caved into the soft ground beneath him. A second later, the buzzing of wasps increased tenfold, and a cloud of angry insects surrounded him. The sound was deafening, but not as horrific as the stinging. He flailed his arms about his head, trying to fend them off.

"They're all over me!"

He heard Geneva shout, "Run! Drop everything and run!"

He didn't have to be told again. He took off blindly, crashing through bushes. The next instant he felt a hand tightly grasp one of his own. Geneva was pulling him, her stride as long as his, guiding him into the forest. He followed her lead, not caring where she led him, aware only of a terrible burning over his face and ears and forearms.

Finally she slowed. He noticed the stillness first. No longer were there angry insects clamoring all over him. Geneva stopped and so did he, bumping into her briefly. She led him to a patch of sunlight, still holding his hand.

"Sit down," she said softly. "Let me look at your face."

She held him gently by the chin, careful not to touch the skin that had been bitten. She turned his head first one way, then the other.

"They got you pretty bad. What happened?"

"I don't know. My foot sank in the ground, and then it was as if hordes of them were over me."

"You must have stepped on a nest. Sometimes they build them underground in a hole." She sighed and let his chin go.

"We'd better get you back. I can put something on the bites, at least cool them down a bit."

"What about the berries?"

"Don't bother about them. It's more important to get you back first. Some people get mighty sick from so many bites. Wouldn't want you to pass out on me." The first hint of a smile crossed her face.

"No. I think you're capable of many things, Geneva, but not of carrying me."

He watched the color suffuse her cheeks, and thought how perfectly flawless her pale skin was, and how attractive the blush made her.

They walked back through the forest. Geneva kept hold of his hand, and he let her lead him, having no idea how she found her way through the trees.

By the time they reached her place, his face felt aflame, and he didn't care where he was or what was done to him. All he wanted was some relief. As if sensing his discomfort, Geneva took him by the hand again and led him to her narrow bed. She helped him lie down, fixing the pillow under his neck.

"Don't move. I'll be right back." She spoke in a soothing voice.

He could hear sounds of a door opening and closing, water being poured into a metal basin, and other rummaging about, but was in too much discomfort to open his eyes and follow Geneva's movements about the one-room dwelling. In a few moments, she was back at the bedside, kneeling beside him. When he made to rise, she pushed him back with a gentle pressure against his forehead.

He could hear her wringing water from a cloth. Then cold compresses covered his face and arms. She unbuttoned a couple of his shirt buttons to loosen his collar. More cold, wet towels surrounded his neck.

"That feels good," he said. "Just water?"

"Saltwater."

She changed the towels often, then rose from the bedside.

"Where are you going?" he asked immediately.

"Just getting something to put on the bites."

When she came back, she carried a bowl containing a white paste.

"What's that?"

"Saleratus mixed with water. It should help bring the swelling down." She briefly felt his forehead, her touch as soft as a butterfly's wing. "You feel a little warm. Might have a fever. I heard tell of people get bit just once and get a fever, even die."

"Well, let's hope it doesn't come to that." He chuckled at her look of alarm.

She knelt beside the bed and began working methodically on each bite.

"Oh, my, they even got you on your ears," she said, moving his head slightly away from her. Gently, she held his earlobe and worked on a bite on the rim of his ear. When she finished on that side of his head, she turned his head toward her again.

He watched her face as she worked, though she never met his gaze. She focused on each bite with steady concentration. He thought she had the most beautiful neck. It had the grace of a swan's. Looking at it made him wonder what it would feel like to nuzzle it.

He took a deep breath, determined to concentrate on other aspects of her neck. If she had on an evening gown, the kind he'd seen Arabella and other women of his acquaintance wear, its neck wide and low, Geneva could outshine them all.

The realization stunned him. How could he come to such a point, in a scant week, from not seeing her feminine attributes at all, to thinking her beauty superior to Arabella's?

Geneva finished with his face and neck, then proceeded with his forearms. Finally she completed her task and sat back to inspect her work.

"Think I'll live, Doc?"

She gave a slight smile. "You'd better, after all that."

She tidied up, putting everything into the empty bowl. "You'd better lie down a little while," she said, rising and turning away from him. "I'll be outside. Try and sleep."

His head ached. He yawned, then cut it short as he felt the swelling on his face. "Aye, aye, Captain."

He heard the door shut and heard the silence all around him, but didn't have the energy to do anything more than sink deeper into the pillow cradling his neck. Suddenly it felt good to have someone else take over for a little while....

When he awoke, Caleb could tell some time had passed by the lengthening shadows in the room. He judged it to be around four o'clock. He didn't move at first, comfortable just to lie there. His head no longer ached, and the burning sensation in his face and arms had subsided. He noticed Geneva had draped a quilt over him, carefully placing his arms above it so they wouldn't rub against the cloth. He wondered that he hadn't noticed her touch him.

He looked at the quilt. It had a mustard-yellow border and lots of lavender flowers throughout. Although it was faded, and some of the squares threadbare, showing the gray ticking beneath it, the fineness of its workmanship was evident in the minute stitches piecing the squares together. It smelled good. The soft fragrance of wild rose permeated it and the pillowcase his head rested on. He smiled, feeling the dried soda on his skin cracking.

Caleb studied the room. It was the first time he'd been in Geneva's home, her sanctuary. He dismissed the day he'd entered and seen her in the washtub. That day he'd only had eyes for her. Now, he felt curious about the place that she inhabited. Accustomed to thinking of her as a woman of the outdoors, he had difficulty picturing her sitting by the fire.

The house was only one large room. Opposite him on the far wall was an iron cookstove. A white-speckled, blue enamel coffeepot sat atop it. Beside the stove was a long table fashioned out of planks of wood with a faded calico cloth forming a skirt around its legs. The table held a washbasin and pail. A few pots and pans and a washboard hung on the wall above it. A rocker sat by the stove, a rag rug beneath it.

There were two windows in the house, one at the front and one at the back, beside the bed he lay on.

A few potted geraniums lined the sill of the front window, and a ruffled white curtain edged it. The other window, at his side, faced the bay beyond her sloping back lawn. A few boats were moored in the bay, their bare masts tall against the shimmering water. The low-lying sun sent its rays to bounce against the water, creating a blinding, silvery scene.

Caleb's gaze came back to the interior of the house. The windowsill beside the bed held a jar filled with colored bits of beach glass. Blues and greens, browns and whites, their edges curved and roughly honed by countless grains of sand, they created a colorful arrangement. A few sand dollars and scallop shells were neatly arranged along the rest of the sill. He picked one up and rubbed his thumb against its surface, wondering about the whimsy that would cause such a practical person as Geneva to collect treasures from the sea.

Caleb got up gingerly from the bed. The pain had disappeared, but the skin of his face and arms still felt tight and warm. He walked the perimeter of the room. A round table held a kerosene lamp, Geneva's slate, covered with words she'd written out, and a worn-looking piece of paper. He picked it up with a smile. It held the simple words with accompanying pictures he'd drawn that day they'd begun their first lesson. He set it back down beside the stack of books he'd given her, including the one he'd brought along earlier in the day. At the back edge of the table, near the window, stood a little jar of water. It held the posy he'd picked. Already some of the flowers had wilted, but the yarrow and vetch stood straight, forming a colorful blend of purple and white.

Caleb turned to the last wall of the room. A cedar chest stood by the bed. A few pillows, their edges ruffled, their fabric covered in lace doilies, were arranged on it. A small, hand-hewn table held a bowl full of pink rose petals. Some were deep pink with white centers, others were pale pink. He dipped his hand into them, feeling the velvety petals against his fingertips. The fragrance rose to his nostrils.

He didn't know what he'd expected, but he knew it wasn't this. The room was much more feminine than he'd have supposed. A lot of things were worn, but everything looked spotlessly clean, not a thing out of place.

He had just returned to the bed when the back door opened. Geneva entered carrying a large pan, which she placed on the worktable by the stove. Then she turned toward him, surprise on her face.

"You're awake."

"Yes. How long did I sleep?"

"Couple o' hours, I guess."

"What have you been up to all this time?"

She gestured toward the pan. "Soaked some salt fish and picked some greens for supper. You're welcome to stay if you'd like." She didn't meet his gaze as she extended the invitation.

"Thank you. I'd like to stay." He thought of all his hours of work. "What a waste, all those berries I picked."

She smiled sheepishly. "I got most of them."

He looked at her in amazement. "You went back there?"

She nodded.

"You didn't get bitten?" he asked in quick concern.

"No. There were a few yellow jackets still buzzing around like they didn't have anyplace to go, but most had gone." She shook her head in amusement, her hands in her trouser pockets. "They'll have to rebuild their nest. You wrecked it some good.

"But your pail was right where you'd left it, just tipped over. I managed to pick up most of the berries you dropped."

"You found the posy." As soon as he said it, he regretted drawing attention to that.

She flushed and looked away from him. "It was right at my feet. You seemed so interested in the names of the flowers."

He changed the subject, wanting to put her at ease. "I should have helped you gather those fallen berries. I guess I wasn't much use to you today. I caused you double work."

"Don't say that. It could've happened to anyone. It could've been me stepped on that wasps' nest."

"I'm glad it wasn't you."

She approached closer to the bed. "How do you feel?" She put her hand on his brow.

"Better." *Keep your hand on me,* he begged silently, but her hand went quickly back to her pocket. "My face has gone from feeling as if it's on fire, to just a dull smoldering."

He could detect another faint smile.

"You're describing it just about how it looks."

He grinned. "I suppose I shouldn't look in any mirrors for the time being?"

Her smile deepened, although he could see she was trying to suppress it. "You're lucky—" She put a hand up to her mouth, hiding her widening smile. "You're lucky I only have a tiny one in this place. I'll turn it against the wall."

She started chuckling. He smiled to see her amusement. It was infectious and he began to laugh, but that only stretched his skin, making the soda crack.

"I—I'm sorry, I shouldn't. It must hurt to laugh—" She turned away from him, trying to stifle the sound.

"It was so awful—" she giggled "—going and stepping on a wasps' nest. And so funny! Your pail almost full." By this time, they were both laughing.

"I was so hot and tired, just looking to the moment you'd tell me it was time to quit," Caleb told her, cradling his swollen cheeks.

They wiped their eyes as the room grew quiet again. Geneva was on her knees on the floor. She looked up at him. "I'm sorry," she said, more calmly. "I felt so bad. I shouldn'a let you go with me." Her dark eyes glistened and her cheeks looked rosy from the exertion.

"Don't be," he said with a smile. "I'd do it all over again just to hear you laugh like that. It was worth it."

She sobered up immediately, her eyes full of appeal and fear at the same time.

"You probably haven't laughed nearly enough in your young lifetime."

She shrugged, getting back to her old self. "Reckon I've laughed as much as anybody's got a right to."

"Life isn't always easy here on Haven's End, is it?" he asked.

"I don't have any right to complain. I have plenty to eat and a warm place at night. That's about all a body's got a right to ask, isn't it?" She turned away from him, clearly wanting to steer the topic to more practical matters.

"Are you ready for your lesson now?" he asked.

She turned back to him, seeming thrown off balance. She nodded. "If you feel up to it."

"Let's look at your work," he answered promptly, rising from the bed.

He was amazed at her progress and could see she'd studied everything he'd given her. "I'll have to order you some new books," he told her. He had the gratification of seeing her flush with pleasure.

After the lesson, she prepared some creamed cod and served it with new potatoes and beans. For dessert they had raspberries and cream.

She didn't let him help her clear the table, but refilled his coffee cup and told him to stay put. Caleb sat back, Jake at his feet, watching Geneva work, admiring the way she always moved quietly and efficiently. He was surprised at how much he'd missed her in the intervening days. It was not just having seen her in her tub. He'd missed the companionship he'd grown used to with her.

As he was mulling over this discovery, Geneva finished drying the dishes and hung up the dish towel. Without looking at him, she crossed to the opposite side of the room. He could hear her clear off the chest and open its lid. He watched her delve inside, carefully laying things aside until she extracted what she'd been looking for. He remained silent as she repacked everything but what appeared to be a bolt of cloth.

She walked to the table, placing the fabric on it. "Would you like some more coffee?"

He shook his head. "I'm fine. What's this?" he finally asked, touching an edge of the pretty, sprigged material.

"It was Ma's." She fingered the muslin. "She was going to make us each a dress out of this. I was a lot smaller then." She smiled, smoothing the material.

He took the bolt of cloth from her and spread part of it out. It was a pretty pattern, pink with tiny navy-blue and white flowers sprinkled over it. It would suit her.

"Geneva, what I said the other day—I didn't mean to be critical. I had no right to question how you dress."

"That's all right. There was some truth in what you said."

"No, I said a bunch of foolishness."

She continued speaking, as if it was important to make him understand. "There was a time I wore dresses. Ma used to make them for me, but I outgrew them long ago." She took a deep, shuddering breath. "And unfortunately she wasn't around long enough to teach me to sew, except mending. It just got to be easier wearin' Pa's old things. When those wore out, I just kept buyin' men's things. It made it easier to keep men like Lucius away from me."

"Men like Lucius should be strung up. Has he been pestering you any more?"

She shook her head. "I haven't seen hide nor hair of him." She smiled. "I think you shook him up good."

Caleb didn't share her amusement. "If I ever catch him nosing around here again, he won't be *capable* of bothering you again."

Her smile widened. "Much obliged to you, Cap'n." She blushed, realizing her mistake. "Caleb," she amended. "There'll be no need. I got Jake, and my pa's shotgun." At his name, Jake stirred, lifting his head in question. "You said it right. Lucius won't be *capable* of botherin' me again." She picked up the bolt of cloth, smoothing out the wrinkles.

Before she could turn back to the trunk, Caleb said, "Maybe you could get someone in town to sew this material up for you."

She flashed him a look of annoyance, as if he hadn't understood anything she'd said. "It'll sit in my trunk 'til it rots!"

"You really don't know how to make up a dress?" he asked her retreating back.

"After Ma died, there wasn't anyone to teach me. Besides, I had a lot more important things to learn. How to survive, for one thing."

"Did your father teach you to fish and garden?"

"Pa didn't teach me nothin'. Anything!" she amended angrily. She hugged the material to her chest, her gaze traveling past Caleb to the front window. "No," she answered more calmly, her eyes once more looking into the past. "There was an old fisherman, lived up in the next house. He's dead now. His house is gone, too. Burned down.

"He must have felt sorry for me or something. He'd take me out on his boat. Taught me to plant, too. Couldn't teach me my letters, though," she said with a fond smile, "because he didn't know them very well himself."

Caleb eyed the material held against her. He'd been right. The pink complemented her creamy skin, picking up the tint in her cheeks, and the tiny navy-blue flowers looked black like the dark mass of hair he remembered.

"I should feel lucky I did a turn before the mast," he said, almost without thinking. He replied to the question in her eyes. "I learned to ply a needle aboard ship." He grinned. "I must say, I never thought I'd need that skill once back on land."

"You know how to sew?" She looked at him fully, her face registering disbelief. At his nod, she scoffed. "Men don't sew!"

He shrugged. "Any common sailor does, you must know that. There's no other way to replace your clothes on a Cape Horn voyage, except by taking needle and thread. During a storm your clothes stay wet nearly all the time, and the salt-water wears them out pretty quickly."

She smiled. "I always picture you pacing up and down on the stern, issuing orders." She lowered her eyes. "I'm sorry, it's just so hard for me to think of you as a common sailor, though I know what you're telling me is true."

"It's probably no harder than for people to picture you in a dress."

Her head snapped up.

"Wouldn't you like to shock them a bit, shake them out of the image they have of you? Walk along the harbor, wearing a dress made out of your mother's material?"

She just kept looking at him, until he grew uncomfortable, remembering the welts along his cheeks.

"Well, are you going to stare at me all night, or are you going to bring that material here and let me take a look at it?"

"What are you saying?" she whispered.

"Do you want to learn how to sew or not?"

"You—you'd teach me to sew?"

He felt as if he'd already lived this scene a few short weeks ago, when he'd found himself agreeing to teach her to read. Caleb touched his face gingerly, wondering if perhaps the wasp stings had affected his brain. But he knew he couldn't crush the shy hopefulness he saw written in her face, not after the way he'd hurt her just a few days ago with his careless remark about her clothing.

"I can show you how to cut a garment and put it together, but I don't know anything about sewing dresses," he answered.

She handled the material as if it were more precious than the finest silk. "I suppose I could buy a pattern and make it up after I've practiced some."

He nodded in encouragement. "It can't be so different from shirts and trousers." He thought of something. "Do you have any of your mother's dresses?"

She nodded. "But they wouldn't fit me. I'm too tall."

"It doesn't matter. We can use them as rough patterns. That's what we sailors did. We used our old clothes to form the patterns for our new garments."

Her growing excitement infected him, and he helped her unfold one of her mother's faded dresses.

Later that evening, when Caleb bid Geneva good-night, she walked him to the door. The evening was beautiful, the sky black with a thousand twinkling stars and a small sliver of moon above them. The scent of roses surrounded Geneva like an aureole as she stood in the opened doorway.

He couldn't help himself. He leaned over, placing a fingertip on her warm, velvety cheek. "Thank you," he whispered. His face came down to hers, his lips touched her other cheek. He heard her intake of breath. In one motion, his lips could cover those soft lips.

Instead, he turned on his heel and left, seeking the cool darkness.

When Caleb entered his house, he paused for a moment in the hallway, contrasting the large, dark, empty house with the warm, cozy room where he'd spent the last few hours. He thought about how easy it would be to draw Geneva out, build up her confidence, and watch her blossom. She'd turn to him as the first man to treat her like a lady. She'd assuage his loneliness. He could make her feel cherished as never before.

Ever since formalizing his engagement with Arabella, he'd been saving himself for her.

He gave a mirthless laugh. A lot of good that had done him. She had turned right around and gotten herself engaged to Ellery the moment Caleb had left Boston.

So, what was stopping him now from seeking Geneva's companionship? A picture of Lucius Tucker, his dirty hands groping Geneva, her legs thrashing beneath him, rose in his mind.

How different was Caleb from all the men who'd harassed Geneva since she'd been left alone in the world? From all the men she'd hidden from behind those baggy overalls and shirts he sought to free her from?

More to the point, how different was Caleb from Arabella, if he could get over the years of fidelity and devotion so quickly and turn to the first woman who'd befriended him?

Chapter Eleven

The following Sunday, Geneva sat on the blanket Mrs. Bradford had brought for the church picnic. The elderly lady sat in one chair beside her, and Bessie on another. They had just finished the picnic lunch Bessie had prepared. Jake lay at Geneva's feet, sleeping off his meal. Every once in a while, his tail moved back and forth a few times on the heavy blanket.

All around her on the sloping green overlooking the harbor, Geneva could see couples and families sitting as she was, chatting in groups or promenading from group to group. They were dressed in their best—women in starched white aprons and bonnets, men in their shallow-crowned, wide-brimmed felts. Children with their boundless energy ran around their elders. All about the harbor, there were more people than usual as the village was filled with summer visitors.

Geneva could easily spot the summer people. The women were more colorfully dressed; their silhouettes were tighter, the only fullness the gathered bustle at the rear of their gowns. Pert little hats perched high on cascades of curls. The men wore a variety of sporting clothes, sack coats and straw hats, checked or striped pants or knickerbockers. She could see more of these summer people at the hotel on another slope above the harbor. Emerald-green lawn stretched out all around it. Both ladies and gentlemen sprang up and down on the tennis courts beside the hotel. More sedate couples played croquet. She watched a man stand behind a woman, his arms around her as he guided her mallet. She turned her head around to him and laughed.

Geneva felt out of place in her trousers. Out on the Point where no one saw her but her few neighbors—hardworking farmers and fishermen, who had seen her all her life—she passed unnoticed. But here, she felt like a freak. She always managed to avoid the harbor on Sundays and festival days. Seeing girls and boys she'd known since childhood, all dressed in their Sunday best, beginning to walk arm-in-arm with each other, only made her own isolated position more painfully obvious.

The only reason Geneva had come today was that she didn't want to disappoint Mrs. Bradford. She glanced down at her dungarees, then peeked sideways at Bessie on one side, sitting straight in her chair, and Mrs. Bradford on the other side, looking with pleasure at the picnickers around her. Never before had Geneva wished so desperately that she owned a dress.

Mrs. Bradford had invited Geneva to spend the afternoon with her, and Geneva hadn't been able to say no. But she hadn't realized the older woman meant for her to spend the afternoon at the church picnic.

"Well, I could sit here all afternoon. But I think I'll go and say hello to a few people." The wicker squeaked as Bessie pushed herself up.

"Yes, it's very pleasant to sit here," Mrs. Bradford agreed. "It's such a beautiful day."

"Don't forget your nap, Mrs. Bradford." Bessie gave Geneva a sharp glance, as if reprimanding her for her employer's lapse.

Geneva stood. "I'll be going on along."

"Oh, not quite yet!" Mrs. Bradford's voice was so full of lament that Geneva hesitated.

Bessie smoothed her hands over her starched, white apron. "Would you care for anything before I go?"

"No, thank you. Geneva?"

"No, thank you, ma'am. I ate more'n I should have. Everything was delicious."

Bessie nodded. "Very well."

When Geneva was sure Bessie was out of earshot, she sat back down and turned to her hostess. "Mrs. Bradford, do you think I ought to wear dresses?"

Mrs. Bradford expressed no surprise at her question. Geneva could hear the sounds of voices around them, but they were distant and held no meaning for her. All she cared about was the elderly woman's opinion.

"I'm sure you dress in the most practical manner for your occupation. I don't imagine you could handle a fishing line very easily in a skirt and couple of petticoats, could you?"

Geneva smiled, shaking her head.

"I would imagine it would feel nice to put on a dress once in a while, though, don't you think? Perhaps on a Sunday, when you're not working in your garden or going out in your boat?"

Geneva was startled at the lady's perception. But she wasn't yet ready to let anyone see the truth. "I pretty much work all the time. I don't guess I'd have much use for dresses."

"A lady always has a use for a dress."

"I'm no lady," Geneva mumbled.

She felt Mrs. Bradford's hand on her arm, forcing her to look up into her gray eyes. "You're *better* than a lady. If you abide in Jesus, and He abides in you, you're a child of God. Think of that—a child of the most high God."

The words thrilled Geneva. They made her feel that she was truly worth something, that she had a right to wish for things she had never thought she deserved.

Mrs. Bradford patted her arm and let it go. "I don't suppose you have any dresses, do you, my dear?"

Children's voices rose and fell in the distance.

"No. That is, I have one of my ma's, but she was smaller'n me."

"Than I."

"Than I," Geneva corrected immediately.

"It's most likely outdated as well. Goodness, to see some of the fashions in Boston now, makes one wish to don trousers like a man. I certainly wish I had your courage sometimes, my dear, when I go bird-watching. I think it must be liberating to dress like a man.

"On the other hand, there is nothing like feeling feminine," she added with a smile.

Was that how Geneva had been feeling each time she remembered Caleb's look when he'd seen her in her washtub? As if her thoughts could conjure him up, Geneva saw him walking across the green. She drew in her breath, observing how handsome he appeared. He was wearing a dark-blue jacket and light-colored trousers. The next instant, he turned her way.

Geneva lowered her eyes, but not before she saw his upraised hand. She hadn't seen him since the night he'd promised to teach her to sew. The night he'd kissed her. Her hand went involuntarily to her cheek, remembering the soft feel of his lips upon it.

She glanced over at Mrs. Bradford, wondering whether Caleb's wave had been meant for her. After all, the older woman was an acquaintance of his.

"Why, I believe that's Caleb Phelps." Mrs. Bradford sat up. "He lives just below you on the Point."

Geneva swallowed. "We've met a time or two."

Mrs. Bradford raised her hand. By then Caleb was within calling distance.

"Hello, Caleb. Come by to greet an old lady?"

Caleb glanced at Geneva before taking Mrs. Bradford's hand. "I've come to call on the most charming lady in all Haven's End." Geneva looked at the two, hearing Mrs. Bradford's chuckle, witnessing their warm regard, and wishing she could be Mrs. Bradford and enjoy that easy friendship with Caleb. She was glad to see his face completely healed of the insect bites. It gave her pleasure to know her ministrations might have helped speed his recovery.

Before she knew it, Caleb turned to her. "Hello, Geneva, how have you been keeping?"

She raised her eyes only as far as the vicinity of his nose. "Well enough."

"I haven't seen you around lately. Busy fishing?"

She dared inch her gaze up farther, and wished she hadn't. She could read a thousand things in those blue depths. Why hadn't she been back for her lessons? How was she? What had she been thinking in the intervening days?

It was all in her imagination, she told herself. She nodded, hoping her own eyes weren't asking him questions of her own, nor giving any replies to his.

"It's good to see you out and about, Caleb," said Mrs. Bradford.

Geneva breathed a sigh of relief as Caleb turned his attention back to Mrs. Bradford. She watched his profile as he replied.

"I thought I'd take a rest from my labors and put in an appearance at this picnic. Pastor McDuffie invited me a while back."

"Oh, that was nice of him. He's a good man. Have you seen him?"

"Yes, I've already greeted him and his wife."

"You're looking well." Mrs. Bradford's voice was soft.

"Am I?" he asked lightly. "It must be the sea air."

The older lady chuckled. "I shall tell your mother that."

Caleb smiled at her. "I sent her a line."

Although his tone was casual, Geneva noticed the look he exchanged with Mrs. Bradford.

"Oh, I'm so glad."

Caleb turned to survey the harbor. "Any new ships come in?"

"I believe the *Anne Marie* anchored this morning."

While Caleb glanced at Mrs. Bradford before scanning the harbor for the Boston schooner, Geneva busied herself with brushing away the few remaining crumbs from her trousers.

"Would you care for a glass of lemonade? Some cookies? Do stay," Mrs. Bradford's voice entreated.

Geneva clasped her ankles as she awaited his reply.

"Thank you kindly, perhaps on another occasion. I believe I'll just continue on down to the harbor and see what's new."

Geneva's grip tightened. Boston was intruding more quickly than she could bear.

"Would you care to take a stroll down with me, Geneva?"

At the sound of her name, her head popped up like that of a puppet on a string. "Me? Uh…"

At her confusion, Mrs. Bradford intervened. "Geneva and I were just discussing something, which I believe we need to finish. What do you think, Geneva?"

"Yes, ma'am." Relief and regret met and clashed inside her. What would it be like to walk arm-in-arm with Captain Caleb, the way Miss Harding had been privileged to do? How could Geneva bear the humiliation of being seen side by side with such a handsome, elegant man, the way she looked? She could feel the rough denim of her trousers beneath her fingers.

"Well, seeing as how I'm interrupting what must be something important, I'll take my leave. Goodbye, Maud. Be seeing you, Geneva." His eyes held a question as well as a command, which scared and thrilled Geneva down to the tips of her toes.

The two women watched his descent toward the wharves. People stopped to greet him, and he spoke with everyone who addressed him. Geneva was glad people no longer avoided him, nor he them. At the same time, she felt a certain sadness, knowing her own special relation to him was coming to an end. He would no longer need the friendship of an outcast like her once the ordinary citizens of Haven's End embraced him.

Mrs. Bradford's voice interrupted her thoughts. "I'm sorry if I intervened. I sensed Caleb took you by surprise with his invitation. I didn't mean for you to stay with me, if you wanted to go on down to the harbor."

"Oh, no, ma'am," Geneva hastened to assure her. "I wasn't interested in going. Thank you. You did right."

Mrs. Bradford contemplated her clasped hands. "I'm so glad Caleb seems to be recovering from his misfortunes."

"He…he went through a lot, didn't he?" Geneva ventured.

Mrs. Bradford sighed. "Yes, yes he did." After a pause, she continued. "I'm not just referring to his recent troubles in Boston, but long before that."

"How do you mean?"

Mrs. Bradford looked beyond the crowd of picnickers to the harbor. "Caleb Phelps didn't have a normal upbringing. He was brought up in the fo'c'sle of a ship. He was wrenched from his mother's bosom at the tender age of eight and sent to sea."

At Geneva's look of amazement, Mrs. Bradford nodded her head. "Oh, yes. The only son of one of Boston's leading families never knew the warmth of family life, never knew a life of luxury. All he knew as a youngster was the company of hardened sailors." Mrs. Bradford clucked her tongue. "I can hardly bear to think what it must have been like for the poor lad."

How could it be? "But he's Caleb Phelps! His father owns all those ships—" She gestured toward the wharves. "Why, he even owns the biggest wharf all the way down here."

"Mr. Phelps Senior is a hardworking man who has only one fear in life, that his only offspring might destroy the company he spent so many years and so much of his life's blood building up.

"Unfortunately," she continued with a sigh, "Mr. Phelps was so careful not to spoil his son that he withheld any indulgence from Caleb. He's done everything imaginable to suppress any natural tendency in the boy toward any sort of enjoyment.

"Poor Caleb." Mrs. Bradford shook her head. "Indeed, he was always such a cheerful, stalwart little lad. Throughout it all, young Caleb retained such a good-humored air. I think deep down he must have been trying to please his father. But everyone has a breaking point, and I so feared that this would be it.

"When these awful accusations surfaced, Caleb left everything in Boston, and came here, as if—" Mrs. Bradford's hands gestured, indicating a loss for the right words "—just giving up. Today is the first time I'm seeing him anything like he used to be."

Geneva could only listen, fascinated. Her heart went out to the little boy who'd been shipped to sea. Why, one could say he'd lost his mother at about the same age as she.

Caleb breathed a sigh of relief when he entered Mr. Watson's store a few days later and found it empty. He'd deliberately timed his visit for the noon hour, hoping most people were at home eating their dinner. He closed the screen door softly behind him. The floor creaked under him as he made his way to the counter.

"I'm in the back." Mr. Watson's voice came to him from the other room. "I'll be right out."

"That's fine," he answered. He went to the far end of the counter where he'd remembered a group of ladies looking at bolts of fabric the first time he'd come in here. The look of frosty disapproval they'd given him was quite a contrast to the smiles and hellos he'd received during the church picnic when he'd spent the day strolling among the crowds, greeting and being greeted in turn.

Caleb's gaze skimmed the articles along the back counter until he found what he wanted. Spools of thread, lined along the edge of a shelf between skeins of yarn and yards of ribbon.

"Good afternoon, Cap'n," Mr. Watson greeted him, running his tongue along the inside of his mouth to dislodge any last particle of food from his last mouthful. "Haven't seen you about in a while."

Caleb decided not to enlighten the storekeeper about his run-in with the wasps and his reason for staying put for a few days. "Sorry to interrupt your dinner."

"Don't give it a thought. Happens all the time. Someone's got to have something that just can't wait 'til afternoon." The storekeeper chuckled.

"Well, I won't keep you. I need a couple of spools of thread."

"What color?" asked Mr. Watson, his hand resting lightly in front of the colorful array. "Black or gray?"

Caleb almost blurted out "pink." He shut his mouth as he considered. Whatever he did here today would be all over the village by suppertime. "Give me white." That should do fine. White could be used for anything. "And black." That should cover everything.

"Anything else?" asked the storekeeper, setting the spools down on the counter.

"Yes. A paper of pins, some needles, a pair of shears." He paused, giving the storekeeper a chance to reach for those items on the shelves behind him. "A tape measure, a pin cushion. Some buttons." Caleb went over his mental list. The dark-blue ribbon looked tempting, but he'd better wait. Geneva could buy that herself later.

"What color buttons?"

Again pink would have been the best choice. "Let me see what you have in navy blue." Actually, that would probably be better, the more he thought about it. He examined the tray Mr. Watson set before him. Yes, just the thing, little round blue buttons. He could picture a row of them curved down the front of her dress—

"Ahem." He cleared his throat. "I'll take two dozen of these."

"Need to do some mending? I know a few women that take in sewing," Mr. Watson said in a friendly tone as he separated the buttons.

"Oh, it's nothing I can't do myself," he replied. His mind was on undergarments. He wondered whether Geneva owned any of her mother's petticoats, or whether he should just buy a length of muslin. While he was pondering this difficulty, the door opened. Caleb swung his head around guiltily, then groaned inwardly as he identified Pastor McDuffie entering the store.

He'd much rather face a whole battalion of nosy matrons than the discerning pastor.

"Good afternoon, gentlemen," the pastor said with a smile. "Quite a warm day today."

"Sure is, Pastor," the storekeeper agreed. "I'll be right with you, soon as I finish with the captain here."

"That will be all," said Caleb, already removing his wallet. "Just wrap it up."

Pastor McDuffie ambled up to the counter. "No hurry. Just need to pick up something for the missus." He smiled at Caleb. "I was working out in the yard, and this was a good excuse to take a breather." He took out his white pocket-handkerchief and wiped his brow. "How is everything down at the Point? I've been meaning to come by, but my parishioners have been keeping me busy this week."

"And I've been meaning to stop by to thank you for sending the two girls for me to interview. Marilla is coming by a couple of times a week now."

The pastor nodded. "Yes. How's she working out?"

"Very well. She comes in, does her work, cooks me a meal, and is gone by mid-afternoon. Most efficient soul I've ever come across," Caleb said with a grin.

"That sounds like Marilla. I thought she might suit you." As he spoke, he watched the storekeeper wrap up Caleb's purchases. He turned back to Caleb, an eyebrow upraised. "You know how to sew?"

"Learned how to ply a needle aboard ship," he answered easily, feeling more comfortable now that the items were wrapped up.

The pastor nodded. "I guess there's a lot more to you than meets the eye."

"I suppose you could say that about anyone," he replied, thinking about Geneva.

"'For there is nothing covered, that shall not be revealed; and hid, that shall not be known,'" McDuffie quoted with an oblique smile.

Before Caleb could figure out what the pastor intended to convey with the Scripture, McDuffie smiled broadly. "I expect Christ's words are particularly appropriate to you at this time."

"I don't follow."

"I refer to the cloud of calumny that has been lifted from your head."

Caleb leaned back against the counter. "You've heard, then?"

"The whole village has heard the good news from Boston. I want to tell you how pleased I am—I know everyone is." He turned to Mr. Watson for corroboration. "Isn't that so, Mr. Watson?"

The storekeeper, who'd been listening to the exchange with growing interest, turned to snip the piece of string tying Caleb's parcel. "Oh, yes. I meant to tell you myself, Cap'n, just how relieved I was—I mean, that it all came out—you were innocent of—" He coughed.

Caleb looked from one man to the other, not quite sure what to say. In all fairness, the storekeeper had always treated him courteously. The same went for the pastor. "Thank you," he said quietly. "I'm not sure I agree with you concerning the sentiments of the rest of the village."

"Oh, I think most folks are ashamed of their suspicion toward you," said McDuffie. "Don't be surprised if you start seeing a change in their behavior."

"I already have," he said dryly. "I didn't know what to attribute it to at first, but I'm certain now."

"Don't be too hard on them," the pastor said. "Folks around here are generally suspicious of outsiders." He chuckled. "It took me a couple of years just to be accepted on the pulpit."

"If that's so, I just find it funny they should have accepted me so readily before, whenever I came into port."

"I didn't say their attitude is correct. I'm only stressing tolerance on your part."

"How tolerant is one required to be?"

"You mean how tolerant does the good Lord require? I'd say He requires mercy and forgiveness if we expect to receive mercy and forgiveness from Him."

Caleb turned to the storekeeper, replacing his hat. "Just put it on my bill." He picked up his parcel. "I have to be honest with you, Pastor. I don't find myself feeling too merciful and forgiving of late."

"Good luck with your sewing." The pastor's cheerful voice followed him out of the store.

The sewing project was turning into Caleb's worst nightmare.

Oh, everything had started out fine. He'd shown Geneva how to clip out the threads in her mother's old garment.

Luckily, the dress had been a simple calico one, which among the country women of Haven's End, was scarcely outdated. A full, gathered skirt attached to a plain bodice with rounded collar and long sleeves.

For the past week, they had taken apart the old dress, then laid each piece flat on the new fabric and pinned it down, leaving a generous margin all around, to increase the size of the new garment. After cutting out the pieces, Caleb had shown Geneva how to pin them together, then baste, using wide stitches. But spending a part of each day with her was taking its toll. Sitting so close to her, watching her gleaming hair bent over her stitching or her reader, and not permitting himself to touch her was becoming pure torture.

But Caleb refused to give in to his feelings. Even that simple peck on the cheek had been a mistake. If he permitted himself the least liberty, he didn't know how easy it would be to stop the next time.

Caleb glanced at Geneva, the truth belying his thoughts. He knew exactly how easy it would be. Just about impossible. And he wasn't ready yet to face the implications.

Now Geneva stood awaiting his instructions. The moment of truth had come.

"All right," he said, shaking out the basted garment. "Except for the sleeves, the dress is put together temporarily. Now we need to sew it with smaller, permanent stitches."

He paused. They couldn't go any farther until they fitted the dress on a real, live person. He looked at Geneva, standing there. He'd avoided using the tape measure on Geneva's body, convincing her—and himself—that all they needed was to make the new dress longer and wider all around than the original.

But if she were ever to have a dress, there was no avoiding the next step. Caleb cleared his throat. "I guess you'd better try this on to see how it fits before we begin sewing it with the final stitches."

They both eyed the sleeveless garment.

"It looks well enough—a little large," she began.

"Women's skirts take a lot of material," he explained. He wanted to ask her whether she owned any petticoats, but felt such a question would be the height of impropriety.

That presented a new problem. He looked at her in her trousers; she certainly wasn't wearing petticoats now. The situation was unconventional enough as it was. He could just picture what McDuffie and his flock would say….

Geneva stared at him as if following the direction of his thoughts clearly. "Try it on?" Her voice sounded fearful.

He grasped at the first thing that came into his head. "You can just put it on over your clothes," he said gruffly. That took care of matters. Yes, that was the solution.

She nodded, relief showing in her expression. Slowly, she extended her arm, and he handed her the dress, neither of them taking their eyes off each other. As soon as the garment had exchanged hands, they separated quickly.

"I'll be in the kitchen," Caleb called over his shoulder. "Just shout when you've got it on."

Geneva's heart began beating like a woodpecker against a tree the moment Caleb looked at her and told her to try the dress on. The thought of standing there in just her drawers and chemise, with only a thin dress covering her, filled her with fear. Great had been her relief when she'd realized he meant for her to put it on over her clothing.

She positioned the dress in front of her, looking down at herself, unable to picture herself as a woman like the ones living down at the harbor. Like Arabella.

Before her excitement could be smothered by images of the fashionably clad Miss Harding, Geneva stuck one leg in the opening of the skirt, scared for a minute that she'd rip the fine thread with her boots.

"Are you ready?"

Caleb's voice broke into her thoughts, and she practically jumped, thinking he might be standing in the doorway.

"Just about," she answered in a hurry, pulling her arms through the armholes. Luckily the sleeves hadn't been sewn on yet. "All right. I've got it on." She looked down at the bodice and skirt doubtfully. It seemed pretty lumpy over her clothes. Of course the front hung open. She couldn't do anything about that; the buttons hadn't been sewn on yet.

She could hear Caleb's footsteps approaching but she didn't dare turn around. She fixed her gaze out the window instead, looking at the sea.

Caleb stopped behind Geneva. Well, it didn't look too bad from the back. At least it looked like a dress. Of course, it seemed a little bulky, but that was to be expected. He grabbed up the pincushion.

"Here, hold this, will you, while I pin?" he told her, handing her the red cushion.

She took it wordlessly. He paused for a moment, but when she didn't look at him, he proceeded with his task, concluding she was probably more nervous than he.

He planted his two feet apart, standing directly in front of her, deciding he'd better take the bull by the horns. He cleared his throat. "I have to do...up...the front." By this time, he didn't dare look in her face either. "The buttons have to...have to go here," he muttered, trying to fold the material down on either side of the front opening and bring the two sides together to overlap. Quickly he stuck a pin to mark the fold. He stepped back quickly. "That should do it."

He shifted position. "All right, we have to pin this part tighter. Can you lift your arm a little?" She did so immediately, and he wondered whether she was as tightly wound as he felt at the moment. He carefully adjusted the side seam of her garment, bringing the dress together as tightly as he dared, then sticking a pin through it. He stepped back to inspect his work. That didn't look too bad. He went down a few inches, trying to ignore the contours of her breasts as the bodice became tighter.

Oh, no! He'd pinned a piece of her shirt to the dress material. It would be much easier if she weren't wearing so much underneath the dress, but he wouldn't even consider that alternative. No, they'd do it this way, or not at all. He stuck a last pin down one side and went on to the opposite side.

He stood back for a moment when he'd pinned both sides. "There," he said. When she started to move away, he said, "Wait, we need to pin on the sleeves." He grabbed one up from the table and began slipping it over her hand. Halfway up, it caught on the flannel sleeve of her shirt. He shoved at it until it reached the top of her shoulder, then began pinning it around the armhole.

"Ouch!" she cried.

"Sorry," he mumbled. "That'll do it, I guess. I can't pin under your arm. We'll just sew it together afterward. It seems to fit about right." He gave a final upward tug to the sleeve to make it look right. After finishing the other sleeve, he knelt beside her and began folding up the hem.

"We're ready to sew it together," he announced minutes later, sitting back on his heels, feeling the sweat running down his back. "You can take it off now." He rose to his feet and began helping her off with it, feeling as if he'd exercised more self-control in the last few minutes than he had in all his years of courting Arabella.

Chapter Twelve

Two evenings later, Jake got up from the rug at Geneva's feet and started barking. Next he trotted over to the door, getting her attention to open it.

Only then did she hear the knock. She was sitting, stitching a seam of her dress. She knew it must be someone friendly by Jake's stance—perhaps Mrs. Stillman. Although, what would she be doing here at this time? It was long past supper. Geneva had already shed her clothes and was sitting in her rocker in her nightgown and robe.

"Who is it?" she called out, stopping her rocker with the toes of her slippers.

"It's Caleb."

She glanced down at her nightclothes and hesitated.

Caleb's voice came through the door. "If you're in bed, I won't disturb you."

"No, no, you're not disturbing me." She hurried to the front door, realizing it was ridiculous to carry on a conversation through the planks. She unlatched the door and opened it about a foot. "Hello! What are you doing here?"

He grinned sheepishly. "I don't know. I was just out for a walk. It's such a beautiful night." He glanced up at the pattern of light and shadow the full moon made through the thin patch of clouds. Then he noticed her clothing, his smile disappearing. "I'm sorry, I did get you up."

"No, come on in," she reassured him, stepping back so he could enter. "I was just sitting here—" it was her turn to smile self-consciously "—doing some sewing. I haven't had much time during the daylight hours." She continued speaking as she turned back to her rocker, which she'd drawn up close to the table, and took up the dress. "There are a lot of vegetables to be harvested now. Between selling them and putting others up for the winter, there ain—isn't—much time left for anything else."

Caleb shut the door behind him, greeting Jake with a pat but remaining by the door, as if reluctant to come in any farther. Geneva thought of the afternoon when he'd barged in and seen her sitting in her tub. She wondered whether he was thinking the same thing.

His glance took in the room. She wondered what he saw in its shadowy depths.

"Are you hungry? Would you like some coffee?" she asked.

"Yes—no—I'm fine." He ran a hand through his hair, looking as if he might step right back out of her door.

Afraid he'd leave as quickly as he'd appeared, she said, "How's my stitching?" She held up the dress for his inspection. She could hear his footsteps approaching. Then he knelt beside her rocker and took the section of dress from her hands. Geneva looked at his dark hair, the waves glowing red where the lamplight hit. She could almost reach out and touch the thick locks. She clenched her hands beneath the dress.

"You're doing very well." He smiled up at her. "Small and even. My mother would be proud of you."

She smiled in gratitude. When she realized it was the first time he'd said anything of his family, she ventured to ask, "Your mother's in Boston?"

He nodded. She didn't think he'd say anything more, but as he rose to his feet, he added, "I'm afraid I haven't been a very good son of late." He walked around the table and gestured to the other chair. "May I?"

"Of course." She picked up her needle again and found her spot on the dress. "What have you done to her?"

"Nothing. That's just the point. Since I left Boston, I haven't written her but once."

Geneva studied his face across the table. They were both encased in the lamplight, the rest of the room in shadow. She remembered Mrs. Bradford's words. "Your mother must miss you."

"I imagine so. I'm not proud of myself. I have no excuse, except…" He fell silent, his hands clasped loosely on the tabletop. "So much time has passed, it's hard to know what to say. I felt nothing but emptiness for so long. Can you understand that, Geneva?"

She nodded, remembering the months after her mother's death and then her father's. Even though she hadn't loved her father, he'd been her last link to anyone. She took another stitch. "Mrs. Bradford says if you have Jesus in your heart, He'll fill that emptiness."

Again Caleb was silent long enough that Geneva didn't think he'd reply.

"I used to believe that, too." He rubbed a hand across his forehead. "It's not that I don't anymore. I think I've been angry at God for a while." He smiled. "I've treated Him as shabbily as I have my mother. I didn't like the hand I'd been dealt, so I came away to sulk."

"You're being pretty hard on yourself." She hesitated again, scared to break the fragile link between them. "What happened in Boston?"

He sighed wearily. "I won't bore you with all the details. The long and short of it is that someone was jealous of what he supposed I had. He was jealous of my position as the son of Caleb Phelps Senior and all the privileges that went along with that." He gave a bitter laugh.

"I was unaware of this…person's jealousy. I trusted him. There was a large amount of money stolen." He paused, his eyes on his clasped hands.

"This person, knowing I was innocent, did everything short of accusing me directly, to make me look like the guilty one. The charges were ludicrous. I thought anybody would see that right away, most of all my own father.

"But, as always, I was wrong about him. After all those years, I still hadn't learned that whatever I did, it would never be enough. Do you know what it's like, to be continually found wanting?"

Before she could reply, he nodded and said softly, "Of course you do. You tried to tell me the other day about your own father, but I was too wrapped up in my own self-pity."

"No—"

"I'm sorry, Geneva."

She shook her head. "You didn't do anything. Tell me about…about Boston."

Caleb gave a bitter laugh. "My father never made any of this public, although the story got out. He confronted me in private, treating me as if my guilt were already proven. He acted as if I'd fulfilled his worst fear. That's what hurt the most, that all along he'd been expecting me to fall. After trying his best to keep me on the straight and narrow, it had all been in vain.

"So, I walked away and came up here," he ended simply, "leaving my father to handle the rumors and aftermath by himself."

He stared ahead of him. "Now they've found proof of my innocence. My father has made a point of speaking to the press and proclaiming it to all and sundry."

"Isn't that good?" she asked hesitantly.

"That's what everyone here keeps telling me. Pastor McDuffie down in the village makes it all sound so simple. Just forgive and forget."

Geneva's whole being longed to reach out and offer him comfort, but she knew it wouldn't be adequate. He needed something more, something she didn't have the power to give him.

Whatever it was, when he did get everything worked out, what then? He'd return to Boston, to his people.

Geneva bent back over her sewing and jabbed the needle into the cloth. "Ouch!" She brought her pricked finger to her mouth.

"I forgot to buy you a thimble!"

"That's all right—" she looked across at him "—I forgive you." She hadn't meant to say that, to make light of all he'd just told her. But suddenly, the two began laughing.

"I'm sorry," she said in her mirth, "I didn't mean it to come out like that."

"You have nothing to be sorry about. You made me laugh, and I'm grateful." In the peaceful silence that followed, he reached across and took the hand she held up to her mouth. He turned it over. Taking her pricked finger in his, he rubbed his thumb lightly against the moist skin. "I should have remembered a thimble."

"I've gotten pricked so many times since I started this, I don't think my skin has space for any more punctures."

He looked at her. "Geneva, all anyone's ever taught you is how to be a man. It's tough learning how to be a lady, isn't it?"

She could scarcely believe the tenderness she saw written in his eyes. She must be dreaming it all—the dress in her lap, the feel of his thumb against her skin, the look in his eyes.

She was going to wake up soon and find it all a cruel joke. She'd fought it so long, fought believing that Caleb might be seeing the person—the woman—inside her, and now all she wanted was to stop fighting her disbelief and yield.

She looked down at their hands, both sun-browned. Was the good Lord telling her to reach out and believe all this was possible?

She cleared her throat. "I guess I'm not doing something so ladylike tomorrow night."

"What's that?"

"I'm going on a herring run with some of the men from the village."

Caleb sat back, intrigued. The look of tenderness was gone, and once again Geneva was left to doubt—was it real, or was it all in her imagination?

She continued speaking, to mask her yearnings. "It's a full moon—a spring tide. We go out to Black's Cove, run a seine along its mouth during the flood, then sit and wait 'til dawn when the tide's on the ebb." She pictured the fishermen as they all fell into action and heard their shouts and the scream of the gulls above them, all as the sun was just beginning to tinge the horizon. "It's some exciting the moment the tide turns."

"Do you mind if I join you tomorrow night?"

Her eyes widened at his request. Then slowly she shook her head, feeling the anticipation begin to build. "No, you're welcome to come along."

Her fears were forgotten as her heart stepped out into the awaiting tide.

As Geneva went about her usual chores the next morning, her heart thrummed at an accelerated beat every time she thought of the coming night. During the worst of the afternoon heat, she sat in the shade of a birch tree, talking to Jake as she sewed on her dress some more.

"What do you think, Jake?" she asked, giving the skirt a shake and spreading it over her outstretched legs. "Can you picture me in one of these? What will Caleb say? Think he'll like it on me?"

As dusk approached, she ate her meal in silence, thinking about rowing out under the night sky, alone with Caleb. She worked a little in her garden in the cool of twilight, then tried to lie down for a nap before midnight, but her thoughts chased each other, tumbling from the previous evening's conversation to the coming night's herring run.

Finally, she tried praying, remembering what Mrs. Bradford had told her about Jesus. He'd promised that when a person prayed, he should believe he would receive the things he asked for, and he would have them.

"Dear Lord, I don't want much." She thought about it, and realized that wasn't true. "Oh, yes, I do want so much, so very much. I want him, Lord. I want Caleb."

Caleb sat across from Geneva in her boat, noting how the full moon illuminated her features. The night was calm, the stars dimmed by the moonlight.

The peapod lay rocking gently at the mouth of the cove. The tide was coming in, higher along the marsh grasses during the full moon than it would be at any other time of the month. Caleb was surprised that Jake wasn't with them, but at the last minute, Geneva had left him behind, saying he'd probably get wound up in the net and get himself drowned.

"Now what?" he asked Geneva.

"We wait for the others to arrive, then we'll string the seine across the mouth of the cove." She turned at the sound of oars. "There they are now. Ahoy!"

"That you, Genevar?" came a voice across the lapping of the waves.

"Yep. That you, Shirl?"

"Right heah. Ozzie hasn't showed up yet. Where is that lazy rascal?"

"Right behind you, makin' sure you don't drift out to sea. Hank's aboahd with me. Tom with you?"

"I'm right heah," echoed another voice from Shirl's boat. "Who've you got with you theah, Ginny?"

"Cap'n Caleb. He asked to come along."

The men chuckled. "Evenin', Cap'n. Glad to have you with us."

"Evening," Caleb answered.

"Ever been on a herrin' run?" Shirl asked, rowing the boat alongside theirs, his oars knocking against the wood of their boat.

"No, can't say as I have. What can I do to make myself useful?"

"For starters, you can make sure Geneva stays in line," Hank quipped from the second boat, which had drawn up on their other side.

"What *else* can I do?"

They all chuckled. Geneva took one of the oars and threatened to hit him over the head with it.

"See, there she goes," one of the men said.

"Enough!" said Geneva. "If I'd known he was going to cause so much trouble, I'd never have brung—brought—the cap'n along tonight."

"We're just havin' a little fun, Ginny. No need to get riled."

"I'll show you fun," she answered. "Just wait 'til you're hanging over the side of the boat trying to steer those little herring, you don't find yourself overboard. I'll be the first to swat you through the gate."

After some more bantering, they finally got to work. Each party took a portion of the seine and dragged it across the mouth of the cove.

"Careful," Geneva told him, "the twine's got to stay straight down. Don't let it get caught on any rocks. Otherwise, the fish'll escape out the bottom."

Caleb could already see the schools of tiny fish swarming below the surface of the water. "There seem to be millions of them."

"Reckon so." She pointed. "See the way they jump up out of the water?"

Sure enough, he heard the *plop-plop* all around him as the silvery fish leaped into the air and fell back down into the water.

The men in their double-enders took up their positions along the seine. Once the net was spread across the mouth of the cove, Geneva turned to Caleb.

"Hope you're good at waiting."

Caleb thought of the years he'd waited for Arabella to be his. "I know how to wait."

"We've got to sit here 'til the tide turns. That'll be just around dawn." She glanced toward the sky. "Won't be long now."

"How will you get the herring?"

"We'll attach another net to this one. It's called a 'stop seine.'" She grinned in the moonlight. "Actually, it's called something else but it's not polite."

"I think we've been through enough together so you can tell me, Geneva."

She sobered at his words, but still didn't explain. "Shirl or one of the others can tell you."

"They seem like good men. How did you get together with them?"

"Through Ezra. The fisherman who taught me most everythin' I know," she explained.

Caleb nodded. Around the cove, the tall, dark silhouette of spruce stood out against the sky. The reflection of moonlight shimmered over the water and bounced off the backs of the fish. He gazed up at the big, pale orb, remembering countless watches aboard ship, in different oceans.

"'Lady Moon, Lady Moon, where are you roving?'" he recited, his glance straying to Geneva sitting opposite him in the stern. "'*Over the sea.* Lady Moon, Lady Moon, whom are you loving? *All that love me.*'"

Geneva's gaze directed itself to the moon as she listened to his words. The moonlight shone on her upraised neck, making him think again of a swan. She was an ugly duckling turning into a swan. He could picture her gracing a ballroom in Boston. Her pale shoulders would rise above a satin gown, her cheeks would glow, her dark eyes would stare at him—

He shifted in the boat, stopping the direction of his thoughts. His gaze went back to the moon. "I remember what a comfort it was on my first sea voyage to look up, so many miles from home, and see the same moon and stars above my head."

"How old were you?" Her voice came softly from the other end of the boat.

"Eight. My father put me aboard a San Francisco-bound clipper. He told the captain to make sure I didn't fall overboard, but for the rest, to make sure I became a man."

"How…how did your mother take it?" she asked hesitantly.

He shrugged in the dim light. "I don't know. She wasn't there to see me off. She did tell me, when we parted at the house, to make sure to make my papa proud. I can still see her kneeling before me, straightening my collar."

"How long did that voyage last?"

"I was gone for a couple of years. By the time I returned, my younger cousin, Ellery, had come to live with us. At least I knew Mother would have someone besides me, so she wouldn't miss me too much."

He risked a glance at Geneva and marveled to see her listening attentively. He didn't know what made him talk like this—possibly the moonlight, and the isolation of a peapod upon the water.

"How did you manage?" she asked him when he fell silent. "You were just a little tyke."

"I served as an apprentice and worked my way up to able seaman, then second mate, first mate, and finally to captain. My father didn't believe in giving family members shortcuts. I had to prove myself every step of the way.

"Unfortunately the other sailors didn't believe this. It didn't set too well with them to have the owner's son in their midst. They taught me good and quick not to be carrying any tales back."

She gave an understanding laugh. "I hope you found someone bigger and tougher to befriend you."

He smiled in agreement. "Eventually, or perhaps I wouldn't be sitting here telling the tale. There was another lad, a few years older than I. He'd already made one crossing, a veteran 'shellback,' whereas I was still a polliwog, having not yet braved the Horn. Yes, Nate considered himself quite a man of the world." Caleb grinned, remembering Nate's bravado when they'd first met. "You saw him when he came up from Boston."

Geneva nodded. "I remember."

"You didn't stick around long enough for me to introduce you."

She turned to look into the water. "I didn't figure you needed me there. The moment you saw him, you seemed to forget all about Haven's End."

Caleb wanted to reach out and take her hand, to tell her that no matter what pull Boston had on him, he'd never forget Haven's End. But he realized what she said was the truth. "I probably did then. It was a bit of a shock to see someone from home so soon."

Caleb went on to tell her about the boyhood friendship he and Nate had formed, how Nate had taught him all about the stars in the sky, the different stars they'd seen when they'd sailed in the Southern Hemisphere, how Nate had guided him around the ports of call in South America, how he'd seen him through the rough passage across the Cape.

He gave a laugh. "And then he showed up here trying to talk me into returning to tell Arabella the truth."

"What is the truth?" she asked softly.

He rubbed a hand across his eyes. "That the man she turned to is the man who virtually framed me."

He heard her sharp intake of breath.

"You mean Ellery's the one who allowed your father to believe the worst of you?"

Caleb nodded, knowing she could see his face in the moonlight.

"How can you bear it?" Her whispered words sounded harsh. "How can you bear knowing she's going to marry the man who took everything away from you?"

He looked across the cove to the shadowy figures huddled in the other boats. The question caught him unawares. If she'd asked him how he'd borne it a few months ago, he could have formulated a response. Now, everything in Boston seemed far away, and he realized how little he'd been thinking of it of late. His gaze rested on Geneva, wondering how much was due to his recent preoccupation with her.

He shook his head. No, he couldn't accept that simplistic answer. He hadn't spent half his adulthood in love with a woman—though it may have been a false, romanticized image—only to be cured in a matter of weeks by a...a...fisherwoman. For all her qualities, for all his admiration and respect of her, she was still that—a simple fisherwoman.

Yet Geneva seemed so self-sufficient and complete in herself. "Don't you ever get lonely?" he asked her abruptly, watching her reaction. She began to shrug, but then stopped as her gaze met his. It was as if the moment demanded honesty of them both.

"Yes," she replied simply. When he said nothing more, she added, "You learn to live with it. Loneliness has become a companion of sorts." She smiled at how that sounded. "So, you see, I'm not really alone."

He smiled in answer, recognizing what she said. He'd felt that constant companion of loneliness since the day he'd arrived. No, he admitted to himself. Far longer than that. Only she had managed to put it into words for him. A simple fisherwoman. The two fell silent. They could hear the murmur of the other men in the boats across the water, as well as the continual lap of the waves against the boat and the slap of the jumping fish hitting the water.

The tide hadn't yet turned. Caleb and Geneva watched the few stars visible in the moon's glow. Caleb told her different legends he'd heard about the constellations from the lands he'd visited. Geneva told him of navigating through the night sky with the old man who'd taught her to fish.

As the moon and stars traversed the sky toward the western horizon and a faint light tinged the opposite shore, Caleb could feel the tension building in those around him. A two-masted Quoddy schooner had come in with the tide, and lay anchored behind them. He could hear the men aboard begin to move about, preparing for the fish that would be loaded soon.

"Where will they take the herring?" he asked Geneva.

"Straight to the cannery for sardines. They set out as soon as the hold is full and head out at full sail. They've got to make it to Eastport with the fish still fresh."

She lifted an oar. "It's almost time. As soon as Shirl gives the signal, we've got to use our oars to move the fish toward him. Bang your oar against the side of the boat to scare the fish toward the center. Shirl will open the gate so they'll swim into the other net."

Just then, they heard Shirl's shout. After that it was pandemonium, as they all yelled and struck their oars at once. The sound was deafening. Caleb could see the fish in a frenzy, seeking the open sea, but instead finding the ebbing tide pushing them against the net.

The men swung their oars into the water along the length of the net, urging the fish toward its center. Caleb watched Geneva and copied her every move. She was kneeling in the boat, swinging her oar. Her hair was plastered to her head, her clothing soaked.

Caleb inched the boat toward the center of the net as he saw the other boats around him do the same. As they neared Shirl's boat, he saw the other seine attached to the net, forming a circle at its opening. The herring swam through the opening as their only escape out of the cove, unaware that they were being trapped in another net.

"Heah they come! No escape for them!" yelled one of the men as he swung his oar like a scythe, and Caleb heard the other name for the stop seine. As fast as the herring filled up the second net, they were scooped up into the awaiting schooner.

The noise was deafening. Water splashed everywhere. Geneva suddenly caught his eye and laughed, a rich, exultant sound, as if to say, *Didn't I promise you it would be exciting?*

In that instant, Caleb realized he could deny it any which way he wanted, but it was more than simple loneliness, it was more than a physical craving for a woman, that kept him coming to Geneva. For the past few weeks, she'd kept him wound as tight as a windlass, and he was only now beginning to get an inkling of just how serious the attraction was.

The whole summer he'd been working side by side with her, the way he'd never done with any woman. He'd only experienced this type of comradeship with the crewmen on a ship.

That was it. Geneva was a *helpmate*. The word came to Caleb out of nowhere, but he realized it described their relationship perfectly. He mouthed the word as his mind tried out the unfamiliar concept.

For a seaman, a woman was someone to see and cherish for short periods of time, to kiss farewell at the beginning of a voyage, whose memory one treasured during the long, lonely voyage, and whose face one sought at journey's end.

For the heir of a shipping empire, a woman was a crowning achievement, to show off in a crowded ballroom and to come home to at the end of a busy day.

His own mother had been like that, an unattainable princess, waving her hankie to him from the pier, at his homecoming from that first voyage. He could barely remember crying himself to sleep, trying to muffle the sounds in his bunk, until his need for her had become a dull ache, fading with each passing year. Now, his mother was someone whom he admired and respected, but whom he didn't confide in.

Geneva was neither princess nor prize. She would be right there, alongside her man, through thick and thin, getting her hands dirty, helping him in all his endeavors, for better and for worse.

For better and for worse. The words hit him like an oar against the head.

After that, Caleb went through the motions of the herring run. Even the sounds of shouts and splashing seemed to ebb, as his attention turned inward. When finally the last fish was scooped up into the net and taken aboard ship, and the boats turned homeward, the sky had gone from gray to brilliant pink to pearly silver as the rising sun disappeared behind a film of mist, the color of the horizon like the inside of a mussel shell, a barely tinted pink and blue. Caleb took the oars silently and directed their own boat homeward.

Chapter Thirteen

Geneva knotted the thread, then brought it to her mouth to break it off. She stuck the needle in the pincushion and removed the thimble from her middle finger. The thimble Caleb had given her. She held it up for a second, smiling.

She remembered how bad he'd felt when she'd pricked her finger. The very next time he'd gone into the village, he'd brought her back the thimble.

She stood and shook out her dress. It was finished. She'd never owned anything so beautiful. She held it against her body, imagining how it would transform her. She'd worn only dull colors for so long, she could scarcely picture herself in the vision of pink and dark blue and white that she held against herself.

She'd never know if she didn't try it on. She took a deep breath, then laid the dress down on the bed, smoothing out the skirt. Slowly she undid the clasps of her overalls and let them fall to the ground. Then she unbuttoned her shirt. It joined her pants. She glanced in distaste at the crumpled pile. For a second she considered burning the heap, but then thought better of it. She knew she'd have to go back to them.

Her life wasn't going to magically change because of one dress.

She looked down at her drawers and chemise, wishing she had nice undergarments to put on under the dress. But all her mother's petticoats had been cut up for pillowcases and rags and towels.

She had the urge to take a bath before letting the new material touch her skin. But she reminded herself this was only a fitting. She'd take it off as soon as she saw how the dress looked.

Finally, she picked up the dress as if it might fall apart as soon as she touched it. But the stitches held. Geneva slipped first one leg, then the other into the full skirt. Her legs felt strange under the skirt, as if she were wearing nothing but air. But she supposed it was the absence of petticoats that made her feel naked.

Next, her arms went into the long sleeves. She began to have her first inkling that something might be wrong with the dress when the sleeves didn't look as fitted as those she'd seen on other women. Her worry grew as she began to button the tiny row of buttons up her front.

Instead of hugging her contours as a dress should, this dress bagged out. The waist hung loose around her. Geneva walked toward her little glass. She took it off its nail. She angled it over her body, catching sight of different parts of the dress.

But she didn't need a full-length mirror to tell her it looked awful.

She looked like a badly repaired rag doll. A caricature of a woman. She was nothing but a misfit, neither man nor woman. She should have known better than to change what she was. Geneva yanked at the baggy bodice, then tried to cinch in the waist with one hand, but it didn't help. The garment looked as ill-fitting as it had a moment ago.

The image came to her of Arabella's perfectly fitting, periwinkle-blue skirt and jacket. A moan escaped Geneva as she thought what Caleb would say if he saw her now.

She couldn't bear the pitying look in his eyes as he surveyed the dress they'd both worked on with such hopes. He'd never be so cruel as to tell her how awful it looked. He'd just look sad, realizing, as he must, that he could never make a woman out of her. What was it they said—you couldn't make a silk purse out of a sow's ear? That about summed it up.

Well, she wasn't going to be the object of someone's pity!

Geneva yanked at the buttons, not caring if she tore the material. She pulled off the dress as fast as possible. Looking around her room, seeking some kind of hiding place, her gaze finally alighted on her trunk. She gathered the dress in a bundle and headed toward the trunk. Pushing everything off its top, she opened the lid. She tossed aside all the carefully packed things, until she could safely place the garment far enough down so that no evidence of it would be visible. She stuffed everything back into the trunk and shut the lid with a *bang*.

If she never had to look at the offending reminder, it wouldn't be soon enough.

Geneva was sitting at Caleb's kitchen table copying a column of new words from her spelling book onto her slate, when his voice interrupted her.

"How's your dress coming?"

It had been about a week since she'd tried it on, and she'd been dreading this moment ever since. In vain she'd hoped that with all the work and activity in between—the harvesting and canning, the berry picking, the haying, all of which Caleb had joined in—the dress would have been forgotten. The *dress*. What an ugly, menacing word it had become, taking on a life of its own, as much a threat to Geneva's well-being as her fear of Caleb's return to Boston.

So, she reacted as she always did when cornered. She shrugged and pretended indifference. "It's coming."

"You should be about finished, shouldn't you? The last time I saw you sewing—" His voice softened, and she could sense the smile on his face, though she didn't dare look up to see for herself.

"—it looked pretty nearly finished. What do you still need to do, the hem? I could help you with that if you like. Just bring it on over some afternoon…"

On and on about the stupid dress. Geneva clutched her chalk so hard against the slate it snapped in two. "Look what you've made me do!" She pushed up from her chair, knocking it over Jake. The dog bounded up with a yelp. "It's just a dress. What do I need one for anyhow? Lived this long without one."

She stood staring at him, her fists clenched at her sides.

Instead of losing his temper, Caleb smiled. "What's the matter, Geneva? Scared to put it on? Afraid all the young men in town will come knocking on your door?"

She turned to stomp out of the kitchen. "Oh, just forget it, will you!"

He was up before she could reach the door.

"No, I will not *forget* it." He took her firmly by the elbow to prevent her escape. "Not until you tell me exactly why you don't want me to see it."

"Because it looks awful on me, that's why!" She glared at him. "Now, are you satisfied? Will you stop pestering me about it?"

"Awful how?" He looked genuinely puzzled. "The pattern was a simple one. The style wasn't really outdated. The color of the fabric suits you."

At his last words, Geneva's mouth trembled. She looked away, afraid she'd break down completely if her anger left her. It was her only shield against the pity she knew would come. She had to get away.

"So, what is it that makes you think it's so awful?"

It was clear he wasn't going to let the subject drop until he knew it all.

"You want to know?" She thrust out her chin at him. "All right, I'll show you! Don't say I didn't warn you." Geneva stormed out of the kitchen, hearing Jake's bark, but ignoring it.

She didn't slacken her pace until she stood once more in front of the chest. He wanted to see the confounded thing, then let him, she fumed, as she threw everything back off the chest and lifted its lid.

He'd see what a waste of time it was to make a woman out of her. Out came the blankets and landed on the floor. She'd known all along what a mistake it was. Out came her mother's wedding dress and fell in a heap on top of the blankets. She should never have let Caleb's soft words fool her into thinking she could be someone she was not. Out came the linens and scattered across everything else.

She grabbed the bunched-up fabric that was her dress. She hated the sight of it. Once again, she flung her trousers and shirt off, and yanked the dress on. With shaking fingers, she fumbled at the buttons. She grabbed up her clothes from the floor and tucked them under her arm. With her work boots still on, she headed back to Caleb's.

By the time she stood in front of him again, her anger had dissolved and she was left with only embarrassment and tattered dignity. She couldn't even look up at him, waiting for his laughter. The silence lengthened as Caleb walked slowly around her.

His words, when they finally came, shocked her into attention. "Take the dress off."

Her head jerked up. He wasn't looking at her, but at a point above her shoulder. "Put it back on inside out."

Then he left the kitchen.

Geneva struggled with the garment, her hands shaking this time not out of anger, but out of fear. Why was she so nervous all of a sudden? Just the shame at his having seen her in such a ridiculous garment? She shivered in her thin undergarments. She felt different, conscious of herself in the captain's house. Referring to him as "the captain" instead of "Caleb" made her feel a little better. It made things less personal.

Geneva turned the dress inside out and quickly shoved it over her head. Her hands trembled so much that she could hardly do up the buttons inside out.

"All finished?"

"Yes," she called out hastily, shaking the skirt around her ankles. She heard Caleb's tread approaching and turned to look out the window toward the sea.

"The only thing wrong with this dress," she heard him say as she followed the flight of a gull across the blue sky, "is the fit, and that should be easily enough fixed."

As he spoke, she felt him tug here and there. She flinched, moving her arms out of his way when he grabbed a piece of material at either side of her waist and pulled. She inadvertently let go of the collar, and the dress gaped open where she had missed the last buttons. She could feel the color rush into her face and down her neck. She kept her eyes fixed on the gull, watching it glide, its wings not even moving, across her field of vision.

"Now, where did I put those extra pins?" she heard him mumble over the rushing in her ears.

He walked over to a table. When he came back, he gave her the pincushion to hold, then stood looking at the front of her dress. She concentrated on the waves in the far-off distance. She spotted a pair of seals, and kept her gaze glued on them until their bobbing heads plunged one last time in the sea, and she could no longer see them.

When she thought she could bear it no longer, he moved and began sticking pins into the sides of her dress. His knuckles and thumb pressed against the tender flesh of her sides.

Caleb concentrated on the fabric between his fingers, trying desperately to ignore the body beneath it. When he'd finished pinning each side of the bodice, he went to work on her arms. Then he stepped back and took a look at the fit.

He surveyed the dress from all angles. Although improved, it still didn't look right. Caleb frowned, not sure what to do. He'd taken in the sides, but the dress still bagged in the front. He'd been right: making a female garment was nothing like making a man's shirt. A man's shirt could hang loose; a woman's bodice was supposed to be contoured.

He knew if he didn't get it right, Geneva would never wear a dress again. He had to prove to her that she could look just like any other young woman. Better, even. But it would mean making sure the top portion of the garment fit like a glove. He tried to picture the women's dresses he'd seen up close. He'd usually been too dazzled by Arabella's presence to stop and examine the workings of her gown.

He approached the matter scientifically. There had to be a way to form a woman's shape out of a flat piece of cloth. His mind went over the old dress they'd taken apart, and then he understood.

He would have to tuck up the fabric at her waist. Caleb stared at Geneva's bodice, wondering how in the world he was going to dare touch her there. He could feel the pounding beginning at his heart and reverberating more and more until it sounded as if his pumping heart lay right between his ears.

Caleb took a deep breath and reached out, not quite sure if he'd hit on the solution. His hands took a piece of material at her waist and pulled it tight. Then he took a pin and stuck it into the material, and then another above that. He worked his way up the material until the fabric lay flush against her. He didn't look at her.

Stepping back, he was able to breathe normally again. The dress did look better on that side. Now for the other side.

When he had finished, the bodice was vastly improved, and he thought the trick would work on the back as well. He circled Geneva and began the same procedure. Then he ordered her to revolve slowly. Looking at the dress, he began to feel a spurt of optimism return.

"This time, we'll just baste everywhere I've pinned. When that's finished, I want you to try it on one more time, to make sure we've taken it in enough."

She nodded. At her serious expression, he couldn't help chucking her under the chin. "Don't look so worried. We'll get through this."

The line of her mouth softened and began to turn upward. He smiled in return. She didn't realize how beautiful she could be, but he'd help her find out.

* * *

Caleb walked back from the village. He'd been to look at the progress on his boat and to stop by the village store to pick up a copy of the weekly paper. Now, as the afternoon shadows lengthened on his walk homeward, he saw Geneva bent over her garden. Jake barked at him, and she looked toward the road, returning Caleb's wave.

He walked into his kitchen, his mind on his boat. He was pleased at the progress. It should be ready by the beginning of the fall. He set his parcels on the kitchen table. The kitchen was empty. Marilla had been and gone. He could smell the lingering scents of a clean house. He glanced at the stove. His dinner was probably sitting in the warming oven.

His empty kitchen. His empty house. The good feeling that had accompanied him home since seeing the frame of his boat dissolved as he surveyed the neat and lifeless kitchen.

In the kitchen in Boston, there was always a staff present. If they weren't working, there'd at least be someone sitting at the table drinking a cup of tea.

Here, Marilla made sure the kitchen was left spotless. Not even a bread crumb escaped her eagle eye. She had set his place on a tray on the table. Knife, fork and spoon, neatly folded linen napkin, crystal glass...

Suddenly, Caleb felt depressed. No matter how tasty the food Marilla left him, Caleb couldn't help comparing it to the savor of food eaten in the company of another human being. He couldn't help remembering the night he'd sat in Geneva's small house, gazing at her smiling face.

He laid his folded newspaper beside the tray and proceeded to the sink to wash up. With a final flick of his hands, he reached for the neatly folded towel and dried them. Instead of replacing the towel, though, he stood for a moment, staring out the window. A boat was sailing past, back to port. He wondered what the men were returning to. Wife, children. Home and hearth. Was he condemned to spend the rest of his life eating alone? Why was he going through this self-imposed exile from all he'd ever known?

He'd even exiled himself from God, he realized, recalling Geneva's simple words about Jesus, and his own lame response. Caleb leaned against the sink, peering at the horizon and sea, as if they held the answers. He got the same feeling he did whenever he attempted to sit down and pen a letter to his mother. He didn't know what to say. It had been so long that he no longer knew how to take up the thread of communication.

Where are You, Lord? he asked the expanse of sky and sea. *Have I walked so far from You that You're incapable of hearing my voice?*

A Scripture he'd learned as a youth came back to him. Something about His yoke being easy, His burden light. *What is Your burden, Lord? To live out the rest of my days here in solitude?*

Forgiveness. The word came to him suddenly, like a non-negotiable item on a contract.

His mind balked at the simple word and he tried to dismiss it from his thoughts. He must have thought of it only because Pastor McDuffie had brought the topic up. It was not some kind of direct command from God.

He turned from the sink and found the oven mitts where Marilla had hung them. He opened the oven door and took out his dinner.

Was he expected to forgive Ellery for setting him up, for trying to destroy his career, for succeeding in destroying his plans to wed the woman he loved? Was he expected to forgive all those who'd believed the false accusations against him?

He'd done so, he argued back to the silent voice. It no longer mattered to him what people had done to him or what they thought of him.

He banged the plate down on the table. Had he forgiven his father for believing Ellery's word over his? Of course. The question persisted. Really forgiven his father for not being the father Caleb had wanted him to be?

He sat down at the table, deciding against taking his food to the sitting room. He removed the cutlery from the tray and began cutting his chop. The question refused to go away, but prodded at his heart like the fork picking at the piece of meat on his plate. By this time, the food held little taste for him. He took a sip of water.

Again, he remembered a lesson learned in a long-ago Sunday service held aboard ship. "Forgive us our trespasses as we forgive those who trespass against us." The message was as unmistakable now as it had been then, delivered by a fiery-tongued captain who'd vividly painted the flames of hell to the eight-year-old Caleb. He'd imagined himself in those very flames if he didn't forgive one of the sailors who had taken the locket with his mother's miniature and threatened to throw it overboard if Caleb ever thought of squealing on any of them for the teasing they gave him.

If we didn't forgive, our heavenly Father couldn't forgive us. The message was clear and immutable.

Is that why he felt this terrible distance from God? Because he hadn't made his peace with his own father?

Caleb stood up, scraping his chair back. He wouldn't be easy until he'd worked this out.

He searched his bookshelves until he found his Bible. Back at the kitchen table, he opened to the gospels, his food forgotten. He knew the Lord's Prayer was in there some-where. In leafing through the pages, he began to read the first gospel he came to, the Book of Matthew. The further he read, the more the words drew him in, soothing him in a way he'd never experienced. The life and teachings of Jesus began to speak to him in a personal way. By the time Caleb raised his head from the text, he felt the words "be of good comfort" were being directed to him personally.

He'd believed he was free of the past, but now realized it would take more than just shoving it behind him. He wasn't sure what the next step entailed, but one thing he did know—he smoothed down the Bible's black leather cover with his palm—he needed to continue seeking the answer between the pages of this book.

Caleb glanced down at his cold food, the pine table be-neath his hand, across to the window at the ocean beyond. He thought of the things he'd lived since coming here to Haven's End and realized they had been good. No matter what the future held, he was glad he'd come. He no longer felt the time had been without purpose.

He thought of Geneva. How did she fit into his life?

He'd never known anyone quite like her. He'd never had a woman for a friend, the way she'd become. She'd seen him at his best and worst—more worst than best. How would she react if she saw him in his former life in Boston? It was one thing to put a dress on her, teach her the basics of reading. It would do for a life in Haven's End, but the demands of Boston were far greater.

What was he thinking? He shook his head vigorously as if to banish what he *might* be thinking.

He wondered how she was coming with the dress. Would he have to demand to see it, as he had the last time?

With a sigh, he took a forkful of the hardened potatoes. Laying open the newspaper beside him, he began scanning the headlines.

The paper was published in the next town, so most of the news was unfamiliar to Caleb. A fire put out at the lumber mill, the launching of a ship at the shipyard, the names of the ships in port that week, an ad for the new goods available at the local emporium. Caleb flipped desultorily through the pages. Weddings, obituaries, tidal chart, planting news…

An announcement in the bottom right corner of the page he was ready to turn caught his eye. The local farmer's club was holding a dance and supper at the end of the week. Caleb pictured the rustic country dances, the girls being swung around by their partners.

He pictured Geneva making her debut into local society at such an event…. The idea appealed to him. The dance was close enough to get there in a day, far enough away for her not to have to face all the people who knew her, at least not until she was ready. Who knew, she might even attract the attention of some young farmer or fisherman?

He frowned at the thought. He knew it was for the best. Whatever he was feeling didn't matter. It was too far-fetched to put into words. The important thing was not to hurt Geneva in any way. It would only be a matter of time before people began gossiping if they saw her in his company.

All he had to do now was figure out how to get her to the dance—taking her himself was out of the question. Maybe with some local family? And then he must convince her to go. He immediately pictured her chin thrust out and her eyes flashing in outrage.

And last he must make sure the dress was passable. He'd promised himself to help her better her life, and he intended to keep that promise. Even if that meant securing her future to a nice, young man who would protect her from the Lucius Tuckers of Haven's End.

Why couldn't he himself protect her?

But Caleb shut that voice off as firmly as he would an annoying drip at the pump. He'd done enough soul searching for an evening. For a lifetime.

Chapter Fourteen

"You want me to *what?*" Geneva stared at Caleb in complete disbelief. She was standing in his sitting room in the basted dress. She couldn't see herself in any mirror, but Caleb had assured her the dress looked fine. He'd just made a few more adjustments with pins before stepping back and expressing approval.

That was right before he said she needed to try the dress out on the dance floor.

"You heard me" was all he replied, before walking away from her.

He came back holding out the weekly newspaper. "Show me how well you can read." With that he thrust the paper into her hands.

She frowned at him in question, taking the paper and staring down at it. He'd folded it over so that all she was looking at was a quarter of a page. She scanned the words, making out several. When she said nothing, his finger pointed her toward a square at the bottom.

"Sat."

"That stands for 'Saturday.'"

"Saturday," she repeated. "Night. Au—"

"August," he prompted her.

"Saturday night. August tenth. Come join the m-uh-sic music." She continued downward. "Dance…to…the… s-ow-nd…of fid-dle and banj-o."

Caleb smiled. "You're doing very well."

She shook the paper at him. "What does this have to do with me?"

"Exactly what I told you before. I read this announcement and thought it would be the perfect time for you to try out your new dress."

"You want me to go to a dance?" She knew her face looked just as horrified as her voice sounded. At his nod she began backing away from him. "You—you can't be serious."

But the look in his eye said otherwise. He began advancing toward her with a wicked grin on his face. She kept stepping backward until she bumped into the door frame.

"It won't help you to run away."

"What would I do at a dance?" The mere idea of it was ludicrous. Why, she didn't even know *how* to dance. And even if she did, a person had to have a partner, didn't she?

"You would dance, the same as everyone else there."

She folded her arms across her chest. "I don't dance."

"You *don't* or you *won't*?"

She looked away from his too-understanding eyes. "I don't know how," she enunciated between gritted teeth.

"I can teach you."

"Why should you want to?" she mumbled, looking away. Why, indeed, did he do so much for her? Her heart yearned for a certain answer, but she was afraid to hear what the reality might be.

He approached her and took her by the elbows. "Because I want to show you that you're no different from any young lady there. Look at me, Geneva." His fingertip forced her chin upward. "You have no reason to feel afraid to go to a dance. You've as much right to be there as anyone else."

She gazed into his eyes. His words recalled Mrs. Bradford's. "You are a child of the most high God." Why indeed did she have to feel ashamed? Suddenly her heart began to sing. Caleb had called her a lady. Did that mean she was equal to Arabella in his eyes?

Before she knew what was happening, he was swinging her into his arms and swept her around the floor, repeating, "One, two, three…one, two, three…" She stumbled after him. They ended up on his new sofa, laughing, their legs extended outward.

"I can hardly walk in this rig." She took a bunch of her skirt in each hand. "Now you expect me to dance in it!"

"It's not so difficult if you know how to count up to three."

She gave him a sidelong look. "I don't know…. You've only taught me the alphabet. We never went over any numbers."

He laughed again and she joined him, taking pleasure from watching his enjoyment. Then he rose and reached for her hand.

"Let this be your first arithmetic lesson—the basics of the waltz. There'll be some set dances as well, but those are even easier. Someone will be calling out the steps, and if you watch for a little while, you'll catch on."

He showed her where to put her hands, and her hand trembled as she laid it on his shoulder. She glanced at him, but he seemed intent on counting as he showed her where to put her feet.

"I shall talk with Maud Bradford about taking you. I know she'd love to. She's grown quite fond of you. And I shall be there. You must promise to save me a dance…."

She hardly heard what he was saying. If dancing meant she could touch him this way, and feel his arm around her, then she would gladly do it. She'd do it forever.

It must be only she who felt as if her heart would burst with longing. How could she wait until Saturday night?

On Friday afternoon, Geneva stood in Mrs. Bradford's parlor, holding her folded dress in a satchel in her hands. She cleared her throat. "I—I brought something to show you."

"Is it the dress, my dear?" Mrs. Bradford smiled in anticipation from her rocking chair. "Caleb told me you had been working on one."

Geneva perched on the edge of a seat near the rocker and carefully removed the dress from the satchel. "Yes." With that, she unfolded the dress.

"Oh, my, that's lovely." The older woman fingered the cloth as Geneva held it up for her. "You say you made it yourself?"

"Yes. It's the first thing I ever sewed. I—I just learned."

Mrs. Bradford gave her a look of admiration. "I'm glad. I wish I'd known you didn't know how to sew. Bessie and I could have taught you. It's certainly a useful thing to know."

"Did I hear someone say my name?" Bessie marched in carrying a tea tray.

"Look at Geneva's first sewing project! Isn't it beautiful?"

Bessie set the tray down. Taking her half-moon glasses out of an apron pocket, she walked over to inspect the garment. Geneva's heart sank. All her pleasure in the dress would disappear after Bessie had raked it over the coals.

Bessie took it from her and held it up to the light, with a frown. "It looks well enough made. Pretty material. It could use a bit of ribbon and lace, I'd say."

Before Geneva could take the garment back and stuff it in her satchel, Mrs. Bradford exclaimed, "That's a wonderful idea! Could you see what I might have at my sewing table? I'll look in my sewing basket." Already she was groping at the side of her rocker for the basket.

Mrs. Bradford looked over at Geneva when she had the basket in her lap. "You don't mind a couple of old women interfering, do you? If we just add a little lace at the collar and cuffs, it will soften the dress. Not that the dress isn't lovely as it is. It will just add a little feminine touch to it."

Mrs. Bradford didn't need to explain any further. Geneva clearly remembered the cascade of lace at Arabella's throat and wrists. She nodded to the older woman. "No, it's all right. I appreciate your help. Isn't it too late to add anything to the dress?" Suddenly she was afraid Mrs. Bradford and Bessie would want to keep the dress for a few days.

"Oh, no," Mrs. Bradford answered with a laugh. "We'll have it done in a jiffy, in time for tomorrow evening. Women do this all the time. We're rarely satisfied with a dress just as it is, but we like to fuss with ribbons and lace until we have it to our liking."

Bessie returned with a length of navy-blue grosgrain ribbon and some white lace.

"Oh, just the thing." Mrs. Bradford took it from her, seeming as excited as a child on Christmas.

Together the two older women began clipping at the dress with their sharp little scissors, showing Geneva how the lace would be inserted at the collar and cuffs, and how the ribbon would be stitched at the edge of each.

Geneva sat, marveling at what they were doing.

"Now, you go try this on and see what you think." Bessie thrust the dress at her in a no-nonsense way.

Before Geneva could protest, Bessie shooed her through the doorway into the washroom. Geneva took a moment to admire the elegant porcelain washbasin, the plush towels, the pink soaps, comparing everything to her own primitive facilities of outdoor pump and privy. She held a soap carved in the shape of a rose to her nose and inhaled. It really did smell like a rose.

Then she remembered where she was. Quickly, she removed her clothes, glad the other ladies couldn't see her shabby undergarments. She went back out into the parlor in her bare feet.

The two women looked at her. Geneva stopped, embarrassed, afraid the dress looked as horrible as the first time. Her toes curled on the soft carpet. She wished the dress had pockets—there was nowhere to shove her hands.

"Come here, child," Mrs. Bradford said.

When Geneva hesitated, Bessie spoke up. "Come along, girl, where we can see you."

When she stood before them, Bessie continued to eye the dress critically through her glasses. She fussed at the lace at Geneva's wrist, then tugged at the ribbon at her neck.

Mrs. Bradford didn't touch her. She had her hands together at her mouth. Was she going to laugh? But her expression looked serious. There was something of wonder in her expression.

"Turn around, dear," she said.

Geneva complied, revolving slowly.

When she faced Mrs. Bradford once more, the older lady was smiling. "My, my." She shook her head. "I always knew you would look lovely in the right dress, but you've outdone my imaginings."

Geneva couldn't believe what she was hearing. *Lovely?* She'd only hoped to pass inspection, but the way Mrs. Bradford was looking at her made her believe she might not shame Caleb by being seen on his arm.

"What do you think, Bess?" Mrs. Bradford turned to her cook with a conspiratorial wink.

Bessie pursed her lips, taking a step back when the lace and ribbon hung to her satisfaction. "I think Miss Geneva looks mighty pretty."

Geneva stared at the cook, scarcely crediting the words coming from the woman's mouth.

"She needs to dress her hair, though, and get some color in her cheeks. A smile wouldn't hurt."

Bessie went down the list, and Geneva felt almost relieved at hearing the return of Bessie's critical speech. It made her believe that perhaps Bessie had spoken the truth when she'd said Geneva looked pretty.

Mrs. Bradford was staring at Geneva's toes peeking out from beneath her hem. "Do you have the proper shoes to wear with a dress?"

Geneva hadn't even thought about her footwear. Her spirits sank as she pictured herself on the dance floor in her heavy boots.

"I have some shoes. Our feet are probably similar in size." Mrs. Bradford tapped a finger against her lips. "What about petticoats? Would you like one?"

Geneva didn't know what to say. The look in her eyes must have answered for her, for Mrs. Bradford spoke softly to Bessie. "Why don't we see what we can find?"

The two women left her standing there, fingering the lace at her wrist. The dress now felt snug—tighter around her chest and looser around her legs—than anything she'd ever worn. She wished she could see it for herself.

When the other two women returned, it was Geneva's turn to marvel at the fine, lacy undergarments and the silky softness of the kid boots with the little buttons running up the side. On top of the pile, nestled among the satin and lace, lay a little bottle.

At her questioning look, Mrs. Bradford smiled. "A little rosewater. There's nothing like a dab of perfume to make one feel feminine."

The boots were a tight fit, but the petticoats were just the right length. She tried her best to thank Mrs. Bradford, but the older woman just waved a hand at her.

"It gives me joy to see you so pretty. I'm so glad I shall have the honor of taking you to your first dance. What a wonderful thing that Caleb thought of it."

Geneva swallowed and found the courage to ask the question that burned on her lips. "May I...may I look in a glass?"

Mrs. Bradford glanced at Bessie in chagrin. "Oh, my! Why didn't we think of that? Of course you may see what your new dress looks like. Come along, I'll show you the way myself."

When Geneva stood in front of the heavily carved oblong mirror in Mrs. Bradford's dressing room, she could only gape at herself. The person staring back at her wasn't the person she knew. The dress hugged the curves of her body, contours she'd always tried to hide. Her bosom was so apparent and her waist so small in comparison. She could only stare.

Mrs. Bradford stood behind her. She laid her hands gently on Geneva's shoulders and smiled at her in the mirror. "You are a lovely young woman. Don't you ever forget it."

"Thank you, ma'am."

Mrs. Bradford squeezed her shoulders before stepping away again. "I can't wait until tomorrow night. It's just the occasion to try out this beautiful dress." As Geneva continued to admire the dress, Mrs. Bradford added, "How about coming to church with me on Sunday morning? I think the people of Haven's End should be permitted to see the new Geneva."

Geneva looked dumbly at Mrs. Bradford's beaming face, not wanting to disappoint her but not sure what to say. She thought of the dance Saturday night. What if the dress were wrinkled or dirty by Sunday? Worse yet, how could she enter the church? She'd have to walk down the aisle; all the people she knew would just turn in the pews to stare at her.

"I don't know, ma'am. I—I'll think about it."

"Of course. If you decide, just come on Sunday at ten o'clock. I'll keep an eye out for you and save a place for you beside me."

Caleb stood on Geneva's step, his hand poised to knock. It was late afternoon. The August sun was still high in the sky. It would remain light for a while, but it was time to drive her to Maud's as he had arranged.

The aroma of roses filled the warm air. Caleb turned toward the vines covering her doorway. It was laden with pale pink, five-petaled flowers. On impulse he plucked a stem, getting pricked in the process. He sucked on his finger, reflecting how like the rose Geneva was. Soft…and prickly.

He knocked on the door, loudly. At her "Come in," he entered. He scanned the room, fearing for a second he'd walked in on her toilet. But no, she was fully dressed. She sat at a chair at her table. A small mirror was propped against her kerosene lamp. Her hands were raised above her head, holding her hair up.

Her dark eyebrows scowled at him from under one of her arms. "What are you looking so fierce for?" he asked, walking toward her.

"I can't get this hair of mine to stay put."

"Is that all? Here, let's see what we can do."

She lowered her arms, releasing her hair, which immediately fell down her back. "I think I've been here an hour, but whatever I do, it just slips out. I might as well just braid it the way I usually do."

Caleb hardly heard what she said. He was looking at the mass of dark hair down her back. Cascading ebony. He saw her reflection in the mirror on the table. He'd never seen her like this before. She always wore her hair tightly pulled back in a braid, except for the one time it had been in a loose knot on her head. But that had been for only an instant, almost like a dream he'd managed to convince himself had never actually taken place....

Now she sat before him. He could reach out to her, feast his eyes and hands. Without a word, he set down his things, then reached for her hairbrush.

With long strokes, he pulled the brush through her hair. It was glossy, thick and straight, reaching almost to her waist. He set the brush down, then plunged his fingers into her hair. It was slippery as silk. He pulled it upward, attempting a knot. He watched her face. Large brown eyes, framed by inky lashes and arching black brows, dominated her face. Her nose was arrow straight. Her lips were red and looked temptingly soft. He concentrated once more on her hair.

He rolled it clumsily in his hands, then picked up a hairpin. When he'd stuck in all the ones lying on the table, he reluctantly let go of her hair and stepped back. Geneva turned her head back and forth doubtfully. "I hope it won't fall out."

He thought of all the women in Boston and their intricate coiffures. "It shouldn't if it's pinned up right."

"I don't know." Even as she spoke, gravity began its work on her heavy tresses, and they began to fall.

He wanted to laugh, but refrained when he saw the consternation on her face. If he weren't careful, she'd burst into tears, or even refuse to go at all. He wanted to ask her how she'd managed to keep her hair up the day he'd seen her in the tub, but thought better of mentioning that day.

Instead, he reached for the hairpins sticking out of her hair and helped her pluck them out. Once again, he brushed it smooth.

"Why don't you wear it down?" he asked. "Just tied back with a ribbon?"

She looked uncertain, but finally reached across the table to rummage in her sewing basket until she found a length of dark blue ribbon, which she held out to him. He took it, his hand coming into brief contact with hers, sending a sensation through his body.

He pulled the ribbon under her hair, feeling the downy softness of her nape, and formed a knot with a bow atop it. She reached up a hand to touch it, meeting his gaze in the mirror.

"I don't know. Is it proper?"

"It looks fine," he assured her, not caring whether it was proper or not.

When her fingers grasped an end of the ribbon as if to pull, he said, "No, leave it." He saw her looking at him through the mirror and realized his words had come out like a command. The last thing he wanted was to have her put her hair in a braid.

Slowly, she let go, her hands going to rest in her lap. She looked as young and demure as a schoolgirl. That relieved his mind somewhat. He'd spent too much time as it was debating the merits and drawbacks of having her go to the dance. What if it was a disaster? He'd told himself over and over that it was harmless. Few people would recognize her in the town of Hatsfield. She might even meet an eligible young man or two, who wouldn't know anything of her life here. If all else failed, Mrs. Bradford would be there to help Geneva through any difficulties.

Putting aside the ongoing mental debate, he turned his attention to the items he'd set on the table earlier.

"Here, I brought you something for your outfit." He handed her the parcel.

Her eyes widened as she twisted around in the chair. "For me?" She took the brown paper package in her hands. Instead of opening it, she sat staring at it.

"Aren't you going to open it?"

She nodded her bent head, her fingers fiddling with the string around it.

"Here." He handed her a pair of shears from her work-basket.

She cut the twine. Slowly, as if handling the most fragile object, she unwrapped the paper. He heard her indrawn breath as she looked down at the shawl.

A navy-blue paisley shawl. He'd had to ride all the way to Hatsfield earlier in the week to purchase it.

"It's beautiful." She reached out her hand, and then stopped as if afraid to touch it.

He took the shawl in his hands and unfolded it. "Try it on."

She stood, her back to him. He draped the shawl around her shoulders. As she pulled it around herself, he took her hair once more in his hands and released it from the shawl. Reluctantly, he let it go, and stepped back.

Slowly, she turned around, her eyes lowered. She lifted them, meeting his gaze.

"You did something to the dress."

"Mrs. Bradford sewed on the lace." She lifted up her wrists, opening the shawl. "Maybe it's too much—"

Now it was his turn to draw in his breath. This was the first time he was seeing her finished dress. The bodice molded her body, emphasizing her slim waist and arms. The narrow rim of lace at the neck and wrist took away the severity of the dress. It drew attention to the slim column of her neck and her long, tapering fingers. The full pink skirt, dotted with dark blue and white, encased her long legs. He could imagine it swinging around her ankles as she danced.

Without a word, he picked up the small cluster of wild roses he'd picked, two buds and one half-opened, and one of the forgotten hairpins. He twirled the flowers. "They reminded me of you." With the back of his fingers he touched her cheek. "Petals as soft as your skin. Like touching the very air." He deliberately pressed his thumb against one of the thorns. "But deadly…ready to defend itself at the merest threat."

He broke off the thorn, then placed the posy in her hair, above her ear, securing it with a pin. The color was perfect, complementing the tint in her cheeks as well as the rose of her dress.

Taking her elbow, he led her outside to the horse and buggy he'd hired.

What had he gotten himself into? he wondered as he helped her up and breathed in the scent of rosebuds in the warm air. Try as he would to deny it, he knew taking her to this dance was only tightening the ties that bound them together.

Chapter Fifteen

Geneva hesitated at the doorway to the dance hall. Although the Farmer's Club in Hatsfield—about an hour's ride from Haven's End—was holding the dance, she was suddenly afraid of meeting someone from her village. What would people say, seeing her at a dance?

She glanced at Mrs. Bradford, who patted her arm.

"You look beautiful."

"What's the matter?" Caleb asked, coming up behind her.

She looked grimly at the couples laughing and talking around the edges of the large hall. "You know what they say—when the crane attempted to dance with the horse, she got broken legs."

"Geneva Samantha Patterson. I'm amazed at you. Are you going to tell me at this late date that you're scared?"

She glared at him. Seeing the twinkle in his eyes, she couldn't help smiling back.

"That's better. You're not someone who backs down from a challenge out of fear. Remember, you haven't spent all this time perfecting that dress, just to let it hang on a hook."

He escorted Mrs. Bradford and her into the room, which

was rapidly filling up with local families. As the musicians warmed up, the sound of discordant instruments rose above the buzz of voices. Geneva dared a look around, and began to relax when she didn't recognize anyone.

Caleb led them to some empty chairs, then turned to help her off with the shawl. For a second, she resisted, wishing she could keep it clutched around her shoulders, as if it would hide her from view. But she made an effort to sit back in her chair and breathe deeply.

Once the music started, she could watch the dancers. Everyone formed their sets as if they knew exactly what they were doing. She tried to follow the words of the caller and the steps of the dancers, but it seemed impossibly complicated to her.

Caleb remained standing behind the ladies and began talking with the men at his side. Several people stood or sat around the sides of the cleared space of the dance floor. Geneva found herself tapping her foot to the lively beat of the piano and fiddles and banjo as they played "Oh, Susanna."

When the set ended and the next dance was called out, Caleb bent and took her hand. "Come on. We'll get in on this one."

She pulled back. "Not yet."

"Nonsense. Come along. You can't learn by watching. You have to jump right in. Besides, this one's an easy one, the Virginia Reel."

"Go on, Geneva," Mrs. Bradford urged.

Geneva dragged her feet as she was tugged forward by Caleb. Caleb put her between two ladies, then stood in the row of men opposite, giving her a reassuring smile as they waited for the music to begin.

The music was lively, and Geneva found there was time to carry out the moves by listening carefully to the caller and watching the other dancers. Geneva watched as the first couple in the line swung each other around, then joined arms with the couple next in line.

By the time the man diagonally across from her stepped forward to swing her around, she not only felt capable of carrying out the swing, but also was anticipating it with pleasure. She smiled as the two pivoted to face her, her smile growing broader as she approached Caleb and took his arm. The two swung, then separated, turning to the next couple in the line. By the end of the set, she was sashaying with the best of them.

Then came a schottische. Caleb took her hand and led her into position. The music was slow enough for her to follow his lead without too many mistakes. Even when she gained confidence, she was still too focused on conforming to his steps, to be conscious of the fact that she was in his arms.

Another line dance followed, to the lively tune of "Turkey in the Straw." Geneva and Caleb stayed on the dance floor for every dance after that. Partners changed with easy familiarity, and Geneva found herself enjoying the hand-clapping, foot-stomping camaraderie of the dance hall.

Suddenly, she found herself face-to-face with a young man, who looked familiar, though she couldn't place him right away. He seemed glad to see her, so she smiled and accepted his invitation to the next dance. She saw Caleb over the young man's shoulder, heading toward her, but when he noticed she was partnered, he changed his course and approached one of the young women sitting on the sidelines. Geneva felt a small pang when she saw their set had already filled up and he would be in another one.

"You don't remembah me, Ginny, do you?" the young man asked with a smile, while they stood waiting for the music to begin.

She hesitated. "You're from Haven's End, aren't you?"

He nodded enthusiastically. "Sam Giles. Ira Giles' son, on the Mill Road."

"Oh, yes." She remembered a tall, gangly adolescent on his father's fishing schooner some years back. This Sam Giles was taller and still gangly, but with the assurance of a full-grown man. "You went away, didn't you?"

The music began and all he could answer was "Yep." When they came together, he continued. "I left home when I was eighteen. Went to sea for a few years, but didn't really take to that life— I almost didn't recognize you. You look mighty fetchin' this evening."

"Thank you," she murmured, wondering if he was finding it incredible that she was the same "Salt Fish Ginny" he had known as a boy. But he made no reference to her past.

Instead he filled in the gaps of his own life each time they stepped close to each other. "Now I'm back. Living in Hatsfield. I got me a job at the lumbah mill."

Geneva shook her head in wonder. She couldn't believe she was conversing in such a friendly fashion with someone she'd grown up with. Not that she'd known him that well. He'd lived up at the head of the bay. But she'd seen him on the wharf off and on, or at the village store. He and a group of boys his age would tease her, but only when they were out of her father's hearing, since they were afraid of him.

When the caller announced the last dance before the break for supper, Caleb stepped up to her and took her hand.

Sam gave her a wink and smile as he relinquished her to Caleb. "Be seein' ya."

The fiddles began a strain for a waltz. Caleb took her in his arms the way they'd practiced in his sitting room, and she forgot all about Sam Giles. She placed her hand in Caleb's, feeling his encouraging squeeze as he looked at her, a smile playing at the corners of his mouth.

"Just pretend we're back at home practicing."

She looked in his eyes, marveling at the thought of just the two of them, in a place called "home," holding each other. She didn't know how she followed the music or the steps. Everything faded except the feel of his hand on hers, his other hand on the small of her back, hers on his shoulder. He looked unbearably handsome, in his dark jacket and starched white collar with its dark string tie. But she didn't dare look any farther than the smooth jaw and cleft chin. The interval was magical, as if all her dreams were culminating in one brief space of time. She didn't know how she could keep from bursting with happiness.

As the last notes ended and the other couples began breaking apart, Caleb held her an instant longer, loath to let her go. If they were all alone under a starlit sky, he knew he would kiss her. Her face glowed, her lips parting as if in anticipation.

The caller's voice boomed out behind them, announcing the refreshments and supper being served below stairs. Caleb reluctantly released Geneva. "I guess I should take you back to Mrs. Bradford," he said, his voice sounding strange and unsure.

She nodded. "I guess so."

He laid a hand against her back, needing to keep the connection between them unbroken. They maneuvered through the milling crowd of acquaintances greeting each other, as they headed toward Mrs. Bradford, all the while maintaining contact with each other. Caleb could feel the warmth of Geneva through her dress. He remembered the feel of her cheek earlier in the evening against his fingertips. Her back, too, would feel just as soft.

He escorted the ladies down the stairs to the ground floor. There were several long tables set up, and Caleb led them toward the most vacant section, in the far rear corner, hoping it would remain unoccupied. He helped Geneva and Maud into their seats, then sat beside Geneva, hoping it was not too obvious that he was her partner, but not wanting to have even the table separating them.

"I'm so glad you had a chance to dance," Mrs. Bradford was telling Geneva. "You must be hungry now. How lovely everything looks. Thank you so much, Caleb, for bringing us this evening."

Before he had a chance to reply, a shrill voice came across the din. "Is that you, Geneva?"

Caleb recognized the farmer's wife from up the hill, and groaned inwardly. By tomorrow noon, word would be all over Haven's End of their attendance at the dance. He gave Geneva a reassuring smile.

"Hello, Mrs. Stillman. Mr. Stillman," Mrs. Bradford greeted the couple, as Geneva nodded to the tall, quiet man following his buxom wife. Behind them came five younger versions of the farmer and his wife—their children, Caleb presumed, watching the three young men and two young women stand awkwardly in back of their parents.

"Why, I never!" Mrs. Stillman exclaimed, crossing her hands over her chest. "You're all dressed up, Geneva. Look at her, Asa. Did you ever see such a thing?" When he shook his head, she turned to Geneva. "Stand up, child, and let us look at you. Oh, my. Turn around." Her forefinger directed Geneva to rotate.

"Who would've thought! Oh, my goodness. But your hair! Just hanging down like that?"

Geneva sat down again. "I couldn't get it to stay up."

"Well, no matter. Sarah'll come by tomorrow to show you how to dress it, won't you, Sarah?" Mrs. Stillman turned to the oldest-looking, flaxen-haired girl behind her. The girl merely nodded, her gaze still on Geneva.

"The dress is lovely, perfectly lovely," Mrs. Stillman continued. "Haven't I told you all along to stop dressing like a man?"

Mrs. Stillman pulled a chair out across from them, turning her attention to Mrs. Bradford. "You brought her to the dance? Oh, how nice of you. If we'd known she was coming, we could have brought her ourselves."

Caleb's heart sank. So much for a quiet supper. Mr. Stillman took the chair opposite Mrs. Bradford, with a nod to Caleb. Caleb returned the nod. He'd made the farmer's acquaintance during the week of haying. He respected the man, and his wife as well, he admitted grudgingly. They were good neighbors to Geneva.

Their offspring arranged themselves along the length of the table as the servers began bringing in platters of food.

Mrs. Stillman asked Geneva a battery of questions concerning the confection of the dress. To her credit, Geneva was holding her own, responding truthfully but with a minimum of information.

"Your dear mother's fabric? Did you hear that, Asa?" Mrs. Stillman tapped her husband on the arm, taking her gaze from Geneva only long enough to get her husband's attention. "The dress is made from the last bolt of fabric Marie Patterson purchased, God rest her soul. And you kept it all this time?" Mrs. Stillman focused on Geneva once more.

To make Caleb's evening complete, a young man stepped over to Mrs. Stillman and asked if the seat beside her were taken. At her reply, he pulled out the chair and sat down, diagonally across from Geneva. He nodded a greeting to the Stillman family. Caleb frowned, recalling the man who had just danced with Geneva and had carried on a very friendly conversation with her.

Mrs. Stillman had no doubts about his identity. "Samuel Giles, is that you?" At the young man's nod and smile, she opened her eyes wide. "Not young Sam from over by the dam?" Mrs. Stillman's face lit up. "When did you get all grown up? Went to sea, didn't you? Why, last time I saw you, you were the village's most mischievous young lad. Asa, children, Geneva, you all remember young Samuel?"

Caleb sat back, drumming his fingers on the tablecloth. Just what he needed, a village reunion. As he half listened to Mrs. Stillman's recitation of all that had occurred in Haven's End for the last decade, Caleb's good mood evaporated, leaving behind a vague dissatisfaction. He watched the rest of the tables fill up. Everyone was talking and laughing merrily together as they helped themselves to the food. Their families went back for centuries. Their ancestors intermarried and were buried in the same cemetery. Myriad generational ties bound them.

As he felt the loneliness of an outsider enshroud him, he asked himself if these people were so different from his own family in Boston. The Phelpses had come over with the Pilgrims and settled in Boston by the early eighteenth century, and today they associated themselves with only those families of similar lineage. Arabella's family had qualified.

Suddenly his family's whole Boston social circle appeared incredibly stultifying. He'd accepted it up 'til now without question. It occurred to him that it was an absurd presumption to base a marriage on one's family's longevity in a particular geographical area.

Geneva would be like a breath of fresh air in the midst of those Boston Brahmins.

His glance strayed to her. He'd achieved what he'd set out to—help Geneva gain acceptance in her community. Now she sat basking among her own. This was what he'd wanted, wasn't it? He should be feeling proud of himself. Instead, he felt only empty and unnecessary.

He stabbed at his string beans, glaring at them as if they alone were responsible for the evening's fiasco.

"So, you came back!" Mrs. Stillman beamed at Sam. "But you've decided to settle in Hatsfield rather than Haven's End? I suppose the village is just too small for you after seeing the world," she added with a laugh. "Hatsfield is a thriving town, with a lot more to offer an ambitious young man!"

"Just exactly what is it you do?" Caleb asked, looking across the table at Sam.

If the young man noticed any hostility in Caleb's tone, he didn't show it, but answered eagerly, "I got a job at the sawmill. The pay's good. If I do well enough, I might make foreman one day."

The boy sounded like a real bundle of energy and enthusiasm. Once, Caleb had sounded that way, too. He remembered his own eagerness when he'd left the sea and begun working in his father's office. He'd had all kinds of ideas, convinced he'd make it to the top on merit alone and not by right of birth. No task was too big, no undertaking too daunting, if it would please his father.

That attitude hadn't gotten him very far.

As the dinner plates were cleared away by members of the Farmer's Club, and people sat back, waiting for their coffee cups to be refilled and the wide wedges of blueberry pie to be set before them, Caleb continued listening to the interchange between Mrs. Stillman and "young Samuel." The appellation was beginning to make Caleb feel as if he himself were ancient at the age of thirty-three.

"I admire a young man with gumption, don't you, Geneva?" Mrs. Stillman asked her.

Geneva nodded, looking startled at finding her opinion called for.

"How old are you now, Sam?" Mrs. Stillman continued her inquiry.

"I'll be twenty-six next month," he answered, immediately taking a large bite of pie.

"Did you hear that, Geneva? Twenty-six. How old are you now, Geneva? Twenty-two, twenty-three?"

"She's twenty-three."

Mrs. Stillman turned to stare at Caleb, her mouth agape.

To further aggravate her, he deliberately added, "She'll be twenty-four next May."

Now, why had he done that? Wasn't it just lovely that a nice, young, eligible man with steady employment was sitting there looking at Geneva as if he'd never seen an attractive woman? Caleb slammed his coffee cup down. He should be pleased as punch at how well his scheme for turning Geneva into a lady was working out.

Mrs. Stillman shut her mouth with a snap and turned away from Caleb. She wasn't silent for long, however. "Did you hear that, Sam, Geneva's just twenty-three?" Before the young man could comment on the fact, she added, "Have you thought about settling down?"

Caleb's fork clattered down on his plate. Would the woman never cease? Before they even got up from the table, she'd have maneuvered young Sam into proposing to Geneva there in front of all seven witnesses of the Stillman clan.

"Oh, yes, ma'am. I mean, I nevah did 'fore now. But, as a man gets older—" young Giles sat back, his pie plate scraped clean, and took a deep, satisfied breath "—he starts thinking about having a place of his own, raisin' a family."

Caleb's own breath caught somewhere in his windpipe. "I think I need a little air. Will you excuse me?" He pushed his chair back, nodding at the company present. When he stood, he looked at Geneva. "Care to come with me?" His eyes brooked no refusal, but not wishing to create a scene, he didn't know what he'd do if she declined. He could only pray she would acquiesce quietly.

He was pleasantly surprised when she rose at once. The constriction around his neck began to ease. He turned to Mrs. Bradford. "I'll bring her right back."

She nodded, her keen eyes fixed on him, as if sensing his turmoil.

By the time they were outside the dance hall, the soft night air cooling their cheeks, his mood had lightened considerably. They walked in silence for a while, their footsteps crunching on the gravel. Caleb had no idea where they would go, as long as it was away from the dance hall, with all the horses and buggies hitched there, and men standing around talking over their pipes and cigars.

Geneva, as if sensing his mood, remained quiet. He thought about the night they'd gone on the herring run and his realization at how right her company always felt. On an impulse, he took her hand in his. She didn't resist the contact. He smiled, remembering how she used to pull away from his touch.

They crossed a stone bridge over the rushing water of a river. When they got to the other side, Caleb guided Geneva toward a small green overlooking the water. The two leaned against the stone parapet. The summer sky had at last darkened and was beginning to twinkle with stars. Caleb let the sound of water soothe him, until he could begin to chuckle over what had happened at the supper.

Geneva glanced at him. A street lamp on the bridge illuminated her questioning gaze.

Instead of telling her the source of his humor, he said, "You look beautiful, you know that?"

He saw her swallow and face the water, not answering.

"Have you enjoyed yourself so far?"

She nodded.

"Look at me, Geneva."

At the sound of her name, she turned to him. He reached out a hand and brushed its back against her warm cheek. But the light touch was no longer enough to satisfy. He'd been holding himself back too long. His hand turned, and he enfolded her cheek in his palm. He could hear her intake of breath. His own breathing had long since ceased to function rhythmically. Slowly, he drew her face upward as his own came down.

The tension that had begun building between them was finally out in the open, acknowledged by them both, and given an outlet. Their lips came together, barely grazing. Caleb stroked Geneva's cheek with his fingertips, his eyes closed, reveling in the sheer touch and scent of her. He'd waited so long for this moment, he was in no hurry to complete it.

He'd been right. She was a wild rose, soft, velvety, with a scent sweet and fragile on the warm night air. His fingertips drifted over her upturned chin and down her neck. He encircled her nape with his hand, drawing her closer. He heard a soft sigh escape her lips, and that sound was the undoing of him. He pressed his lips to hers, softness and firmness fused. His hand flattened against her back, molding her body to his.

Her lips parted beneath his, welcoming him with no reservations.

"Geneva." He breathed her name, releasing her lips only far enough to draw breath before seeking them again. He took one of her hands in his and guided it up to his neck. She needed no further prompting, but clasped both her hands around his neck, entwining her fingers in the hair at his nape.

Their kiss deepened as he wrapped his arms around her, pulling her to him. Why had he waited so long? The question reverberated in his mind as his body sought hers.

He pulled at the ribbon that held her hair. The heavy, silken strands fell at once, surrounding her face. He stuck the ribbon in his pocket and burrowed his nose in her hair, wanting to absorb the very essence of her. He grew still when he felt her hands begin to explore his own face. Timidly at first, her fingers touched the sensitive lobes of his ears, then swept downward more boldly, exploring the contours of his jaws and cheeks. Caleb moved his head, giving her better access, and closed his eyes. Her slim fingers touched his lips softly, and he kissed them in response. This time it was she who brought his face back to hers, and their lips met once more to draw life from each other, as their arms held their bodies fast.

Even when their lips had drawn apart, they stood for a long time in a silent embrace, as if there was no need for words just then. Her hands and head rested against his chest. No doubt she could feel the thudding of his heart, which was gradually returning to a regular beat. He felt protective of her, as if his arms could shield her from all the gossip of Haven's End and Boston combined.

"I suppose this wasn't very wise," he said when he heard a shout of laughter from over the bridge near the dance hall. He grinned. "What will Mrs. Stillman say when she sees your hair in disarray and—" his finger rubbed her bottom lip "—the unmistakable signs of your having been thoroughly kissed?"

She looked downward. He could feel her body stiffen and he tightened his hold, not letting her draw away from him.

"I didn't think—" she began.

"I don't think either of us *thought*." He chuckled at her look of dismay. When she didn't respond to the humor, he strove to reassure her, though he didn't know what to say. He was in no state to assemble a rational thought. He sighed, running a finger along the edge of her face. "I'm sorry, Geneva. I probably shouldn't have kissed you. I would never want to do anything to hurt you." He smiled, as something occurred to him. "I wouldn't want to ruin your chances with the up-and-coming 'young Samuel.'"

She tried to draw back then, but he wouldn't let her go. He took her head in both his hands, plunging his fingers into her mass of hair. Unable to loosen his hold on her, she tried to turn her head sideways, but he forced her to face him.

"Don't say those things! I know we all seem silly to you, most of all me in this getup—"

"Geneva! Geneva!" He wanted to shake some sense into her. "You look beautiful in your *getup*. More elegant than the finest lady in Boston." As he said the words, he realized they were true.

Geneva stared at him as if willing herself to believe what he was telling her.

He took a deep breath, trying to make sense of the evening. "All of you form an adorably funny little community, and I love every part about it. Well, almost every part. I'll have to withhold judgment on 'young Sam.'" He sobered, frustrated at being unable to express himself adequately. "I am truly sorry about—" he made an ineffectual gesture "—this. No, that's not true! I'm *not* sorry. I've been wanting to kiss you for a long time."

There, he'd admitted it, as much to himself as to her. He didn't think she was going to say anything, but then he saw a smile tug at her lips.

"So have I," she whispered, as if making a shameful confession.

An incredible tenderness stole over him at the admission. He tilted her chin up with his thumbs, his hands still framing her face. This time she met his gaze straight on. It was he who suddenly had the need to shut his eyes. Her utter trust in him was daunting. It would be so easy to throw all caution to the wind.

Arabella had had such a wide-eyed, guileless expression, never more so than the day she had calmly given him his ring back. Caleb desperately wanted to dispel the image.

He reopened his eyes to find Geneva waiting, her heart in her eyes. He cleared his throat. "Have you indeed? Since when?" Suddenly he wanted to know every feeling Geneva had been experiencing for him since they'd met, as if those details would overshadow the reminders of the past.

But she wouldn't answer. She just shook her head. "It doesn't matter."

"It does to me." When no revelations were forthcoming, Caleb loosened his hold on Geneva and stepped back, feeling the cool breeze off the river for the first time. He noticed Geneva give a slight shudder. "Cold?" he asked her, reaching out a hand. She stepped aside deftly from his touch, shaking her head.

Sensing a withdrawal, he walked to the parapet. The dark, turbulent water rushed beneath the bridge, cascading over the rapids on its way to the sea. "I don't understand what's happened tonight. You'll have to excuse me if I take a little time to adjust myself to it." He looked over to her. "I meant what I just said. I would never do anything knowingly to hurt you. Do you believe me?"

Mutely she nodded.

Caleb wanted to kiss her until there was no tomorrow or yesterday. But he had no right. He thought about the supper they'd just enjoyed. Geneva's life was just beginning.

What right had he to destroy her world before she'd even had a chance to find her place in it? If this evening had shown him anything, it was that Geneva deserved so much more than she'd ever enjoyed in her community. He must step aside and let her come into her own. Unless he could offer her something more...

Could he?

Chapter Sixteen

When they returned to the hall, Caleb asked Mrs. Bradford if he could drive them home instead of staying for the remainder of the dance. She agreed immediately. After they dropped her off, Caleb cradled Geneva in his arm. By the time they entered Haven's End, she had fallen asleep against him. Caleb suspected she'd been up at dawn. He kissed the crown of her head, enjoying the clean smell of her hair.

When they arrived at her house, she awoke before he had a chance to pick her up and carry her to her door. The image of a bride and groom flashed through his mind. He bid her good-night with a chaste peck on her forehead, knowing if he did any more he likely would not be able to leave at all.

He had already started walking back down her path when he changed his mind. He retraced his steps and reached for her one last time. As if they both sensed that their lives would be different when the sun arose in a few short hours, they held tightly to one another, not saying anything. Reluctantly he let Geneva go and returned to his home.

Once there, Caleb went out to the back veranda, knowing he wouldn't be able to sleep. The sky, pitch black with myriad pinpoints of light, blended into the dark ocean. Only the ceaseless sound of waves told him the water lay out there in front of him. He settled into his hammock, hoping to find some answers.

He'd put off thinking of the growing tension between Geneva and him, telling himself he needed time…not realizing he was running out of it. Tonight had proved that. So much for deluding himself he could keep things under control.

Ever since he'd seen Geneva as a woman, he'd pretended he could keep her at arm's length, continuing his "project" of making her into a woman—even going so far as thinking he could settle her with the right young man.

Seeing her in Samuel Giles' arms on the dance floor had put an end to that particularly foolish notion.

What was preventing him from pursuing Geneva himself?

Caleb had dodged the answer to that question long enough.

How could he offer a woman anything after the recent events in Boston? He'd left his family, his friends, a career, a future—everything that made a man what he was.

Deep in his heart he knew none of those things mattered to Geneva. He was hiding behind those reasons.

He got up from the hammock, too restless to settle the issues in his head while lying down, and he paced the floorboards of the porch. He kept returning to thoughts of his father and the unresolved issue of forgiveness between them. Caleb knew someday he'd have to face his father and make his peace with him.

But that still didn't account for his hesitancy where Geneva was concerned.

Was he discriminating against her background? God knew her upbringing had been different from his—but had it been so different? Hadn't they been but two lonely children? Yet his world in Boston was far removed from her sphere of knowledge at Haven's End.

For an insane moment he told himself he didn't care about all that. She'd never have to come to Boston if she didn't want to. He could keep her here, protected from the cruelty of that society.

Caleb stopped in the center of the porch and gripped the railing, facing seaward. The stars gave him a sense of infinity. He was such a tiny mortal speck down below. The least he could do was be honest with himself.

He knew he had to think about Arabella, and he didn't want to do that. That was the one thing he'd been avoiding all evening…all summer. The one night he'd opened up to Geneva had shown him it was just too painful. He'd succeeded in numbing his heart by not thinking about Arabella and all the years he'd wasted loving her. No, it was worse than that. He'd wasted all those years loving a person who didn't even exist.

His heart, if not healed, had reached a comfortably numb state. He could live for years if need be, as long as his heart weren't jarred into remembrance.

But his newfound feelings for Geneva demanded just that. He knew he must examine his heart with the thoroughness of a surgeon to see what still remained in it for Arabella.

Caleb put his face in his hands. He'd give anything to avoid this confrontation with his heart. Even now he could feel the pain swelling there, demanding release.

He'd spent his entire young manhood building his dreams around Arabella. She'd become the substitution for his inability to please his father. The fact hit him like an ice pick against the tender swelling of his heart. Caleb's fingers dug into his forehead as he steeled himself against the pain. But he had to go forward, exploring this discovery.

When he'd come up against his father's exacting criticism time and again, Caleb had gradually replaced his need to gain his father's approval with a desire to build an empire for Arabella. He'd take over his father's company and expand it for *her*. Their children would be the crowning achievement of all his work and ambitions.

His plans had crashed to nothing that fateful day when Arabella gave him his ring back. Caleb remembered how the numbness overtook him as he listened to her tell him that under the circumstances she could not continue her engagement to him, not when there was a cloud of suspicion above his head.

She'd broken the engagement only days after his own father had confronted him, almost as if she'd been privy to the inside workings of the firm. Now, he had no doubt she had—through Ellery.

It was as if she couldn't wait to be free. All the years Caleb had been striving for her, had she been seeking an escape?

Had she been seeing Ellery even then?

The sickening knowledge, once released from his hidden thoughts, contaminated his reason. He gripped the wooden rail beneath him, wishing he could rip the whole balustrade apart and fling it into the ocean.

Instead, the anger went out of him, deflating him like a sail in the middle of a tack. His knees collapsed under him, his hands slid down the balusters, and he fell to the floor, letting go of the emotions he'd kept under control for so long.

He hadn't cried since that first voyage out, when he was eight. Before then, he'd cried easily as a lad, until he'd seen how it infuriated his father to see the tears welling in his eyes. *"Clara, I will not have you coddling that boy and turning my son into a weakling."* That had been the reason for shipping him off to sea, no doubt—to turn Caleb into a man.

Now, the tear ducts had been dry so long, they didn't open easily. Great, gasping heaves erupted from somewhere far down Caleb. He could only kneel there on the wooden planks, his hands on his knees, letting the dry sobs rip through his chest.

Finally, as if breaking some barrier, the tears began to flow.

His face and hands were suddenly wet, and he felt like a baby, but he couldn't stop. Too much disappointment and hurt had broken through the dam of self-control to be stopped until they had spent themselves.

"Oh, God," he cried. *"Help me! Sweet Jesus, help me."* His thoughts were incoherent. He could only crouch there against the pain, with no strength to stop it. He had to submit, let it shred his heart, knowing there was no other way to come through to the other side.

"Help me, Lord! Help me to forgive them...to forgive myself."

So he cried until there were no tears left, until the racking sobs subsided, and he lay down on the wooden planks, curled on his side.

Tentatively, as if still tensed for pain, his body unfurled itself. He lay on his back and gazed at the stars once more. High above him, untouched by his pain and sorrow. When his body had fully relaxed, he realized he was feeling something he hadn't felt for a long time. Peace.

He began to breathe in and out deeply, testing the sensation to see if it would hold. Or was it another illusion, as his life had been from beginning to end?

The stars still glinted above him and this time he thought of their Creator. The words crossed his mind, "For we have not a high priest who cannot be touched by our infirmities." Had God been touched by his pain and replaced it with peace?

Caleb sat up and clasped his hands loosely about his knees. He sat there until light began to tinge the eastern horizon and he could make out the outline of the spruce and firs atop the cliffs above the cove. He watched the tide on the ebb as it dragged itself seaward, exposing the rockweed-covered boulders in its path, leaving them like black-shrouded humps upon the sand and muck.

How could he claim any feelings for Geneva if what he'd felt all these years for Arabella was a falsity? If after a few short months here, his sentiments for Geneva were already displacing his love for Arabella, how was he any different from the woman he wanted to despise? How could he feel in any way superior to Arabella? Could she help it if she fell in love with someone else?

Caleb stood, placing his hands once more upon the balustrade, but this time not in despair, but with purpose. He needed to know if what he was feeling for Geneva would stand the test of time. How could he be sure it wasn't just the result of his loneliness and desire for female companionship? That as soon as he returned to Boston, the passion he'd felt for her last night would dissipate as quickly as a fog by midmorning?

Boston. As soon as he'd thought it, he knew he'd come to the decision that had been hovering on the edge of his thoughts since the evening he'd sat down to read the Bible.

He must return.

Caleb looked up at the glorious expanse of sky, darkness
fading before the light. He was willing to obey the Lord's
command. Now it was up to God to show him the rest of the way.

Geneva rose with the dawn. A feeling of well-being
such as she'd never known pervaded her whole body. She
rested for a few moments on her pillow, turning her head
to look at the lightening sky outside her window. Gradually the events of the previous evening returned to her,
and with them, the feeling of anticipation at seeing Caleb
once again.

She relived each dance with him, the feel of him guiding
her to supper, his presence beside her at the table, and finally,
the walk they'd taken together outside.

She burrowed her face in the pillow, feeling his kiss once
more. Had it been nothing more than a dream? Suddenly, she
threw back the bedcovers and rose. She ran to her glass, took
it off its nail and ran back to the dim light of the window to
stare at her face, focusing intently on her lips. Her cheeks
looked flushed, her hair—she'd been too tired last night to
braid it—was in disarray about her face. She touched her lips,
remembering the feel of his lips upon hers. Could it really
have happened as she remembered? Would it happen again?

The only thing to mar her memories and expectations was
Caleb's reaction after their kiss. His remark about not spoiling
her chances with young Sam had hurt her to the quick. How
could he even think of giving her to another man? That she'd
even consider anyone else after him? And as soon as Caleb
had let her go, she'd felt alone once again. His claim that he
didn't want to hurt her in any way had only filled her with fear,
but he'd been so insistent on her understanding that she'd
finally given him the answer he so clearly wanted.

Jake's scratching to be let out brought her back to the present. Hurriedly, she let him out, then turned to dress. She eyed the dress hanging on a hook. She went to it, and held it up, inspecting it. Could she wear it again today, one more time before washing it and putting it away for another occasion? She remembered Mrs. Bradford's invitation to church. Perhaps she would go. She smiled. It would give the older woman pleasure to see the dress on her. With that she hurried to wash and dress and prepare her breakfast.

By midmorning, she'd finished her chores. Everything was neat and tidy, including herself, and she stood outside her door. Mrs. Stillman and her family hadn't yet gotten their wagon hitched up to go to church, so she knew there was still time. She glanced toward the Point. When she spotted Caleb kneeling in the middle of his garden, her heart quickened its beat. She could feel the blood begin to race through her veins. If only she could see him before she left for church. How could she endure those hours before being able to see him again, to assure herself that last night had really happened?

Without conscious thought, she began walking down the road to the Point. Jake followed quietly beside her.

"You want to see him, too, don't you?" she asked, bending to give him a pat.

She walked across his yard. He heard Jake's bark and turned to watch their progress.

Geneva almost turned back. What if she were wrong? What if it had all been some mistake?

She scolded herself for being so silly and forced her footsteps forward. The way Caleb had held her and kissed her so ardently was too clear for her to have misconstrued.

Caleb was in the middle of his potato patch, loosening the roots with a fork. A pile of small spuds sat on the grass at the edge of the garden.

"You know, you should wait 'til the plant withers before digging them up. What're you in such a rush for?" she joked.

He didn't answer right away, but continued forking the earth. Then he laid down the fork and began to pull up the plant. He shook the dirt off the roots and pried the potatoes loose, carefully setting them down beside him.

Finally he looked at her. "Good morning, Geneva."

Geneva started to feel a hammering in her chest. Was this the way it was supposed to be? Caleb staring at her as if she were a stranger? He looked more solemn than she'd seen him look all summer.

Once again she wished she had some pockets in her skirt. Instead she spread out her hands. "It looks like it's going to be a fine day."

Caleb continued feeling around in the dirt for any stray potatoes. When he was satisfied, he sat back, removing his gloves, one at a time. "Yes—" he answered, looking toward the sea.

"Geneva—"

Why was he saying her name like that? Like a teacher calling a pupil up to the front of the class. "What is it, Caleb?"

"I'm thinking of going down to Boston soon."

His words echoed in the stillness. The moment she'd expected and dreaded all summer was here. Geneva wanted to laugh. Here it was, and she wasn't prepared.

Suddenly, she felt like a fool, standing there in her dress— her "finery." It was nothing but a calico frock. Who had she thought she was, trying to compete with Arabella Harding's silk and lace?

"Did you hear me, Geneva?"

Geneva bent down and began to spread out his potatoes. "You've got to lay these flat to dry. But don't leave them out in the sun too long. They'll turn green and not be fit to eat."

"Geneva." His voice cut through her.

"I heard you."

Her world was crumbling beneath her and here she was worrying about his potatoes. Of all the places she'd imagined she'd be when he broke the news to her, it hadn't been kneeling in his garden. But it was fitting. She'd better just grab herself some handfuls of his dirt, for that's all she'd ever have of him.

She continued with her task, wanting to laugh at the absurdity of last night compared to this morning. Here Caleb was leaving, and she was concerned about his potatoes being edible. Who was going to eat them, for pity's sake? She pressed her lips together, afraid even to smile for fear she'd start to sob instead.

They continued for a while longer in silence.

Caleb must have finally realized the way she was dressed. "Look here, leave those. You'll get your dress soiled."

What did it matter if her dress got dirty? Would he be here to see it?

As if reading her thoughts, he straightened. "Look, Geneva, the reason I have to go—"

Just then, Geneva heard the Stillmans' wagon moving down their drive. She grabbed at the sound like a lifeline. If she stayed around for even a few more seconds, she'd be down on her knees, begging him not to leave.

She stood in one swift movement. "Oh, my, it's time I got going." She brushed her hands off and even managed a smile. "I'm going to church this morning. Mrs. Bradford invited me."

Caleb looked relieved to hear her speak so normally. "That's great. You'll see, people will start treating you like the lady you are."

He didn't realize how close her voice was to breaking. She inspected one of her palms, making a show of brushing off the remaining dirt, until she was sure her words would come out evenly.

"Well, I'll be seein' ya." With a small wave of her hand, she moved off. She whistled to Jake, and walked resolutely toward the road, out of Caleb's life, knowing he was watching her. She straightened her shoulders and kept marching.

She didn't bother to stop by her house to wash her hands at the pump, but kept walking on up the slope. She walked the entire way to church, arriving hot and sweaty, but not caring. What did anything matter anymore?

A rousing hymn was in full swing when she opened one of the heavy oak doors. A few people in the back pews turned to look at her. She stuck her chin higher, not meeting anyone's eyes, and shut the door behind her. She would have slipped in the last pew, but as the folks in the back rows caught sight of her, they turned and nudged or whispered to others. Soon, the entire body was aware of her entrance and her new appearance. Mrs. Bradford, who sat toward the front, was one of the last to turn. She immediately beckoned to Geneva, who had no choice but to walk up the aisle.

By the time she slipped into her seat, the last chorus of the hymn had been sung. Pastor McDuffie rose and introduced the next one. Geneva stood beside Mrs. Bradford, who placed a hymnal in her hands. The tiny print began to swim before her, but Geneva swiped angrily at her eyes and concentrated on reading the words.

Although she was able to read several of the words and make out others from the singing voices around her, they made no sense to her. She kept on mouthing the words, knowing if she stopped to think of anything else, she'd break down.

By the time the next hymn began, the meaning of the verses was beginning to penetrate. "Rock of ages, cleft for me, Let me hide myself in Thee…." How much she desired to have someone to hide in.

"Could my tears forever flow…." She was afraid to let them come, precisely for fear they'd never stop. "Thou must save, and Thou alone…." How she needed salvation at that moment. Never had she felt so lost. "In my hand no price I bring; Simply to Thy cross I cling…." She felt her strength slipping and could imagine herself like a shipwrecked person, just clinging to a wooden spar. "Rock of ages, cleft for me, Let me hide myself in Thee."

When everyone was seated, Pastor McDuffie began to preach. His voice ebbed and flowed, reaching heights of passion and coming down again to a near whisper. Geneva didn't hear half of it. Her thoughts flooded with memories of how Caleb had looked and what he'd said this morning. She dared not think of the previous night or she would surely weep.

Why now? Why had he decided to go to Boston now? It must have something to do with last night. Had he regretted it so quickly?

The pastor's voice lowered. Geneva raised her eyes, caught by the change in tempo. McDuffie's gaze swept the congregation as he spoke. "Jesus said, 'Lo, I am with you always, even unto the end of the world.'" At the last words, his gaze came to rest on Geneva and held her.

She felt as if Jesus Himself were talking directly to her. Her whole being reached out to believe in that promise. How she longed for someone who would never leave her nor forsake her.

Caleb tightened the final strap of his leather satchel. He wasn't taking much with him. He glanced down the hallway of the house before closing the front door behind him. He wouldn't need much. He'd be back soon.

He laid the bag by the front door. Old Jim would be by shortly to pick him up to take him to the harbor.

Caleb stood outside the door and glanced up the hill to Geneva's house. Only one thing remained. Saying goodbye.

He hadn't seen her since her abrupt departure Sunday morning. He knew he'd handled things badly, springing the news on her. But she'd clammed up as if she didn't even want to hear any explanation of his reasons for returning to Boston.

There was so much he wanted to say to her, but couldn't. Not yet. He no longer wanted promises of any kind.

Her silence worried him. He would have preferred anger or tears. But she'd brushed off his words as if they didn't mean anything at all to her. He couldn't help contrasting it to her passion the night he'd kissed and held her. Could it have been the same woman?

Caleb straightened, knowing he didn't have much time. The sooner he went to Boston, the sooner he'd be back. There'd be time enough then to explain things. A lifetime, if it was meant to be. But no—it was premature to think such things.

When he entered Geneva's yard, there was no one there. The pathway in front was a profusion of flowers. Jake approached him with a joyful bark, stretching up for a pat, then walked along beside Caleb as he circled the house.

She was standing in her garden, half hidden behind the stalks of beans. If she heard him, she gave no sign, but continued to pick beans. He could hear them drop into her pan. It irritated him, being able to read her so little. Arabella had vocalized every grievance. But then she'd cast him aside, giving her heart to Ellery…. How well *had* he been able to read her?

"Good morning," he said.

Her glance flickered over him before turning back to the vines. "Morning."

Caleb's annoyance grew. She was dressed once more in her overalls, her hair tightly plaited in one long braid down her back. She looked exactly as she had when he'd first met her. So much for his efforts to make her into a woman.

"Your garden's doing well." What a brilliant observation. When she didn't reply, he could hardly blame her.

"What's that you're picking, string beans?" At least she gave him a nod. His efforts at making conversation were going from bad to worse. He gave a quick glance at his pocket watch. He didn't have much time left.

He looked up to see Geneva catch him tucking his watch back into his pocket, and cursed himself. He tried again to establish a normal conversation. "You're taking them down to the village to sell?"

"'Swhat I been doing all summer." Her hand never stopped plucking the beans off the plant.

"Feel free to take any vegetables from my garden. To sell or use yourself."

"I got more'n I need with my own."

Again the only sound was the *plop-plopping* of the beans into the pan.

"I reckon your boat must be near finished. What're you going to do with her?"

It was her first reference to his departure.

He wanted to tell her he'd thought of asking her to keep it for him. But he'd decided he didn't want to leave her under obligation of any kind. "Winslow will keep it there for me for the time being."

She gave him a sharp look.

"I'm leaving today. For Boston," he added unnecessarily when she didn't react. But he knew she'd understood.

"Figured you'd be heading out soon."

"The sooner I go, the sooner I can get back."

She finally stopped her work long enough to look at him. As he gazed into her dark eyes, Caleb had the sudden impulse to go over and kiss her and find out if what they'd shared Saturday night had been real. Forget Boston.

But he stood where he was. He knew he must go through with what he'd decided. And he'd better go quickly before he changed his mind altogether—or before he became convinced he had to have his head examined for leaving such a beautiful young woman just when he'd discovered her. For she was beautiful to him, even standing there in those work clothes, her eyes hard, her stance belligerent.

His throat ached with the longing to tell her what was in his heart. He wanted to tell her to wait for him…no matter how long it took. He wanted badly to promise her he'd come back. But he remained silent.

Experience had taught him well. Never again would he exact promises from someone he loved. Geneva was too beautiful. Before long, she'd have honorable men vying for her attention. Men like Sam Giles. It wasn't fair to bind her with promises she couldn't keep.

He didn't think he could survive another disappointment.

Geneva was only now discovering her wings. He would do nothing to prevent her soaring.

He cleared his throat. "Sam Giles seems like a good man."

Her black eyes flashed him a look of anger—the first reaction to anything he'd said since he'd first told her he was leaving for Boston. But immediately she went back to her task, yanking the beans off and flinging them into her pan. "What's that to me?"

"He seemed taken with you at the dance."

Her lips were a straight line, as if she were holding back a retort.

He held his hat in his hands, and began turning it around, studying its brim. "Geneva, there is a lot I have to do in Boston. You were right a long time ago, when you said I was running away from my troubles." He smiled, remembering how convinced Geneva had been when she'd first met him that he'd soon hightail it back to Boston—and he'd so vehemently denied it.

He looked at her. He finally had her full attention, though it was disconcerting to meet her gaze. Her dark eyes stared at him unflinchingly, demanding no less than complete honesty.

"You made me see I can't run away. I need to go back and make my peace with…with what I was running from."

His fingers tightened on the brim of his hat. "I have no future—" His arm swung out, encompassing everything around them. "I can't begin anything new until I settle the past. Can you understand that, Geneva?"

Suddenly, it was extremely important for him that she do so. He stepped toward her and reached for her shoulder, but stopped short of touching her. He couldn't trust himself to.

"I don't want to be a man shackled with bitterness or regrets. I want to be able to make a genuinely fresh start."

He could see her swallow. But still she didn't give him the words he wanted to hear.

"Can you tell me you understand?"

She was no longer looking at him, as if what she'd hoped to read in his eyes wasn't there and he had disappointed her in some profound way. Finally she just gave a brief nod. "You'd better go, or you'll miss your boat."

"I'm going to miss you." He touched her cheek with his fingertips, knowing he needed to feel its petal softness one last time, to take it with him.

She didn't react but continued to look at the vine in front of her.

He cleared his throat and took a step back. "Well, I'd best be on my way."

"Goodbye," she answered, not looking at him.

Geneva waited for Caleb to leave, her mind screaming, *Leave. Leave. Just leave!* Her fingers tightened on a string bean and she focused all her attention on the poor pod in her grip. She could feel Caleb hesitate as if he wanted to say more, then sensed more than saw him nod and put his hat on. She refused to acknowledge him, to look at him directly, to give him anything. His departure was hurting her too much, and her only defense lay in not letting him see how devastated she was.

He raised his hand in a final farewell, and then he was gone.

Geneva kept on picking beans.

They had to be picked within the next day or so or they'd get tough. She decided to make a delivery tomorrow to her customers. At all costs, she'd avoid the harbor today. Mentally, she went over the list of her customers. She glanced at the sky. The good weather should hold another day.

The beans made a soft *thud* in her pan now as they fell against each other. They felt warm and smooth. She didn't stop her rhythm until the pan was full. Then she went to her house by the back, avoiding the front yard. She heard the wheels of old Jim's trap when he rode toward the Point, but she didn't look up.

She packed the beans in her baskets, filling up the individual orders. She'd wait to pick the greens first thing in the morning.

She heard the rumble of wagon wheels go by again. She glanced up quickly as the horse and trap passed her house and continued on up the slope, only to make sure old Jim had his passenger with him.

She didn't slacken the pace of her work until the last murmur of wagon wheels had died completely. Then she sat on her back stoop, her hands lying idle between her knees.

He wasn't coming back. That fact stood clearest of all before her. She knew Caleb was gone for good. Once back in Boston, there would be too much holding him there to allow him to return. She gave a shuddering sigh, accepting the fact.

She was happy for him that he was through with running away. That was right. Whatever had happened here in Haven's End had produced something good in Caleb if it helped him face things back in Boston.

In the silence that followed that conclusion came the thought, How was she going to bear the burden of Caleb's departure? A moan escaped her lips, and she clutched her knees for support. She couldn't give in to it. She *wouldn't!* No! No! Geneva fought the rising tide of despair, knowing she mustn't let it flood over her.

But her heart was breaking with pure longing, and she didn't know how she was going to be able to bear it.

She'd experienced an ache when her mother died, but then childish ignorance had cushioned the impact of loss. She'd been too young to understand the full implications of being left in her father's hands. When her father died, she'd known only release. His death had given her freedom, but at the same time, it had severed her last known tie to any human being…until Caleb had walked into her life that fateful day upon the wharf.

And now he had walked back out again.

Chapter Seventeen

It seemed that Caleb had left Haven's End and taken the good summer weather with him. The day after he departed, the fog rolled in and hadn't budged since. The very clouds had descended and seemed to push down on Geneva's soul.

Her bay was like a large cauldron full of white vapor. She could find no release out on the water. Her boat remained beached, high tide and low. All she could do was pick her vegetables and put them up for the winter. She shelled peapods and bean pods, their husks papery dry, the beans inside hardened like little stones. As long as she could remember, she had always been able to forget her troubles in her work. Whenever he was home, her father had never allowed her to sit and play. Ezra, who'd taught her of the sea, always said, "The idle man tempts the devil."

She thought of another one of his sayings: "Like plays best with like." She'd remembered that one too late.

"Better to be alone than in bad company." She repeated the adage over and over in her head, trying to convince herself. The trouble was, Caleb hadn't been bad company.

He'd been the best company she'd ever known. Strong, yet so gentle. Handsome enough to take her breath away, yet completely unaware of his looks—or of the way women looked at him. A gentleman through and through, but a man who knew what it was to work from the bottom up.

Why had he ever bothered with her? She was a fool to have imagined he'd ever come to feel anything for the likes of her.

Wearily, she split open the yellowed peapod and extracted the hard wrinkled peas, hearing them clatter onto a tray, where they'd finish drying. If she'd imagined keeping busy would alleviate the ache of missing Caleb, she'd miscalculated. This month, one of the busiest of the year, held enough chores to keep her working from sunup to sundown. Unfortunately, she could no longer find the energy or enthusiasm to carry them out. She dragged herself through the most necessary ones with utter lassitude.

This afternoon she didn't even have Jake to unburden herself to.

"Where has that fool dog gone off to?" She'd seen him chasing after something a couple of hours ago. Now she realized she hadn't heard his bark in some time.

"I'd better go looking for him before he gets himself lost in the fog."

Outside, the evergreen trees at the edges of her fields were scarcely visible in the white mist. Everything was damp. With a deep sigh, she began calling for Jake as she trudged around the yard.

She could taste the salt on her tongue from the droplets of moisture that hung suspended in the air. She called across the street and received no response. She called down toward the Point, seeing only the tip of Caleb's roof, and heard nothing. Wearily, she made her way to her backyard and called over the field before walking down the path to the shore.

She heard the gentle lap of waves through the cloud of mist.

"Jake! Answer me, confound you! Jake!" Her voice was growing hoarse and her fingers were feeling chilled.

Then she heard it—a soft whimper.

She hurried toward the sound.

There, at the edge of the beach where the goose grass grew and the rockweed was stiff and black, lay her dog.

"Jake!" As soon as she reached him, she knelt and began to examine him.

"Oh, Jake, what have you got into, ol' boy?" Her fingers probed his fur. He could barely keep his eyes open to look at her. She lifted one lid and saw his eyes glazed with pain.

"Poor fellow, your belly's all swollen," she muttered, feeling the distended skin. She could find no other clue to his malady. No bones seemed broken. There were no visible wounds on his fur. Finally she braced herself and picked him up. She'd just have to carry him back up to the house and nurse him.

He was heavy, and the way to her shack was an uphill trudge, but her worry lent her strength. Just when she thought her arms would give out, the house came in sight. She reached the back door and managed to kick it in. Then she laid him down by the woodstove and brought his blanket to cover him.

She lit a fire to get the chill and dampness out of the room. Then she grabbed an old towel and began rubbing Jake dry, not bothering to take time with her own damp garments. He didn't react until she tried rubbing his stomach, and then he whimpered so much that she knew he must have eaten something he shouldn't have.

"You should know better, you foolish dog. You're not a
puppy anymore, getting into everything, as if I don't feed you
here at home."

She rose and fixed some warm water with soda, then tried
to get a few spoonfuls down his mouth. Finally, she just sat
with him, rubbing his forehead, trying to keep him as warm
and comfortable as she could. But he didn't improve. His
body shook, and she knew he must have a fever.

As the day waned, Geneva's alarm grew. She didn't know
what to do for him nor whom to call. By nightfall, when Jake
was barely conscious, Geneva ran across the street and
begged Mr. Stillman to look at her dog.

He came to her aid, but shook his head as he listened to
her tale and examined the animal for himself. Finally, he
straightened. "Doesn't look good. Sounds like he ate
somep'n poisoned him. He'll just have to work it outta his
system."

He took a dark brown bottle out of his pocket. "This here
tonic's what I give my hounds when they seem indigested.
Got a teaspoon?"

Geneva hurried to fetch one. She watched as he administered the medicine.

The farmer sat back. "I don't know. Might as well give him
a double dose. He looks some poorly."

In went another spoonful. Geneva helped hold Jake's
mouth so the tonic would go down.

"All you can do is sit with 'm. Get a basin in case he vomits. Just give a hollah if he gets wuhse."

After Mr. Stillman left, Jake's chills intensified, and
Geneva brought her quilt to cover him. She sat by his head,

her knees drawn up, and kept her hand on his face. She prayed, until the prayers just seemed to go round and round in circles and she couldn't make sense of the words anymore.

Finally, at some point in the night, Jake's breathing became labored. "Hold on, boy. If you can just hold on 'til morning…"

But poor Jake could hold on no more. In the wee hours of the morning, he took his last breath.

The fatigue and tension of seeing Jake suffer left Geneva too disoriented to react. She closed his eyes with her hand, telling herself in her benumbed state that he'd just gone to sleep. She tumbled into her own bed and finally slept, a restless sleep filled with dark images.

When she woke, it was mid-morning. Her head felt like a piece of cordwood split into kindling, her joints as if they had sand rubbing between them, and her throat as if she'd swallowed a whole mess of codfish bones. She tried to rise, but her shirt and trousers felt heavy on her limbs. She must have caught a chill out in the fog the day before.

She saw Jake's still form huddled in the quilt. Forgetting her pains, she pushed herself out of bed and went over to him. When she saw his unmoving face, the previous day came back to her vividly. Gently she removed the blanket. Jake's body was stiff and cold.

"No, no…" she moaned, but each shake of her head brought a thud of pain. Jake couldn't be dead. *No! No! No!* her mind screamed.

She didn't know how long she lay with her pet, her arm wrapped around him. Her own body felt too warm—there must be some warmth she could give him. She dozed off, and when she awoke, chills racked her body. Even huddling under the blanket she'd thrown over Jake brought no relief.

She heard a knock on the door.

"Genevar, you in theah?"

She dimly recognized Mr. Stillman's voice, but her throat was too sore to answer.

The knock came louder. "Genevar!" The door swung open. "Genevar, I came to see how your dog wuz doin—" At the sight of dog and mistress on the floor, he hurried over. "What's happened?"

He was kneeling beside her, pulling her against the floor away from Jake, but she refused to let go. He might wake up and be cold.

She felt the farmer's calloused hand against her forehead. "Land sakes, you're burnin' up! You been up all night with Jake?"

She could only shake her head and try to bury her face in Jake's fur. She could hear the farmer rise to his feet.

"Let me go get the missus. She'll know what to do."

Geneva heard her door bang shut, then silence. She rocked Jake against her. Just as she was on the verge of dozing off again, she felt strong hands pry her away from Jake and carry her across to her bed. She was undressed, and then her nightgown enveloped her like a cold sheet against her shivering flesh.

Footsteps crisscrossed the room, voices murmured.

"Here, drink this, my dear." Mrs. Stillman's voice came to her, as the woman's strong arm came around her neck to lift her head up. Hot, strong tea laced with honey and rum scalded her throat, but felt good going down. It gave her enough awareness to remember Jake.

"Where is he?" she croaked out to Mrs. Stillman. The farmer's wife pursed her lips.

"Don't worry none about him. He's restin'."

"Is he…is he dead?" *Please God, did I dream it all? His poor stiff body?*

Mrs. Stillman busied herself tucking the blankets up around Geneva.

Just then Mr. Stillman came in through the back door. Geneva managed to raise her head enough to see him. He stood at the door hesitantly. Mrs. Stillman spoke to him across the room. "She wants to know if her cur's dead."

Mr. Stillman looked at Geneva. "Best she know the truth. I'm gettin' ready to bury him."

Tears welled up in Geneva's eyes and Mr. Stillman's standing figure wavered before her.

She thought about Jake standing like a sentry on the meadow right above her beach, his legs straight, his muzzle pointing out to sea, until the moment he could pick out her peapod coming back into the bay. Then he'd race down to the beach to be there when she beached her boat....

"Mr. Stillman," she implored the farmer, her voice hoarse.

"Hush, child." Mrs. Stillman's smooth hand came up to her forehead, urging her back against the pillow.

But Geneva found the strength to grab her wrist. "I gotta tell him." The words were pure torture against her throat. "Gotta tell him where to bury Jake."

Mrs. Stillman gave a nod. "Very well." She turned to her husband, who still stood by the door. "Best come closer. She wants to tell you where to bury the dog."

Mr. Stillman approached the bed.

"Bury him at the end of the meadow, right...over the bay." Geneva swallowed. "Where all the daisies and clover grow."

The farmer nodded. "I know the spot. Don't you worry your head about it anymore."

After that, she slept. It seemed as if she slept for days, waking only for sips of hot tea or cool water. She didn't want to awaken from her dreams. They were filled with sunlight and laughter. She could feel the sunlight against her eyelids. She could see herself and Caleb and Jake out in the meadow, upon the sea, in a forest glade.

But the dreams ended and she was forced to awaken. Her head felt normal now, her limbs light. Only her heart remained heavy. If she looked out the window by her bed, she could see the spot of earth at the end of the meadow where Jake lay. She decided to get up then, rather than sit there looking.

When she took up her chores again, she avoided that corner of the field.

Mrs. Stillman came over once a day or sent one of her daughters to check on her, but Geneva squared her shoulders and stiffened her lips when they were there. She displayed an energy she didn't feel, just so they'd see she was well and leave her alone. She didn't want their pity. She didn't need it.

Finally, she took her boat out. She didn't have much strength to row, but there was a stiff breeze to hoist her sail. As soon as she'd left her bay, she headed westward rather than sailing by Ferguson Point.

But avoiding Caleb's property didn't help. It was a sunny day, which turned the ocean into that inky blue that reminded her of Caleb's eyes…their intensity when he'd scrutinized her in suspicion the first time she'd approached him in his garden…their praise when she'd read a passage faultlessly in her primer…their glow in the moonlight the night the two of them had gone seining for herring….

Geneva didn't stay out long in the boat. That afternoon, upon her return, she looked up toward the meadow above her, feeling it was time she faced things. She trudged up the beach path, then turned onto the field. She walked through its high grasses, full of late-summer wildflowers bent in the breeze.

She walked until she came to the mound of earth, the bare patch like a scar upon the land. It wouldn't reseed itself until next spring. Geneva bent to pluck some of the plumpest black-eyed Susans, Queen Anne's lace and goldenrod she could find. Her mind went back to the day Caleb had asked her the names of the wildflowers. He'd handed her a posy, and she'd recoiled, so afraid she might reveal what she really felt for him. Those flowers were now wedged between the pages of her mother's Bible.

She knelt beside Jake's grave and placed her bouquet atop it. She tried not to picture Jake lying down there on his side, stiff-legged, covered in dirt. She preferred to remember Jake as the active dog he was, chasing after rabbits and squirrels, chewing up his toys to obliteration, bounding across the meadow to greet her, or lying contentedly by Caleb's feet.

She wished she could talk to Mrs. Bradford. How much she needed that woman's comforting words! But Geneva had found out that Mrs. Bradford was away and had no idea when she'd be back. It didn't matter anyway. She'd done without a Mrs. Bradford before. She'd get used to being without a friend again. If she just stayed inside herself, she'd be all right. She'd been practicing her whole life. It would come back to her.

But the thought brought her no reassurance. Geneva looked down at the rich brown dirt laced with bits of slate-colored stone. She smoothed an edge of the mound with her palm, then looked up at the painfully blue sky, knowing that with Mrs. Bradford away, she couldn't look for help anywhere but on her own. Unless those words of Jesus were true. "Lo, I am with you always, even unto the end of the world." The song's refrain came back to her: "In my hand no price I bring; Simply to Thy cross I cling."

Looking up at the sky, she spoke aloud. "You've got all I ever loved—Ma, Jake…Caleb. They're all gone. It's just me now. You should know I've nothing left to give."

She remembered Mrs. Bradford's lessons and reconsidered. "Nothing 'cept my soul." She gave the sky a bewildered look. "Is that what you want? Don't know why you'd want it. It's not worth nothing." Correct grammar didn't matter anymore.

She had a sudden clear vision of Jesus hanging on the cross.

Her soul had been worth His life.

She made the decision then, feeling too tired to keep up appearances any longer. "It's not much, but You can have it, too. It's not doing me any good, except cause me pain. Pastor McDuffie said in church You wouldn't cast anyone out that came to You."

The sky looked down on her placidly, a wisp of white cloud floating across it like a woman's hankie waving to a loved one.

Geneva felt foolish continuing to talk to such an empty expanse, but something compelled her. She wasn't willing to go back where she'd come from. "If it's like Mrs. Bradford said, that You died for me up on that old cross, that You paid such a price for me—then I figure I owe You whatever I got. It's Yours, Lord. You got everything else worth having anyway."

She looked down and smoothed the rocky dirt over Jake's mound one last time. "Take care of him, Lord. Take care of him."

She trudged back to her house, feeling she'd done a foolish thing but not really caring much anymore.

That night she didn't feel like eating. In the summer twilight, she sat at her front window, looking down the road toward the Point. Her eyes ran over Caleb's house, alone and empty; his garden, overgrown in late August; and finally, the sea, ablaze with color in the setting sun.

Her heart yearned for the man who'd inhabited that tip of Haven's End for a few months.

The days went by, each one wearing her control down a little more. Each evening she'd take out the Bible Mrs. Bradford had given her and try her best to decipher the words. Although she could make out many words, others were too difficult. She kept herself as busy as she could, but every few hours, she'd have to stop and plead.

"Help me, Lord. I can't make it on my own. It's too much for me." Never had she had to admit her weakness. She didn't know why she felt so helpless, and she blamed it on her recent illness.

One night as she was taking her teacup to the washbasin, she tripped against a floorboard. The cup slipped out of her hands and went crashing to the floor.

She stared at it and then at her hands, which began to shake. The trembling spread to her entire body. She fell to her knees, unable to stop the convulsions. She thought she wouldn't be able to draw breath.

"I can't bear it anymore, Lord," she gasped out. *"I can't bear the pain. I know I'm nothing but a sinner. I know I don't deserve Your attention. I've never given You the time of day.*

"But I need You, Lord!" she whispered. *"Please help me! If You're anything like Mrs. Bradford said You are, please help me."*

The trembling subsided as suddenly as it had started and the stillness resounded all around her.

Then she felt it—a heat beginning at the crown of her head. Like a hand touching the head of a child, but seeping into her skull and extending downward, it expanded to fill the width and breadth of her body, down to her very toes, until she felt she was filled with a warm, radiant light.

She didn't dare move. She knelt in wonder. As the sensation receded, she continued kneeling there, wanting only to relive the experience. She remembered something Mrs. Bradford had read her from the Scriptures: "Be still and know that I am God."

After several minutes, she slowly rose. She looked at her hands and arms, at her legs and feet. Everything was new. She broke into a smile. Joy—she knew what it was she was feeling, though she'd never experienced it before—pure, simple joy invaded her being. She could no longer stay still. She must rise. She must extend her arms upward; her feet must dance, her heart must sing.

She ran to the little Bible Mrs. Bradford had given her before she'd left. She flipped through it, looking for one of those—*Les Psaulmes,* her ma had called them. Mrs. Bradford called them Psalms. She'd even marked a few for Geneva.

She read with difficulty, skipping over some words. Psalm 138: "I will praise thee with my whole heart...I will worship—" her mouth sounded out the two syllables "—praise thy name for thy loving kindness—" she stumbled over that word "—and for thy truth....

"In the day when I cried thou answeredst me, and strengthenedst—" she guessed at that word "—me with strength in my soul."

She looked out her back window to the darkened bay, the trees behind it tall and black against the setting sun. The scene wasn't gloomy to her. She knew she wasn't alone now. She hugged the certainty to her breast. She would never be alone again.

* * *

The next day nothing had changed outwardly. Geneva still felt the silence of her little house, the absence of Jake's early-morning wake-up nuzzle. She still must rise and dress and be about her chores. When she went out to pump some water, Caleb's house still stared at her with its blank windowpanes.

But Geneva went around seeing everything through new eyes. She felt as if she walked hand-in-hand with the Creator, witnessing everything He had made, evidencing His hand in all things.

She'd slept later than usual, the sun was already above the top of the firs across the road, its rays lighting the bay opposite. It was the same scene she'd viewed the evening before, but now the golden sunshine lightened the spruce across the bay, transforming them from black silhouettes to yellow-green boughs. The sky behind the trees was pale blue, promising to turn into an intense, cloudless azure by mid-morning. The sea lay still, the boats moored in the bay like animals quietly awaiting their masters to put them to work.

Geneva kept busy that day and the following ones, hardly speaking to a soul, but learning to speak to God and hear His voice.

Soon Mrs. Stillman came by with a batch of blueberry muffins. "I've hardly seen you since you've been up and about. Don't you be overdoin', you hear?"

Geneva smiled, remembering the woman's kindness during her fever and ashamed that she hadn't expressed her gratitude. "I've been keeping well. I want to thank you for helping me out when I was ill."

Mrs. Stillman beamed. "Oh, think nothing of it, my dear. That's what neighbors are for."

"Well, I'm not used to being a bother to anyone, but I don't know what I'd'a done without you." She looked away. "I was in a pretty bad way for a few days."

"Well, we wuz happy to oblige. Now, you mustn't think of it anymore. You're better now, that's what's important." As if a change of topic would be what Geneva needed, Mrs. Stillman asked her, "You going blueberryin' this year?"

"Yes'm."

"Well, I brought you these muffins I just baked this morning with our first berries."

Geneva took them from her. "Thank you kindly, ma'am."

Mrs. Stillman folded her hands over her apron. When Geneva said nothing more, she jerked her head to indicate down the road. "So, the captain's gone."

"Looks like it," Geneva replied, folding down the napkin that covered the muffins. She was still unsure how to react to her neighbor. She was no longer offended by her curiosity. She realized Mrs. Stillman was also a child of God. But neither was Geneva ready to lay bare her heart to just anyone.

Mrs. Stillman sniffed. "I knew he wouldn't stick it out here. Folks like that belong with their own kind. Fancy folk, like that young lady he paraded all around the harbor last summer." She patted one hand over the other, waiting for Geneva to agree with her. When Geneva remained noncommittal, the farmer's wife peered at Geneva's face. "You're not taking his leaving too hard, are you, dear?"

Geneva met her eyes, hoping nothing of her feelings for Caleb showed in her face. "No. I knew he had to go back."

Mrs. Stillman observed her for a few more seconds. "Well, I must say, you don't seem too brokenhearted. You're looking pretty well. There's something different about you." As she tried to puzzle it out, she gave Geneva a good going-over, from the top of her head to the toes of her boots. "It's certainly not your attire. I thought you wuz going to get rid of those trousers. You looked so nice in the dress the night o' the dance. My, that seems a century ago, 'stead o' just a few weeks. Ever hear from that nice young man, Sam Giles?"

Geneva shook her head. She'd forgotten all about Sam.

Mrs. Stillman nodded thoughtfully. Then she narrowed her eyes again at Geneva. "Why'd you go back to wearin' those things?" She made a gesture toward Geneva's trousers.

Geneva shifted from one leg to the other. "I didn't want to ruin the dress, working out in the garden and all."

"Well, you just need to make yourself another dress—a dress for working—and save that one for Sundays."

"I—I'll think about it." No matter how reasonable the suggestion sounded, Geneva didn't think she'd have much call for wearing dresses from now on.

"Why don't you go blueberryin' with us tomorrow? Do you good to have some company."

Geneva started at the suggestion. While most people went in wagonloads to the various blueberry fields, making a day outing of it, Geneva had always gone by herself, to a field she knew of in her own woods.

The prospect of being stared at by all those people who knew her, who doubtless knew of her friendship with Caleb and would be eyeing her to see "how she was taking it," rid her of any desire she might have to be in the company of people. "No thanks, Mrs. Stillman. I've got to see to my own field."

"As you will." She gave a sigh. "Well, enjoy those muffins."

Geneva watched her walk back up the road to her farmhouse, wondering at the sense of regret she felt, as if her last link to humanity were leaving.

* * *

Geneva spent the next few days at her own blueberry field, filling basket after basket with the little round blue-black fruit, which she took into the village and unloaded at the canning factory. The days were hot and backbreaking. She'd come home weary, almost too tired to eat.

She missed Jake's companionship during the long days, although she no longer felt alone. In every step she took, in every blueberry bush she touched, she felt God's presence.

Whenever her thoughts began to stray to Caleb, she steered them away. She didn't want to torture herself with wondering where he was and what he was doing. Was he being well treated? Didn't people recognize now that he was a good, upright man? Had his father asked his forgiveness?

Back in her house, Geneva filled her washbasin with water. Too weary to take a full bath, she opted instead for a sponge bath, standing at her counter. She unbelted her trousers and let them fall on the floor in a heap, then her fingers slowly unbuttoned her shirt. All she wanted was to fall on her bed. Her shirt slid to the floor and she removed her chemise, then took her washcloth and cake of soap and began to scrub the day's sweat off her skin. She rubbed her face and neck, lifting her thick braid to wash her nape.

"Oh, Lord, help me forget him. I try to keep busy, but it doesn't help stop my thoughts. I can't do it myself."

She sighed, continuing to rub downward. Nights were the worst. She'd get over Caleb, she kept telling herself. She'd survived before, she would again.

She gritted her teeth, leaning over the wooden edge of the washstand. It sometimes took more strength than she had.

She reached for her nightgown to pull it over her head. At the same moment, she heard the latch of her back door click.

She whirled around, clutching the muslin gown to her chest.

The door creaked until it stood fully open. Looming on the threshold stood Lucius Tucker. He looked her up and down, his leer telling her exactly what was on his mind.

"Gettin' all washed and purty for me, are you?"

"Get out."

As if her words were an invitation, he stepped in, closing the door softly behind him. In one hand he carried a rifle, which he leaned against the door. Then he came toward her, slowly.

"I'll leave in my own good time." He planted his boots wide apart when he got to her and just stood there, eyeing her half-clothed body. "Why don't you just go on with your wash? Ain't nothin' I ain't seen already."

Her fingers gripped the muslin tighter, her gaze darting to her back window. "How long you been here?"

He chuckled, following her gaze to the window. "Plenty long enough."

Geneva looked back at him, determined not to let him see that his words made any difference to her. "You'd better leave if you know what's good for you." Her words sounded tough, but her heart was beating half out of her chest as she calculated what course to take. She wouldn't make it to the front door before his hairy arm snaked out.

Before she could decide on anything, he did exactly that. He reached out a hand and touched her bare shoulder.

"Ginny," he breathed, "whattya been hidin' all these years? Dressin' up like a man, when you're all woman inside? It's a cryin' shame to let all this go to waste."

"Get your filthy hands off me." His fingers felt like sandpaper against her skin as he rubbed his hand up and down her shoulder. But as soon as she recoiled from him, his hand tightened on her arm.

He pulled her closer to him, and she could smell the rum on his breath. She gagged, remembering her father, and the way he used to grope and paw at her mother in the dark cabin, sometimes not even waiting until dark. She could feel the bile rising in her throat as she tried to put all the revulsion she felt for the man standing next to her into her stare. Everything about him repulsed her, from his bloodshot eyes rimmed with reddish blond lashes to his coarse beard.

With his free hand, he removed his hat, revealing his red hair combed back in long, oily streaks. Although he wore a suit, it had a sour, unwashed smell.

"I'm glad you got rid of that ol' cur of yours like I told you." He laid his hat aside on her table without letting go of her arm.

"Jake'll be around."

His laugh was low and guttural. "Tell me anothah good story. That Jake up and poisoned hisself."

"Who told you that?" She glared at him, trying to determine whether he'd have heard it from Mr. Stillman. As long as she could make him believe Jake was still alive, she had a weapon on her side.

Lucius scratched his beard, making a rasping noise. "Didn't need no one to tell me." He gave her a long, measuring look. "Didn't I tell you myself, he'd get hisself poisoned one day?"

Geneva felt as if she were riding the swells in her small boat. Everything had suddenly shifted and she didn't know whether she could keep her balance. When she first found Jake, she couldn't believe he would eat something unfit, but with everything that had ensued, she'd put it out of her mind.

"If you know so much about Jake, tell me how he came to eat something poisonous."

His pale blue eyes mocked her. "You're a smart girl. I'll let you figure that out all by yourself."

She looked at him, too incredulous to credit what he was saying. She was reading too much into his words! She thought back on the last time Lucius had come by. His threat against Jake had seemed all too real then. For a few weeks Geneva had hardly let Jake out of her sight. But when Lucius didn't bother her again, gradually her fears faded. Now his warning returned to her in all its malice, as she relived the moment she found Jake lying in pain, then later, stiff and glassy-eyed.

"You poisoned him!" The words came out a whisper. When he made no effort to deny it, she shook her head. Lucius had always annoyed and repulsed her, but she'd never taken him seriously. Now she stared at him in horror. What kind of man would do such a thing? "You said Jake would eat some bad meat." She looked at him steadily. "You gave him that bad meat, didn't you."

He chuckled, a sound so odious that she knew it would ring in her ears for a long time to come. "Shows how bad I wantchya. Have for a long time. When I get through with you, you'll forget all about that cur o' yours, I guarantee." His hand began stroking her arm once again, and she couldn't help the shudder.

"That's right, you just let yourself loose with me. You been hidin' your treasures too long." His two hands came up to grasp her breasts.

She did let loose then, but not the way Lucius expected. *"Jesus!"* she screamed at the top of her lungs. Her breath was cut off as Lucius clapped his hand over her mouth.

A part of her mind took in Lucius' efforts to bring her under control. As one hand covered her mouth, and the other tried to shake her into submission, she kept struggling.

"Quit that caterwaulin'! What are ya, some kind of crazy woman?" His fingers dug into the hollows of her cheeks.

Her rage transferred itself to her legs and she started kicking him with everything in her.

Above the noise of his curses and her muffled cries, they both heard the baying of hounds outside her front door. It sounded as if a whole pack would tear down her door.

At the same moment that the door began opening from the outside, a man's voice shouted, "Genevar! You all right in theah?"

Then Mr. Stillman stood in her half-opened doorway taking in the sight of her and Lucius. His hounds jumped around behind him, but his figure filled the entry, not permitting them inside. To Geneva, he looked like an avenging angel with a whole troop behind him come to her rescue.

Once again her neighbor had arrived just when she needed him. She shut her eyes for an instant, knowing beyond a doubt Who had sent him to her.

"Heard you screamin'." He stared at Lucius. "Think it's about time you took your hands off Ginny."

At that Lucius came to life again. Hastily, he backed away from Geneva. "It's not what you think, Asa. Don't go jumpin' to no conclusions." He reached the back door and picked up his rifle.

"It's a mite late to be payin' calls on young ladies, ain't it?"

Lucius cleared his throat. "Had to talk to her about her taxes."

"You go on home now, Lucius. Go on home to that wife and those kids of yours." Mr. Stillman stood where he was until Lucius unlatched the back door and let himself out.

The farmer turned at last to Geneva. Before she could say anything, he told her, "Shoulda' been here soonah. Missus been aftah me to come look in. She thought she saw someone making his way down heah. Mighty sorry it took me so long."

When she didn't say anything, he asked her, "You all right?"

She nodded, still clutching her nightgown to herself. She could feel her knees begin to tremble.

"I'll send the missus on down. You just stay put. Lucius ain't gonna be botherin' you again."

She wanted to laugh hysterically when he told her to stay put. She wasn't going anywhere, she wanted to assure him, except perhaps onto the floor, if her legs gave out as they were threatening to do.

Mr. Stillman left one of his hounds with her, the rest swarming around him as he departed with a final assurance over his shoulder that his wife would be "over in a jiffy."

He was as good as his word. A few minutes later, not only Mrs. Stillman but also her daughter Sarah walked in.

Mrs. Stillman took one look at Geneva and bustled over. "There, there, it's all over." She put an arm around Geneva and led her over to her bed. "What's the world coming to when a young lady isn't safe in her own house."

As she spoke, she helped Geneva slip the nightgown on over her head and push her arms through the sleeves.

"Sarah, get a kettle goin' and make some tea." She tucked the bedclothes around Geneva. "You just lie down here. Sarah'll stay with you tonight."

Geneva wanted to protest, but found herself mute, wanting desperately to have someone nearby that night.

"We'll fix up a pallet right here beside your bed. I've already sent Mr. Stillman to bring by some bedding."

Geneva just nodded.

"We'll leave the hound here, too. He'll raise enough racket if anyone tries to get in." Mrs. Stillman gave a final smooth-

ing to the bedding. "But don't you worry. That good-for-
nothing Lucius ain't going to be pestering you again. Mr.
Stillman and the boys will have a word with him." She
pressed her lips together.

"When they get through with him, he'll wish he never even
laid eyes on you."

Sarah's bed was made up, and Geneva drank the cup of
tea the girl had fixed for her. When Mrs. Stillman bent over
to take her final leave, Geneva suddenly reached out her hand
to the older woman.

"You know, I called on Jesus tonight, and He sent you."
Her voice mirrored the wonder she felt.

Mrs. Stillman just smiled and patted her hand. "So He did,
so He did." Her expression became fierce. "If there were
more God-fearin' folk around here, sorts like Lucius would
be run out of town.

"Well, good night, my dear. Sarah is right here. She can
always run over to the farm if you need anything. Don't you
fret no more. You just get your rest."

As Mrs. Stillman was leaving she turned back. "One of
my girls can lend you a dress for tomorrow, if you'd care to
accept it. That'll keep your new dress nice."

Again, Geneva found herself speaking words she never
would have dreamed of speaking even five minutes ago. "If
they don't mind, I'd be much obliged."

After the older woman left, Geneva felt cozy and secure
within her blankets, the trembling in her body subsiding.

Sarah sat by the table, the hound at her feet, some mending in her hand.

Geneva spoke across the room. "Thank you, Sarah, for
staying with me."

Sarah looked up from her sewing and just smiled.

"I've been a real bother to your folks lately."

Sarah rested her mending on her lap. "Nonsense. We worry about you, living all alone over here. That's why Ma's always glancing through her window, just to make sure there's a light on, especially since Jake died."

Geneva remembered what a trial Sarah had been to her when they were young girls. She couldn't believe this was the same girl, treating her so nicely. Sarah's next words startled her even more.

"I'm sorry about the captain." The girl's tone was sympathetic.

"What do you mean?"

She could see Sarah's blush in the lamplight.

"Well, he seemed so sweet on you at the dance." Her eyes looked off dreamily into the darkness. "I thought you two were the handsomest couple there. My sister did, too."

Geneva stared at the girl. Had people really thought her a suitable partner for Caleb? These people who had taunted her so much growing up? Had she changed so much, or had they?

Sarah sighed and picked up her sewing again. "What a shame he had to go away. What did he want to go all the way to Boston for, anyway?"

What indeed? echoed Geneva's heart.

Chapter Eighteen

The following day, Geneva sailed to town with her bushels of blueberries. After taking them to the cannery, she headed back toward the wharf.

When she heard herself being hailed, she turned to see the pastor from church walking toward her.

"Good afternoon, Miss Patterson."

"Afternoon, Pastor McDuffie." She looked at him more closely than she had in church, wondering whether he, too, had experienced the touch of God the way she had. Had he felt His very presence?

Pastor McDuffie smiled at her. "I wanted to welcome you to our church, but when I looked around, you were gone. I haven't seen you since then. Mrs. Stillman told me you were ill, that you weren't to be disturbed. She assured me you were being well taken care of."

"Oh, yes, Mrs. Stillman and her daughters took very good care of me."

"I hope you can join us again for service when you're feeling up to it."

Geneva smiled shyly. "Thank you kindly. I'd like that."

The pastor's expression turned serious. "Mr. Stillman told me what happened to you yesterday evening. I want to tell you, first of all, how sorry I am that you had to go through such a terrifying experience. I've had a talk with Lucius. I did my best to put the fear of God in him, but I don't know how well he heard me. He didn't look so good.

"It seems he ran into some trouble after trying to meddle with you. Black eyes, split lip, broken nose, wouldn't be surprised if he had a few broken ribs. I don't know whom he ran into." Pastor McDuffie shook his head. "I shall have to preach a sermon on brawling."

Geneva listened to him, too astounded at what she was hearing. Could Mr. Stillman and his sons have gone and beaten up Lucius for her? It was too unbelievable to credit. But if the pastor was telling her these things, they must be true.

The pastor's pink-cheeked face turned a little pinker. "I see Captain Phelps has returned to Boston."

"That's so," she answered, bracing for the inevitable scrutiny, knowing she'd have to get used to it.

"I'm glad he felt ready to go back."

She realized he understood why Caleb had to leave. "Yes, I am, too."

The pastor seemed to be weighing the truth of her words. She gazed back at him without flinching. He nodded, as if satisfied.

"He'll be back one of these days. He's proven himself a man who doesn't run away from his duty." He touched her lightly on the shoulder. "In the meantime, please come by and call on my wife. She'd be happy to make your acquaintance."

"Thank you."

With a final nod, Pastor McDuffie continued on his way. Geneva resumed walking.

"Hey, Ginny!" The postmaster stuck his head out the door as she passed the little brick post office. "Come on in heah. Got a lettah for you."

A letter? She'd never received a letter in her life. It must be some mistake. She made her way over.

"Good morning," she told the wizened little man with the pencil stuck behind his ear.

He pushed back his blue cap and scratched his head. "I'm glad I caught you. Haven't seen you in a while and didn't know how I was goin' to get this out to you." As he talked, the postmaster moved back behind his window.

"Now, let's see, where did I put it? It came in a couple of days ago, you see. Yes, heah 'tis." He reached up to a shelf behind him. "Right wheah I put it aside. I said to myself, it'll be safe up theah, until I see Ginny come to town."

Geneva didn't dare ask who had sent it. What if she couldn't read it? She was used to reading printed words, what if she couldn't read someone's script? She held out her hand to take the white envelope.

"It's from the captain," the postmaster whispered confidentially. "Postmarked from Boston!"

"Thank you," Geneva told him, touching the envelope as if it were the greatest treasure on earth. All she wanted now was to be alone somewhere so she could savor the feel of it. She looked back at the postmaster, trying to keep her face blank. "Well, I'll be seeing you."

"Be seein' ya, Ginny." The postmaster touched his fingers to his cap.

The little bell on his door tinkled as Geneva left. She slipped the envelope into the bib of her overalls. She wouldn't look at it yet.

When she arrived home, she stifled her impatience at the

sight of Mrs. Stillman making her way down the road as if she, too, had been on the watch for Geneva. Geneva scolded herself for her impatience, remembering her neighbor's kindness the evening before. If it hadn't been for Mrs. Stillman's interest, Geneva didn't know what would have happened with Lucius Tucker.

"You're back, Geneva. How are you feelin' today?"

"Oh, I'm fine, Mrs. Stillman. Right as rain."

"I'm so glad to hear that. Sarah said you slept well."

Geneva didn't know how Sarah would have reasoned that, since her gentle snores had reached Geneva's ears as soon as the farm girl's head hit her pillow.

"I came over to bring you the dress I promised you." She held out a folded garment. "Why don't you go blueberryin' with us tomorrow? It'd do you good to be among some people your own age for a change. We have a grand time of it. We take the wagon and a picnic lunch. Why, it's almost like a sleigh ride in winter."

"I don't know, Mrs. Stillman...." Geneva looked off toward the bay. She felt as if she'd faced a hundred people today in the village instead of just the pastor and postmaster.

"Oh, come on. You've known everyone there your whole life. I'll tell you what, you wear this. It's one of Sarah's old dresses. That way you can save your own for Sundays. If you buy yourself another bolt of material, you bring it over, and we'll have a second dress sewed up for you in no time."

Reluctantly, Geneva found herself nodding her head. She'd probably regret it, but she felt she had to do something to show her neighbor some gratitude for last night's rescue. Besides, she was willing to agree to anything at the moment, if only she could be alone to read her precious letter at last.

When Geneva was finally by herself, she walked to the end

of her meadow, overlooking the bay, and sat down beside Jake's grave.

"Well, Jake, what do you think? He wrote to me!" She traced the outline of her name in the black ink. *Miss Geneva S. Patterson, Haven's End, Maine.*

"Hope I'll be able to read it," she mumbled, prying open the flap. Inside there was a small piece of notepaper folded neatly in half. Half in disappointment for the brevity of the correspondence, half in relief that it would be easy to read, Geneva scanned the neatly printed letters.

Dear Geneva,
How are you? I arrived fine in Boston. All is well. I have to sail for New—

Geneva carefully sounded out the next word

—Orleans!

Her excitement over the new word disappeared as soon as she realized what she was reading. Caleb was going to New Orleans! She looked at the shimmering water before her, trying to come to terms with the fact. If Boston had sounded like the other side of the world, New Orleans might as well be. She bent back over the note.

I wish I could tell you about it. Keep well.
Fondly, Caleb.

Fondly. Geneva puzzled over the word. Did that mean he was fond of her? He hadn't forgotten her? She tried to picture him in New Orleans, but couldn't. She reread the letter several times, trying to decipher the meaning of each sentence, until it was no longer necessary to look at the paper, she knew the words by heart. But still she preferred looking down at the words. She felt closer to Caleb that way, imagining his hand on his pen, forming these very letters, his other hand actually holding the paper she was now holding.

She put the paper up to her nostrils and sniffed, hoping to catch even a whiff of him. But it only smelled of paper. She put it to her breast, wanting to believe she was touching Caleb by touching something he had touched.

He had asked how she was. Did that mean he really cared to know? He said all was well. Did that mean with his father? Did it mean he and Miss Harding had reconciled? He said he had to sail to New Orleans. Did that mean he had been obliged to? Or was it some whim of his own? The only hope she could draw from the brief note was in the last sentence. He wished he could tell her about it. Did that mean he might do so someday? Would he ever come back?

Geneva had tried to banish any hope in her heart of seeing the captain again. She had told herself over and over to accept the fact that he was gone. But the hope refused to be smothered completely. One little spark remained, and it wanted to rekindle.

She told herself the letter gave no hope. It said nothing of ever coming back. It just ended with the words *keep well. Fondly.* He was wishing her the best. That's what people did when they said goodbye. He was telling her in those words that he wouldn't be back.

By the time she went to bed, she was no closer to solving the meaning of Caleb's words than when she'd first read them. But one thing was certain: he hadn't forgotten her.

* * *

Blueberry picking the next day proved much more pleasant than she could have imagined. Although the work was just as hard—even harder hampered by heavy skirts and petticoats than in her usual trousers—the company was so convivial that it made the time go faster. At noon, everyone sat under the shade of the fir trees to rest and enjoy lunch. People exchanged gossip and caught up on the news of the summer. Most of the farming and fishing families had been too busy throughout the summer to visit with each other, so the blueberry picking took on a festive atmosphere.

Nobody mentioned the incident with Lucius, nor was the captain's name brought up. Geneva wondered whether someone had forbidden those topics. She glanced over at Mr. and Mrs. Stillman. No one looked at her curiously nor exclaimed over her appearance in Sarah's old dress. Geneva didn't think she would have minded anything anyone said. She was too caught up in the memory of Caleb's letter to let anything distress her.

One thought kept going through her mind: he had remembered her all the way in Boston, enough to write her a letter!

There was an added distraction at the berry picking. To her surprise, Sam Giles showed up in the afternoon. He came right over to Geneva, as if he'd expected to find her there, and helped her fill her basket for the remainder of the afternoon. He was such friendly company that Geneva was surprised when it was time to go home. Sam rode with her in the Stillmans' wagon, then walked her to her door. After he said goodbye, Geneva watched him leave, wondering at his attentiveness.

The next day, another buggy pulled up to her gate. When she recognized its driver, Geneva ran to it.

"Mrs. Bradford! You're back! Did you have an enjoyable time?"

"Yes, indeed, although it's nice to be home again," Mrs. Bradford said from the buggy. "It's you I was concerned about. I couldn't rest until I came to see you for myself."

Geneva beamed up at her. "Oh, I've never been better. I'm so glad to see you!"

Mrs. Bradford returned her smile. As Geneva helped her down, the older woman kept talking. "Let me look at you. My, you look wonderful. No, more than that, you look radiant. I'm so glad." Mrs. Bradford peered into her eyes. "You know, I've had you on my heart for days. I told myself I was silly for worrying. Why should this past week have been any different from any other?

"Are you quite all right? I've been praying for you. When I came back, I heard a few things in the village."

She looked at Geneva closely, and when Geneva broke into another wide smile, Mrs. Bradford asked, "What is it? Something's happened, hasn't it?"

Instead of answering her, Geneva reached out to the older woman and they embraced.

After a few moments, Geneva stepped back, but kept her two hands in Mrs. Bradford's. "Yes, ma'am, something has happened." She squeezed the older woman's hands. "If you come inside and have a cup of tea with me, I'll tell you all about it."

"I would like that very much."

Geneva did as she'd promised and told Mrs. Bradford about her experience with the Lord. She told her about Jake and about Lucius and about the help she'd received from the Stillmans. She poured out her heart to Mrs. Bradford about everything, except Caleb. She didn't know how Mrs.

Bradford would react to that. Mrs. Bradford came from Caleb's world, and Geneva couldn't bear it if the older woman expressed shock over Geneva's feelings for him.

Mrs. Bradford just sat and listened, marveling at Geneva's words. She clasped her hands to her breast, saying, "Oh, my! Oh, my!" over and over. Their tea grew cold, but neither one noticed.

By the time Geneva had finished, Mrs. Bradford's eyes were moist. "Oh, Geneva, you don't know the joy I feel at hearing your words." She took one of Geneva's hands in hers. "And this is just the beginning. You are going to begin a road that teaches you more and more about your dear Lord and Savior, Jesus Christ. The lessons won't always be easy, but the journey is well worth it. You've only begun to experience the 'joy unspeakable' the Bible tells us about."

Despite her heavy workload, Geneva made time for her outings with Mrs. Bradford. The two had a stronger bond now, and Geneva wanted to spend as much time as possible alone with the older woman before the warm weather was over and Mrs. Bradford headed back to Boston.

They went out to the island where Geneva had first taken her. They hiked up the rocks to the highest promontory to watch the eagles once again.

As they watched one in flight, Mrs. Bradford raised her arms heavenward and spoke aloud some verses from a favorite psalm: "'Bless the Lord, O my soul: and all that is within me, bless his holy name. Bless the Lord, O my soul, and forget not all his benefits: Who forgiveth all thine iniquities; Who healeth all thy diseases; Who redeemeth thy life from destruction; Who crowneth thee with loving kindness and tender mercies; Who satisfieth thy mouth with good things; so that thy youth is renewed like the eagle's.'"

She turned to Geneva with a smile. "You know the Lord uses the image of an eagle many times throughout Scripture. He talks about our hiding under his wing."

Geneva watched the majestic bird soar across the sky, marveling at how apt the image was.

When they sat down to a picnic lunch, Mrs. Bradford said, "The time goes by so quickly. Soon, I shall be heading back to my winter home." She smiled. "Just like the birds I've been watching." She reached over and squeezed Geneva's hand. "You've given me such pleasure, taking me on these outings. I want to tell you how much I've appreciated your company."

Instead of looking away embarrassed, as she would have even a few short weeks ago, Geneva smiled and squeezed her hand back. "You're the one who's given *me* the pleasure. You'll never know how much I owe you."

"I'm sure you're overstating the case, but I'm happy that you've enjoyed these outings as well. I'm glad we've become friends." She let Geneva's hand go. "I meant to tell you again how nice you looked in a dress. I hope you have plans for making another?"

Geneva colored and nodded. "Yes, I bought some more fabric and started cutting one out. One for everyday," she hastened to add.

"That's delightful. I know soon there'll be a young man who'll come calling on you—"

Geneva shook her head. "No, I don't think so."

"You sell yourself short. You don't realize how attractive you are. And now you have an added beauty, a beauty that comes from within. 'The Lord has made His face to shine upon thee.'"

Geneva could feel the pinpricks of tears in her eyes. The euphoria that had come after receiving Caleb's note had faded, leaving a renewed conviction that he was out of her life for good. She swiped at her eyes. "It seems as if all I've done is cry since I found the Lord."

"He's filled you with joy, and it's difficult to contain that with mere words."

Geneva wanted to tell her so badly about Caleb, but she still didn't dare.

When the afternoon waned, they began their descent. Geneva turned to help Mrs. Bradford down a steep slope, which was made up of dried spruce and balsam fir needles wedged between the exposed roots of a tree.

"Oh, dear!" Mrs. Bradford cried as the toe of her foot caught on a root. Her weight came forward upon Geneva, who braced herself to support it.

"Easy there," Geneva told her, trying to cushion the older woman's fall as much as possible without losing her own balance. When she'd managed to secure her footing, she tried to help Mrs. Bradford regain her balance.

"Ow!" The older woman winced as she placed some weight on her foot. "I must have twisted my ankle." She tried again. "Oh, dear."

Geneva eased her onto the slope, so she could sit while Geneva examined her ankle. After removing Mrs. Bradford's boot, she probed it gently. It was swelling and painful to the touch.

"Oh, what will Bessie say! She's going to give me such a scolding. And my daughters in Boston!" Mrs. Bradford seemed more concerned about those at home than about her injury.

"Let's see if we can get down if you lean on me," Geneva suggested, standing and giving her a hand.

Together the two worked their way down the slope, with much stopping along the way. When they finally returned to Mrs. Bradford's home, Bessie was waiting at the foot of the lawn, her arms folded. Geneva could understand why Mrs. Bradford's fear had been greater for her cook than for her injury.

Geneva saw Mrs. Bradford settled on a couch. When Bessie didn't allow her to do anything more, Geneva returned home. The very next day, she received a note from Mrs. Bradford asking her to stop in and call. Geneva changed into her dress and hoped Bessie would allow her in.

Mrs. Bradford was lying on a settee in the sitting room. "Thank you for coming right away."

Geneva approached the settee. "How are you feeling, ma'am? Did the doctor come?"

"Yes, someone was sent to Hatsfield to fetch him. I'm just fine, except for the bother I've caused." She chuckled ruefully. "Bessie has done nothing but scold. She says I should know better than to be traipsing up hill and down dale. But I was fortunate. It's only a sprain. I shall just have to keep off of it for a few days. Come, sit down, Geneva, I want to have a talk with you. Would you like some tea?"

"No, thank you." Geneva took the chair closest to Mrs. Bradford, eager to find out what the older woman wanted to talk with her about.

"I've had some news from Boston that makes it necessary for me to return there immediately. I'm involved in certain charity work, and people need my advice. Anyway, the point is, I need to return, but I'm going to need some help getting around. Bessie shall go back with me, but…" She sighed. "I'm afraid I'm becoming just a little weary of the scolding. Besides, she'll have enough to do, keeping track of the luggage."

Mrs. Bradford leaned forward, eager as a child. "That brings me to my question. Would you consider coming with me to Boston as a companion?"

Geneva stared at her. "I don't rightly understand you, ma'am. You're asking me to come to Boston?"

Mrs. Bradford beamed and nodded. "Yes. I know it's asking a lot of you. You have your work here. That is why I wouldn't just ask you to come for a few weeks and then return here. I would like you to come and stay with me the winter. I want you to consider yourself part of my family."

"Oh, Mrs. Bradford, oh…I…I don't know what to say." Boston was another world.

Boston meant Caleb.

Geneva put her hands to her cheeks, filled with confusion. She couldn't believe she was being given an opportunity to live in his city. Her heart began to soar at the thought. The next instant her hopes plummeted.

All kinds of stumbling blocks came to mind. She didn't belong in a place like that. She would die if Caleb ever thought she'd gone running after him. What would she do in a grand city like Boston?

She shook her head. "Oh, I couldn't possibly go with you." She looked at Mrs. Bradford's stricken face, and immediately reached out a hand. "Oh, not that I wouldn't want to. I do want to help you. Perhaps I could just accompany you on the ship and then come right back?"

"Are you sure you couldn't leave your house behind for the winter? Or is there someone you don't want to leave behind? Has a young man already stolen your heart? I'll understand."

The words were so close to the mark, in a way Mrs. Bradford couldn't begin to imagine, that Geneva felt her cheeks go warm. She shook her head, trying to think of plausible reasons why she couldn't come.

"I would be no kind of companion for you. I don't know any good manners. I wouldn't know how to act among your people."

"All those things can be learned. I shall teach you myself."

"But I'm not a lady. You couldn't take me anywhere. I'd shame you."

"Nonsense. You're a fine young woman. Anything that a lady knows, you can easily learn."

"I can barely even read and write." There, she'd played her trump card. "I didn't know anything at the beginning of the summer, but I— I've been taking lessons."

"And you shall continue to learn."

Geneva stared at Mrs. Bradford. She'd blurted out her most shameful secret, and the woman remained as calm as always. "You make it sound so easy." Geneva's gaze alighted on Mrs. Bradford's well-worn Bible, and she picked it up in frustration. "I still can't even read this. How am I supposed to know who God is if I can't even read His word?"

But Mrs. Bradford was completely unfazed by Geneva's shortcomings. "Why, that's all the more reason you must come with me. The Lord doesn't want you to stop where you are. You must continue learning what He has in store for you." She patted Geneva's knee as if the matter were all settled.

"I shall engage a tutor for you. You can study in private in my home. You're a bright girl. You shall see how quickly you'll learn. It's perfect, Geneva." Mrs. Bradford smiled, warming to the idea. "I'll even bring someone in to give you lessons on deportment, if you think that will make you comfortable among people."

The more she talked about it, the more excited Mrs. Bradford became. Geneva tried to bring up more objections—Mrs. Bradford's children, her charity work, her social engagements, her status in the community, even Bessie—but for every objection, Mrs. Bradford had a ready reply, until Geneva's resistance began to cave in.

What finally allowed her to accept Mrs. Bradford's offer was the knowledge that Caleb was not in Boston. His note had said nothing about returning there from New Orleans. Geneva knew trips so far away meant months at the very least.

So, she finally nodded to Mrs. Bradford, feeling she was committing herself to some great, unknown adventure.

Chapter Nineteen

"As you can see, this painter is presenting light and dark in a strong contrast, the way you see in photographs. There is no chiaroscuro as in the works up to this period. The woman's body is harshly lit. Do you see the difference between this painting and the ones we saw last week?" Miss Talbot turned her face from the canvas to Geneva.

"Yes, it certainly looks different from those others." Geneva marveled at how real the people looked. Only last fall she hadn't even imagined that anyone could with paint and brush bring alive a scene on canvas.

"Come," said Miss Talbot in her brisk voice, "let's look at the next canvas. This one is a landscape."

Geneva let Miss Talbot's words drift past her ears as she looked at the next picture, but her mind was no longer on the art lesson. So often during the preceding autumn and winter she had felt her puny mind could not hold all the information being fed it. Since the moment she'd stepped off the steamship onto

the wharf in Boston harbor, she'd barely had time to get her
bearings before finding herself with a rigorous schedule to
follow. Dress fittings, selection of a tutor and dance instructor,
and setting up a timetable for lessons had filled her first few
days.

If she'd feared an encounter with Caleb in his native city,
the possibility seemed so remote now as to be nonexistent.
Miss Talbot, the woman Mrs. Bradford had selected as Geneva's tutor, kept her mind filled with facts and figures. Geneva had little time to worry about the world she imagined
Caleb inhabited.

Miss Talbot, a fair-haired woman in her early forties, was
kind, but very serious about her duties. Geneva spent six
hours a day with her, with a break at the noon hour for dinner. She studied reading, writing and arithmetic, as well as
religion, history, geography, and art and music appreciation.
As part of the latter two disciplines, Miss Talbot took Geneva
to the Athenaeum and other, smaller, galleries certain after-
noons of the week, alternating with musical performances.

On Saturdays she was taken into the world of Mrs. Bradford's charities. She worked at a settlement house, where she
learned about the other side of life in the large city, the life of
the recently arrived immigrant, the drunk, the fatherless
child....

Sundays were spent at church and in visiting. That was the
only time her world touched Caleb's, but after the first few
Sundays, any worry subsided. Mrs. Bradford's world involved
elderly ladies, and her own children and grandchildren, as
well as consultations with the minister on helping the needy.

Geneva wanted so badly to learn everything Miss Talbot
took the time to teach her. More than anything she didn't want
to disappoint Mrs. Bradford, whose belief in her never waned.

Miss Talbot took Geneva to the next painting, her clipped voice seldom at a loss to explain something puzzling. Geneva sometimes wondered what her tutor would say if she knew her full story.

"Well, I think that's enough for one afternoon. How about a brisk walk along the Commons?"

"That sounds perfect." She gave Miss Talbot a grateful smile. At least her tutor was a strong believer in exercising both the mind and the body.

What Geneva missed the most in Boston was the outdoors. Since her arrival she felt she hadn't breathed real air, except for the few times she'd stood at the harbor. And that was so clogged with ships' masts, she could scarcely see the ocean.

The gray, bare look of winter dominated the park. Dirty snow edged the walks, but in the central areas, pure white still blanketed the Commons.

Geneva wondered when this interlude in her life would come to an end. She would always be grateful to Mrs. Bradford for giving her the opportunity to learn. In the deepest recesses of her heart, she was also glad to have seen Caleb's city. By the time she returned to Haven's End, it would be easier to live without him, and yet know more about him from the place he came from. This knowledge would fill her storehouse of memories, just as the secret cache of treasures he'd given her filled her chest—the paisley shawl, the posy of dried flowers, the faded rosebuds....

Geneva arrived at the imposing Beacon Hill town house cold but refreshed after the walk.

Siobhan, the young Irish maid, helped them remove their wraps. "Might brisk out there, 'tisn't it?"

"Yes," Miss Talbot answered. "But invigorating, wouldn't you agree, Geneva?"

"Oh, yes. I feel so much bett—" She stopped as she realized what she had been about to say. She didn't want Miss Talbot to think she hadn't enjoyed the outing to the gallery. "I mean, the air inside the gallery was a bit stuffy."

Miss Talbot didn't seem to notice Geneva's remark, her mind already on the next item on their schedule. "Has Mrs. Bradford taken tea yet?"

"Oh, yes, miss." The maid gave them an eager look as she came closer to them. "She would'a waited for you, but she had some callers. Fine gentleman and his mother. Ever so handsome, he is. A friend of Mrs. Bradford's, I believe."

"Thank you, Siobhan." Miss Talbot turned from the young maid to curtail any gossip. "We'll go on up, then. Would you ask for a fresh pot?"

"Yes, ma'am." The maid bobbed a curtsy.

"Maybe we shouldn't intrude," Geneva ventured.

"Siobhan would have informed us if it were a private call. Think of this as part of your education, Geneva. Mrs. Bradford wants to introduce you gradually to society. She has held off until now, wanting to prepare you better. This is a perfect occasion to practice some conversational skills. You must be at ease conversing with anyone over a wide range of subjects."

They had reached the drawing room. Miss Talbot grasped the handle firmly and pushed the door open.

"Good afternoon," she said.

"Oh, good, you're both back. I was hoping you'd be in time to see my visitors." Mrs. Bradford looked past Miss Talbot to Geneva. "Look who's here! Caleb Phelps, your neighbor back in Haven's End."

Facing her across the room was Caleb—more imposing than she'd ever seen him. As soon as she'd entered, he'd stood, and immediately dwarfed the four women present.

Geneva barely registered Mrs. Phelps at the edge of her vision.

Against all hope, she'd dreamed of this moment. At the same time she'd dreaded meeting him on his own territory, and now the reality was much more daunting than any of her imaginings.

He was so elegant, dressed in a fine black cutaway with impeccable white shirt beneath. His narrow, fawn-colored trousers only served to emphasize his height. His hair, closer cropped than he'd worn in Haven's End, gave him such a formal appearance.

Gone were any vestiges of the broken man she'd befriended early last summer. Gone was the casually dressed man playing at gentleman farmer. This was a man of the world. This was the scion of an old, aristocratic family. One of the Boston Brahmins. The heir of an empire. Oh, yes, Miss Talbot had instructed her thoroughly about Boston society!

Geneva's mind could formulate nothing beyond these thoughts of Caleb's superiority.

Then she remembered her experience in her room at Haven's End and who she was.

Already Caleb was advancing toward her. Miss Talbot, interpreting Geneva's abrupt halt as fear of talking to a member of society, intercepted the captain before he could reach Geneva.

"How do you do?" She extended her hand.

Caleb looked at the woman's hand as if he didn't know what to do with it. But he couldn't ignore it for long. "How do you do," he answered, taking Miss Talbot's hand, although his gaze reverted to Geneva.

"Caleb Phelps," he added automatically, since no one had a chance to introduce him.

"Edith Talbot." Geneva watched Miss Talbot give Caleb's hand a firm shake. Then her tutor turned to her. "I understand you are already acquainted with Miss Patterson."

"Yes." Now there he was, standing before her, his hand held out. "How are you, Geneva?"

Her name on his lips took her back to their time together in Haven's End. Like a sleepwalker, she extended her own hand and felt it enfolded in his warm one. His other hand came up to cover the top of hers.

"Hello—" her voice came out like a breath "—Captain Phelps."

Something flickered in his blue eyes at her polite address. Was it disappointment? Of course not, she scolded herself. Most likely it was relief. He was probably wishing she wouldn't reveal to everyone that they used to be on a first-name basis.

"You look wonderful."

How could he know what she looked like—his blue gaze had never left her face. She must look a mess. After that brisk walk home, she hadn't even glanced in the mirror to smooth her hair before entering the drawing room. Her nose and eyes and cheeks must all be red, her hair windblown. As hard as she tried, she never managed to look neat the way Miss Talbot did.

"You two must be chilled to the bone. Come have a cup of tea." Mrs. Bradford's voice drifted over to Geneva.

"That would be just the thing." Miss Talbot's brisk tones cut through the unreality enveloping her.

Caleb reacted more quickly than Geneva was capable of at that moment. He released her cold hand, now warmed by his touch, and took a step back.

"Yes, you look chilled. Mrs. Bradford has been telling me you were at the Athenaeum, looking at a new exhibit. Realism, I believe they call it?"

"Yes, indeed," Miss Talbot answered, as she made her way to a chair.

Geneva felt a twinge of gratitude for her sober-minded tutor, who seemed the only one aware of Geneva's sudden and complete loss of all social skills—skills that had been drummed into her over the past months.

"It is quite a good exhibition with the works of Manet, which caused such a stir when they were first shown in Paris. They are almost scientific in their detached quality. But they are now accepted by the art community in view of the latest uproar in Paris by artists such as Monet and Renoir. But those haven't reached our shores as yet."

The voices of the others faded behind Caleb's shoulders as Geneva continued to stare up at him. He met her gaze as if he, too, found it difficult to break the connection.

"You came back," she finally said.

"I always intended to."

Before she could fathom what his eyes were telling her with his reply, he took her elbow and escorted her to one of the settees by the marble fireplace. "Excuse me just a moment."

She watched him walk to the tea table and take the cup Mrs. Bradford held out to him. Before he returned to Geneva, he stopped by his mother's chair and said something to her. Mrs. Phelps blinked at whatever it was, then rose and came with him to where Geneva sat.

Geneva had only met Mrs. Phelps once before, at another tea last fall. Although she seemed a pleasant woman, she'd appeared so refined and elegant that the recently arrived Geneva hadn't dared utter a word. When Mrs. Phelps had heard that Geneva came from Haven's End, she'd turned to her with friendly interest, but Geneva could barely answer in

more than monosyllables. Mrs. Phelps had turned back to
Mrs. Bradford and they'd spoken of Caleb for a few minutes.
Geneva had hungrily garnered every word. She'd managed
to find out the reason for his trip to New Orleans was to set
up his cousin in their shipping office there. One thing that
stood out in the conversation was when Mrs. Phelps had
said, "He didn't want to go. He did it for Ellery and Arabella."

And now that same woman, escorted by her son, was approaching Geneva again. All she could do was lift a silent
prayer heavenward, asking for help.

Caleb held a cup of tea out to her. Geneva concentrated
on the simple act of taking the cup and saucer from him,
stilling the trembling of her hands as his fingertips brushed
hers. Carefully she lowered cup and saucer to her lap.

Caleb seated his mother beside her.

Geneva was afraid to lift the cup to her lips for fear of
spilling something.

"Before you came in, my son was telling us what a great
help you were to him at Haven's End."

Geneva looked from mother to son, unable to hide her astonishment. "He did?" Then, recovering, she shook her head.
"Oh, no, ma'am, I didn't do anything."

"Among her many virtues ranks modesty," Caleb put in
from where he stood by the marble fireplace. "If it hadn't
been for Geneva, I don't know how I would have kept my
sanity."

Geneva thought she must be in some dream where
everyone was saying funny things. Things that had the sound
of reality while the dream lasted, but which would appear ludicrous as soon as she awoke.

"When—" She cleared her throat and began again. "When
did you return from New Orleans?"

"Yesterday."

Again Geneva knew it must be a dream. He'd just arrived yesterday and he was already visiting her? No, no. It was Mrs. Bradford he'd come to see.

"How was your journey?" she asked, glad her voice, at least, was coming out normally.

"Very satisfactory."

Geneva wished she could get through the mire of this dream. All his answers sounded fraught with meaning, but there was no way, in her current state, of getting to the bottom of them. She knew from Mrs. Phelps' previous visit that Caleb had accompanied both Ellery and *his wife*, Arabella, to New Orleans.

At the time, Geneva had thought perhaps Caleb wanted to be with Arabella at all costs, even if it meant having to be beside her new husband. But here was Caleb—looking extremely well—expressing gratification with his trip, and no shadows apparent in his features.

"Caleb's father and I are holding a soiree for him this weekend to welcome him home. There will be music and dancing, but we hesitate to call it a ball, since we're giving it on such short notice. We just want all his friends and acquaintances to know he is home. He was here so briefly in August before he sailed to New Orleans, as a favor to his father and me, that most people didn't even know he had returned."

"I see." Geneva gathered strength enough to lift her cup to her lips.

"Would you do us the honor of attending?"

Geneva's hand jerked forward, and she took far too big a swallow of tea. It went down the wrong way, and she began to cough. The cup clattered against the saucer. Caleb's hands took it from her.

"Oh, my dear, are you all right?" Mrs. Phelps' kind voice came to her, and she could only nod.

Caleb was kneeling in front of her, offering her his handkerchief. She took the crisp white cloth and put it against her mouth. She could smell the fragrance of his cologne against her nostrils.

Finally the coughing subsided. She couldn't even meet Caleb's gaze so close to her. She turned to Mrs. Phelps instead. "I'm sorry."

"Would you like some water?" Caleb's mother asked, her face expressing concern.

"Oh, no. I'm quite all right, I assure you. Please go on with what you were saying."

"Oh, yes, about the homecoming party for Caleb. You will come, won't you?"

Geneva's gaze flew to Mrs. Bradford. What was she going to say? She began to panic. She'd never intended to see Caleb in Boston. He would think she had come looking for him. She should never have left Haven's End.

"Will you be there, Geneva?"

Slowly, she turned to meet Caleb's blue eyes, which she had felt on her the entire time. "I don't know— I…I wasn't planning on attending any parties." She floundered for a valid excuse. "Mrs. Bradford…I came only as her companion…."

"Mrs. Bradford—" Caleb's voice rose over the gathering. "What do you say to coming with Geneva to an evening's festivities at our house on Saturday evening?"

Mrs. Bradford clasped her hands together and gave a smile of enchantment such as a girl of eighteen would, at hearing of such an event. "How delightful! And just the thing. I've been trying to figure out how to introduce Geneva to some people her own age. This would be perfect."

Caleb turned his smile on Geneva—the same smile that had dazzled her so long ago on the wharf. "So, it's settled. Saturday evening at eight o'clock."

Caleb and his mother left shortly after that. Both Mrs. Bradford and Miss Talbot went up to their rooms to rest. Geneva stayed in the drawing room and did nothing but alternately roam its perimeters and stand at the window gazing out. By the time she went upstairs to change for dinner, she'd made up her mind about something. She knocked on Mrs. Bradford's door on her way to her room.

"Come in," Mrs. Bradford called out.

Geneva's hostess reclined against a sofa by her window, a book in her lap. "Geneva, come in, dear."

"May I talk to you a moment?"

"Of course."

Geneva sat on the edge of a salmon-pink, velvet-upholstered chair and clasped her hands above her knees. "Mrs. Bradford," she began.

"Yes, my dear?"

"I'm very grateful for all you've done for me since I arrived in Boston."

The older woman smiled. "It's been my pleasure."

"When I came, I only expected to be a helper to you. I didn't expect you to hire people to teach me so many things."

"Have I given you too much? I know you've been kept very busy." She looked down at her book. "I think I feared you'd be so homesick for Maine and if I kept you busy enough, you wouldn't have a chance to have second thoughts. I'm sorry, my dear."

"Oh, no, that's not it at all," Geneva hastened to reassure her, thinking how much harder those months would have been if she hadn't been so occupied. "I—I'm glad to have my time filled. I'm grateful for all the learning you've given me. It's just that it's not what I expected. You've been more than generous. I had no right to receive so much."

"Oh, Geneva, you'll never understand the satisfaction it's given me to see you learn. You know my children are grown. Having you here has been as if the Lord has granted me another daughter to cosset and encourage."

Geneva stared at Mrs. Bradford. She could scarcely believe her hostess had likened her to one of her daughters. She knew how close Mrs. Bradford was to her daughters, and how good they were to their mother. The woman certainly was in no need of any more daughters. Such generosity of heart on the older woman's part moved Geneva so much, she didn't think she could say what she needed to say.

"No one's ever said anything so nice to me before," she said finally.

"Well, you deserve it."

Geneva smoothed her skirt down over her knees, knowing she must proceed. "The reason I needed to talk with you was…was…to tell you—" she gripped her knees for support "—I think it's time I thought about getting back. Back to Haven's End."

Mrs. Bradford showed the first concern she'd exhibited during all of Geneva's narrative. "Oh, dear, no! I thought you'd wait at least until summer. Then the two of us could travel together. What's the matter, dear, aren't you happy here? I know it's so different from what you're used to. But just give it a little time.

"I know Miss Talbot has been pushing you hard. But it's only because we wanted to prepare you to begin enjoying a little entertainment while you were here in Boston. And now we have just the occasion to begin. Caleb Phelps' homecoming will be just the thing. He's such a nice young man, and you already know him."

"That's just it, ma'am. I didn't come here to go to dances and such."

"Oh." Mrs. Bradford waved a hand. "If that's what's worrying you, you can set your mind at rest. I'd already talked with both Miss Talbot and with your dance instructor. They both assured me you are ready to begin having some social life with people your own age."

"I'm fine here. I enjoy my time with you."

"I know you do, and I do, too. You'll never know how much these times mean to me. But it's important for you to be among young people as well. Now, don't look so scared. You're capable of a lot more than you give yourself credit for. And you'll never know, until you go out there and do it.

"This soiree is the perfect opportunity to introduce you." She chuckled. "You've got to get your feet wet sometime. You'll meet lots of young people. You'll also see many of my acquaintances, ladies you've already met at tea or at the settlement house."

As if sensing Geneva's continued resistance, she went on. "If it's the dancing that scares you, your dance instructor assures me you can handle any of the popular dances well. In fact, he says it's precisely what you need—to practice in a real situation. But if that is what is holding you back, you needn't dance. You can sit out the dances with me in the old ladies' corner," she added with a smile, trying to ease Geneva's nerves.

When Geneva said nothing at all, Mrs. Bradford asked her softly, "What's really bothering you, my dear?"

Geneva looked down at her splayed fingers, debating. She'd told Mrs. Bradford just about everything of her life.

Everything but her friendship with Caleb. Why not tell her? She trusted Mrs. Bradford. And if anyone would understand why she couldn't go to the party, it was this kind woman.

So, slowly, her words coming out hesitantly at first, Geneva told her of meeting Caleb. Once she began speaking, the words began to flow, as she described how he'd first picked her up off the wharf, and how she in turn had helped him when he'd returned to Haven's End, and from that, how a friendship had grown. Mrs. Bradford never once interrupted, merely nodded her head from time to time. If Geneva had feared shocking her hostess with such a tale, she needn't have.

Finally, Geneva got to the dance in Hatsfield. She hesitated, but then plunged on.

"He— He kissed me. And—" She shrugged and tried to smile. "And then, I did something foolish."

"What was that?" Mrs. Bradford asked softly.

"I fell in love with him.

"And then the next day, he told me he was leaving for Boston. It was silly of me, I know, to hope he'd stay. I knew all summer long that someday he'd leave."

When Mrs. Bradford didn't say anything, Geneva tried to explain. "I never expected him to feel anything for me. I never even hoped to see him again after he left. Why, the only reason I agreed to come with you here was that I knew he was in New Orleans."

Mrs. Bradford looked puzzled. "How did you know that? I don't think he himself had any idea when he returned to Boston."

"Because he sent me a letter." Geneva smiled at the memory of her pleasure. "It was the first time I'd gotten something addressed to me by mail. I was even able to read it myself," she added proudly.

"What did he write you?"

"He wrote to say he was sailing for New Orleans."

Mrs. Bradford nodded. "So, you knew he'd be away."

"I knew enough to know that New Orleans was far enough that he wouldn't be back soon." Suddenly she remembered the soiree. "But time has a way of slipping by. Now he's back. It gave me quite a turn when I first walked in today."

Mrs. Bradford smiled. "I thought you acted a little strangely. I just attributed it to spending too many hours looking at paintings."

Geneva looked down. "I don't think I should be here. I mean—" She clenched her fists. "I wouldn't ever want him to think I'd followed him here."

"You know what they say about running away. It's no good."

"I won't be running away. I never ran away." She answered sadly.

"No, indeed you didn't. He left you." The older woman gave a deep sigh. "Geneva, I need to do some thinking about all you've told me, but there is one thing I'm sure of right now. Caleb is not the type of man to trifle with a young lady's feelings—"

"But I'm not a young lady. I was just a—a farmhand to him."

"Nonsense!"

"But you remember how I was. Going around in trousers. I don't blame him for not seeing me as a woman—"

Mrs. Bradford snorted. "He might have started out not seeing you as a woman, but a man like Caleb doesn't go kissing a 'farmhand.'"

"Anyway, he might have seen something in me at the dance, but that still doesn't make me a lady. Everything's different now. This is Boston."

Mrs. Bradford gave her a severe look. "Don't ever think you're not a lady. You're much more than a mere lady. You're a child of the most high God. You've been purchased by the blood of Jesus. He paid a high price for you, so don't you ever sell yourself short."

Mrs. Bradford straightened and swung her legs down from the settee, as if coming to a decision. "You'll not only go to that dance on Saturday, but you'll outshine every other young *lady* there. And, although I don't normally agree to such breaches of etiquette, we shall both arrive fashionably late. Because, you, my dear girl, are going to make an entrance."

The afternoon before the soiree, Caleb called again at Mrs. Bradford's. Geneva was out with Miss Talbot, so he swallowed his disappointment as he sat alone with Mrs. Bradford. He'd waited this long, he supposed he could manage one more day.

"It's so good to see you back to your old self," Mrs. Bradford told him.

Caleb thought about the events of the last year. "Not quite my old self."

Mrs. Bradford gave him a knowing look. "Better, then. You've taken your experiences and used them to learn."

"I hope I've learned something." He eased back in his chair and thought about the things he'd realized since his return from Haven's End. "I learned to let go of some of the sentiments I'd been clinging to for far too long."

"Which sentiments were those?"

Caleb grinned. "I've managed to make some sort of peace with my father…if that's possible."

"He's a strong man, with strong beliefs."

"That he is."

"I'm glad, for your sake, if you've learned to accept him for what he is."

"Yes. I always expected more from him. And I finally realized he's given me all he can. In his own way, he's proud of me."

Mrs. Bradford reached over and patted his hand. "Of course he is. He loves you very much, but he doesn't really know how to show it."

Caleb ran a hand through his hair, thinking of the trying months in New Orleans, doing his best to see Ellery and Arabella settled, hoping Ellery would succeed at his new post, far away from him and all sense of competition with him—

"Any other sentiments?" Mrs. Bradford's soft tone broke into his thoughts.

"Other sentiments?" He smiled, remembering his original line of thought. "Oh, yes. My infatuation for Miss Harding."

Mrs. Bradford raised an eyebrow. "Infatuation? For the woman you intended to marry?"

He grimaced at the reminder. If he'd had any doubts about it before he left for New Orleans, a few days aboard ship with Arabella, followed by several months in almost daily contact with her, had convinced him for a lifetime.

"Yes." The word came out decisive and emphatic. "No doubts about it."

The entrance of a maid with the tea tray interrupted them. After Mrs. Bradford poured them both a cup and the maid dispensed the platter of cakes, they drank in silence for a few moments.

"So, then, your heart is now free?"

He looked down into the clear tea, remembering his amazement at seeing Geneva again. She'd looked exquisite, elegant, fashionable—and all he'd wanted to do was crush her in his arms and assure himself that she was truly standing in front of him, not the dream he'd pictured for months.

He remembered Maud's question. "No, I wouldn't say my heart is free now."

Before his friend could comment, Caleb sat forward in his chair, addressing the older woman earnestly. "Listen, about Miss Patterson, I didn't have an opportunity the other day to express my admiration for your decision to bring her along with you to Boston."

"Well, as I explained to you and your mother, it was really she who helped me out at a trying time."

Caleb tried to imagine what Geneva must have felt. She'd never been farther away than the next town. Boston would seem like another country. Had she been at all curious about his city?

"What made her finally give in to your arguments?"

"I don't really know. I promised her everything I could think of—tutors, lessons—but I don't think those enticements really helped. To every suggestion, she had a reason why she shouldn't come. I think I finally got through to her when I convinced her that in no time at all she'd be able to read the Bible."

Caleb remembered Geneva's reverent handling of her mother's Bible, and the few remarks she'd made to him about Jesus. Had she been searching, too?

He set down his cup. "What you've done with Geneva is wonderful—more than anyone else I know would have. You've made her into the young lady I knew she could become."

Mrs. Bradford gave him a penetrating look. "Geneva told me how you began to teach her to read. I admire you as well for seeing the potential in her."

"I did very little. The real credit belongs to Geneva."

"Oh, yes, indeed. She's a remarkable young woman." Mrs. Bradford paused, as if debating something. "You know, she didn't have an easy time of it last August, right before she came here. That's perhaps one of the reasons I pushed so hard for her to come with me. I thought a change of scene would do her good."

Caleb frowned. "What happened to her in August? What happened?" he repeated.

As Mrs. Bradford explained, his agitation grew. He heard about the death of Geneva's dog. *Oh, God, no!* Caleb felt Geneva's pain. Had she felt abandoned as well? First him, then her beloved pet. Too restless to sit any longer, Caleb rose and crossed the room. He scarcely heard Mrs. Bradford's continuing narrative until she mentioned an incident and a familiar name stuck out.

Caleb whirled around. "What did you say?" he demanded.

"I said it was a local man, Lucius Tucker, who came to her door. It seems he had pestered her in the past, but then she had Jake. This time he found her alone. To think of her alone on the Point…" Mrs. Bradford shuddered.

"The good Lord watches over His sheep. Mrs. Stillman happened to see a male figure approaching Geneva's place, too stealthy for her liking."

With a sick feeling in the pit of his stomach, Caleb listened in silence to the rest. His responsibility—to take care of Geneva—had fallen to Mr. and Mrs. Stillman. Even as he breathed a prayer of thanks that they had been there, he condemned himself for his lack of vigilance. That good-for-nothing Lucius, he'd just waited for an opportunity to find Geneva alone. Caleb's instincts had been right about him. It was all too clear that he had waited until Caleb left.

He never should have left her alone. The agony of impatience and frustration that had plagued him with each passing week in New Orleans should have been heeded. He should have dropped everything and come back. He should never have gone out in the first place. Caleb felt impotent rage rise up in him.

The realization of what Geneva had gone through hit him full force as he thought once again of the loss of her dog. Jake! How she'd loved that dog. It was the only creature he'd ever heard her speak tenderly to.

"I hope they did something to that scoundrel that attacked Geneva. If they didn't, I'm going to see to it myself as soon as I get back to Haven's End."

"Oh, they did something all right. The only reason he wasn't run out of town was pity for his wife and offspring. And now Pastor McDuffie is watching him like a hawk, visits him twice a week or sends one of the deacons around. I wouldn't be surprised if Mr. Tucker decides of his own accord to move to another village."

Caleb stopped his pacing and looked at Mrs. Bradford as the significance of what she was saying penetrated.

"You make it sound as if she had the whole village behind her. The Geneva I knew didn't think much of the villagers. She acted like an outcast."

"I think Geneva came to discover a few things about her own long-held opinions." Mrs. Bradford smiled. "Believe me, there were many who were quite disappointed when I whisked Geneva away from them to Boston."

Caleb smiled. "Like a fairy godmother."

"No." She shook her head. "I've done little enough. I think—in fact, I know—she would have been in good hands had she stayed." She sighed. "Sometimes I wonder whether I have done the right thing in bringing her here and opening up a whole new world for her. She really was beginning to enjoy an acceptance in her own village that she'd never found before."

Mrs. Bradford met Caleb's gaze and smiled. "In fact, I hear there was even a young man, very personable, who was beginning to pay her some marked attention."

Caleb frowned, knowing already who it was. "Not a young man by the name of Giles?"

"Yes!" Mrs. Bradford opened her eyes wide. "You know him?"

"I know of him," he answered grimly. Caleb realized he must stifle his frustration each time he heard the name and consider things rationally. After all, he was the one who'd left Geneva in the lurch, all because of his selfish preoccupations. He clasped his hands behind him, pretending an ease he did not feel. "He seemed a decent sort."

"Yes. From the little she told me, it sounds as if he was sweet on her."

Caleb's grip tightened. "Do you think she returns his affections?"

Mrs. Bradford made no reply at first, looking at him with her usual serene expression. "You'll have to ask her that."

"I shouldn't have left her the way I did," he blurted out, wondering how Mrs. Bradford could possibly know anything he was feeling, and not caring anymore how much he betrayed. At the moment, he desperately needed some good advice.

"You must have had good reasons for leaving Haven's End so abruptly."

Caleb looked away. "I thought I did at the time." After a pause he continued, "I didn't declare myself to Geneva. To be truthful, I wasn't even sure what I was feeling, but one thing was certain. It scared me.

"I could have asked Geneva to wait, but I wanted her to make whatever decisions she might about her own life, even if it meant marrying someone like Giles."

Mrs. Bradford's eyes held compassion. "Perhaps Geneva had a right to make that kind of decision with some knowledge of what you were feeling."

"But I wasn't willing to take the risk a second time."

"Geneva is nothing like Arabella."

He gave a laugh. "I know that now."

"Geneva has turned into a striking young woman. Whether she stays in Boston much longer or returns to Haven's End, I very much doubt she'll remain unspoken for, for very long."

"You can't imagine what I experienced when I heard she was here, right under your roof, and then to see her, such a proper young lady—and still free."

Mrs. Bradford smiled. "I think it's time you stopped telling me how you feel and started talking to the young lady."

"I don't know. After what you've told me, I feel I have much to be forgiven for. When she truly needed me, I failed her. There's so much to make up for."

"Perhaps you should start immediately." She gave him an approving look. "That soiree you've invited her to is a nice start."

Chapter Twenty

Geneva stood at the doorway of the magnificent ballroom of the Phelps' residence, waiting to make the entrance Mrs. Bradford had insisted upon. The older woman held her hand against Geneva's gloved wrist, preventing her from stepping any farther into the gilded room.

There was a greater crowd than Geneva had anticipated when Mrs. Phelps told her it was to be merely a soiree. To Geneva, it looked like a full-blown ball. She wondered what the difference was.

The large room was awash with golden light from the crystal chandeliers above. The light was multiplied by its reflection off the wide mirrors around the room and the more muted glow of the polished, parquet floor. Deep-red velvet drapes framed the floor-to-ceiling windows. Gilt tables and chairs lined the walls.

Even more striking were the guests who'd come to welcome Caleb home. She'd never seen so many elegantly dressed people crowded together in one room. Colorful ball gowns intermingled with the stark black and white of the men's attire, forming a palette of colors from pale blues and pinks to deep crimson and silver. If Geneva had thought her own dress overloaded with ruches and ruffles, she saw now she was not alone.

Mrs. Bradford, for the first time since Geneva had known her, had been firm about her wardrobe. She'd taken over Geneva's toilette like a commander, selecting the dress, overseeing the hairdressing, choosing the wraps. No detail had been too minor, no effort spared.

Geneva fingered the silk tulle of her white gown. She'd never felt so delicately feminine as she did tonight. Her skirt billowed around her like a puff of clouds that at the merest breath of wind might blow away. The deep, heart-shaped neckline exposed more neck and shoulders than she'd ever allowed anyone to see.

The bodice, molded like a second skin, accentuated the bosom Geneva had striven so long to hide. The stiff-boned corset underneath threatened to cut off her breathing. It had been difficult enough becoming accustomed to wearing one every day, but tonight, she could vow the maid had laced it up a couple of inches tighter.

Geneva didn't dare sneeze for fear the fastenings of her bodice would pop off. If she managed to avert that calamity, there was the danger of one misstep and the train trailing several feet behind her would get caught under someone's foot, ripping the delicate fabric clean off her skirt.

Two long trails of red roses and greenery had been fastened down the front of her skirt, relieving the purity of the white tulle. More roses adorned each tiny cap of sleeve at her shoulders and the nape of her neck.

She didn't dare touch her hair, for fear the elaborate coiffure at the back of her head would come tumbling down. She remembered the night she and Caleb had tried to dress her hair, and wondered how the maid had managed it so deftly in such a short time. The girl had mercilessly brushed her hair before pulling it straight back. Then the real work had begun. Braids and coils had been twisted around at the nape of her neck and finished off with the posy of roses.

Geneva twisted the little beaded evening bag and fan in her gloved hands. They were about the only part of her costume she dared fiddle with. Mrs. Bradford had commissioned a lady to come in the day before to drill Geneva in the use of the fan and the maneuvering of her train. But Geneva had no confidence that she'd mastered either lesson.

"He's coming."

Mrs. Bradford's quiet announcement snapped Geneva's attention back to the ballroom. Sure enough, there was Caleb, walking straight toward them. If she'd thought he had looked impossibly elegant the other afternoon, his present attire managed to make the afternoon calling outfit look downright rustic. His black evening coat and trousers contrasted sharply with the pure white of his jacquard silk waistcoat and starched shirtfront. A white neck cloth and high collar framed his jaw.

He cut through a sea of beautiful women without sparing them a glance.

"Good evening, Mrs. Bradford…Geneva." He bowed to the older woman with a smile, then gave his full attention to Geneva. His blue eyes crinkled at the corners.

"Thank you for coming. I was beginning to wonder whether you were going to make it." He smiled ruefully. "But I'm glad you're here."

"Excuse our tardiness, my boy, but you know how we women are. We can't arrive at a ball without all our finery." Mrs. Bradford smiled at him. Geneva looked from her to Caleb, hardly believing the older woman's flirtatious tone.

If she didn't know any better, she'd say Mrs. Bradford was fishing for a compliment.

And she got it. Geneva blinked at hearing Caleb's reply. "I'd say the wait was well worth it." His gaze swept over Geneva. "You both outshine any woman present tonight."

"Save the compliments for the young lady, Caleb. Otherwise, she'll know they're just flattery."

Caleb smiled at Mrs. Bradford before turning to Geneva. "She's right. Although Mrs. Bradford knows I think she's beautiful, I shall save my compliments for you tonight." In a lower tone, for her ears alone, he said, "You take my breath away."

Geneva felt the heat steal into her cheeks until she was sure their color must match the roses at her shoulders.

"This corset just about takes mine away," she blurted out.

She was aghast at what had come out of her mouth. Caleb seemed startled, then threw back his head and laughed, a deep, rich sound that surrounded Geneva like warm molasses.

"Oh, Geneva, how I've missed you! I'm glad you haven't disappeared completely under all the finery."

Mrs. Bradford interrupted. "I think you've managed to intrigue everyone in the room before you've even entered it. This is better than I'd hoped."

Geneva tore her gaze from Caleb's and glanced into the room beyond. At the sound of Caleb's laughter, several people paused to give Geneva a thorough perusal. Their eyes lingered on her. She took a step backward. Before she could withdraw from the doorway, Caleb stepped between her and Mrs. Bradford, holding out an arm for each woman.

"Shall we proceed?"

Geneva found her gloved hand tucked in the crook of his elbow. With him beside her, she felt ready to brave the crowded room.

Caleb took them to greet his mother first of all. Afterwards, Mrs. Bradford stayed to chat with Mrs. Phelps, while Caleb made the rounds of the other guests with Geneva. They approached a distinguished, silver-haired man who was talking with another gentleman. When he turned toward them, Geneva sucked in her breath, noting Mr. Phelps Senior.

"Father, may I present Miss Geneva Patterson?"

Mr. Phelps gave her a piercing look, which made her draw back slightly. His eyes were the same hue of midnight blue as his son's. He, too, was slim and tall, although Caleb's height topped his father's.

"Miss Patterson." He took her hand and bowed over it.

His focused attention seemed all out of proportion to her status. She tried to remember the things Mrs. Bradford had told her. She had no reason to be ashamed before any of these people. She asked the Lord to help her watch each word she spoke, that she might not embarrass Caleb.

"You come to us all the way from Haven's End, do you not?"

"Yes, sir."

"How do you like Boston?"

"It's mighty large."

Mr. Phelps' chuckle eased the severity of his face somewhat. "Compared to Haven's End, it is."

"But not so large when you compare it to the ocean and sky which surround us there."

He narrowed his eyes at her. "Yes, that's so. We have our own share of ocean and sky here as well."

"Somehow they seem vaster down at Haven's End."

Caleb spoke for the first time. "Geneva's accustomed to being out on the water."

"Is that right? Have a boat, do you?"

Geneva nodded. "I fish for a living."

If he seemed fazed by the information, Mr. Phelps didn't show it. "And I sell them for a living."

"Yes, sir, I know. I've sold many a catch at Phelps' Wharf."

Mr. Phelps chuckled. "Well, go on, Caleb, take your guest out on the dance floor. No use wasting your time with an old man."

"Aye, aye, sir." Caleb touched Geneva lightly at the elbow.

Geneva, remembering her lessons under Miss Talbot, held out her hand again. "It was a pleasure, Mr. Phelps."

He took her hand in a brief handclasp. "The pleasure was all mine."

Caleb led her to the area reserved for dancing. "Not afraid of breaking your leg this time?"

She shook her head, smiling that he should remember her fear the last time they danced. She felt his arm go around her, something she'd never thought to experience again. Everything seemed a wonder.

All at once she felt the fullness of joy in her breast, remembering how good the Lord had been to her since that day she'd cried out to Him in her room. Her joy burst forth, widening her smile as she met Caleb's gaze.

If she had nothing more than this moment with Caleb, she would be forever grateful. He regarded her as if entranced. She would keep that in her treasury of memories.

"You dance as if you'd been at it for years," he told her after a few moments.

"I've been practicing. Does it show?"

Caleb didn't answer her. He couldn't keep his mind on the conversation. All he could do was behold her. She looked more than beautiful. She looked radiant. She was someone completely transformed from the woman who'd hidden any glimmer of feeling the day he'd come to say goodbye to her. That woman had been taciturn and sullen.

The woman before him wasn't afraid of showing her feelings. Her countenance exuded pure joy. Ever since he'd seen her again, he'd noticed something different about her, but tonight she absolutely glowed.

He remembered the thread of conversation. "You dance superbly. Whom have you been practicing with?" His mind pictured her in young Giles' arms, being swung around vigorously.

"Mrs. Bradford hired a dance instructor for me."

Caleb felt the sense of relief wash over him. "Mrs. Bradford is a marvel."

Geneva laughed, a jubilant, full-throated laugh. Caleb gazed at her alabaster neck and shoulders.

Her laughter ended and she met his gaze once more. Her smile faded. Color stained her cheeks.

"Why are you looking at me like that?" she asked.

He swallowed, trying to dispel images of the night he kissed her. "I thought perhaps it was Samuel Giles you were practicing with."

She looked confused, then shook her head. "Oh, no, of course not."

"He seemed quite taken with you the last time I saw him."

She blushed again and denied it so strongly that it made Caleb only more convinced there had been something between Geneva and Giles.

"There's nothing to be ashamed of in the fact that a young man admired you."

"Well, it doesn't matter what he thought about me. I never let him say anything about it, even if he did."

"So, you did sense something on his mind?"

She refused to meet his gaze. "No, no!" In her vehemence, she missed a step, but Caleb guided her through to the next.

She made an effort to explain. "Sometimes you can tell what's on a man's mind by the way he looks at you. That's the way it was with Samuel. And, well, I didn't want him to say anything."

"Geneva." He looked at her steadily until he had her full attention. "Can you tell what's on my mind by the way I look at you?"

The two gazed at each other wordlessly. Finally, she gave a timid shake of her head.

They twirled around the ballroom in silence for a while.

"I salute you, Geneva. I always knew you had it in you."

As if sensing the serious intent of his words, she asked gravely, "Had what in me?"

"The potential to become the beautiful young lady dancing with me now."

"Now you are ribbing me." As if to prove her point, she asked, "When did you first suspect a lady hiding in my trousers? When you saw me fall flat on my face on the wharf, my vegetables rolling all over the place?"

He smiled back at her, surprised and gratified at finding her so at ease with her former self. "Do you really want to know?"

She nodded.

Although he thought about seeing her in her washtub again, he didn't voice that thought. Someday—he hoped—he'd be able to tell her. Instead, he replied, "It was when you told me how badly you wanted to learn to read."

She flushed under his gaze once more, making her appear all the more beautiful to him, with her dark hair and pale skin tinted so prettily at the cheeks. Her lips were slightly parted, and he longed to taste them once more. Her dress was a vision, the crimson roses accenting the color in her face.

Caleb wished again that he could take her in his arms fully and tell her he loved her.

The only thing that held him back was the regret that he hadn't done so before she came to Boston. How would she ever know that it wasn't the transformed Geneva he'd fallen in love with, but that young woman in her men's trousers and dirt-encrusted boots?

"Geneva, there's so much I want to tell you—"

The dance ended before he could say anything more. If he couldn't speak to her in private tonight, he determined that at least he was going to do his best now and in the coming days to show her how proud he was of what she had accomplished without him.

He began introducing her to his friends and acquaintances. His tongue itched to claim her as his betrothed, but he held back, knowing the declaration was still premature. He knew that people would know how special she was to him by the marked attention he was giving her.

"When are you going to introduce me to your beautiful partner?" a voice said over his shoulder.

"Nate!" Caleb turned to clap his hand on his friend's shoulder. "I've been looking for you to do precisely that."

Nate wasn't looking at him but at Geneva. "I must have been away from Boston far too long to have missed you. Where has Caleb been hiding you?"

Geneva's cheeks glowed and her dark eyes seemed to radiate light. "I don't think Caleb's been hiding me. But I have been keeping myself at Haven's End."

"Haven's End!" Nate took her hand and bent over it. "How

did we miss making an acquaintance? I bet you had something to do with it, Caleb!"

Caleb grinned. "You met Geneva briefly the day you were up to visit me. So briefly, in fact, that Geneva didn't even stay around for an introduction." As Nate puzzled, trying to remember the details, Caleb just smiled, not caring to enlighten his friend just yet.

"Well, I shall just have to question Miss Geneva myself to get the particulars." He turned to Geneva with a courtly bow. "May I have the pleasure of the next dance?"

The beginning notes sounded like those of a lively polka. Geneva's glance quickly met Caleb's. He read fear and trepidation. He patted her fingertips, which rested in the crook of his arm, and smiled, giving her a slight nod. "You dance superbly."

She laughed. "Don't listen to him, Captain—"

"Nate," he corrected.

Caleb stood for a few moments watching his two best friends dancing. Geneva was going to be all right on the dance floor. After a while he was no longer seeing them. Instead he began imagining what it must have been like for Geneva after he'd left Haven's End. The way she'd responded to his kiss the night of the dance showed she had strong feelings for him. But whatever those feelings had been, she'd hidden them awfully well as soon as he'd told her he was leaving.

Leaving her like that had been unforgivable, he saw that now. He had not given her the least shred of hope! What good had he done her—offered her a friendship and then left her to fend for herself, just as she'd had to do all her life?

He didn't deserve her.

But never had he dreamed he'd be forced to be away so long. *Dear God, Why did You send me so far, so long? I thought I was doing Your will! Did I misread You? Was it pure obstinacy on my part? Was it pride, that I felt I must put Ellery's life back together again? You know it wasn't those things!* Caleb didn't know what to think anymore.

Oh, Lord, he prayed, *I have no right to ask anything of You. I turned my back on You. But if You can spare any of Your mercy for me, I beg You, give me the means to win this woman. I know I don't deserve her affections. I ran away from her like the worst coward—out of pride, stupidity, fear...*

But I swear to You, Lord, if You let me win her back, I'll honor her and cherish her all the days of my life.

He was so intent on his words that he didn't hear his father's approach. Caleb started at the sound of the older man's voice at his side.

"So, that's the young lady I'm to have as daughter-in-law?"

Caleb turned to his father, who stood watching the dancers as he had. "If she'll have me."

His father nodded. "Your mother told me how you broke the news to her the other day, just a few seconds before introducing her to the young lady."

"I wanted the fact perfectly clear to both of you before I declared myself to her."

"And what are you waiting for now?"

"If you don't mind, Father, I'll handle this in my own way. But I'll tell you one thing, if Geneva agrees to be my wife, I shan't waste any time with long engagements as I did before with Arabella."

His father looked at him with approval before cracking a smile. "But aren't you glad now that it took so long with Arabella?"

Caleb reclaimed Geneva after the polka, and they continued dancing until the musicians paused for a break. Caleb turned to Geneva. "Would you care to come with me for a moment? I can't invite you for a stroll outside, but perhaps a few moments in the conservatory with some refreshment?"

She agreed, filled with trepidation at the thought of finally, after so many months, being alone with him. What would he say? Would he wonder what had brought her to his city?

He led her to the warm, shadowy room on the ground floor that smelled of earth and plants. They sat together on a wrought iron bench. The sounds from the ballroom provided a muted backdrop.

She glanced around her at the silhouette of the potted plants. "It's nice and quiet here," she said after taking a careful sip of punch, trying to will her heartbeat to slow down.

"Was my mother's soiree too overwhelming for you?"

"I thought it would be, but everyone has been so gracious." She was afraid to look at Caleb. It still seemed unreal that he was really here beside her after so many months…so many days….

"It isn't hard to be gracious to such a beautiful, gracious young lady."

She set down her glass, afraid of another upset.

"Geneva, may I tell you a story?"

She raised her eyes to him and found herself unable to look away, so she merely nodded.

"You recall the time on the wharf last summer when I came to your rescue?"

She smiled. "There stood all those fine-looking folks gaping at me, as if they'd never seen anyone trip before. I was just wishing the planks of the wharf would widen to let me through. And then you came along. You didn't care how I was dressed, or how dirty my hands were. You didn't treat me any differently from those city folks you were with…just like tonight."

"I've been wanting to finish your story." He looked down, rubbing his knees, suddenly appearing ill at ease. "But I haven't had a chance until now. You see, the day I rescued you, little did I realize my life was about to change forever—that someday I'd need someone to come to *my* rescue."

He lifted his eyes to hers then. "When I thought I'd lost everyone's respect—including my own—there was one person who held out a hand of friendship. She didn't care anything about my past, what I might have done or not done. Who my family was, what I came from, or what I had walked away from. She became my friend, and little by little, gave me back hope and self-respect."

He paused. "Before I realized it, I fell in love with her."

Geneva, her hands clasped tightly, was afraid to breathe for fear of losing one word of what he was saying.

"The problem was," he continued, "I was too blinded by my own problems to take a chance on what I was feeling. I'd given my heart to someone once—" He stopped. "Even though this young woman of Haven's End had already proved her friendship, I couldn't bring myself to trust that someone would remain loyal and true to me even if I had to go away."

Geneva was finally beginning to understand. She reached forth a hand to cover one of his. He clasped it firmly. "I'm sorry, Caleb. I didn't realize—"

"So, I went away and left her all alone, when she needed me the most."

"But I wasn't alone," Geneva whispered. "I found that out after you left. I might never have found it out if you hadn't gone away."

His gaze met hers, questioning and beginning to hope. "What are you saying?"

"I found Jesus. Or He found me. I felt His very presence. I knew then how much He cared for me—that I'd never be alone again. Ever."

They looked at each other for a long moment. Then Caleb reached for her, and she came toward him with a half laugh, half sob.

His arms enveloped her as his lips met hers, and all the yearning of the past months was expressed in that kiss.

"Oh, Geneva, this is the moment I've longed for…every day…every night since I left you…the moment I dreamed of," he murmured between kisses on her lips and cheeks and temples. "I counted the days…I thought I would never get back from New Orleans…."

Could this be happening to her? Geneva thought she'd extinguished every last hope of a moment like this—to be in Caleb's arms, loved by him, his lips covering hers, his breath brushing hers, her fingers touching his smoothly shaven jaw, the cleft in his chin, the rough hair of his sideburns….

"I tried to convince myself you weren't coming back," she murmured in turn. "Tried so hard to believe it…." A laugh gurgled up from her throat.

He parted his lips from hers just enough to ask, "Why are you laughing?"

"During our dance you asked if I could tell what you were thinking."

"You shook your head."

"Because I was afraid. If I'd been truthful, I'd have said you looked as if you wanted to kiss me, but I didn't dare. I didn't think it could be possible."

His lips touched hers gently again and again as he whispered, "It was not only possible, it was absolutely true."

A while later, when the two of them were seated side by side, with Caleb's arm around Geneva, Caleb asked, "Tell me about Jesus."

"Oh, Caleb," she breathed, remembering her experience as if it were happening all over again. "It was so extraordinary. Just when I was so down I didn't think I could go down any farther. You had left without saying anything—"

"I'm so sorry, my dear," he said, squeezing her to him and kissing her brow. Then he looked at her. "Can you ever forgive me for leaving you alone there in Haven's End? Mrs. Bradford has told me about Lucius Tucker."

She smiled at him. "Of course I forgive you. I did then, but it was because all along I'd been telling myself you were going to go back to Boston someday. Then, when you made your decision, I just told myself you owed me nothing. You had every right to go back to your former life."

When he would have said something, Geneva silenced him with a finger to his lips. "Then you sent that letter and I tried to figure out what it meant. Did you care at all? But try as I could, I couldn't tell. You hardly wrote anything—"

Caleb groaned. "I wanted to pour out my heart in pages and pages, but I didn't dare. If I'd written anything more, I'd have asked you to wait. So, I left it like that, hoping you could tell that I cared about you and hadn't forgotten you. I could only trust in the Lord that He would take care of you."

She laughed, her hand touching his cheek. "Oh, He did, He did! But then I didn't understand why you had left. Now it's different." She looked downward. "I'm sorry about Arabella. I know how deeply she hurt you and why you couldn't trust me."

Caleb kissed her fingertips, then drew her hand down to his, his eyes looking deeply into hers. "I made a mistake. Not just about Arabella but, more importantly, about you. And through that mistake, I hurt you very deeply. I'm truly sorry."

"When I arrived in Boston with Mrs. Bradford, I heard that Arabella had gotten married. For a while I wondered whether you'd gone to New Orleans just to be near her."

He shook his head, a wry smile on his lips. "No, my dear. I wanted nothing more than to come back to you." His smile disappeared. "But I felt the Lord—" He smiled. "Yes, I think He's been dealing with my heart as well. I felt He was telling me to go with Ellery and Arabella to New Orleans.

"It was as if that was the only way to show Ellery I truly forgave him for what he did to me. He was desperately unhappy about his part. I had a talk with him as well as with Arabella when I came back here. I understood how much he needed a fresh start, somewhere far away from here. He also needed to see that I no longer felt the way I used to about Arabella, that I was no threat to him in any way. I think he's truly free of the feelings that made him act the way he did."

He squeezed her hand. "But continue with your story. You said you discovered you weren't left alone."

She looked down at their joined hands. "Well, I was trying so hard to be strong. I never felt I needed anyone, and then I came to need you. I was determined I would get over you. But then— Then Jake… I couldn't do anything to help him—" Her voice broke. She felt Caleb's arm tighten about her shoulder once again. "I tried so hard to be strong on my own. Just like before. After Ma died and after Pa…I was always able to go on. Thumbing my nose at everyone. But I couldn't do it anymore." She smiled up at Caleb, feeling her lips trembling. "You did something to me, Caleb. I couldn't be strong on my own anymore.

"One night, I just broke down. I just told the Lord I couldn't go on." She looked past Caleb, remembering the presence of God. "He touched me. I felt this warmth come into my body. Jesus let me feel His very presence. It was the most wondrous thing in all the world—words can't begin to describe what I experienced." She met Caleb's gaze once more. "I knew I'd never be alone again. He'd always be with me."

"You look so radiant when you talk about it that I know it's real. I noticed something different about you when I first saw you again. Every time you smile at me that joy is there."

She smiled at him then, happy there was something in her that reflected what the Lord had given her.

"The night…the night that man, Lucius—"

Caleb's voice soothed her. "I know, Mrs. Bradford told me."

She stared at him before nodding. "That night I didn't know what I was going to do. I think he'd been watching for me. He knew I couldn't get to my gun. He knew I didn't have Jake. But I just called on Jesus to save me." She looked at Caleb in awe. "*And He did.* Just at that moment Mr. Stillman came by and poked his head in the door."

Geneva laughed. "It was the funniest thing. I'd never thought much about my neighbor, Mrs. Stillman. Thought she was just a busybody, sticking her nose in my business. But it was she who'd seen Lucius. She made Mr. Stillman come by. If it hadn't been for her pestering, what would've happened?" She shivered at the recollection. "Then, afterwards, I saw that she wasn't just a nosy neighbor. She really cared about me."

Caleb drew her to him. "Oh, Geneva," he breathed. "If I hadn't left you alone—"

"Don't ever say that again. You had to go."

"But I wanted to tell you I'd return. I wanted to so badly, but I was afraid." He drew her back far enough to peer into her eyes. "I didn't want you to promise you'd wait for me. I knew there would be other…men."

She looked at him angrily. "How could you think that?"

"Geneva! Don't you know how beautiful you are? You weren't going to stay single long. I saw the way that young man, Sam Giles, took to you. I knew when I left Haven's End that it wouldn't be long before there'd be other young men calling on you. I didn't want to force you into a situation where you felt you had to remain loyal to me."

"But when you said nothing to me at all, I never thought you'd come back!"

"I had every intention of returning. In fact, I still want to return as soon as possible."

She widened her eyes in disbelief. "Caleb Phelps, you're not going to make me believe you'd go live in Haven's End!" She gestured around her. "Not when you have all this."

He caught her hand in his. "But I don't have you here."

She knew in that instant that she must take a risk of her own. "You have me if you want me."

His eyes regarded her tenderly for several seconds before he whispered firmly, "I want you for the rest of my life. Will you do me the honor of becoming my wife?"

Although he was speaking the words, she could hardly believe she was hearing them. They expressed an impossible dream, one that she had not even been able to confess to herself.

"I'm never going to fit in very well in your world here," she replied.

"I think you're doing better than you imagine…by far," he added with a smile.

She swallowed. "If you're sure," she said, giving him a last chance to withdraw his offer.

"I've never been more sure of anything. Except to know that the Lord has blessed me incredibly. He brought you here. He kept you for me." He chuckled in recollection. "You don't know how terrified I was that when I finally managed to make it back to Haven's End, I'd find you already married to Sam Giles."

She laughed incredulously. "I never heard anything so preposterous."

"Be that as it may, you will never know the relief I felt—after the initial shock of finding out you were here in Boston—to know that you were still unspoken for, living in my very neighborhood." He hugged her tightly to him. "Yes, Geneva, I am very sure I want you to be my wife." He eased away from her just enough to draw something from his pocket. "I was even certain of it before I left for New Orleans. It only took me a few days to accomplish what I'd set out to, when I came back here. I had just bought this and was ready to return to Haven's End when I was asked to go to New Orleans." As he spoke, he opened the small jeweler's box.

Geneva drew in her breath at the sight of the diamond solitaire resting against the velvet cloth. Caleb removed the ring and held it out to her. "Can you believe that I loved you before you were transformed into a Boston society lady? That you were already a lady to me?"

"I can," she replied slowly, "if you can believe that I have loved you since the moment you came to my aid on the wharf."

They smiled at each other. Geneva could feel the tears filling her eyes once again as Caleb slipped the ring on her finger.

"You know that we won't have to live in Boston all the time," he continued, as she stared down at the ring gracing her finger. "I've been thinking about living part of the year here and part of it at Haven's End. Would that suit you? More importantly, what is your answer? Can you bear the thought of having me for a husband?"

She looked at him. "I would be honored."

"I think we've done enough talking, don't you?"

She gave a barely perceptible nod. "You're the captain."

His eyes alight with amusement, he bent his head. Then his eyelids came down, leaving Geneva only a vision of his dark lashes against his skin, before her eyes shut, too, and she felt the sensation of his lips against hers.

Epilogue

Haven's End, Maine, July 1874

"Coming, my dear?" Caleb stood above her on the wharf and held out his hand to her.

She smiled up at him, never tiring of hearing the tenderness in his voice. Her hand joined his, and she climbed the last few rungs onto the wharf.

Together the two of them walked arm-in-arm the length of Phelps' Wharf toward the village street.

"Hello, Captain Phelps, Mrs. Phelps. Welcome home." Fishermen doffed their caps and bowed to them both.

Geneva had had a few months in Boston, following a honeymoon in New York, to get used to her new title, but it felt new all over again, hearing it from the mouths of people she'd known all her life.

What was most amazing was the way they were looking at her. Smiling and welcoming, as if it were the most natural thing in the world for Salt Fish Ginny to be strolling down the wharf, dressed in city finery, with the town's most prominent citizen.

The appellation made her recall that summer day when circumstances had been different. She glanced down at her silk traveling suit, comparing it to her dirt-stained overalls.

"Glad to be home?" Caleb's touch on her arm brought her attention back to him.

He was smiling at her, and she returned the smile.

The one thing that hadn't changed was her husband's manner. She gave his hand an answering squeeze. He was the same knight in shining armor he'd been that long-ago summer day.

"Yes. Very glad."

* * * * *

REQUEST YOUR FREE BOOKS!

2 FREE INSPIRATIONAL NOVELS
PLUS 2
FREE
MYSTERY GIFTS

Love Inspired®

YES! Please send me 2 FREE Love Inspired® novels and my 2 FREE mystery gifts. After receiving them, if I don't wish to receive any more books, I can return the shipping statement marked "cancel." If I don't cancel, I will receive 4 brand-new novels every month and be billed just $3.99 per book in the U.S., or $4.74 per book in Canada, plus 25¢ shipping and handling per book and applicable taxes, if any*. That's a savings of 20% off the cover price! I understand that accepting the 2 free books and gifts places me under no obligation to buy anything. I can always return a shipment and cancel at any time. Even if I never buy another book from Steeple Hill, the two free books and gifts are mine to keep forever.

113 IDN EF26 313 IDN EF27

Name	(PLEASE PRINT)	
Address		Apt. #
City	State/Prov.	Zip/Postal Code

Signature (if under 18, a parent or guardian must sign)

Order online at www.LoveInspiredBooks.com

Or mail to Steeple Hill Reader Service™:

IN U.S.A.: P.O. Box 1867, Buffalo, NY 14240-1867
IN CANADA: P.O. Box 609, Fort Erie, Ontario L2A 5X3

Not valid to current Love Inspired subscribers.

Want to try two free books from another series?
Call 1-800-873-8635 or visit www.morefreebooks.com

* Terms and prices subject to change without notice. NY residents add applicable sales tax. Canadian residents will be charged applicable provincial taxes and GST. This offer is limited to one order per household. All orders subject to approval. Credit or debit balances in a customer's account(s) may be offset by any other outstanding balance owed by or to the customer. Please allow 4 to 6 weeks for delivery.

Your Privacy: Steeple Hill is committed to protecting your privacy. Our Privacy Policy is available online at www.eHarlequin.com or upon request from the Reader Service. From time to time we make our lists of customers available to reputable firms who may have a product or service of interest to you. If you would prefer we not share your name and address, please check here. ☐

LIREG07